*A So Sophisticated Publication*

# When the Lovin' Gets Good

## K. Lowery Moore

So Sophisticated Publications
Adult Literature with a K*I*S
(Keepin' It Sophisticated)

## Author's Note

Although this is a work of fiction, some of the characters and situations presented in this book were inspired by actual people and events. Most of the situations were embellished for an extra dramatic appeal. All parties presented in the book have been notified, however, the names were changed to protect the innocent, as well as the guilty.

∾ ∾ ∾ ∾ ∾

So Sophisticated Publications
P.O. Box 23002
Washington, DC  20026-3002

All So Sophisticated books may be purchased for education, business, or sales promotional use. For information, please write: Special Markets Department, So Sophisticated Publications, P.O. Box 23002, Washington, DC 20026-3002.

ISBN-13:  978-0-9795333-3-4
ISBN-10:  0-9795333-3-3

Printed in the United States of America

Photo Credit: Kara Colleen
Cover Models: Marcus and Ash'Leigh Gunn
Cover and Interior Designed by TWASolutions.com

# Dedication

This book is dedicated to those in pursuit of unconditional love...
Keep believing that you are deserving of the kind of love you
desire!

## Also by K. Lowery Moore

*When I'm Loving You*
*Moments in Love: Reflections through Poetic Expressions*

# Acknowledgements

Lord, I thank You for giving me life. I thank You for my talents and the courage to express myself freely. It is because of You that I am able.

Antonio and Andray, there is nothing in this world more important to me than being your mother. It has been a joy watching as you grow into handsome, young men. Life will try to beat you down, but do not let it. When all else fails, call your mother. I will always have your back!

Mama, your life was cut way too short; however, I think of you every day. I wish we had more time together, but I remain faithful that God knows best. I want you to know that I am doing just fine because you set the perfect example to follow.

Dad, your words, *that one there is going to be somebody*, have stayed in my mind all these years. Back then, I did not realize that the words you spoke would contribute greatly to my self-esteem.

Mary, I could not have asked for a better stepmom. You have been my biggest supporter, and I am glad you are in my life. Thanks for accepting me as your own.

My siblings, Judy, Angela, H. Marcellus, and Marcus, I want to thank each of you for your continued support.

Shadonne Brown Harris, thanks for always having the "what do you need me to do" attitude. I do not know what I would do without your support.

My extended family and friends, thanks for your support. Jamie Scipio, Patrice Johnson, and Regina Robinson, you deserve honorable mention. Thank you for the many years of friendship.

It takes a team of great people to produce a novel to be proud of, and there are so many people who have helped me through this journey. Sometimes a thank you is not enough, but it is all I have to offer. *Smile!*

Jessica Tilles, you are an amazing person. Thanks for the advice over the years. I appreciate your patience with me, but in the end, you always bring my vision to life.

The editors on this novel, Lisa DiGloria and Carla Dean, thank you so much. You played a very critical role in this process. I took editing for granted, but I will not anymore.

Kara Colleen, thanks for allowing me to use your photographs for my book cover. Also, thanks for being my photographer at the pre-release party for *When the Lovin' Gets Good*. It was great finally meeting you.

Ash'Leigh and Marcus Gunn, you are a beautiful couple, and I am honored to have you on the cover of my book. Ash'Leigh, I have watched you grow into a lovely woman. Marcus, I know my cousin is in good hands with you. Congratulations on your marriage, and may you have a wonderful life together!

Najah Ryles, thank you for reading the manuscript. Sorry I teased you with bits and pieces of the story. However, I cannot promise I will not do the same thing with the next book.

Leo Gordy and Tai Saunders, thanks for your hospitality at the Borders Bookstore in Largo, Maryland. I was deeply saddened by the closing of Borders, especially this location, because I always felt at home during my book signings and discussions. Tai, the Lord called you home, but your beautiful spirit lives on through the lives you have touched.

Michael Baisden, it meant the world to me to be able to give a pitch about my book during your live tour in 2008. I was not prepared to speak in front of so many people, but it was an honor to stand beside one of my favorite authors.

Mary B. Morrison, it was a pleasure finally meeting you. Thank you for all of your encouraging words and the information you shared with me. You are an amazing author.

J.J. Michael, I am glad I met you early in my literary career because you were the first to give me the honest 411 on the industry. You will forever have my gratitude.

Bill Holmes, China Ball, Daamon Speller, Dawayne Williams, James A. Jimason, Jihad, Marc Lacy, Matthew C. Horne, Monda

Webb, Monica Mathis-Stowe, Moses Miller, Richard Jeanty, Ronda Rountree, S. James Guitard, Tariiq O. Walton, Victoria Christopher Murray, and Yonder, I am very thankful I had the pleasure of networking and bonding with such great authors.

Jocelyn "Jacki" Lawson, thank you for introducing me to your book club, The Sweet Soul Sisters. You are an amazing group of women. I cannot wait until our next discussion.

My readers, especially those who made an advance purchase, thank you for all of the support and feedback you have given me over the past few years. The e-mails I received were used as ammunition to keep going when I wanted to give up! A special thank you goes to the past and present members of Sircles, Inc. and Silk Social Book Club.

Of course, I could go on, but I am sure you are eager to read the story. If you feel I left you out, let me know and I will make it up to you in the next book. Enjoy!

# When the Lovin' Gets Good

# CHAPTER 1

## *Dianne*

❧

*LORD, GIVE ME THE STRENGTH not to hurt this little girl up in here. I know raising a child can be challenging, but damn! If this child stomps up one more stair, slams one more door or sucks her teeth again, I have no idea what I might do to her.* Nihya knew she was supposed to come home immediately after she got off the school bus, no exceptions. That little girl decided she wasn't going to follow the rules, and it took her almost forty minutes to get home. I wanted to know what the hell she was doing and what was so important that she felt the need to deliberately disobey the rules. I called her cell phone a few times, but it went straight to voicemail each time.

When I heard her key in the door, I almost snatched her through the doorway, but I thought she would immediately offer an explanation when she saw me standing there.

"Hi, Dianne," Nihya said in a dry tone, attempting to walk past me.

"Um, excuse me. Why did it take you so long to walk home from the bus stop?"

"I guess I wasn't walking fast enough," Nihya answered nonchalantly. *Lord, help me. I'm about to grab her!*

"Nihya, I'm not sure how you turned a five-minute walk into a forty-minute stroll. So, I'm going to ask you again. Why did it take you so long to walk home from the bus stop?"

"Because I had to get something from a friend's house."

"Your friend who and something like what?"

"Dang, you act like I'm always doing something wrong."

"Well, you know the rules. And watch your mouth."

"All I said was dang."

"Nihya!"

Nihya sucked her teeth. "Okay, okay. I'm sorry."

"Let's not get off the subject, young lady. What were you doing? And I'm hoping it doesn't involve a boy."

"Am I in trouble for thirty or forty measly minutes?"

*Lord, I'm about to knock her out. Help me!*

"How many minutes is not the issue, Nihya! What were you doing?" I raised my voice significantly because I was definitely losing my patience.

Nihya responded in a sassy tone, "Well, I wasn't with a stupid boy. I went to Jenny's house to get some female stuff."

"Female stuff? Oh, my goodness, Nihya. You started your period?"

"Yes, in school today. I went to the school nurse, and she gave me some thick ol' pads that I didn't want to use. Jenny said her mom had the thin kind, so I went over there to get some."

"Well, I don't understand why you didn't just come home and tell me, because I have some here."

"I didn't want to tell you just yet."

"Why, Nihya?"

"Because you would make a big deal about it, then get on the phone and tell everybody like you always do."

"Oh." I couldn't even say anything else because she was right, but her damn mouth was going to get her ass in trouble.

"And please don't tell my dad."

"Why not? He's going to figure it out. I can't keep something like that from him."

"Oh, my goodness," Nihya mumbled and walked away.

"Nihya, get back here."

"What?"

"What do you mean *what?* Never mind. Just go to your room and get your homework done. We'll talk about your sassy mouth later."

"But it's Friday!" Nihya yelled disrespectfully.

"Well, read a book then!"

*Wouldn't you know it?* After sucking her teeth and mumbling under her breath, that child stomped her way up the stairs, dragging her book bag behind her. I wanted to go up there, snatch her butt back down the steps, and make her walk up them over and over until I was tired of watching her. *Lord, I'm not ready to deal with her hormones. She's already sassy enough.*

Nelson and I agreed not to physically punish Nihya after all she had been through; however, I didn't know how long I could hold to that agreement. Nelson wasn't home with her as I was because of his new work schedule. He had left his senior executive position at the Pentagon for a lower-level management position at the Department of Transportation. Nelson earned the same salary, but with fewer responsibilities; however, after almost one year in that position, he indicated he was bored and was interested in pursuing another senior executive position making substantially more money. As a result, he had accepted very demanding work commitments. Based on several conversations with Nelson, I figured he wanted to show the top management in his department that he was dedicated enough to take on extra projects. Subsequently, he put in a lot of overtime to assist with end of the fiscal year activities. I knew the position was important to him, so I was willing to do most of the hands-on parenting; however, I was losing my patience with Nihya.

I decided not to return to the federal government since we unexpectedly had the responsibility to raise Nihya. When I initially left my job at the Office of Personnel Management, my intention was to go back to my position as a training specialist after I pursued some other career interests for a while. During that time, I was completely burnt out from the monotony, and I desperately needed a break from the corporate world. Nelson was extremely supportive. He didn't see the benefit of me going back to do something that I didn't have the desire to do anymore, especially since my juvenile counseling practice was successful. Moreover, Nelson and I figured one of us should be home when Nihya got out of school to make sure she completed her homework and to be there for any after-school activities she participated in. Not to mention she was a preteen, which was around the time hormones started to kick in. Nelson had expressed his apprehension about allowing her to be home alone for too long.

School began about two weeks prior, and we wanted Nihya to get off to a good start. The last school year was extremely difficult for her following her mother's death. She had a series of outbursts in the classroom, and we never knew when the emotional trauma would fuel her anger. After a steady year of counseling, her psychologist felt Nihya was making tremendous progress channeling her emotions more constructively. She seemed to resent me, and I tried not to take it personally in the beginning, but I wasn't going to continue pacifying her situation. I didn't want to bother Nelson with some of the minor issues that I could handle myself, but I had to talk to him after the crap she pulled with not coming straight home as instructed.

While Nihya was in her room, I cooked dinner. Normally, I wouldn't make an elaborate meal on a Friday night, but I needed the distraction so I could think about how I wanted to approach Nelson about Nihya's behavior. I prepared one of Nelson's favorite meals: chuck roast, potatoes, and carrots along with stir-fried cabbage. Once dinner was completed, I showered quickly. Nelson arrived home from work about 6:30 p.m., just in time to have dinner with Nihya and me. Most of the time when he arrived home, Nihya was already asleep. He wasn't happy with his work schedule, but I kept reminding him that it was positioning him for better career opportunities.

Nelson walked into the kitchen, loosened his tie, and pulled me in his arms. He gave me one of those quick, but passionate kisses on the lips that said, "I can't wait to get you alone."

*My God, I love this caramel sensation of mine.* If we were alone, I would have sexed him right in the kitchen, no conversation necessary. Afterward, he kissed Nihya on the forehead, rolled his sleeves to his forearms, and proceeded to wash his hands in the kitchen sink.

I figured I wouldn't bring up Nihya's behavior at dinner because I wanted to talk to him alone first. Plus, when I had spoken to him earlier that day, he expressed that he was glad to be getting off work early enough to spend time with Nihya and me, so I didn't want to ruin it for him. He had been working extremely hard, so I was going to allow him to enjoy a nice, peaceful dinner without me being the complaining wife.

During dinner, Nihya talked about her first two weeks of school. She expressed her excitement about making new friends, and she mentioned she wanted to try out for the dance team and cheerleading squad. I thought it was a great idea for her to participate in more school activities, although Nelson's demeanor alluded to the fact that he wasn't so sure. Depending on her grades and her behavior, I would try to convince him to allow her to participate. Those kinds of activities were important to me growing up.

After dinner, Nelson showered and was in bed by the time Nihya and I cleaned up the kitchen. Since I showered before dinner, I entered our bedroom, undressed, and eased under the covers. I kissed Nelson passionately on his lips, and he was instantly aroused.

"Damn, baby, I've missed this," Nelson said, as he softly traced the shape of my vagina with his finger.

"I know, Nelly. She's missed you, too."

When I kissed him again, I knew we wouldn't be doing any talking that night regarding Nihya's behavior. Nelson and I used to make love almost every night until we no longer had the house to ourselves. I was still getting comfortable with the idea of being a stepmom, and although it may have sounded selfish, I missed having my husband to myself.

After a few minutes of grinding, Nelson penetrated me slowly, erasing all of my worries and concerns immediately. With each passionate thrust, he gently grabbed my hair and whispered in my ear how much he missed making love to me. The passion was somehow different, though. Normally, Nelson reached his peak first and I would have to wait for round two, but not that time. After about twenty minutes of constant stroking, my sugar walls pulsated with pure satisfaction.

"Oh, damn, Nelson. I'm cumming, baby," I managed to moan.

"I know. I can feel you. I'm about to cum, too."

That was the first time in a long while that we reached our peak together. To my pleasant surprise, Nelson maintained an erection and continued stroking even after his release. His strokes became more intense, and the pleasure started to mix with pain.

"Nelson, baby, calm down. You can't have me screaming up in here with Nihya in the next room, especially since we don't know if she's already asleep."

"Yeah, you right. Shit!"

"What's wrong?"

"Nothing, babe, but you feel so amazing. Damn, I can't help it," Nelson said, as if he had been running a marathon.

"Um, so you've noticed, huh?"

"Yeah, what've you been doing, them pussy exercises?"

"You so stupid," I said, laughing. "It's called Kegel exercises, and it's supposed to help keep the vagina nice and—"

"Can I get the Kegel lesson tomorrow, baby?" Nelson interrupted. "Right now, I want you to turn over for me."

"For what, Nelson?" I instantly got an unpleasant flashback of our first anal experience.

"Scared? Say ya scared. But naw, I know you didn't like the anal thing, so I won't do that again unless you're ready. Now turn dat ass over for me, mami."

"When you start talking like that? You must be looking at them rap videos again, with your nasty self."

"Woman, you talking too much."

Nelson laughed as I reluctantly turned over on my stomach. I couldn't believe how hard his erection remained, but I sure wasn't mad. My husband must have had a lot of pent-up sexual frustration to release because I hadn't seen him with that kind of stamina in a while. With his hectic work schedule for the past few months, our sex life had pretty much been filled with quickies. I despised quickies, especially if I didn't have an orgasm prior to Nelson's release. Thank goodness it was a Friday night. We could keep on making love until he could no longer maintain an erection or until my coochie was too sore to handle it.

After the second round of lovemaking, we needed another shower. And since both of us refused to sleep in the wet spot, the linens on our bed needed to be refreshed.

When we were back in our bed, Nelson kissed my cheek and caressed my stomach. I wasn't about to ruin the night we had with the conversation regarding the problems I was having with Nihya. It was going to have to wait until the morning. My mind was filled with so many random thoughts that I almost didn't hear Nelson say my name.

"Dianne?"

"Yes, baby?"

"I love you."

"I love you, too, Nelson."

"You and Nihya are my world. You know that, right?"

He always made me nervous when he talked like that, almost as if he was about to follow up with some kind of bad news or something.

"I can't wait until you're carrying my baby." Nelson continued to rub my stomach as if I was already pregnant.

"I know. Neither can I," I replied sadly.

Immediately, thoughts ran through my mind about the baby I lost prior to Nelson coming into my life. He still didn't know anything about that part of my past. When Nelson and I first got married, neither of us was in a rush to start a family. We wanted to enjoy each other before the babies started coming. After he found out he already had an eleven-year-old daughter, he constantly talked about adding to our family. I knew he wanted a son; so, I hoped I could give him one or maybe even two.

"Dianne?"

"Yes, Nelson?" I answered, somewhat annoyed. *If he has something on his mind, I really wish he would just say it.*

"Thank you for being the woman you are."

"Nelson, is there something you need to tell me? You sound guilty about something."

"No, sweetheart, I just—"

"You just what?"

"Love you, that's all. I work with a few guys that dread going home. They would rather go to the bar and get drunk before going home to deal with their wives and children. Listening to them made me realize how much I look forward to coming home to you."

"Aw, Nelly, that's so sweet." I kissed his lips.

Nelson smiled and continued. "Yeah, at work, we were talking about the movie *Why Did I Get Married?* The fellas laughed and said they ask themselves that question every day. One guy said he felt like he only got fifty percent of the kind of woman he wanted and not the eighty percent that's mentioned in the movie, so he gets the other fifty elsewhere from several different women."

"Damn, really? Unfortunately, that's not uncommon for a lot of folks these days."

"Yeah, so I went back to my office and wrote down all the things I ever wanted in a woman. Then I wrote down all the things I love about you. And, baby, I got pretty much one hundred percent of the kind of woman I wanted."

"You wrote a list? Isn't that taking the movie too seriously?"

"Did you hear what I said?"

"Yes, yes. I'm perfect. Thank you!"

We both laughed.

"No, woman, you are *not* perfect."

"Dag, you didn't have to emphasize it like that."

Nelson continued. "What I said was that I basically got the right woman for me. I don't feel like you are only eighty percent."

I had a very passionate and sensitive husband, so I knew he was sincere about what he shared with me. *I wish I didn't always think he had an ulterior motive.*

"Thank you, baby, but where's all this coming from?" I stroked his five o'clock shadow that would be a full beard if he would let it grow.

"I just wanted you to know that."

"Are you sure there's nothing else on your mind that you want to talk about?"

"Yeah, baby, I'm sure. I was just listening to how those dudes were talking about their wives and not wanting to go home. I mean, I don't know. I want you to know that as your husband, I'm here to make your life easier in every possible way. We're already living comfortable financially. But, with this new position I may get, you, Nihya, and the baby—or babies we may have—will not want for anything."

"I know, Nelson. You are an excellent provider and a great lover I must say," I told him while stroking his semi-erection.

"Oh, I get it. You only want me for my money and my body," he said jokingly.

"And, of course, your mind, Nelly."

"Come here, woman." Nelson playfully grabbed me in his arms.

"Nelson, we just got out of the shower and put clean sheets on the bed. Don't start."

"So, what does that mean? I can't have any more tonight?"

"You can have anything you want from me, baby."

"I tell you what. Hand me the towel on that chair."

I obliged. "What are you getting ready to do?"

"You'll see."

Nelson put the towel underneath me and parted my legs as he kissed each of my inner thighs. It had been such a long time since he pleased me orally that I immediately got excited and felt my vaginal walls contract in anticipation.

He licked his lips and asked, "Where's the honey?"

# CHAPTER 2

## *Lynda*

***THE THOUGHT OF ZION AND*** *Jasmine together is too much for me to digest at this point in my life; it's supposed to be a happy time for me.* My debut novel was due to be released in a couple of months, and I didn't have anyone to share the occasion with. Well, I did have my girls, Natasha and Dianne, but I was ready for a significant other to share these kinds of milestones and accomplishments. I could've called any one of my male friends, but spending time with a man that I didn't anticipate having a future with was getting extremely old.

To be honest, I didn't know if Zion and Jasmine were together. I let my assumptions take over after she called his house. But why would she have called him? I wouldn't allow Zion to explain the situation because I didn't think I could handle whatever he was going to say. The hurt in Zion's eyes quickly turned to anger the day I questioned him about Jasmine. I had never seen him so angry before, and it really startled me. My thought was if he wasn't messing around with her, then why did he allow himself to get so angry?

I was still in love with Zion, but I had to admit to myself that our relationship faded once his literary career took off. His success as an author was evident as he made the ESSENCE® bestseller's list for several consecutive months. I was indeed happy for him, but we appeared to move in different directions. He made a lot of effort to ensure I was a part of his life, but I could sense he felt pressure from our relationship. I knew I would have to let him go anyway, eventually. The call from Jasmine just sped up the process.

Jasmine and I used to be good friends until the day she pulled that stunt while we engaged in a threesome with the male dancer, Long Stroke. She knew it was clear that we weren't supposed to interact with each other, only to take turns with him. The fact that she went *down* on me without my consent validated we could never be friends again; however, I let her continue pleasing me, which still bothered me. I couldn't blame anyone for that but myself.

I also had to blame myself for what was going on with Justin and me. Although Justin was currently separated from his wife, he was still a married man. Apparently, his wife found the poem I wrote to him, or at least that was his story. From what he previously told me, their marriage was pretty much over, so maybe that was the last straw for her. Other than Zion, no one else pleased me sexually like Justin. Well, then again, Maurice was great in bed. As far as Justin was concerned, the lovin' was too good to give him up now. He was the only man I had in my life since I stopped seeing all the other men I once indulged myself in, especially Maurice. *Lord knows I can't go back down that road.*

As I settled into bed, my house phone rang, startling me. I knocked over the glass of wine that rested on my nightstand as I grabbed the phone off the cradle. Not too many people even knew I had a house phone, and I didn't recognize the number on the Caller ID.

"Shit," I said, not realizing I had already hit the talk button. "I'm sorry, hello?"

"Hello, is this Lynda Davis?"

"Yes, it is."

*Please don't let this be a business call,* I thought to myself. Then again, they wouldn't have been calling on that number. I had a separate business line.

"Hi, Lynda. You don't know me, but I wanted to talk to you about Taylor Dixon."

"Who?"

"I'm sorry, you may have called him Taye."

"Who is this, and why are you calling me about Taye?" My eyes watered as painful memories surfaced.

"I apologize for calling you like this. I'm Taye's brother, and I found your number on one of Taye's cell phone bills."

"That doesn't make sense. My name is not shown on the actual bill, so how did you get my information?"

"Since your number was listed so many times on the bill, I Googled it. Your information came up, so I figured I would call you."

"Okay, and you're calling me because…"

"I'm not sure. I guess I wanted to find out what happened with my brother."

"Well, Taye tried to kill me. That's what happened!" I screamed into the phone before slamming it down. "Why is everyone fucking with me?" I asked aloud.

My phone rang again.

"Hello?"

"Lynda, please don't hang up. I'm sorry if I'm upsetting you. I'm Taye's younger brother, Xavier. I was away at college when I found out that Taye was killed in a high-speed car chase with the police. It didn't seem like Taye to be in trouble with the law, so I thought maybe I could talk to his friends to find out some of the missing pieces."

"Well, I'm not the *friend* to get information from, okay? I dated Taye for several months, things didn't work out, and he tried to kill me. He shot me." The tears fell.

"Oh, I'm sorry. I didn't know. But that doesn't seem like Taye's character."

"Of course you didn't know. I didn't mean to yell at you, but this is too much for me. I don't know if I can be of any help to you. I hope you understand."

"Yes, I understand. Again, I do apologize for calling you, but my mother isn't doing well after all of this. I just wanted to see what I could find out about Taye to help ease her pain."

I took a deep breath as the tears continued to fall. "Xavier."

"Yes?"

"Listen, Taye was a good man. I don't know why he snapped, but he almost killed me. At one point, I really cared about him. He seemed happy, so I don't know what he was going through."

"I appreciate your time. If anything comes to mind that Taye may have mentioned that would help us understand his behavior, then please call me."

"I will. I have your number on the Caller ID."

"Thank you. Goodnight, beautiful."

"Excuse me?" I asked, a bit startled.

"Oh, your name means beautiful one."

"I guess it does," I answered with hesitation.

There was something definitely strange about the phone call. *I hate Google.* Someone could be after you, and Google gave them all of your damn information. I needed to change my number to unlisted.

"Well, take care, Lynda."

"Goodnight, Xavier."

As I hung up the phone, I remembered I had spilled my glass of wine. I desperately needed a drink after that phone call, so I went into the kitchen to refill my glass with Moscato. I grabbed the roll of paper towels so I could clean up the spilled wine. A bit distraught over the phone call from Xavier, I decided to place a call to Justin hoping he could make me feel better. When Justin didn't answer, I immediately got annoyed, wondering if he was with his wife. I didn't understand why some people stayed in a situation they claimed they didn't want to be in.

For the rest of the night, I sat on my bed and cried while watching *Waiting to Exhale* repeatedly. *When the fuck am I going to exhale? I'm so tired of the bullshit.* After I drank almost an entire bottle of wine, I eventually drifted off to sleep.

Around three o'clock the next morning, my cell phone rang, disturbing me from my sleep. In a near delirious state, I checked my phone, and it was Justin. He probably wanted some of my good lovin' since he was done playing house with his wife and children. *I don't think so.* I ignored his call and sent his ass straight to voicemail. *Fuck him!* I was able to immediately return to a deep slumber.

After sleeping for what seemed like a few hours, I woke up to use the bathroom. It must have been all that wine I consumed. I checked the time on my cell phone and realized I had only been asleep for about forty-five minutes. On my way into the bathroom, I noticed the light blinking on my answering machine. *I wonder who left me a message at this time of the morning.* And yes, I still had an old school answering machine.

I didn't hear the phone ring nor did I remember turning off the ringer. I tried to resist checking the message because I figured it was from Justin since he was the only person who had called me recently. I checked the message anyway. Justin's sexy voice asked me to return his call because he wanted to come and see me. Come and *sex* me was more accurate. He claimed he had fallen asleep watching football and that was why he had missed my call. It was possible he was telling the truth, but who knew? I didn't feel like analyzing the situation anymore, so I decided to return his call. He answered on the first ring.

"Lynda?"

"Hey, Justin," I responded flatly.

"What's wrong, baby? Why do you sound like that?"

"I'm tired, that's all. It's nearly four o'clock in the morning."

"I was hoping you would call back. I want to come over."

"Justin, I don't know if that's a good idea."

"Why? I don't have to work tomorrow, so I could just spend the day with you."

"How do you know I don't have anything to do?"

"Do you?"

"No, not really."

"See, so let me come over there. I know you want me to."

"How do you figure that?"

"You called me back, didn't you?" Justin laughed.

I managed a slight smile because he was right. I wanted him. I didn't know how much longer I could continue to sleep with a married man, though, because I was ready to be in a committed relationship. Justin didn't consider himself to be married since he was separated. I probably should've asked to see the separation papers to see if it was legit. For some strange reason, he thought we were going to be in an exclusive relationship while he was still married. I didn't understand his logic. *How is that possible?*

"Justin, if you're going to come over, then come now. I would like to go back to sleep," I lied. Truthfully, I was ready to get down to business.

"Okay, I'm on my way."

"Call me when you're outside, Justin, and hurry up."

"A'ight, bet."

# Chapter 3
## *Natasha*

*I DON'T KNOW WHY I* allowed Tyrone *to talk me into moving to Columbia, Maryland.* I was sure someone told him that it would be better to raise our children in Howard County instead of Prince George's County. It didn't take us long to discover that even some of the best counties had its own hoods. Since I previously rented a condominium in Upper Marlboro, it wasn't a difficult process to move. However, during our first few months in our new place, we encountered more drama than I could stand.

When I brought my babies home from the hospital, I was greeted by yellow police tape surrounding the entrance of the building next to mine. After talking to one of my neighbors, I learned that apparently, a sex offender living in the building committed suicide after he was accused of molesting his girlfriend's son. *What is the world coming to?* I was appalled at the news. That was almost two months ago. Unfortunately, I didn't know most of my neighbors, so there was no telling who lived close to me.

The constant police activity was too much for me to deal with, especially since I found out I was pregnant again when I went for my six-week check-up after having my son, Tyler. I almost lost Tyler after Tyrone's ex-wife kicked me in the stomach, causing him to be born a month early. He was a fighter, though.

Being pregnant twice within one year wasn't the main issue, but carrying twins was a lot to digest. Tyrone appeared ecstatic about the situation because he had the family he told me that he wanted for such a long time. I didn't know for several months that I was pregnant with twins. The doctor said sometimes, one baby was positioned behind the other one, so it appeared there was only one heartbeat. I didn't mind having another baby because although I loved my son, I wanted another girl, and God blessed me with two.

Life was definitely going to be challenging with three babies to take care of. Tyrone occasionally made comments to me that I was trying to replace Aisha. No matter how many kids we had, that wasn't what I was trying to do. Aisha could never be replaced.

Tyrone and I were returning from the two-month check-up appointment for the girls when we noticed several police cars in our parking lot. Tyler was spending the night with Tyrone's cousin, Anita, who lived in the area. Before Tyrone moved from Georgia, I wasn't aware he had any family in the Maryland area. He said it was a cousin by marriage, and they grew closer after his mother died. Anita had a small child around Tyler's age; therefore, it was a smooth transition for him to stay with her during my first few days after leaving the hospital. Tyler enjoyed being there since he had someone to play with, so we occasionally let him go over there.

"Tyrone, I'm not comfortable with all this police activity. We've been here less than a year, and there's already way more drama than I care to see."

"Natasha, please. This can happen anywhere."

"Well, it's not happening *anywhere*. It's happening too close to my home."

Tyrone sighed as he carried Natalia in his arms. I was still sore from the delivery, so I moved slowly up the two flights of stairs as I held Nevaeh tightly in my arms. *Now, I wish we had purchased a house instead of a condo.* I experienced something painful during delivery that I wouldn't wish on anyone else, not even my worst enemy. Natalia was born first without any complications; however, Nevaeh was turned around backward, and the doctor had to reposition her in my womb. As the doctor reached into my vagina and turned Nevaeh around to the appropriate birthing position, I let out a piercing scream as if I was in a horror movie being chased by Freddy Krueger. I squeezed Tyrone's hand so hard that I broke his skin with my fingernails. *I don't wish a breech situation on anyone.*

The hardest part of the delivery with the twins was that I thought I had lost Nevaeh because she wasn't breathing. I was in shock, so I couldn't react to what the doctors had said. After a few seconds— although it seemed like hours—she started breathing. It was as if angels were watching over us when she cried, so I decided to name her Nevaeh, which is 'heaven' spelled backward.

I hoped my baby girls would sleep through most of the night so I could get some much-needed rest. Although I missed Tyler, I was glad he was spending time with Tyrone's cousin. He had a lot of energy. I was amazed that Tyrone and I got the twins to fall asleep almost at the same time. That was the first time we were able to do that. Once they were asleep, he insisted I get some sleep immediately. I was exhausted, so he wasn't going to get an argument from me.

"Natasha, baby, don't try to do anything right now but rest."

"Okay, you're right. Are you going to lay with me?"

"I mean, I can't get *any*. Can I?"

"Tyrone!"

"Girl, you know I'm kidding, but it has been eight long weeks. What happened to six weeks?"

"Remember, I had two babies this time. I'm still sore, and I don't even want to think about you poking around inside of me."

"I know you needed more time to heal from that minor complication. But as soon as you're healed, all I'm gonna do is tear that ass back up."

"You know what, Tyrone?"

"What?"

"You got issues."

"No, I'm horny."

"Your horny ass is why I have given birth twice in a year's time."

"Well, your tubes are tied now, so I can get it as often as I want without you worrying about getting pregnant again."

"Yes, you can. I got you in about two more weeks." I kissed Tyrone softly on his lips.

"Well, lay down so I can grind on your ass."

"Tyrone, come on now." I couldn't help but laugh at his teenage request.

"I'm serious. Why you laughing?"

"I know you are, but we're not fifteen." I remember how Tyrone used to grind on me before we actually had sex when we were teenagers.

"Yeah, okay. Wait until you go to sleep." Tyrone laughed and kissed the back of my neck. "I'm going to be grinding all up on that ass."

Although I loved Tyrone, I was nervous about our new family status. Things were moving so fast that I hadn't taken the time to process it all. Tyrone wanted us to have more than one child so they could grow up without being an only child. He hated being an only child, and I did, as well. *I wonder if Aisha felt the same way about being an only child.* I decided to get my tubes tied right after delivery, and Tyrone agreed without a question. Tyrone was ecstatic that he had a son, and I now had my girls.

"Natasha?" Tyrone spoke, interrupting my thoughts.

"Yes, Tyrone?" I asked sleepily.

"Are you too tired to help me with this erection?"

"How do you *suppose* I do that?"

"Come on, babe. I know you can be creative," Tyrone responded with slight laughter in his voice.

I was a traditional, missionary position woman; however, being friends with Dianne and Lynda, I learned to experiment more sexually in order to keep Tyrone home and satisfied. They talked me into purchasing a Super Stretch Sleeve from the last toy party we attended, which I initially thought was going to be a waste of money. Dianne warned me that after having my babies, I would need to be creative and please Tyrone for the next six to eight weeks. *I really hate when she's right!* Along with the sleeve, I had to get a lubricant to put inside, and it was supposed to feel like a vagina once placed around a man's penis. That night, I put that theory to the test with Tyrone.

"Tyrone, are you sure you can't help yourself?" I asked sarcastically.

"Very funny, Natasha. Why can't you just kiss *him* for a while?" Tyrone caressed himself.

"Because, Tyrone, you want me to come home after giving birth to your *babies* two months ago and please you like it's business as usual. Selfish!"

"You did last time."

"Well, this isn't last time."

Tyrone stood there looking at me with eyes that said, "Please." I tried to give him oral sex often since we got married, although it wasn't really my thing. Most men seemed to need that as part of their sex life; however, I wasn't in the mood.

"All right, never mind, Natasha," Tyrone said, as he walked closer to me. He grabbed my hand and placed it on his full erection. He was so hard. "Can I at least get a hand job? You have no idea what your fat ass and those huge breasts are doing to me."

"Tyrone, stop it!" I pulled my hand away. I was a bit self-conscious since I still looked pregnant.

"What? Baby, you look good. Look at all this." Tyrone pulled down my panties and caressed my ass, as I looked over my shoulder.

In the mirror, I could see what he was referring to. I looked back at Tyrone and kissed him passionately. Then I pushed him on the bed and said, "I'll be right back."

When I came back with the Super Stretch Sleeve and lubricant in my hand, Tyrone looked perplexed.

"Baby, what's that?"

"Wait and see," I replied.

I filled the sleeve with the lubricant just like the consultant showed us at the toy party. She suggested using a flavored lubricant in case we decided to combine that technique with using our mouths, as well. I decided on a strawberry flavor. As I rolled the sleeve onto Tyrone's erection, he immediately closed his eyes and moaned, indicating he was very pleased. I stroked him in a back and forth motion while kissing him softly all over his upper body. I concentrated on his nipples because I knew that was one of his hotspots. Within a few minutes, he acknowledged that he was about to cum. He grabbed one of the pillows off the bed and covered his face so he could yell out in pleasure. I figured he did that so he wouldn't risk waking the babies.

Once Tyrone was done, I rolled the sleeve off his limp penis. The consultant also instructed collecting his sperm inside. I went into the bathroom, cleaned the sleeve thoroughly, and smiled at myself in the mirror. I had stepped out of the box to please my man. The sound of Tyrone's light snores let me know he was content. I eased into the bed beside him, laid in the spooning position, and he immediately placed his arm around me.

Tyrone awoke briefly to whisper, "Thank you, baby. That felt good," before he continued snoring.

*Men!*

# CHAPTER 4
## *Dianne*

*AFTER A NIGHT OF PASSIONATE* lovemaking, I woke up feeling amazing, and I didn't want the feeling to dissipate; however, I couldn't prolong having the conversation about Nihya's behavior. Nelson was already out of bed, although it would've been nice to have some early morning sex. The water running in the bathroom suggested to me that he was taking a shower, so I decided to join him. I was going to let him know that we needed to talk about Nihya's behavior.

"Nelson, baby?" I called, tapping on the bathroom door.

"Yes, baby. Come in. Why you knocking?"

"I don't know. Good morning," I said, stepping into the shower with him.

"Good morning, baby," Nelson responded, kissing me softly on the lips. "How did you sleep?"

"I slept well thanks to you," I teased.

"Thanks to me, huh?" Nelson laughed, as he gently caressed the lips below my waist.

"Yes, we haven't made love like that in a while. It was long overdue."

"Yes, it was."

I took Nelson's washcloth out of his hand and washed him. He looked into my eyes and apparently sensed there was something bothering me.

"Dianne, what's wrong? It looks as if something is on your mind."

"Nelson, we need to talk about Nihya and her behavior lately."

"What's going on?"

"She's just become increasingly disrespectful."

"Are you going to be more specific?" Nelson asked, sounding defensive on Nihya's behalf.

"Well, when I tell her to do something, she has to be told several times, and I'm getting tired of it. Some of her teachers are saying the same thing."

"So, when were you going to tell me?"

"I'm telling you now, Nelson. Why are you so defensive?"

"Because I'm her father, and I don't understand why you have been keeping this from me."

"In the beginning, there were certain things I could handle on my own. I didn't want to bother you since most of the time you were so tired when you got home. I was hoping it was just a phase Nihya was going through. I wasn't trying to keep this from you."

"Well, *as her father,* I don't need to be in the dark about what's going on around here."

"Why do you keep emphasizing that you are her father? I know who you are, but do you realize who I am? I'm the only mother she has now, and I need the same amount of respect from you and her. Maybe I'm overreacting, but I don't like the way you keep saying, *I am her father.* I know who the hell you are."

"Wow," Nelson responded sarcastically.

"Wow what? Never mind. Forget I said anything," I said, before dropping Nelson's washcloth and stepping out of the shower.

"Dianne."

"What!" I shouted.

"Okay, I didn't know you were so upset. Baby, we can talk about this when I get out of the shower."

"Whatever!"

When Nelson finished showering, he dried off and put on lotion for what seemed like an hour. It appeared to me as if he tried to avoid having the conversation.

"Dianne, please tell me what's going on. I do appreciate you trying to handle things while I was trying to get this new position, but baby, my household is more important. We need to handle things together."

I didn't respond.

"Dianne, I'm sorry if I upset you, but talk to me. We can't work through this if you shut down."

"Nelson, look. I'm not trying to replace Nihya's mother, but sometimes you act as if I don't know what I'm doing. Or maybe that's just how I'm taking it. I don't know. If I tell Nihya to do something, I have to repeat myself several times. But, if *her daddy* tells her to do something, she gets up immediately. I feel disrespected."

"I understand."

"Do you really?"

"I'm trying to at least. Come on, Dianne, don't act like this now. You know all that she has been through."

"How long are we going to allow her to use what has happened to her as an excuse? She isn't the only person who has to deal with situations like this, Nelson. You have no idea what it was like when my mother first died."

"She didn't only lose her mother. She was molested, too, Dianne. Or did you forget that?" Nelson lowered his tone.

Avoiding Nelson's last response, I got up off the bed and walked out of the room. Nelson followed me and grabbed my arm. I was somewhat startled by his aggressiveness.

"Stop walking away from me. We need to talk about this."

"Okay, um, maybe you forgot whose father you are, but surely it isn't mine." I pulled away from Nelson's grip and headed downstairs to fix myself something to eat. Nelson and *his daughter* were on their own with breakfast.

"Dianne." Nelson followed me downstairs to the kitchen.

"Nelson, you've made it clear how you feel about the situation. You don't care that she's disrespectful to me because of what she has been through. I get that now, so I have nothing else to say about it."

At that moment, Nihya came downstairs and joined us in the kitchen. "What's for breakfast?"

"Ask your father," I snapped.

"Dianne!" Nelson responded quickly.

"What, Nelson? Shit! This is exactly why I haven't said anything to you, because I knew you would make excuses for her behavior. So, never mind. Let it go!"

Nihya looked confused. "Did I do something?"

"Obviously you're doing something. Dianne's very upset."

"She's *always* upset about something, Daddy," Nihya responded with a sassy tone.

"That's exactly what I mean. No respect," I said, shaking my head as I continued to scramble my eggs.

When I finished cooking my breakfast, I sat down and ate. Nelson seemed in disbelief. I could see him looking at me from my peripheral vision, but I refused to acknowledge him. I was tired of feeling unappreciated.

"Dianne, that was very petty of you not to fix us anything to eat," Nelson stated.

I continued to eat as if he wasn't there. Nelson sat down next to me and caressed my back when the tears welled up in my eyes. As they fell, he wiped them away. After a few minutes, Nelson spoke again.

"Baby, I'm sorry. I didn't know this was so difficult for you. I see you're really upset, and I will make sure I have a talk with Nihya right away. You're right; she has no business disrespecting you."

Somehow, that didn't make me feel any better, so again, I didn't respond.

"Daddy!" Nihya yelled from the living room where she watched cartoons.

"Nihya, go upstairs so I can talk to Dianne." Nelson spoke in a soft tone. I shook my head.

"But, Daddy, I'm hungry."

"Nihya!" Nelson said, this time in a stern voice.

"Okay, okay," Nihya said, as she hurried up the stairs.

"How long has this been going on with Nihya?" Nelson asked me.

"Months."

"Months?"

"Yes, months, and I guess I should have told you sooner. From now on, when the school calls, I'll tell them to call you instead of me."

"That's not necessary."

"Why isn't it? You need to experience the phone calls for a change. I counsel children all day. The one thing I stress to them is, no matter how bad their situation was in the past, they have to be held accountable for their actions. The law doesn't always take into consideration a child's past if they become juvenile delinquents. The system will detain them, regardless."

Nelson looked defeated. "I know, but I'm not sure how to handle this, Dianne. It's not like I've raised her since birth. This parenting thing is new to me. At least you have experience working with children."

"Nelson, there's nothing wrong with wanting to protect Nihya, but you also have to find a way to discipline her before her behavior gets out of hand."

"I know. You're right."

Nelson kissed me on the cheek and got up from the table. He prepared breakfast for Nihya and himself. No longer hungry, I left my plate on the table and went upstairs to lie across my bed. I was deep in thought about the situation with Nihya until I drifted off to sleep.

Finding out you had a child after eleven years had to be hard for anybody. I knew this situation with Nihya was especially hard for Nelson because he was a very gentle person. I figured when we had children together, I would have to be the one to do most of the discipline. It wasn't in his nature to spank children, and he probably never got a spanking when he was a child. But me, I would beat a child's ass if I had to, and I wouldn't feel bad about it either.

# CHAPTER 5
## *Lynda*

*I WOKE UP AT APPROXIMATELY* eight o'clock in the morning and immediately realized that Justin had never showed up. *Asshole!* I checked the Caller ID on my cell phone and house phone, but his number wasn't on either. I was so sick of his lies, but I had allowed this bullshit to continue. *How are you on your way, but then never show up?* Why did I even ask myself that question? My ex-boyfriend, Maurice, did that frequently during the time we were involved. *I must like self-inflicted pain, choosing to deal with men like this.* Well, enough was enough. It was time I made a few changes in my life as far as men were concerned because my current path was leading me down the road to nowhere.

Justin was lucky I hadn't called his wife yet. He called me from that number a few times, so what made him think I would never call back? Usually, I wasn't one for that kind of drama, but there was something about when the lovin' gets good that would make a sane person act totally crazy. Due to the way I felt in regards to Justin playing with my emotions, I was tempted to pay a visit to his wife. *Oh yes, I have the address!* What would that accomplish, though? I didn't know, but I would find out when I got there.

I needed to get my mind off Justin before I ended up doing something not just immoral, but illegal. My cell phone rang, interrupting my thoughts of Justin. I didn't recognize the number, and the name displayed as, "Do Not Answer." Shit, that could have been any man I had dealt with during the past two years, and that list was about as long as a five-year-old girl's Christmas list. Zion was even on that list.

Regretfully, I answered the damn phone. *Why me?* It was Maurice. Speaking, or should I say thinking, of the damn devil, and I meant that literally. I didn't make it to his housewarming party, so he was calling to invite me over to see his new place. Presumably, he was trying to prove to me that he could be stable. Please! He was about as stable as a chair with a missing leg.

After several minutes of his normal act of persuasion, I decided to visit Maurice to see his new place because I was a bit curious. I left my house almost immediately after I hung up the phone. I had taken a shower the night before since I thought Justin was coming over, so I slid on my clothes and grabbed my purse. On the drive over there, I contemplated turning around several times. *Why am I going over there?*

When I entered his house, he immediately started kissing me on my neck as if he missed me. The look I gave him must have shown exactly what I was feeling, because his attempts at turning me on came to a halt. I had to admit he had a nice house; however, I wasn't all that impressed because deep inside, I knew he was the same ol' Maurice. Damn, he looked deliciously good, though. I tried to seem unaffected by his presence, but the sight of him made me want to wrap my legs around his waist and not let go until they were trembling with satisfaction. *Damn! I may have set myself up with this visit.*

"What's up, Ms. Davis? Long time, no see."

"Yeah, whatever."

"What's up with the attitude? What did I do or didn't do this time?"

"It doesn't matter anymore, Maurice. Just show me around your place."

"Damn, okay. Are you in a rush or something?"

"Not really, but I do have some things to do today."

"Oh, okay. As long as you aren't mad at me."

I didn't respond to his last comment. I stayed mad at Maurice for one reason or another. He didn't know how to be consistent. Well, he was not consistent with me anyway. It appeared I wasn't that important to him, and I was glad I made the decision not to have his baby. *Who needs a constant reminder of someone who doesn't love you the same way you love them?*

"Lynda?" Maurice called my name to get my attention. My mind had wandered for a minute.

"What?"

"I asked you a question."

"What's the question?"

"I asked if you were mad at me."

"Actually, you made a statement about me being mad. As long as you aren't mad at me and are you mad at me is two different things. One is a declarative, and the other is an interrogative."

"There's that smart mouth of yours. It just doesn't stop, does it?"

"Well, it's the truth. And please just show me around. Goodness."

"Okay," Maurice sighed.

I no longer had the same desire to be in his presence. And quite frankly, he had started to get on my nerves. I felt as if he enjoyed playing with my emotions. With men, as long as you talk to them, they feel they still have an opportunity to get some ass from you. Well, he was wrong if that was his thought process. My ass was tired, and my heart simply couldn't take it anymore. I still didn't know why he invited me over to see his new house. I could've cared less about him, his house, or anything else concerning him. Then again, I lied, because my ass wouldn't be over his house if I didn't care. I was indeed curious to see how he was living these days. A part of me also wanted to see if I was actually over him before I tried to mend things with Zion.

"I'm going to give you the quick tour and then save the master bedroom for last," he said and kissed the back of my neck.

"You know what, Maurice? Stop playing games. I'm not sleeping with you anymore."

"You mean to tell me you don't want any of this?" he asked, stroking his pride and joy.

He was well endowed, and in the past, I couldn't resist his 'pride and joy' being inside of me. But it was a new day, and I needed more than a stiff one. *Although it would be nice to sit on his face right about now so he could lick Ms. Kitty. She really needs to purr!*

I couldn't believe how weak I was for him because before I could even answer him, he managed to unbutton and unzip my jeans and had pulled them down past my hips, exposing my sexy thong.

"See, you even wore my favorite thongs. So, you stop playing games."

Maurice kissed the back of my neck again, which he knew drove me crazy, while one hand wandered across my breasts and the other eased inside my thong, teasing my clit.

"Damn, and you're wet. Let me feel you, girl. You know you miss me."

The truth was I didn't miss him, but I was horny. I was tempted to allow him to sex me, but then I realized he tried to enter my sweetness without a condom. *When did I step out of my jeans?*

"Maurice, stop."

"What's wrong?"

"Look, I came over to see your place, not to have sex with you. Plus, you don't even have a condom on. We're not together like that. That's how I ended up pregnant the last time."

I couldn't believe I slipped and told him the secret I had been keeping from him.

"What do you mean pregnant? Pregnant by who?"

"You, Maurice. Okay, I was pregnant by you," I said, pulling my jeans back up.

"So you had an abortion?"

"Obviously so. You don't see me with a baby, do you?"

"I wish your ass would stop being so damn sarcastic all the time. You know what, get the fuck out."

"Fine with me. Remember, you called me over here in the first place. And I'm sorry if you're upset about the abortion or the fact I didn't tell you. It's not like you're consistent and was going to be there for me."

"How do you know? You didn't even have enough decency to tell me and give me a chance. But, whatever, Lynda. What's done is done. I see now you only really give a damn about your feelings. How could you kill my baby without even telling me?"

"You're making it seem like you wanted to be with me. You always had an excuse as to why we couldn't take our relationship to the next level. So, please, let's not talk about decency. There were times when your ass stood me up, but I'm not going to get into all of that. I'm over it now. I simply didn't want to be a single mother. You know as well as I do, you would have wanted me to have an abortion."

Maurice just stood there with anger in his eyes. When he finally spoke, he said something I would never forget. "That bullet should have killed you."

I had never seen Maurice with so much hatred in his eyes. I couldn't believe how angry he was about the situation. I decided not to respond; instead, I got my purse and left his house hoping I would never hear from him again. Whether he meant it or not, that was something I would never forgive him for saying.

When I got home, I checked my voicemail messages on my home phone. There were two messages; the first message was from Justin. I deleted it as soon as I heard his voice. At that moment, I didn't care what he had to say. The other message was from Xavier, Taye's brother. I listened to his message and decided to call him back. *Loneliness makes you do some foolish things.*

"Hi, Lynda. Thanks for calling me back."

"No problem. What's up?"

"I was just wondering if you would meet me so we could talk."

"I don't know if that's a good idea, Xavier."

"I understand, but we could meet in a public place. I want to talk to you in person before I go back to school. It would only take about an hour of your time."

"Let me think about it and touch base with you later."

"Okay, sounds good. Thanks, Lynda."

I wondered why it was so important to Xavier to meet with me. A part of me believed he wanted to talk about Taye and to get closure; however, another part of me felt that maybe he actually wanted to hold me accountable for Taye's death.

My curiosity took over and I decided to meet Xavier at a Starbucks in downtown Washington, D.C. I didn't want to be too close to my place because I didn't want to risk him finding out where I lived. *Then again, he probably has my address, thanks to Google.* I should've told Dianne and Natasha that I was going to meet with him in case something went down, but they would have only tried to talk me out of it. Therefore, I would tell them afterward. I wasn't too worried about meeting him since we would be in public. I just hoped he wasn't as sexy as Taye because that could be an area of concern!

# CHAPTER 6
## *Natasha*

~ ∽ ⊙⊙ ∽ ~

**THE SOUND OF SOMEONE BANGING** on my door startled me
out of my sleep. I hated to be awakened in that manner. I rushed to the
door to see whom it could possibly be knocking like the police early
on a Saturday morning. I noticed the time on the clock was about 8:15.
*Who in the hell?* I thought as I looked out of the peephole.

"Who is it?" I asked, obviously annoyed.

"Janiquisha, your neighbor from next door."

*Janiquisha? I'm sure her mother thought that was a really cute name.
Good grief!*

"Yes, how can I help you?" I asked through the door.

"I was wondering if you had some kind of juice I can have to go
in my vodka."

"Excuse me?" That was when I looked through the peephole again
and noticed the glass in *Janiquisha's* hand. *Did she really bring the glass
of vodka with her?*

"I know it's early in the morning, but this is how I like to start my
day, girl."

"I'm sorry, I just brought my babies home from the hospital. I haven't even had time to go to the grocery store yet," I lied. The twins were two months old.

"Okay, girl, I understand. Thanks anyway."

*The nerve of some people! How do you knock on a stranger's door with a glass in your hand, asking for juice to go with your vodka at eight something in the morning?*

When I got back into my bedroom, Tyrone asked who was at the door. I told him about Janiquisha's request. He laughed and rolled over as if he thought of going back to sleep; however, Natalia cried. It was amazing that I could tell which baby was crying. Natalia had the stronger cry; I hoped that wasn't a sign she was going to be a hell raiser! I knew it wasn't going to be long before Nevaeh started crying, so Tyrone and I went to get them for their morning feeding. They only woke up twice in the middle of the night, and we were happy.

One thing I could say was Tyrone was willing to be there every step of the way. When the babies cried, he immediately went to their room. I didn't have to ask him for help; it seemed instinctive. Initially, I didn't want to breastfeed because it seemed like it was going to be too much with two babies. After a long discussion with Tyrone, I decided to try it, but I had to constantly pump the milk into bottles to keep up with two greedy babies. I wasn't sure how long that was going to last, but he couldn't say I didn't try.

Being a stay-at-home mom was great, but occasionally, I missed my job at the Department of Education. I was one of the few people who actually liked their job with the federal government. Considering the high cost of childcare, it didn't make sense for both of us to work, though. Once my maternity leave was over, I was going back to work to officially resign. Tyrone and I agreed that I would stay home until the girls were ready for pre-kindergarten. Even then, we planned to consider home schooling if private school was too expensive.

Tyrone earned a handsome salary as an accountant, and he was studying to become a Certified Public Accountant. I was shocked to discover how smart he really was because he was a consistent C student in high school. Seemingly, he did just enough to pass. His mother would constantly say to him, "If you can get C's without opening your books, imagine what you could accomplish if you actually studied." I wondered if Tyrone got caught up in that "too cool to be smart" nonsense. I figured his mother was right because when I saw his college transcript, he graduated with a 3.7 and all the A's were in his core accounting classes. There was nothing sexier to me than an intelligent black man with a little bad boy in him. I had what Lynda often described as a "refined roughneck."

Once the twins were back to sleep, I decided to talk with Tyrone so we could plan our financial schedule since we would be using his salary and any savings we had accumulated.

"Tyrone?"

"Yes, babe?"

"When do you go back to work?"

"Dag, are you sick of me already?"

"No, I was just asking."

Tyrone was hesitant in his response. "Well, it's hard to say right now."

"Why?"

"Tash, I don't know any other way to say this."

"Say what?"

"I kind of quit my job."

"What? Why? You loved your job."

"I love you guys more, and they were trying to work me to death. No consideration for new babies at home."

"I don't follow you."

"Well, just like women get maternity leave when they have a baby, at my firm, fathers get paternity leave, and they were trying to deny my request."

"Yeah, it's like that in the federal government, but why were they denying you?"

"My boss made a comment that this wasn't a good time for my wife to have a baby."

"Can't you report him for saying that?"

"Yes, but all he would probably do is make my life a living hell, and I don't want that kind of stress."

"I understand, but, Tyrone, do you think that was smart walking away like that, burning your bridge?"

"Baby, this wasn't something I planned to do. My boss pissed me off, so I just walked out."

"So, you haven't officially resigned? How is this going to affect us financially?"

"No, and we're fine financially. You know that. Nelson helped me with some investments that are doing exceptionally well."

"Nelson?"

"Yes. Why? What's wrong?"

"You're just doing all kinds of stuff without including me. I didn't know you even talked to Nelson like that."

"On business matters, yes."

"Um, oh, okay."

"Natasha, please don't act like I'm hiding something from you. Everything I do is for us, not me. Besides, we agreed on having yours, mine, and ours. That was your suggestion, remember?"

"That was when I was working, Tyrone. Things are different now."

"Baby, listen. We're fine, okay?"

"Men say that, and then their wives come home to eviction notices."

"That's not going to happen. And just so your mind is at ease, the mortgage and car payments are paid for a year. I figure that's how long it may take me to find a federal government position."

"More plans without me?"

"Come on, Natasha. We've talked about this before."

"I guess I don't remember, but that's fine, Tyrone. What about health insurance? You know what? Never mind, forget it. I don't want to talk about this any further right now."

"Natasha, understand something. I love you and the kids so much. Everything I do is for you guys. Please don't worry about money because we have plenty in the bank. If my mother never taught me anything else, she taught me to save money. She was very frugal, and so am I. I actually have money still saved that she left me when she died."

Tyrone lowered his eyes when he mentioned his mother. I could see the pain surfacing on his handsome face. Before I could respond, he got up and went into the bathroom, I assumed to cry. Tyrone wouldn't shed any tears in front of me unless it was over Aisha. When it came to the loss of our daughter, he didn't care who was around if he felt like he needed to cry.

Several minutes later, Tyrone came out of the bathroom and went back into the bedroom. I started to follow him, but he looked as if he wanted to be alone, so I went into the kitchen to cook breakfast. I knew he was really trying to make me happy, and I planned to surprise him with breakfast in bed.

Although I raised Aisha, being a mother of three small children was a difficult reality for me to process. On top of that, I had to figure out how to be a good wife to Tyrone. Our family situation was new to me, and it was becoming extremely overwhelming. I was quiet and reserved; however, I wasn't much different from Dianne and Lynda. I was definitely a part of the "strong, black, independent woman" club, and women like us needed to learn how to be submissive. It wasn't a natural feeling, and it required work.

# CHAPTER 7
## *Dianne*

❧

*I DIDN'T MEAN TO HIT NIHYA,* but I was tired of her disrespecting me. She had mumbled under her breath one too many times, and Nelson talking to her about her attitude didn't help. After the conversation I had with Nelson, I contacted Nihya's school and told them to call her father whenever there was a disciplinary issue. I wanted him to see just how much her behavior was a problem for some of her teachers. When he got tired of getting the phone calls, he would do something about it.

It wasn't even a week after I notified the school to list Nelson as the first point of contact that he received his first phone call. Of course, he was preparing for an important meeting, and guess who he called to handle it? When I saw his office number appear on my cell phone, I took a deep breath and rolled my eyes.

"Yes, Nelson?"

"Baby, I need you to contact Nihya's school for me."

"Nelson, I told you that I can't deal with Nihya's outbursts anymore until she starts respecting me."

"Dianne, please. I know you're trying to prove a point to me, but now isn't a good time for this."

"That's not how parenting works. There are many parents who have to leave their job and go up to their child's school, even on days when it's not a good day."

"I know, baby. You're right. I already apologized to you. What else do you want me to do?"

"So you want me to get involved in Nihya's disciplinary actions when it's convenient for you?"

"Dianne, I have a meeting in less than ten minutes. I was only asking you to just let me know what was going on and not wait so long to tell me. Can't you understand that?"

"I guess so, Nelson. I'll call the school and go meet with her teacher, if necessary. We can discuss the meeting when you get home from work."

"Thank you, baby."

"Yeah, whatever."

"Dianne, we're going to work through this together, okay?"

"Okay, sure, Nelson. Bye."

*If I go up to this school and that little girl shows off, I'm going to jail. I just know it,* I thought while preparing to go handle Nihya's outburst in class. I figured she was going to probably have some emotional problems, but damn. Lately, her counselor had been having a difficult time getting through to her, so I wasn't sure what we were going to do to get her to open up.

I agreed to meet with Nihya's teacher right after the school day ended. During the meeting, Nihya's teacher informed me that her grades were drastically slipping because she often refused to do any class work and spent a lot of time gazing out the window. Her teacher said when she asked her to turn in her work assignment, Nihya yelled out, "I don't have to listen to you!" I wondered if she was going to grow up and have a problem with female authority. *She sure lashes out at me!*

It appeared she didn't behave the same way in the classes where there were male teachers. Maybe she was scared of them because of what Walter did to her. It was hard to tell because abused children had different ways of coping with their hurt. I wanted to help Nihya, but she wouldn't let me in either.

When I arrived home with Nihya, I asked her to go up to her room until her father got home. I didn't feel like dealing with her attitude. As she stomped past me to go up to her room, I heard her mumble, "You're not my mother." Before I knew it, I smacked her in the mouth.

"Why did you hit me?" Nihya cried.

"Because I'm tired of your mouth."

"I didn't even say anything to you."

"Well, I heard what you said, and I'm tired of you mumbling under your breath like I can't hear you."

"I'm calling the police."

"Little girl, if you don't go up to your room, you're going to need more than the police!"

"I'm telling my daddy that you're threatening me."

"See, you're still running your mouth."

"But you didn't have to hit me. I said you're not my mother because you're not."

"No, I'm not your biological mother, but I'm the one raising you whether you like it or not. I know you have been through a lot, Nihya, but I'm not going to tolerate your disrespectful behavior. You can't have these outbursts whenever you feel like it and expect not to be disciplined for it."

"You just don't like me, so you don't want me here."

"Nihya, I told you once before that I was a stepchild, and I know the adjustment can be hard. You have to try to make this work just like I do."

"You're not trying because you don't want me here, and I know it. So, maybe I'll leave and go live with my grandmother."

Nihya finally went into her room when I didn't respond to her last comment. I didn't care if that little girl didn't like me; however, I knew she wasn't going to continue to disrespect me in my house. It hurt my feelings that she didn't accept me as her mother figure. In all fairness to Nihya, I would bet most stepchildren have made that comment. I said it myself once or twice to my stepmother. When a person was hurting, he or she wanted others around them to hurt as well. It didn't make it right, but that was reality.

When Nelson arrived home, I told him what happened at the meeting with Nihya's teacher. I also let him know that I smacked her in the mouth because of what she had mumbled under her breath. His response wasn't anticipated at all. He didn't acknowledge what I said about her behavior.

All he managed to say was, "I thought I asked you not to hit my daughter?"

My response to him was simply, "Fuck you and your disrespectful-ass daughter." As I walked past Nelson to leave the house, he grabbed my arm.

"Dianne, this conversation isn't over."

"You better get off me before this marriage is."

Nelson looked at me with pain in his eyes. "Dianne, I didn't mean to say that to you. It's just..."

"It's just what, Nelson?" The tears fell rapidly from my eyes.

"Dianne, she's been through so much. I really think this is a phase."

"So what do we do until then? Just let her act however she wants?"

"I'm sorry for what I said to you."

"No, you're not sorry. You meant it, and it's now clear how you really feel. She's not my daughter. I want you to understand something. We can't have a marriage like this, Nelson."

"What are you saying, Dianne?"

I walked away with nothing else to say. I went upstairs to my room before I said something I didn't mean. It felt as if I was losing my husband. I tossed and turned all night because Nelson never came upstairs to bed. I was sure he didn't know what to make of my comment, but how could we have a functional marriage where I was reminded constantly that I wasn't Nihya's mother? I didn't get married to get divorced, but I also didn't get married to live in dysfunction. I figured I would go visit Natasha, Tyrone, and the kids the next day. I felt the need to be surrounded by love.

# CHAPTER 8
## *Lynda*

"*I AM SO SICK OF* men right now that I don't know what to do with myself," I said aloud, noticing Justin stood me up again. *He did the same shit last week!* I knew I had to take responsibility for the kind of men I chose to deal with, but damn! I was so frustrated with men that I was tempted to call Jasmine. *Wow, did I let that thought creep into my mind?* It still felt awkward not knowing Zion's association with Jasmine. I eased out of bed to check my mail. I never understood why I allowed my mail to pile up for several days. I figured mainly because I wasn't waiting for anything specific. The few bills I had I paid online.

Sifting through the stack of junk mail, I was immediately reminded as to why I rarely checked my mailbox. You knew it was bad when your mail carrier left you a note on your door asking you to please check your mail because your box was too full to add anything else. I laughed to myself. My mail carrier was a cutie, too. I needed to find out his relationship status the next time I saw him.

After tossing most of the store sales papers and setting aside the coupons to my favorite stores—Express and Victoria's Secret—I noticed an envelope with the return address of my brother's P.O. Box.

*I haven't spoken to Langston since shortly after our father passed away.* He was bitter about the money our father left to me. Although I wasn't close to my mother, I hoped it wasn't a letter telling me that she had died. I would like to think he would have more decency and call me for that kind of news. I always wondered why my grandmother named my father after her favorite poet, Langston Hughes, and then why my mother thought it was a good idea to pass it down to my brother. Maybe it wasn't so bad. *I'm just surprised I wasn't named after Maya Angelou.*

Before I opened the letter from my brother, I glanced at another envelope from the company in California where I submitted several samples of my writing for consideration for a screenwriter position. I froze for a few seconds and then placed the letter on the table. I wasn't ready to read their response yet. I also applied for similar positions in the New York and Atlanta areas, but I hadn't heard back from them yet.

I turned my attention back to the letter from Langston. Opening the letter, I braced myself for any bad news. He must have remembered how I didn't like to anticipate bad news because the first line read, "All is well, so you can stop worrying."

I smiled. My brother and I were once very close when we were kids. While most siblings fought each other, my brother and I rarely even argued. We had dreams of making movies together one day. We would walk around the house and neighborhood making short documentaries using my father's camcorder. I was proud of my brother because he continued with the dream of making films, and some had won independent film awards; however, I wished he were more stable. Langston normally lived with whatever girlfriend he had at the time instead of getting his own place. I never understood why some men did that.

The letter from Langston was very brief. He just said that my mother had been asking for me, and he thought maybe I could pay her a visit. I still felt she only wanted to know how much money my father left me, and why he didn't leave anything to my brother. I actually planned to share the money with my brother, but I didn't want him to give any to my mother. I knew it was cruel, but that woman was horrible to me when I was a teenager. *Maybe it's time I let all of that go.*

It was still early in the morning, so I decided to call my brother sometime after noon. I was glad he put his current telephone number in the letter because he was another one, like Maurice, who had a different cell phone number every few months. I couldn't believe Maurice said he wished that bullet had killed me.

I was tired of the random thoughts. I needed to find something to do to get my mind off a few things. I decided to call Dianne. She was the only person I knew that didn't mind an early phone call. I didn't call Natasha early anymore because I didn't want to risk waking up the babies too early. Dianne's cell phone barely rang before she answered.

"Hello?" a chipper Dianne answered.

"Hey, Di. What's going on?"

"Just visiting the most beautiful babies in the world."

"Huh? Why y'all heifers didn't call me? Y'all get on my nerves."

"Well, I figured Justin would have still been over there, so I didn't want to *disturb* your groove."

"Justin who?"

"Oh, goodness! Did he not show up again?"

"Exactly! And I have definitely had it this time."

"You say that like once a week, girl."

"I mean it this time, but I'm on my way over to Natasha's. Is her babies' daddy home?" I said, laughing.

"Would you stop calling him that, and no, he went to do some grocery shopping."

"How cute. Anyway, I'm on my way." I hung up and immediately headed for the shower.

Columbia wasn't a short drive. It was going to take at least forty-five minutes to get there. *Shit, why did they move all the way out there?* I planned to go to the mall out there after I left Natasha's, so I put the coupons to Express and Victoria's Secret in my purse as soon as I got out of the shower. Somebody was going to appreciate whatever I bought from Vickie's, preferably Justin. Damn, I really needed to get something else on my mind other than Justin. I felt the situation with him had the potential to get really ugly.

When I arrived at Natasha and Tyrone's place, I greeted her and Dianne with a hug. The babies were both asleep. I hadn't seen them in about a month, but this gave us girls a chance to catch up until Tyrone returned home.

"Remember I told y'all that Taye's brother, Xavier, called me and wanted to talk about Taye?" I started the conversation.

"Yes," Dianne and Natasha said in unison.

"Well, I finally agreed to meet with him to talk."

"Really? Why?" Dianne asked.

"I'm not sure. He just seemed like he really needed to talk about his brother. To hear that his brother was killed must have been rough on Xavier."

"Yeah, I'm sure it was," Natasha responded.

"It was big of you to meet with him after what Taye did to you. Just be careful," Dianne chimed in.

"Why you say that, Dianne?" I asked, already knowing why.

"How do you know that he doesn't want revenge or something?" Dianne said, getting serious.

"Revenge? I didn't kill Taye," I snapped.

"But he might find you responsible somehow. I don't know," Dianne replied. "Don't get upset. I'm just saying."

"Okay, but did I tell y'all that I purchased a gun?" I asked.

"What!" Dianne and Natasha both screamed.

"Yeah, considering what happened to me, I figured I would get something to protect myself. I thought I told y'all?"

"No, and, Lynda, do you think that's a good idea with your attitude?" Dianne asked.

"Excuse me?" I said in my defensive, 'how dare you' tone.

"Now, you know you have a quick temper, G.I. Lynda," Natasha chimed in, laughing.

"No, I don't," I said, sucking my teeth.

"Okay, Ms. I'm In Denial," Dianne responded, laughing.

"Anyway, back to what I was saying. I met Xavier for coffee, and you wouldn't believe how much he looks like Taye."

"Oh, Lord," Dianne mumbled.

"He claims his mother doesn't think Taye tried to kill me."

"Why doesn't she think that?" Natasha asked.

"Well, he said his mother has a copy of his police report where he reported his car stolen two days before I was shot."

"Are you serious?" Dianne asked.

"Wait, I'm confused. So his mother thinks someone stole his car, used it to try to kill you, and then returned his car?" Natasha interjected.

"Doesn't make any sense to me," Dianne remarked.

"Yeah, that could have just been his cover up," Natasha said.

"I agree. I thought about that, too. But I have to consider the possibility that there's someone out there who still wants to hurt me," I responded with tears in my eyes.

"Is that why you bought the gun?" Dianne asked.

"Yep, that's the reason." I wiped away the few tears that fell.

"Lynda, just be careful with that gun. I don't want you to panic and accidentally shoot someone 'cause you are kind of crazy," Dianne joked.

"Did you say kind of?" Natasha remarked with a bit of sarcasm.

"I got y'all crazy. But naw, I'm taking some lessons. I have a police officer friend who's assisting me with my lessons, so I didn't just go buy a gun. Plus, I want my aim to be on point if I need to use it to defend myself," I replied with a slight smile.

Dianne responded, "A police officer friend? Girl, you can't stand cops, so when did one become your friend?"

"Chill, Dianne. Goodness. He's a friend of my cousin's who is with the Prince George's Police Department."

"Oh, yeah, I forgot you have a cousin who is a PG cop," Natasha included.

"Okay, so what about Xavier?" Dianne switched topics.

"What about him?" I asked, as if I didn't know what she was talking about.

"Yeah, something tells me there's more to this story," Natasha said.

I sighed. "I didn't sleep with him, if that's what you're insinuating."

"No, but you thought about it. I see that guilty look you always get when you're up to something," Dianne responded.

"Well, we did sort of kiss."

"How do you *sort of* kiss someone?" Dianne asked. "Either you did or you didn't."

"Look, Dianne, I'm not in the mood for your judgment today."

"I'm not judging you, but I am somewhat appalled," Dianne replied.

"Why, because he's Taye's brother?" I asked.

"Yes, Lynda. Damn!" Dianne said.

"Well, be appalled then. I don't care. I'm grown, and you know I don't need your approval on anything that I do or *whom* I do."

"Lynda, are you planning to continue to see him?" Natasha asked.

"No, because the attraction is too strong. It's almost like looking at Taye."

"Good!" Dianne said.

"But what difference would it make if I did? Y'all sitting over there like two little Miss Goody Two-shoes, and we all know that's not the case."

"Okay, now you're in defensive mode," Dianne said.

"Yep, because y'all have done some unspeakable shit before, also. Like you, Dianne, all bent over in the conference room. Oh, what? You think I forgot? Plus, he was a damn little boy."

"He was legal," was all Dianne could say at that moment.

"Barely!" When I stood up, it was obvious I was a little tipsy from the coffee and Kahlúa Natasha had prepared. "And let's not forget Mr. and Mrs. Thompson, AKA Mr. and Mrs. Perfect, who slept together on the first day they met."

Natasha put her head down because she knew her turn was coming. When I got tipsy, I was definitely going to speak my mind to everyone in the room.

"And Ms. Innocent Inglewood—oh, I mean Price, or whatever your new last name is. How many men have you slept with before you asked if they were married?"

"What do you mean?" Natasha asked, annoyed at my question.

"When you slept with Tyrone, you had no idea he was divorced, but you slept with him anyway."

"And he was the *only* one," Natasha said in her own defense.

"So you say. You're probably like the quiet girls Eddie Murphy mentioned in his stand-up comedy show, *Raw*. Remember? The ones he said don't talk much because of the skeleton bones that might fly out of their mouths."

I laughed. Dianne and Natasha couldn't help but laugh along with me.

"Forget you," Natasha said, still laughing.

"Damn, see? A bone hit me in the forehead."

We all laughed so hard, we were in tears.

"Okay, y'all, I know I need to think with my head more when it comes to men. I just have so much testosterone in me that I don't know."

"Oh, you're not going to use that excuse, but you do act like a man when it comes to sex," Dianne said.

"Yeah, I don't know how you can have sex with a man and it's not tied to an emotion," Natasha added.

"It is tied to an emotion—horny." We all laughed.

"That's not an emotion," Natasha remarked, laughing so hard she could barely speak.

"Why not? You have happy, sad, and angry. So why not horny?" I shrugged and continued sipping my coffee.

"You're a fool, girl. But this conversation about Xavier isn't over," Dianne said, pointing her finger at me.

Hanging with my girls always put a smile on my face. It soothed the stress away. I didn't know how to tell them just yet that I was considering moving to California, New York, or Atlanta if I got a screenwriter position in one of those areas. I hoped something would come through for me in New York since it was closer to home. They were like family, and it was definitely going to be hard to leave them.

While we laughed, Tyrone walked in with several bags.

"Damn, have y'all been drinking around my babies? I can hear y'all downstairs. What time is it anyway?" Tyrone asked before kissing Natasha.

"Hey, Tyrone. It's never too early to drink as long as it's after noon. And it's always after noon somewhere. Besides, it's only coffee," I said, laughing.

"Hey, Lynda, what's up, girl? When is that book coming out?" Tyrone asked, as he put away the groceries.

"Soon, very soon. As a matter of fact, Dianne, are you still hosting my book release party?"

"Yes, heifer. Maybe next week we could work out the details."

"Cool. Sounds good to me. Oh, yeah, guess what else?"

"Oh, Lord, what now?" Dianne asked.

"Chill. I got a letter from my brother."

"Your brother? You haven't mentioned him in a long time," Natasha said.

"I think about him from time to time, but I just haven't reached out to him."

"What did he say in the letter?" Dianne asked.

"The letter was very brief, but he wants me to consider paying my mother a visit. He claims she has been asking about me. I hope she isn't sick. At first, I thought she wanted to know about all the money my father left me, but who knows?"

"Excuse me?" Dianne shouted.

"I thought I told y'all that my father left me money."

"Yeah, but now you're making it seem like he left some *real money* to you," Dianne responded.

"Well, he did, and I have my reasons as to why I haven't gone into any details. Actually, I have almost one million reasons."

"What! Naw, heifer, start talking!" Dianne exclaimed.

"What's going on?" Tyrone asked, responding to all of the commotion.

"Damn, Tyrone. Would you mind your business? No one is talking to you. Make yourself useful and put the stuff away. Then check on my babies, would you? Thank you!" Natasha spoke in a harsh tone.

Tyrone walked away shaking his head.

"Dag, Natasha. Why are you talking to him like that?" Dianne asked in a whisper.

"Girl, please. He's lucky I'm talking to him at all." Natasha didn't bother to follow Dianne's lead in whispering.

We all sat there in silence before Dianne turned her attention back to me.

"Now, Lynda, explain these 'almost million reasons' as you put it."

"Well, I'm not exactly sure how much it is, but I know everything is worth about seven hundred and fifty thousand. That doesn't include my trust fund, which I was entitled to at twenty-one. I never touched mine, although my brother spent every dime of his chasing his dream. That's why my father didn't leave him any money in his will. He told me to give it to him as I see fit."

"Wow. That's great. Now I see how you're able to not work a full-time job. I was beginning to wonder about you." Dianne managed a half-smile. "I was beginning to think you had an undisclosed sugar daddy taking care of your finances."

"Dianne, are you okay?" I asked because I could see in her eyes that something was wrong.

"Yeah, just tired. Go on."

"Well, remember I was bartending when we first met? That was mainly to meet men. Then I had some other jobs, but I just couldn't find my niche until I started writing again. I get paid well from freelance assignments, but of course, the money isn't consistent. It doesn't matter, though, because I always have money in the bank. I just contact my accountant if I want to do something big."

"Lord, the heifer has an accountant!" Dianne said, sipping on her coffee.

"Yeah, I know it seems strange. I didn't want to let the money go to my head and not pursue my passion. Money doesn't last forever if it's not invested properly. We have all learned that from watching athletes or people in the music industry."

"Like M.C. Hammer," Tyrone commented from the kitchen.

"Leave that man alone. But, yeah, like Hammer." I laughed.

"Lynda, that's smart. Now you can pursue your passion and not worry about your finances," Natasha said, cutting her eyes at Tyrone.

"Exactly, but with this economy, I've been very worried about my investments. I canceled my appointment with my accountant until after my book is released because I don't want any potential bad news to send me into a depression. I simply can't handle it right now."

"Yeah, I understand. Nelson has been worried, as well. He's great with financial stuff, but he's still concerned," Dianne added.

"Well, I wish some of that concern would rub off on Mr. Mom in there," Natasha replied sharply.

"Natasha!" Dianne said in a loud whisper.

"I know. Isn't he an accountant or financial advisor or something?" I asked.

"When he's working," Natasha replied.

Again, there was silence.

"Natasha, don't do this now. A lot of people are getting laid off because of this crazy economy. Don't treat him like that," Dianne whispered.

"You just don't understand what I'm going through. He didn't get laid off his job; he had some kind of grand idea to quit. So, you don't know how I feel. I'm tired." Natasha sounded as if she wanted to cry.

"I wasn't trying to tell you how you should feel. All I was saying was that maybe you should consider Tyrone's feelings. He's your husband

and not a piece of trash. Maybe I'm out of line for saying something, but so are you. One thing I've learned is no matter what your issue is with your man, you don't talk to him any kind of way in front of company, even if it is us."

"So I guess y'all are just going to keep talking like I'm not even here, huh?" Tyrone spoke in his defense. "You know what? Maybe I shouldn't be here right now. Natasha, *your* babies are fine. They're fed, burped, and back to sleep. I'm going to pick up my son. Dianne, Lynda, you ladies have a good one, a'ight?" Tyrone walked out the door.

Natasha just looked as if she hadn't said anything wrong and continued sipping on her coffee. Dianne looked disgusted. I had to agree with Dianne on this one; Natasha shouldn't have spoken to Tyrone like that in front of guests.

Natasha sat there for a while with a blank look on her face before tears fell down her cheeks. She rocked back and forth. I wondered if she was going through some kind of postpartum depression because I'd never seen her so angry.

I went over to their place thinking they would lift my spirits, but I felt worse than before. I needed my girls, but that wasn't the mood I was looking for. I sat there in silence because I couldn't think of anything to say to lighten the mood.

# CHAPTER 9
## *Natasha*

*MAYBE I WAS WRONG* as to how I spoke to Tyrone in front of Lynda and Dianne, but at that moment, I really didn't care. Tyrone may have been trying to do an honorable thing by wanting to be home with the kids and me, but it wasn't the time to lose his job over it. I didn't know why I was so upset with what he did because I wanted him to be home with us, so I was feeling confused over my actions. *I hope I'm not experiencing some kind of anxiety issues or postpartum depression.* I couldn't afford to have a nervous breakdown.

"Natasha, what's going on with you?" Dianne asked, snapping me out of my thoughts.

"Dianne, please. No lecture today, okay? Thank you," I responded.

"What's all of this about? I was asking you to look at how you were handling things with Tyrone. But you know what, Natasha? I won't say anything else to you about it." Dianne sighed and rolled her eyes.

"Again, Tyrone didn't get laid off. He wanted to be home with his babies, so he quit his job. He claims his supervisor was giving him grief about paternity leave, which he should have been entitled to, but he got pissed off and walked off the job. Who does that with children to take care of, and in this damn economy at that?"

"Natasha, look at this from his point of view. He wants to be here with you, Tyler, and the twins full-time," Lynda said.

"Yeah, to make up for not being there for Aisha," I responded.

"So that's what this is about? Why did you marry him if you were going to make him suffer for his past mistakes? You could've just pushed him out the door into the arms of another woman," Dianne said, pointing to the door.

"I'm afraid, okay? I'm afraid to be left alone with not one baby, not two, but three. I have no idea what I was thinking having these babies." I shook my head slowly.

"Are you worried about money or something?" Lynda asked.

I sighed before speaking. "This really isn't about money. We're fine when it comes to that because we have a good cushion saved up. I'm just pissed because he made a decision without even talking to me first. I don't want to end up alone again."

"Okay, that's understandable, but I doubt if Tyrone's thinking about leaving you alone, unless you keep treating him the way you did today. I'm sure he can get another job easily with his financial background. I'm sure Nelson could—"

"Why do you always throw Nelson up in everybody's face? I hate when you do that. If he's so perfect, you wouldn't be having the problems you're having now, would you?" I interrupted before Dianne could finish her statement.

"Excuse me? What the fuck you trying to say, Natasha?" Dianne asked, jumping up out of her seat.

"Nihya isn't your child, and I agree with your *Mr. Perfect*. You shouldn't have put your hands on her. You obviously don't have what it takes to be a mother. Maybe that's why God didn't allow you to carry your child to term, and now you want to tell me how I should or shouldn't feel about losing my daughter whom I raised for sixteen years alone? Do you know what it's like to be alone to raise a child? No, you don't. So, I don't want to hear this from you, Dianne."

"What!" Dianne screamed. "Are you fucking serious? You know what? I'm going to assume this is the postpartum depression talking.

And you're right; I don't have any children of my own, but now I'm just as responsible for Nihya as Nelson is. I have what it takes to be a good mother even if I didn't give birth to her. By the way, giving birth to a child doesn't automatically make you a good mother. Remember that."

"Well, Dianne—" I couldn't believe what I had said, but it was too late to take it back.

"No, Natasha, let me finish. Remember my baby that I couldn't carry to term, as you so *delicately* put it? Well, although I didn't carry him to what's considered a full-term pregnancy, he was fully developed when I delivered him. And, Natasha, just for your information, my son, Daniel, lived and then he died in my arms."

Lynda and I both had surprised looks on our faces.

Dianne continued. "I told everyone I had a miscarriage because I didn't want to keep explaining how I held him until he took his last breath. I didn't want to remember how he died in my arms because his lungs were too thin to continue breathing on his own, and there was nothing I could do to save his life. Nothing!"

"Dianne, I'm sorry. I didn't know," I responded, wishing I could take back everything I said.

"Well, now you do, and you're not sorry. If you truly gave a shit about me, you wouldn't have said something so fucking hateful. You were deliberately trying to hurt me; I guess because you're hurting. I'm tired of you playing victim all the time. You lost your daughter, and I expect you to be hurting. That hurt may never go away. But I don't expect you to treat everyone else around you like we don't know what it feels like to lose someone. The three of us have all lost someone close to us, Natasha. Remember, your husband did, as well. And as far as I'm concerned, this friendship is over." Dianne grabbed her purse and headed toward the door.

"Come on, y'all, don't do this," Lynda finally spoke up.

"Lynda, you and I both know that Natasha is wrong for this. So, I'm leaving before I go back to jail for beating someone else's ass," Dianne said, cutting her eyes in my direction.

There was no excuse for what I said to Dianne, and I had probably ruined our years of friendship. She had always been there for me when I needed her, and I knew she was only trying to help. I hated that she usually turned out to be right about most situations, and my stubbornness caused me to lash out at one of the only people in my life who truly had my back unconditionally.

*What am I going to do without her if our friendship is over?*

# CHAPTER 10
## Dianne

⌒⌒

*THE ONLY TIME I SPENT* in jail was the few hours after I defended Natasha against Tyrone's ex-wife, Annie. Annie had kicked Natasha in the stomach while she was pregnant with Tyler. I could've beaten Natasha down just like I did Annie that day, so I knew it was best I left her place. She had completely crossed the line that time. As I was leaving, I heard Lynda tell Natasha that she would call her later on.

I couldn't believe what Natasha said to me. No matter how mad, friends shouldn't say hurtful things. Sometimes, things are said out of frustration that we might not have meant, but doing so ruined friendships. What made the situation even harder was that Natasha was more than a friend; she was more like my sister. However, I'd had it with her.

By the time I was at my car, Lynda had caught up with me. "Dianne, hold on."

"What, Lynda?"

"I'm so sorry."

"Sorry for what? You didn't do anything."

"You never told me about your son, Daniel."

All I could do was cry. "Lynda, I'm so tired of people lashing out at me because they're mad. We're all mad about something, but that doesn't give us the right to hurt other people. I would never do that to you guys."

"I know, Dianne. Natasha was completely foul for that."

"I'm really tired."

"Do you want to talk about it?" Lynda asked.

I told Lynda about the problems I was having with Nihya and how Nelson treated me when I told him that I had to smack her in the mouth. I told Natasha the story before Lynda had come over, but I didn't think she would turn around and throw it in my face. As I told Lynda what happened, my phone rang; it was Nelson. Out of anger, I threw my phone on the ground.

"Oh, my goodness, Dianne. Come with me. Let's go to my house. I see you're really upset."

Lynda knew how I felt about my phone. One time, I dropped my BlackBerry in the toilet, and I cried as if I was in the first grade and had to stay inside for recess. I was sure Lynda remembered that day because she had to console me.

Lynda picked up my phone, which was now in two pieces, and put it in her purse. "Leave your car here and ride with me. I'll bring you back later to get it."

"No, that's okay. I can drive. I'll follow you to your house. Plus, this is too far to have to come all the way back."

As I followed Lynda to her house, all I could hear in my head were the things Nelson and Natasha had said to me. I wasn't as mad with Nihya because she was a child, but Nelson and Natasha were adults. They should have known better about saying hurtful things to people they supposedly cared about. The difference with Nelson was that I made a commitment to him before God to be there for better or worse. He was my husband, and he deserved a chance to explain himself. I didn't know about Natasha, though. That wasn't the first time we've argued, but it was definitely the first time she said something so hurtful. *Why should I ever forgive her?*

When I got to Lynda's house, I could tell she was trying to hold back her tears. I waited until we got inside her place before I started asking questions.

"Lynda, what's wrong? Are you okay?"

"Yeah, but all this talk about losing loved ones made me think about my father and the Taye situation. Also, the way I've treated Zion is definitely wrong."

"Have you spoken with Zion?"

"No, not lately."

"Well, maybe you should call him to apologize."

"Maybe I should, but I don't know."

"What don't you know?"

"If he will accept my apology."

"Well, you have to call him and find out."

"You just don't understand."

"Look, Lynda. I know you still love Zion, so try to consider his feelings."

"Consider his feelings about what?"

"About how you've treated him. You were wrong for accusing him of messing around with Jasmine without knowing the truth. Do you even know the truth yet?"

"No."

"See what I mean? That's not fair to him."

"I know but—"

"But what, Lynda?"

"Are you going to call Nelson to let him know where you are, or are you going home?" Lynda asked, obviously avoiding my question.

Sighing, I replied, "I guess I should return his call."

"Yes, especially after this third degree you're giving me." We laughed a little. "But here, use my cell phone. You broke yours."

"I know. I'm glad I have equipment coverage. Actually, I'm just going to send him a text message."

"Dianne, no, you're not. Call your husband and talk to him. You have a man who really loves you. Then you're calling Natasha."

"No, I am not calling Natasha! And hold that thought, heifer." I emphasized each word before Lynda could say anything else.

I was glad I got Nelson's voicemail because I wasn't in the mood to say anything to him. I left him a message that I would be at Lynda's for the night and he could call me on her number if he wanted to talk. I decided to use Lynda's phone to check my voicemail messages. I hated not having my BlackBerry, so I planned to call the phone company first thing the next morning so they could send me a replacement phone. I was going to have to tell them it fell out of my hand or something so it would be covered.

One of the messages was from Nelson asking me to call him back. Well, I did that, and he didn't answer. *Oh, well.* Then the other message was from Tyrone. He wanted to know if we could talk. I called him back from Lynda's house phone and gave her back her cell phone. I told Tyrone that I was over Lynda's and he could stop by if he wanted to talk. He agreed and was there within fifteen minutes. I knew I was wrong for not asking Lynda if Tyrone could stop by, but I would have to deal with her later.

⁂

When Tyrone arrived, he looked as if he had one too many beers. I offered him a bottle of water because I knew Lynda always had plenty in her refrigerator. I figured the water would help him sober up since he probably had way too much to drink. He accepted the water, opened the bottle, and took a long gulp. He then looked at me as if he didn't know where to begin with what he wanted to talk about.

In our conversation, Tyrone explained to me that Natasha was upset a lot, and he didn't know what to do to help her. He expressed to me that he felt nothing he did was ever good enough for her, and she often reminded him of not being around for Aisha. According to his side of the story, it seemed as if Natasha had forgotten that she was the one who gave up on Tyrone and left Georgia to move away from him. It appeared Natasha didn't acknowledge Tyrone for the good man he had become, but instead, made him suffer for his past actions.

When a single tear escaped from Tyrone's eye, I wiped it as if I was wiping away a stream of tears. That one tear was long gone, but I still caressed his face. Until now, I hadn't noticed the handsome man that he had become. Since he wasn't currently working in corporate America, he had allowed his beard to grow in fully, and it complemented his strong, masculine features very well. *I wish Nelson would let his beard grow.*

Tyrone turned, looked into my eyes, and said something I wished he had never said.

"Dianne, you know I always wanted you."

"Tyrone, please don't go there."

"When we were in high school, I wanted to be with you, but you introduced me to Natasha. I'm sure it was to get me out of your face. Don't get me wrong, you know I love her, but I always *wanted* you."

I sighed and stopped rubbing his face. However, he continued talking.

"Remember in the ninth grade when we played that truth or dare game and I got to feel you any way that I wanted? Well, I'm thinking maybe I can feel you like that now."

"Tyrone, how much did you have to drink?"

"Not much. Maybe five or six beers."

"Five or six? Okay, um, listen to me. No more reminiscing, okay?"

"Why, you can't handle it?"

"No, I cannot, and I don't want to either. Tyrone, stop it," I said, moving his hand off my leg.

"Do you really want me to stop?"

"Yes, Tyrone."

"I was wondering if you still feel as good as you did when you were fourteen. I'm sure you feel even better now."

"Oh, my goodness, Tyrone. Stop!" I had to remove his hand once again.

"I bet you would never treat me like Natasha does. I know you. I've known you since elementary school. I used to fight boys for bothering you. I bet you forgot about that."

"No, I remember, but we were kids."

"And I see you're all grown up now. The only reason why I'm not going to keep touching you is because I know you love Nelson and he really loves you. I see it in his eyes. Sometimes, I watch him watching you. So, I'm going to respect your marriage."

*Lord, this is too much!*

"What about your marriage, Tyrone?"

"What marriage? Natasha doesn't want me there."

"I don't believe that, Tyrone. I think I was wrong for allowing you to come over here. I just didn't like the idea of you being out there drinking and driving. Natasha would lose her mind if she lost you. She needs you regardless of what she says."

"Yeah, but I want her to *want* me and love *me* for who I am, not just need me."

"I believe the two of you can work through this. You just need to communicate to her how you feel."

"I want you to *communicate* something to me." Tyrone moved closer. "You knew how I felt about you, didn't you?"

"I knew back then, but I had no idea you still felt the same way now. It's been over twenty years." I moved away because I was feeling a bit uncomfortable being that close to him.

*Where is Lynda when I need her?*

"Well, like I said, I love Natasha, but I've always *wanted* you. And the only reason I'm not going to try anything is because—"

"Because you're in my damn house," Lynda interrupted.

*Lynda to the rescue.*

"What the hell is going on up in here?" Lynda asked.

"Right now, I'm thinking a threesome with my wife's two best friends," Tyrone said, as he rubbed his erection.

"Dianne, get him before I get my mace," Lynda responded, pointing at Tyrone.

"He's drunk. He doesn't know what he's saying. Do you, Tyrone?" I yelled in his ear.

"Well, he can't stay here tonight. This doesn't look right."

"I know, and I was just trying to be a friend. Lord, what have I done?"

"Obviously, you brought back a twenty-year-old crush." Lynda laughed.

"This isn't funny," I said, shaking my head.

"I know, girl. I'm sorry. Normally, I wouldn't care if he was married, but I won't cross that line if I'm friends with the wife. He's looking good over there, though."

"Lynda!"

"What? I'm just saying," Lynda said, giggling. "This is going to make a juicy story."

"Girl, don't you add this to your book. You saw the movie, *The Best Man*. This can get ugly."

"Yeah, you right. Although Natasha was foul today, she's still our girl. Yes, *our* girl. Don't look at me like that, Dianne."

I rolled my eyes at Lynda before glancing back at Tyrone. It was a good thing he had fallen asleep while Lynda and I talked. It gave us a chance to think about how to get his drunken ass out of her house. I didn't want Natasha to think he was out in the streets messing around. I couldn't believe I was even worried about Natasha's feelings with all the mean things she had said to me.

Nelson called back on Lynda's phone, so I told him what had happened with Tyrone. Well, most of the story anyway. He immediately came over to help with the situation. Nelson drove Tyrone's car to take him home, and I followed them in Nelson's car so Nelson could ride back with me.

Before Nelson got Tyrone to his car, I heard Tyrone's cell phone ring. Nelson checked Tyrone's phone and said to me that Natasha was calling, so he answered the phone. I could hear him telling her that Tyrone had been out drinking and had way too much and he was driving him home. She had to wonder how Nelson was going to get back home, but she would find out when we got there. I imagined Natasha was pissed that he was coming home drunk, but she needed to be thankful he was coming home at all. There were a lot of women out there who preyed on men who appeared to be unhappily married.

When we arrived at Tyrone's place, Nelson and I walked him to the door. Natasha came to the door, and I could tell she had been crying. I was glad Tyrone had some time to sleep off his alcohol. I was sure he still needed more time to fully recover, though. Only time would tell if he remembered some of the things he had said to me.

"Thank you for making sure he got home safely," Natasha said, as she opened the door.

"It's no problem, Natasha," Nelson responded.

"Goodnight, Natasha. Take care," was my response.

Natasha couldn't make eye contact with me. I was sure she had some time to think about what she had said to me, but I wasn't certain how our friendship was going to be affected. We should all watch the things we say to others because we can't take words back after they were spoken, ever!

"What was that all about?" Nelson asked, as we headed to his car.

"It's a long story, but right now, I'm tired. Are you okay to drive?"

"Sure, baby. Are you okay?"

"I will be. I just need some rest."

Nelson pleaded with me to go home instead of going back to Lynda's. He said he would take me back the next day to get my car. I reluctantly agreed. I called Lynda to let her know that Tyrone was home safely and that I was going home with Nelson, which was where I needed to be. Although lately, I didn't feel welcomed in my own home.

# CHAPTER 11
## Lynda

*WHEN MY PHONE RANG AGAIN,* I thought it was Dianne calling to tell me that she had changed her mind and was coming back over to my place. I was wrong. *Lord, why didn't I check the Caller ID?* It was Justin saying he was outside in my parking lot. I never understood what made some people think they could show up at your house unannounced, especially when you weren't in a committed relationship with them.

"What do you want, Justin?"

"You have company or something?"

"Justin, it's too late at night for your drama. What do you want?"

"You know what I want, so open the door," he demanded.

"Who are you talking to like that?"

"I'm sorry. Whose car is this in your parking space if you don't have any company?"

"Justin, excuse me, but that's really none of your business."

"All right, well, let me in, baby."

"Oh, so I'm your *baby* now? After you stood me up two times in a row?"

"Come on, Lynda. You know I have a lot going on right now. Let me in so we can talk face to face. I miss you."

"Whatever!" He knew damn well he didn't want to do any talking. Who was he kidding?

Against my better judgment, I opened the door for him. He was dressed as if he had just left the club. He looked good, too. He wasn't quite drunk, but he was clearly not sober. Justin immediately kissed me and caressed my body. There was no point of me resisting him because I wanted him as much as he wanted me. He slid his finger inside of my boy shorts to see if I was ready for him to enter me.

"Damn, girl. You're wet already."

"You talk too much," I whispered, pushing his finger deeper inside of me.

"Can I have you right here, or do you want to go to your bedroom?" Justin asked since we were still in my living room.

"It depends. Do you have any condoms in your pocket?" I didn't know why I asked him that because condoms were like his American Express; he didn't leave home without them.

"Yes, I do, but let's go to your room. I want to make love to you. It's long overdue," he responded, still feeling my wetness.

Although I was getting tired of Justin, I wasn't tired of his thick, long manhood that always stood to greet me whenever I saw him. When Justin laid me on the bed, I was no longer mad at him. He eased off my boy shorts and continued to gently slide his finger in and out of me. He went down and hungrily licked my clit as if he needed a midnight snack. *Damn, his tongue feels good.*

"You taste so good, baby," Justin said, coming up for air.

*I'm glad I took a shower.*

"I'm ready to feel you," I responded.

"No, not yet. I know you like penetration, but I want to enjoy you, all of you, tonight."

*Now, who could be mad at that?*

He slid my shirt over my head and gently sucked on my nipples while he resumed fingering me. I could feel my juices flowing.

"Justin," I said, breathing hard.

"Now you're talking too much." Justin released a sinister laugh.

Justin knew he could control me with great sex. As long as he was making my body feel good, he knew I wasn't mad at him for long. That night, I was conflicted. I enjoyed the way he was touching and kissing me; however, my heart was growing cold. I was tired of the emotional rollercoaster he kept me on. Well, it was my fault for continuing to ride the same unstable ride.

Justin was very well *hung*, possessing a good six-inch package without a full erection. It didn't matter to me what his final measurements were when it reached its maximum length because he had the most impressive girth I had ever seen. Justin slowly rolled the Magnum extra-large condom over his eight, maybe eight and a half inches of thickness. His body was extremely remarkable. He looked as if he worked out at least five times a week. Although my body wanted him, tears rolled down my cheeks as he entered me. *Does he even notice?* Maybe he thought I was crying because the loving was so good. That definitely wasn't the case, not that time.

"Cum for me, baby," Justin whispered in my ear.

I tried to refuse, but my body immediately responded to his seductive demand. Justin knew my body so well, and that was only going to make it harder for me to leave him alone. Within seconds after I had an orgasm, Justin reached his peak. I could always tell because his slow, deep rhythm increased in speed. Justin was definitely good in bed. He never came before he made sure I was satisfied. His stamina was amazing, even after a night of drinking. I wondered if he made love to his wife the way he made love to me. I was sure he did, so I tried to shake that thought out of my head.

I wasn't certain when I drifted off to sleep, but at some point in the middle of the night, I rolled over and discovered Justin was still in my bed. I started to wake him up because he was snoring loudly, but I decided to get up and sleep on my sofa. *Obviously, he's tired.* As I left my bedroom, I heard Justin's cell phone vibrate. Normally, I wouldn't bother to look at it, but curiosity got the best of me. Whoever was calling at that time of the morning must have really needed to get a hold of him. I answered the phone upon seeing the word "Home" on the Caller ID.

"Hello?"

The person on the other end was silent. Certain it was his wife, I figured it was time for us to play truth or dare. Finally, the person spoke.

"Why are you sleeping with my husband? You can't find a man of your own?"

"Excuse me?"

"You heard me."

"Obviously, you got it twisted. If you and Justin are separated, then why are you calling him? Is one of your daughters sick or something?"

His wife cried. "Where is Justin?" she finally asked.

"Right here, *asleep*. Is there something I can tell him for you when he recovers?" I asked, being a smart ass.

"Wake his ass up now!" she screamed into the phone.

"I don't take demands from you. I don't care who you are. And to think about it, I had Justin first."

"Well, he married me."

"He sure did because he knew I wasn't going to accept his bullshit."

"Whatever. Like I said, he married me."

"Then why isn't he there with you?" At this point, I just wanted to fuck with her.

"Bitch, wake Justin up and put his cheating ass on the phone."

"Sure, but let this bitch get her gun first," I said, losing my patience with the situation.

"Your gun? No, don't."

I didn't respond until I had my gun pointed in Justin's face. "Don't worry. I'm not going to kill him. No man is worth me going to jail, no matter how good his dick is to me. But he needs to learn a fucking lesson."

Again, I was just fuckin' with her.

"Is this Lynda? Justin told me his ex was stalking him. He told me that you were crazy."

"Crazy? Stalking? Is that the lie he told you, so he could fuck me without a guilty conscience? I might have to shoot him for lying. And don't you tempt me. I know where you live and where your little girls go to school."

"Are you threatening me and my daughters?"

"Take it however you want. Let me wake Justin's ass up because it's time for the moment of truth."

When I finally woke up Justin, he was staring at my gun, not sure what to do. I handed his cell phone to him so he could talk to his wife. His eyes watered as he looked me directly into my eyes, as if to beg for forgiveness. I forgot until that moment how amazing his hazel eyes were. When he licked his lips in nervousness, his dimples almost made me melt. *This bastard is playing both of us.*

Come to find out, Justin had never moved out of his house. The place he had me visit on occasion was one of his rental properties. I wondered how many other women he took there to fuck. Justin had the nerve to try to explain. *How do you explain this shit?* He was lucky I had a book coming out because I wanted to shoot his ass. I wasn't as hurt as I should've been because I wanted to move on anyway. The part that bothered me was that he lied to his wife about me stalking him. *How am I stalking him when he's in my bed?*

Justin confessed and told his wife the truth. I felt sorry for her because he was her husband and the father of her children. I could move on with my life as soon as I put his ass out, but she had to deal with the cheating bastard.

I snatched the phone from Justin before his wife hung up. I wanted to apologize to her because it was not our fault he was trying to have the best of both worlds. When she hung up, I gave Justin back his phone and told him to put his clothes on and get out of my house.

"Lynda, I'm so sorry."

"Are you saying something to me? You have some nerve while I still got this gun in my hand. Justin, just get your clothes on and leave me alone." I fought hard to hold back my tears.

"You know I didn't mean for any of this to happen."

"It's okay. The truth always comes out eventually. I'm not mad, trust me."

"Lynda, I…"

"Stop talking before my finger accidentally slips and I pull the trigger! Don't ever contact me again for any reason, and I mean that shit from the bottom of my heart. I loved you. I trusted you. But you played me and lied to me. Did you really call me crazy? You know what, Justin? It doesn't matter now. I feel sorry for you. I really do."

Justin dressed quickly and left my house. Before he left, he looked back at me as if to say goodbye. He knew it was better not to keep talking. He couldn't be sure that I wouldn't shoot him.

The tears fell rapidly from my eyes once he closed the door. It wasn't because he was out of my life, but I never thought I would have to pull out my gun for anything other than self-defense. Moving past this situation wasn't going to be easy, but I had to manage somehow.

Dianne and Natasha were right; I didn't need to have a gun in my possession. I really wanted to shoot Justin, but I had to keep thinking about my future. At that moment, I knew I needed to make some changes in my life if I was ever going to find the kind of love I desired. I had to find a way to focus on my book release and the literary career I had ahead of me. First, I needed to find some peace. Maybe it was time for me to start going back to church.

# CHAPTER 12
## *Natasha*

~~~

**TYRONE ARRIVED HOME INTOXICATED IN** the middle of the night. The nerve of him! He was seemingly thinking only of himself with his behavior lately. Maybe I was partially to blame for his erratic behavior, though. *I would love to know how Nelson and Dianne ended up driving him home.* I figured I would address that at another time since it probably would be impossible to get a straight answer out of Tyrone while he was under the influence of alcohol. There was no question that I loved Tyrone, but he was getting on my nerves. *Wait, what am I thinking?* I had a man who loved me and sacrificed a job he loved to be home with his wife and children. I was tripping.

I needed to figure out a way to deal with Aisha's death before my actions ruined my marriage. I couldn't continue to blame Tyrone for not being around to help raise her, but I needed someone to blame. Did I blame God for taking her away from me? Did I blame myself for allowing her to go on that college tour? Did I blame the driver of the 18-wheeler that killed her? Because he was truly to blame for what happened. I wished I could confront him, but he was dead, too. It still bothered me that Aisha felt she couldn't come to me if she thought she was pregnant. *Was my daughter pregnant when she died? How do I let all of this go in order for me to live a happy, productive life?*

I let Tyrone stay asleep on the sofa because I didn't want to smell the beer on his breath. I stared at him for a few moments before going back to bed. My husband was exceptionally handsome. *Have I even told him that?* Probably not because all I did lately was take him for granted.

I had also taken Dianne's friendship for granted. *How could I have been so insensitive to her losing her baby?* It would be completely my fault if she never spoke to me again. I kept replaying the situation over and over in my head to see how I could've handled things differently with her and Tyrone, two of the people I loved most in this world.

I entered each room of my condo when I couldn't sleep. Tyrone had done such a wonderful job making sure everything was exactly the way I wanted it, from the shade of the paint to the color of the carpet. I quietly peeped into the twins' room to check on them. The Winnie the Pooh nightlight allowed me enough light to see Natalia and Nevaeh peacefully asleep. I smiled as I headed to check on Tyler who was peacefully sleeping, as well. Tyrone was really good with him, and I could tell when he looked at Tyler that he was happy to have a son. Earlier that day, he had picked up Tyler from his cousin's house, played with him for a couple of hours, and then left, barely speaking to me. He doesn't look at the girls the same way he does Tyler, or maybe that was just my speculation. I was certain he loved his children equally. Did I?

I wandered from room to room until Tyrone woke up. I watched from the kitchen as he stumbled his way into our bedroom. I hadn't treated him as lovingly as I should have since we were married, but I didn't know what I would do without him.

I followed behind Tyrone, who was now stretched out across the bed. Since I had so much on my mind and couldn't sleep, I decided to return to the living room and watch a movie. I didn't want to disturb Tyrone with my tossing and turning. Then again, as loudly as he was snoring, I doubt I would have kept him from sleeping.

I sat on the sofa and stared at the TV, but all I could think about was Aisha. I hadn't burned her diary as I said I would nor had I discussed with Tyrone what I had read. It weighed heavily on my mind that she might have been pregnant when she died. *Was my daughter pregnant?* I closed my eyes, and I was sure within minutes, the movie was watching me.

The next morning, I took Tyler out of his bed and put him in the bed with Tyrone. I wanted to run to the store, but I didn't want to risk leaving the babies with him in case they started crying and he couldn't hear them. Tyler could at least talk a little bit, so he could wake him up. Plus, I showed Tyler how to use the speed dial to call my cell phone. He was very advanced for his age. I left Tyrone a note explaining that I was going to the store before it got crowded; I hated being in any store after noon on the weekend. I didn't have much to get from the store, so I packed two bottles each for the girls, diapers, and a change of clothes.

I was skilled with carrying both babies down to the car at one time; the things you'll learn to do as a mother. Once I strapped Natalia and Nevaeh into their car seats, I headed to the Super Wal-Mart up the road from my house. The double stroller Lynda bought for the babies worked beautifully when I wasn't doing major shopping. The truth was I just wanted to get out of the house to clear my head from the random thoughts I had.

I picked up a couple of outfits for the kids and the *Toy Story 3* movie for Tyler. *Having new babies in the house must be hard for my little man, so I'll get something especially for him.* I had been moody lately, but I needed to spend more time with him alone to give him that one-on-one attention. I didn't want him to feel like I loved his baby sisters more than I loved him.

Once I was headed to the check-out line, I heard someone call out my name. I didn't recognize the voice, but as soon as I turned around, I noticed it was a neighbor from where I once lived in Upper Marlboro, Maryland.

"Hey, Natasha. Remember me? Janice, Jason's mother."

"Yes, hi, Janice. How have you been?"

"I've been okay. I try not to complain. Are these your girls? They are so adorable."

"Yes, and I have a son, too." I showed her the picture sculpture keychain with the picture of all my children together.

"Oh, congratulations."

"Thank you. How's Jason doing?"

"Well, he's doing okay now, but it was rough for him for a while. He took Aisha's accident very hard."

"Oh, I'm so sorry to hear that."

"Yeah, he attempted suicide once."

"What! Oh, my God!"

"Yes, he swallowed a bottle of pills, but I found him in time to get his stomach pumped."

"Thank goodness."

"His grades started slipping, and he was in jeopardy of losing his basketball scholarship."

"Oh, no."

"Thankfully, the school understood that he was grieving and sent him to counseling. I think that saved his life and gave him a chance to further his education."

"Wow, I'm so glad he's doing okay now."

"Yes, thank you. I know they were young, but he really loved your daughter; more than we realized."

"I know. I understand young love. I married my high school sweetheart recently; Aisha's dad."

"Aw, really? Congratulations again."

"Thank you."

"How are you holding up, Natasha?"

"I just take it day by day. It has been extremely hard."

"I can imagine. Watching my son grieve was the most painful experience I've had in my life, especially while he was on suicide watch. I was afraid he would try it again and succeed."

"Sorry you had to go through that with Jason, but can I ask you a question?"

"Sure."

"Please forgive me if this sounds insensitive. Did Jason ever mention that Aisha may have been pregnant when she died?"

"Yes, he talked to me about the possibility, but he told me later that it was a false alarm."

"Really? Okay, thanks." I was glad she didn't ask me any questions because I didn't want to go into detail about how I had to learn about it from reading her diary.

"Well, I'm not going to hold you up. I know you have your hands full. It was great seeing you, Natasha."

"Same here. Take care, Janice."

"You, too. Thanks!"

The news about Jason's attempted suicide broke my heart; however, I was glad he was making progress in his life. He looked out for Aisha the way Tyrone looked out for me when we were their age. I once again reflected on the way I treated Tyrone. He was sincerely trying to be a good husband and father, but I wasn't making it easy for him. I needed to turn that around immediately before I ended up losing him.

I purchased the items I picked up for the kids and headed back home before the girls started to fuss. Tyrone barely spoke to me when I arrived home, but he kissed the twins on their cheeks. I hated when there was tension between us. He started a routine of spending time with the kids and then leaving the house without saying where he was going.

*Is he trying to stay away from me?*

# CHAPTER 13
## Dianne

***THE DAY AFTER THE TYRONE*** fiasco, Nelson drove me back to Lynda's house to get my car. Plus, I had some things at her place that I needed to take home. Nelson went to the gym while I went inside Lynda's place and gathered my belongings. Nelson and I agreed to talk later that day regarding Nihya and her frequent outbursts.

When I arrive at Lynda's house, she wasn't there, but I had a set of keys. It seemed to be too early for her to be out of the house on a Sunday morning, but knowing her, she spent the night out somewhere. As I gathered my things, I received a call on my spare cell phone. Since I broke my BlackBerry, it was going to take a few days to receive a new one. I rarely used my spare phone, so there weren't many numbers programmed in it. Natasha's home number displayed on the Caller ID, so I immediately answered thinking it was her apologizing for the things she had said to me.

"Hello?" I answered in a nonchalant tone.

"Hi, Dianne. This is Tyrone."

"Yes, Tyrone. I don't think it's a good idea for you to call me considering last night."

"I know, but I wanted to say thank you for listening to me."

"You're welcome, Tyrone. Where's Natasha?"

"She got up early this morning and left me here with Tyler."

"Oh, okay."

"I was thinking about taking a drive. Do you mind if I bring him by to see you? I'm sure he would love to see his godmommy."

"Come on, Tyrone. You're killing me with all of this."

"Naw, I thought maybe Nelson would like to see him, too. He hasn't seen Tyler in a while."

"Now you know this has nothing to do with Nelson seeing Tyler. What's really going on, Tyrone?"

"Well, I think Natasha's upset since I came home a little drunk."

"How are you feeling this morning? And why would she leave you home with a hangover with Tyler?"

"I actually don't have a hangover, but Natasha didn't know that when she left. She just got up and rolled out without saying anything to me. Well, she left a note. I really think she's going to end up taking the girls and leaving me to raise Tyler alone. She wants me to pay for not being there for Aisha. When I walked out on my job to be home full-time, I thought she would be happy, but I think she would rather I not be there."

"I think she's happy, but you did make an important decision without talking it over with her. You don't do that when you're married, Tyrone."

"I know. I didn't plan to quit. My boss just pissed me off. I can take off at least a year, and we would be okay financially."

"That's good. Still, you need to talk things over with Natasha."

"Talking to her is becoming impossible, but I could always talk to you. You've never judged me. It must be all that psychology training." Tyrone laughed.

"I guess so, Tyrone." I managed to laugh along.

"Well, can I bring Tyler by?"

"I'm not home yet. I'm still at Lynda's. I had to come back this morning to get my things."

"Oh. Can I come by Lynda's? I promise to be on my best behavior. After all, I'll have Tyler with me." I detected sadness in Tyrone's voice.

"Okay, Tyrone," I agreed against my better judgment. I sensed he really needed to talk.

"Thanks, I'll be there in an hour."

When Tyrone arrived at Lynda's, I noticed he didn't have Tyler with him. *He set me up!* I was fuming with anger, and I started not to let his ass in.

"Hey, Dianne." Tyrone smiled.

I didn't respond right away. I just stood in the doorway with my hands on my hips for a few seconds before I spoke. "Where's Tyler, Tyrone?"

"Natasha came back home before I walked out the door, and she told me that she bought him a movie that she wanted them to watch together. I just left and came on over since I had already said I was coming."

"Tyrone, it isn't a good idea for us to be alone."

"Why? What are you afraid will happen?" Tyrone moved closer to me.

"Nothing. Just come in. I don't know where Lynda is and what time she's coming home, so you need to make this visit quick."

"All right." Tyrone sighed.

"Have a seat," I said, motioning toward the sofa.

He sat down, and I sat on the loveseat across from the sofa.

"Dianne, I'm tired."

"Tired of what?"

"Of the way Natasha treats me. I can't do this anymore. This is why I did some things when Aisha was born. Smoking and hanging in the streets was my way of dealing with her. Nothing I did then or do now is good enough for her."

"She's been through a lot, Tyrone."

"I know that, but we have all been through something traumatic. That doesn't make it right for her to treat me the way she does."

"I know and I agree. That's why we had an argument after you left yesterday."

"Oh, I didn't know because she rarely tells me anything anymore. She's normally fussing about something. She needs some serious help, but I do love her."

"I know. I told her that she should consider talking to someone, but she lashes out at me, too. The only person she doesn't lash out at is Lynda because she thinks Lynda is crazy and will kick her ass."

"She probably takes it out on us because she knows we love her most in this world. Although that sounds backward, some people are like that."

"Yeah, true, but I've had it this time, Tyrone. She said some really hurtful things to me. I've tried to be a sister to Natasha since she didn't have a lot of family, except for her foster family."

"Dianne, I won't leave Natasha, but I'm kind of hoping she leaves me."

"Are you serious?"

"Yeah, I don't want to be the man who runs out on his family, but she's kind of impossible to be around sometimes."

"I'm so sorry you have to go through that. I didn't know it was that bad."

"Yeah, so I figure she'll eventually leave. She did once before. It's not like I don't want us to work, but I can't take too much more."

"I know this may be asking a lot, but try to hang in there. I know it's easier said than done."

"Dianne, I would give anything, including my life, to bring Aisha back to Natasha. I know she would rather have Aisha here than me."

"Tyrone, don't say things like that."

"I don't know, Dianne. I'm tired of feeling like this. Isn't there someone you wish you could bring back?"

"Sure there is, Tyrone. But one thing I've learned is that things happen for a reason, and our lives are the way they are supposed to be.

If I could bring back anyone who has passed on, my life as I know it now would be entirely different. I don't know if I would want things to be changed. I lost my son, but if he would have survived, I probably would have married his father and never met Nelson. I don't know why my son didn't live, but I learned to trust God's plan."

"Yeah, I guess you're right," Tyrone said, then sighed.

When Tyrone stood up, I was hoping he was going to use the bathroom. Instead, he walked over to where I sat and extended his arms as if to ask for a hug. Once again, against my better judgment, I stood up to give him a friendly hug; however, his embrace was more than friendly. He caressed my curves softly.

"Tyrone, stop it."

"Stop what? I told you that I was going to get my chance to see how good you feel, and Lynda isn't here to stop me this time. Maybe this is God's plan."

"Tyrone, stop it, and don't use God's name in vain like that. That's not right, and you know it."

"But it feels so right, doesn't it? Admit it, Dianne."

"Feeling good is one thing, but feeling right is another."

"Oh, so you admit that it feels good? Well, that's a start."

Before I could respond, Tyrone had me up against the wall with his tongue trying to get acquainted with mine. It didn't take me long to give in to his kiss. So many things were going through my head, but without a doubt, we had definitely crossed the line. Tyrone was feeling so good against me that we didn't hear Lynda come in the door.

"What the hell am I walking in on?" Lynda said, as she slammed her front door shut. "And why is he back up in here today?"

I eased away from Tyrone. "Okay, Lynda, please calm down. I can't even say that it's not what you think."

"You sure the hell cannot! I can see, damn it."

"Lynda, you're just in time," Tyrone said playfully.

"For what?" Lynda yelled.

"Tyrone, I think you should go before Lynda gets her gun," I said jokingly.

"Yes, because I almost used it last night. So, don't tempt me, Tyrone. I'm kind of itching to shoot somebody, so don't volunteer yourself to be first."

"Okay, I'll go. Dianne, I'll talk to you later and thanks for listening. Bye, Lynda," Tyrone said, as he walked out the door.

"Now, heifer, you know that you have some explaining to do," Lynda demanded.

"Me? What about you? Who did you almost shoot?"

"Naw, don't try to shift the emphasis on my situation. Please explain to me why our best friend's husband had you pinned up against the wall, Dianne."

"To be honest, I'm not even sure why I let it happen. I think a part of me wants it to happen."

"You want to have an affair with Tyrone and risk losing Nelson? I don't think so."

I sighed. "Nelson doesn't pay attention to me like he used to. I miss the attention."

"Well, you need to talk to Nelson. The last thing you want to do is mess up two marriages by getting this so-called *attention* from Tyrone. Like I told you last night, if we didn't know his wife, then maybe I wouldn't say anything. But, come on, Dianne. This is too much, even for me."

"Of course, I know you're right, but…"

"But nothing. Please put an end to this now before it gets out of hand. I don't like being in the middle of this."

"I'm not putting you in the middle."

"You don't have to. Just walking in the door seeing you two like that puts me in the middle, Dianne."

"Okay, I'm sorry."

"Why was he even here?"

"I guess to talk."

"Uh-huh. Something tells me there's more to this than what you're telling me."

"Lynda, please, I don't want to talk about this anymore."

"All right, fine."

"Now, are you going to tell me who you almost shot?"

"Girl, you wouldn't believe the kind of night I had last night. To make a long story short, Justin's wife called his cell phone and I answered. I don't know why I did, but I'm glad I did. He's been lying to both of us. I'm supposed to be crazy and stalking him. He never moved out! He was taking me to one of his vacant rental properties. He's such a damn loser."

"Well, at least now you know. You even said it yourself that you were ready to move on from that situation. This should make it easier."

"It does. I just hate that he tried to make me out to be crazy. Can you believe that?"

"Crazy? No, not you," I said, laughing.

"Whatever, Dianne. I just better not catch you all up on Tyrone anymore."

"I promise, you won't." I smiled and winked while Lynda gave me the evil eye.

# CHAPTER 14
## Lynda

*THERE WAS SO MUCH GOING ON* around me that I forgot to call my brother as I had planned. I hated that so much time had elapsed since we last spoke, but from this point on, I promised to make a conscious effort to reach out to him more often. Before I engaged in a long, heated discussion with Langston, I needed to inform him that I had already made up my mind to visit our mother, so he didn't have to convince me of that. Otherwise, he would spend most of the conversation trying to get me to visit her.

It was definitely time for my mother and me to make amends, and after watching a televised church service that I had recorded on TiVo, it was confirmed that I needed to let old baggage go. The preacher kept saying you can't expect people to repay debts that only God can repay. He said when people hurt you, only God can heal you, so we should stop living as if someone owes us something. Even if a person doesn't say they're sorry, we have to still forgive them. That was easier said than done, but I was dedicated to trying when it came to my mother.

I dialed Langston's number from my cell phone, and he answered on the first ring.

"Hey, Lynda. I was wondering when I would hear from you, girl. How've you been?"

"No complaints, baby brother. How are you?"

"You know me, living day to day. Nothing's changed much." Langston laughed a little.

"Is everything okay with you?"

"Yes, why do you ask?"

"You know I could always tell when you had something on your mind. With that little nervous laugh you do, you can't keep it from me."

"I guess you're right. Well, Lynda, I might as well just come out with it. You're going to be an aunt."

"Oh, my goodness, Langston! Why didn't you call and tell me?"

"I'm still trying to deal with the news myself. You know I'm not in the position to be somebody's father yet. I'm still trying to get myself together."

"I know, but you'll make the best of it. Let me know if you ever need anything. I hate that you struggle without saying anything."

"Are you going to see Mom?" he asked.

"Yes, but don't try to change the subject."

There was an awkward silence on the phone for several seconds. I knew Langston was still upset because our father left all his money to me.

I needed to break the silence. "Hello?"

"I'm here."

"Don't shut down on me."

"I'm not, but when are you going to see Mom?"

"Very soon."

"I hope so. A Sunday would be a good day to visit. Do you know that she occasionally sets an extra plate at the table thinking you're coming to dinner?"

"What? That's odd. I haven't been there for dinner in years."

"I know, Lynda. That's what I said to her, and she seemed very sad. She said one day you are coming to dinner again."

"Then that's what I'll do."

"Oh, and please do not tell her that I sent you a letter. I want her to feel you did it on your own."

"Actually, I was planning to visit her before I got your letter. I found it very ironic that you sent the letter. I was praying she hadn't passed away or was sick."

"I would've had enough decency to call you, Lynda. You don't put something like that in a letter. Come on, give me some credit."

"I know. I'm sorry. When's your baby due?"

"I have no idea."

"Okay, no comment."

"Thank you. Please don't comment. This girl is driving me crazy already. I'm sure she told me, but I don't want to piss her off by asking again."

"Who is *she*?"

"This girl I was staying with for a while named Deniece. We weren't really in a relationship, but we were kind of seeing each other."

"Okay, I know how that is."

"I moved out and got my own place. It's an efficiency apartment. It's small, but it's mine. Then she calls to say she's pregnant. I just knew she was only saying that to get me to move back in with her."

"How do you know it's yours?"

"I don't, but I'll definitely get a blood test when the baby is born. I already told her that so there wouldn't be any surprises."

"That's good. And I'm glad you finally got your own spot."

"Me, too. I'm struggling, but happy."

"Langston, this money I have is for the both of us. You know you don't manage your money properly, so that's why I got it all. Dad didn't hate you, and I know that's what you've been thinking. Don't ever think that again. You were just a momma's boy and wanted to be up under her all the time. He wanted to go out and throw a ball around with you, but you wanted to be with your mommy. I was daddy's girl. That's just how it was."

"So, are you saying that since I was a momma's boy, I was a punk?"

"I didn't say that, and stop being so darn sensitive."

"Whatever, Lynda."

"Anyway, let me know what your bills are, and I will make sure you have access to enough money to cover your monthly expenses."

"Wow, are you serious?"

"Yes, and if you had called me a long time ago, you would have already had access to it. But don't think you're slick. My accountant is only authorized to give you the amount I specify, or I will do an automatic transfer once a month. But you better use it for bills, Langston. I'm not playing with you."

"Either way is fine with me. Thanks, sis!"

"No problem. Just work on your stability and confidence as a man, and fatherhood will fall into place."

"Wow! Dad used to say that all the time."

"Yes, he did. Please remember that he loved you more than you realize."

"Okay, sis. Call me after your visit with Mom. I love you."

"I love you, too, baby brother."

I hung up the phone and stared at the wall for a brief moment. I tried to imagine what visiting my mother would be like after all these years. I still couldn't believe so much time had passed. I prayed it would be a peaceful visit. I wasn't in the mood for anyone's drama, especially hers. She could really be a drama queen when she wanted to, but I was ready to make amends with her. Hopefully, she was willing to put the past behind us, as well.

# CHAPTER 15
## *Natasha*

*I WAS READING TYLER A* bedtime story when Tyrone arrived home. He came into Tyler's bedroom, kissed him on his forehead, and then kissed me lightly on the lips. The girls were already asleep. There was sadness in Tyrone's eyes when I looked into them.

I heard the shower running, and by the time I was done with Tyler's story, Tyrone was already in bed. When I entered our bedroom, he didn't budge, so I assumed he was asleep. Not to disturb him, I undressed in the bathroom and took a quick shower. Afterward, I slipped on one of his T-shirts and eased under the covers. I really loved Tyrone, although my actions lately suggested otherwise. I had so many bottled up emotions, and I took them out on Tyrone when he didn't deserve to be treated that way. When I touched his face to kiss him goodnight, his wet cheeks suggested to me he had been crying. *I guess men really do cry in the dark.*

"Tyrone, sweetheart?"

"Yeah?" he answered, not turning around.

"Baby, please talk to me. Tell me what's wrong."

"You wouldn't understand. Then again, maybe you would. I miss my mom, Natasha. I would do anything to talk to her right now. She was the one person I could count on, no matter what."

"I know. It's hard for me, too, without my parents. We've both been through a lot. Baby, please turn around and talk to me."

"Why do you want me to talk now, Natasha? I've been trying to communicate with you for a while now, and all you manage to do is find reasons to lash out at me." He still had his back turned.

I put my hand under the sleeve of his T-shirt and caressed his bicep. Tyrone lay on his left side, which allowed me to caress his right shoulder that now displayed a tattoo of the names of our twins and Tyler. I raised the sleeve of his T-shirt and kissed his shoulder. His skin was so soft. I grazed my lips across his ear and followed up with a soft kiss to the back of his neck.

"Tyrone, there is no excuse for the way I talked to you in front of Dianne and Lynda, and I'm sorry. I know I can be difficult to deal with, but I'm trying to handle my emotions better. Please talk to me."

Tyrone rolled over onto his back and pulled me on top of his chest. My head now rested over his heart, and I listened to the rapid rhythm of it beating.

"I feel nothing I do is good enough for you. You always seem to find something to complain about," Tyrone confessed.

I attempted to pull away from Tyrone, but he wouldn't release me from his grasp. He caressed the nape of my neck with one hand and my back with the other. When he kissed my forehead, I felt one of his tears fall.

"I guess I've been an awful wife, huh?" I let out a deep sigh.

I caressed Tyrone's chest where he recently got a picture of Aisha tattooed. Our daughter...gone. I was indeed having an extremely hard time dealing with her death, but it wasn't his fault.

"Natasha, I wouldn't say awful, but it's kind of bad at times. I want you to be happy, and if you're not happy with me, then..."

I cried before he finished his statement. When Tyrone heard my sobs, he held me tighter.

"Don't cry, Tash. We're going to work through this. I love you, but I just need to know that you *really* want me here."

"Of course I do. Maybe Dianne is right; maybe I do need to talk to a therapist. I owe her a huge apology. I said some really mean things to her."

"I know. She told me. Maybe we both should talk to someone. We have three little people that need us now."

"What do you mean she told you? When did you talk to Dianne?"

I raised my head off Tyrone's chest, and he softly kissed me on my lips. He pulled my body completely on top of his, and my legs fell open to a straddle position. My tears quickly evaporated.

"You want me, don't you?" Tyrone grinded against me slowly.

"No, it wasn't like that. I just—"

Tyrone interrupted. "You just came to bed with no panties on so we can make love. I know you, and normally, I have to fight to get them off you. Admit it. Plus, you know I love you in my white T-shirt. You knew what you were doing."

"Whatever," I said playfully, but he was absolutely correct. I wanted him to make love to me, and he did just that.

After he slid off his boxers and a few moments of grinding later, his manhood found its way into my wetness without any assistance. There had been so much tension between us that it had been a while since we made love so passionately. I rode my husband as if I was a jockey desperately trying to race to the finish line. Once I felt Tyrone throbbing inside of me, I made my own release and collapsed on top of him.

"Now that's what I'm talking 'bout, baby. Whew!" Tyrone gently smacked my ass.

I eased off Tyrone and kissed him gently on his lips. "I needed that."

"Me, too."

"Tyrone?"

"Yes, babe?"

"I'm worried about us."

"Don't be. Marriage takes work, and as long as the two people are willing to put in the work, then things will normally work out."

"I guess you're right."

"Tash, I love you and you know that. But you can't keep shutting me out."

"I know. I'm sorry. Forgive me?"

"Give me some more and I'll think about it." Tyrone laughed.

"It's on you."

Tyrone rolled me over onto my back, lay on top of me, and penetrated me slowly. He kissed me softly while easing in and out of me. There was nothing like some good lovin', and it surpassed good. It made me think back to the night we reconnected in the hotel room. That night meant so much to me because it was the beginning of something beautiful, and I was messing it all up with my drastic mood swings. I had to find a way to turn things around for my family's sake.

# CHAPTER 16
## *Dianne*

❦

***THE PAST FORTY-EIGHT HOURS*** replayed repeatedly in my head. The situation with Natasha didn't concern me as much as what I feared could happen between Nelson and me if I didn't get things in check with Tyrone. It weighed heavily on my mind, and I wondered if I should confess to Nelson that I kissed Tyrone. The thought of Nelson's possible reaction erased that option from my mind almost as quickly as I thought it.

Although I had a lot on my mind, if I was going to host Lynda's book release party, I needed to get my house in order. Whenever I was upset, I neglected my house, and now I had so much cleaning to do; however, cleaning my house was fine with me because I needed the distraction to keep my mind off a few things that bothered me.

The sound of my cell phone ringing startled me out of my thoughts. When I saw Natasha's home phone number appear across the screen, I decided not to answer it, assuming it would be Tyrone. After several rings, the call went to voicemail. I was relieved when I didn't get the indication that there was a message, but moments later, my house phone rang. I was nervous as I walked to the phone because I didn't want to believe Tyrone would be so bold as to call my house. I would rather it be a telemarketer. Sure enough, when I looked at the Caller ID, it was Natasha's house number. *Not today, Tyrone*, I thought before answering the phone. I took a deep breath and closed my eyes, dreading the conversation.

"Hello?"

"Hi, Dianne."

"Natasha?" I was glad it wasn't Tyrone, but shocked it was Natasha.

"Yes, Dianne, it's me. Please don't hang up. I really need to talk to you."

"I'm listening."

"I know sorry may not be enough for what I said to you. I was upset, but that's no excuse for what I said. I would understand if you didn't want to speak to me, but I had to at least try to talk to you. We've been friends for a long time, and you're like my sister." Natasha paused before she spoke again. "Hello?"

"I'm still here."

"Oh, okay. Well, I'm not going to hold you up. I just wanted to say how deeply sorry I am, and I pray you will soon forgive me. Love you. Bye."

Natasha hung up the phone before I had a chance to respond. I figured she did that on purpose so she didn't have to hear me out right away, which was cool. Most people utilized that avoidance mechanism when they knew they were wrong. She was definitely wrong for saying those things to me about losing my baby, and I was hurt; however, she would be even more hurt if she knew I kissed her husband. She didn't have tough skin like Lynda and I did. I typically didn't stay mad for too long, and I tried not to hold grudges. I planned to call her back so we could discuss Lynda's book release party, but I needed some time to think first. I had some guilt of my own to deal with. I wondered if Tyrone and I should tell Natasha what happened because I needed to clear my conscience. Of course, I would have to deal with Nelson on my own.

*Several Months Later*

# Chapter 17
## *Lynda*

*MY BOOK RELEASE PARTY HAD* finally arrived, and it was time to celebrate. I decided to establish my own publishing company and continue with my self-publishing plans. Although I had some offers from a few local publishers to publish my book, I couldn't see someone else profiting from all of my hard work. Maybe I would consider signing with another publisher in the future for more exposure. Until then, I was going to enjoy promoting my debut novel.

Dianne offered to host the party at her beautiful home in the Tantallon Community in Fort Washington, Maryland. Since the party was being held at her home, I was very selective as to whom I invited. I wanted it to be an exclusive event.

Although I didn't have a steady man in my life, I had faith there was someone special out there for me. Maurice and Justin were definitely out of my life. I occasionally spent time with Xavier when he was home from school, but it was nothing physical. I wasn't sure if it was a good idea, but I asked him to accompany me at my book release party. I knew Dianne and Natasha didn't approve of the situation with Xavier, so I kept that part of my life a secret. They didn't know what Xavier looked like, so I was probably safe to invite him; however, if they looked at him closely, they would see his resemblance to Taye.

Whom I really missed was Zion. I hadn't found the courage to call him to apologize for my actions concerning the phone call from Jasmine. I still didn't know how they knew each other. I wasn't sure when our paths were going to cross, but since both of us were in the literary industry, it was inevitable that I would see him again; however, I wasn't prepared to see him so soon, and especially not at my book release party.

I turned to Dianne and Natasha once I noticed Zion was there. "Okay, which one of you heifers invited Zion?" I was glad the two of them were able to work things out.

"I didn't. Did you, Natasha?" Dianne asked sarcastically.

"No, it wasn't me," Natasha responded with a devilish smirk.

"Well, one of you had to invite him. You know I have a guest with me."

"A guest, really?" Dianne remarked nonchalantly. "I wonder who your *guest* is, and why haven't we met him?"

"Dianne, don't start."

"Start what? Why do you have that little boy up in here?" Dianne asked.

"To celebrate!"

"Celebrate my ass." Dianne giggled. "Oh, this is going to be interesting."

"Not funny, Dianne."

"Well, next time, you shouldn't keep stuff like that a secret." Dianne winked.

When Dianne walked away, I noticed Zion walking in my direction. I looked at Natasha and begged with my eyes for her not to leave me. Of course, she ignored my signal, smiled, and walked away. It appeared that I wasn't going to be able to avoid him any longer. I had no idea where Xavier was at that moment, but I hoped he was somewhere mingling. Zion greeted me with a tight embrace. The kind of embrace that said, "I've missed you." I held onto him for what seemed like forever.

"Zion, thanks for coming."

"You know I wouldn't miss an occasion like this, and congratulations, Ms. Published Author." Zion handed me a bottle of Cristal.

"Thank you. For the price of this, you should have just bought me something from Tiffany's," I said, giving him another nice, firm hug.

"Maybe we could celebrate later."

"Celebrate how?" I asked, releasing my embrace from him.

"Don't act like you don't miss me."

"Whatever, Zion," I responded, blushing.

"Plus, I think you owe me an apology, so I'm going to let you apologize to me *in private*. I'll let you get back to your little guest for now. Yes, I saw y'all together." Zion then whispered in my ear, "But just let me know when you get rid of him."

He kissed me on my cheek and walked away.

*Does he really think it's that easy?* I smiled and went to find Xavier so I could think of a reason to send him home. After mingling for a while, Xavier must have realized he wasn't going to be able to get any one-on-one attention from me. He thanked me for a nice time and left. *Whew!* I didn't have to come up with a bogus reason to send him on his way.

Zion sent me text messages about how much he missed me and that he couldn't wait to get me alone. His messages got very sexual, and I was immediately turned on by what he said he would do to me. I knew Dianne had a guestroom in the basement, so I sent Zion a text message to meet me downstairs in the second room on the right. Everyone was mingling and having a good time, so I was sure no one would notice my absence for a few minutes. I was glad I didn't see Dianne or Natasha before I headed downstairs because they would have started asking me a series of unnecessary questions. I reached the room seconds before Zion.

"Did anyone see you?" I asked.

"I'm not sure, but we're grown, right?"

"Yeah, but Dianne will kill me if she knew what I was about to do in her house."

"Um, what are you about to do?"

"I'm about to *apologize* to my ex-boyfriend," I said seductively. I caressed the bulge in Zion's pants. He always had a way of letting me know he missed me.

"Oh, yeah? Well, tell me you're sorry, baby. And if you apologize right, maybe he will no longer be your ex."

"Oh, really?" *How arrogant* was what I really wanted to say.

Zion pulled me close to him and kissed my neck. I eased from his grip.

"Zion, wait."

"What's wrong, baby? I have condoms. I know you're about to ask me that."

"Actually, no, I'm not. We shouldn't be doing this."

"Why not?"

"Because, Zion, we need to talk."

"Now? You're killing my erection."

"Yes, now. And trust me; I can get it back up."

"Okay, we can talk now if you want, but somehow, this doesn't sound positive."

"Well, you never told me who Jasmine is." I didn't waste any time saying what was on my mind.

"Because you never gave me a chance. You just jumped to conclusions."

"I know, and I'm sorry. But I would like to know who she is to you."

"A friend. Well, sort of."

"Sort of?"

"It's complicated. Well, not really. Okay, her father used to date my mother."

"Oh, that's not so complicated."

"I guess not." Zion hesitated in his response.

"Sounds like there's more to the story than what you're telling me."

"Can we please talk about this later?"

He was definitely hiding something. "Sure, we'll finish this conversation later."

"Good! Now, back to my apology."

I started to tell Zion that it was possible I knew Jasmine, too, but then he would have asked me for details, and I didn't feel like sharing the whole threesome story anyway. I was sure it would come out at some point, especially if Jasmine surfaced when I was with Zion. I wasn't sure how the whole thing was going to go down, but I would worry about it when that day came. It had been a while, and I simply wanted to enjoy Zion's company.

I eased down to my knees and unzipped Zion's pants, exposing his semi-erection. I welcomed most of his nine inches into my mouth as he moaned.

"Damn. Apology accepted, baby."

Although Zion appeared to be enjoying my oral skills, he stopped me before I could make him cum. "That feels good, baby, but I want to be inside of you. I miss being up in you."

"Okay, but do you..."

"Yes, I have protection. Remember, I already told you that."

Zion kissed me gently on my lips. Damn, his kisses turned me on. They were wet, but not too sloppy.

"Okay."

"First, do me a favor."

"Whatever you like," I said, as I bowed my head and mocked Vanessa Bell-Calloway in the movie *Coming to America*.

Zion laughed. "Strip for me."

When I had stripped down to my bra and panties, Zion motioned for me to stop. "Let me look at you for a minute."

"Zion, we don't have that kind of time. I do have guests upstairs."

"I know, but you look so good in your bra and panties, especially with those heels on. Thanks for leaving them on, girl. Turn around so I can see how your ass looks in that thong."

I obliged to his request.

"Damn, girl. I see you've picked up a few pounds."

"Zion!" I responded impatiently.

"Okay, okay. It's not my fault you look so good to me right now. And when did you get that tattoo on your back?"

"Oh, my goodness, Zion. Can we talk later?"

"Okay, I see. You can't wait for big daddy to tear that pussy up," Zion said, as he rubbed his erection on my ass.

Normally, that would have turned me on, but for some reason, it did just the opposite. I didn't need to be fucked right now in my life. I wanted someone to make love to me. I wanted passion. *I need passion.*

Zion laid me down on the bed so that I was now on my stomach. He entered me from behind without taking my thong off; he just moved it over to the side. *How romantic.* Zion was never the most romantic man, but sex with him was always exciting. As Zion stroked me from behind, the thought came into my mind that I didn't check to see if he had put on a condom. He felt so good inside of me that I didn't bother to stop him so I could check. Once I moaned in satisfaction to signal I was having an orgasm, Zion increased his rhythm, which let me know he was on his way to satisfaction himself.

A few strokes later, Zion pulled out of me, and I felt his warm release all over my ass. I got my answer; he didn't have on a condom. I felt too good to be mad at that point. I would have to address it later.

Thank goodness for the baby wipes I kept in my purse because I needed them then more than ever. I told Zion to get them out of my purse so he could clean up his mess. Once we both freshened up using the baby wipes, we quickly dressed and went upstairs. I decided it was best that we went separately so no one would see us together. I didn't want to leave any room for speculations. Apparently, I dressed too quickly because when I got back upstairs to enjoy the rest of my party, Dianne motioned for me to come over to her.

"Heifer, why is your shirt inside out?" Dianne asked with squinting eyes.

"Oh, shit!" I said and laughed loudly.

"Shh! Go and fix your clothes before anyone else sees you. We'll talk later about what you were doing up in my house."

*Busted!* I couldn't even say anything, I just went into the bathroom, fixed my clothes, and prepared myself for the lecture I had coming later on from Dianne. After fixing my shirt, I grabbed my makeup bag from my purse so I could reapply my lipstick before continuing to mingle with my guests. When I returned my makeup bag, I felt my cell phone vibrate. I had a new text message from Zion, which indicated he wanted us to hook up the following day since he was scheduled to go on another book signing tour. I replied to his message, *definitely!*

For the rest of the night, I was more excited about spending time with Zion than I was about celebrating my book release. Xavier actually popped into my mind a few times because I felt guilty I had neglected him at the party, inadvertently no doubt.

The next day, I prepared for my date with Zion. It had been a while since we were out on a date, so I wanted to look especially good for him to give him something to think about while he was away. I dressed in my stretch jean leggings, a cute off-the-shoulder sweater made of Angora, and my calf-length leather boots. I wouldn't have been complete for my date without my Angel perfume made by Thierry Mugler. Zion always loved when I wore that scent.

When Zion arrived, he knocked on the door. I was glad he didn't call from his cell phone. I answered the door and hugged him tightly around his neck. I was slightly disappointed because he used to bring me white or yellow roses when we went out on a date. *Why did the courting stage seem to end?*

"So, what do you want to do? You want to go to dinner, a movie, skating, all of the above?" Zion asked, caressing my curves.

"Naw, I have something else in mind tonight. Let's do something we've never done together."

"What's that?"

"Take me to a gentleman's club."

"Are you serious? Aw, shit, we can do that."

"Why are you so excited?" I laughed at his anticipation.

"I don't know, but I am." Zion adjusted the erection he had developed.

"I'm just curious as to what goes down in a place like that. Plus, I want to get you all ready for me."

"Shit, I'm ready for you now."

"Is that right?" I decided to get a feel of Zion's erection.

"Girl, stop it, or we ain't going to make it nowhere."

"Okay, let's go then."

When I got into Zion's car, I immediately noticed a beautiful flower arrangement on the backseat. He must have noticed me looking and smiled.

"Yes, those are for you. I meant to bring them to the door so you could put them in water," Zion said and winked at me.

"Thank you. They're beautiful." I retrieved the flowers from the backseat. The flower arrangement consisted of a variety of flowers, but red roses were strategically placed throughout the arrangement. I returned the flowers to the backseat and continued smiling.

It seemed we arrived at our destination extremely quick. I was nervous at first to be in a gentleman's club because I didn't want people to make the mistake of thinking I was into women. After a while, I could have cared less what other people thought about me. I was into Zion and Zion only. I knew he went to see the female dancers from time to time, and I was curious to see what the scene was like for men. That was all a part of the foreplay for the evening I wanted to have with Zion.

Once we were inside, we were seated at a table near the rear of the club. A waitress immediately came over and took our drink order. Zion and I both ordered a Long Island Iced Tea.

"Zion, keep in mind that one of us has to be sober enough to drive tonight. Okay?"

"Well, that's going to be you. I've had a rough few weeks, and I need to get my damn drink on."

"All right, that's cool. I don't have a problem with that. I want you to get all nice and liquored up anyway."

"What are you planning to do to me, mami?"

*Damn, he sounded sexy when he called me mami.* I blushed. Normally, I hated when men said that to me, but of course, Zion could get away with it.

"I have a few things in mind."

"Shit, I'm ready to go now."

"We just got here, Zion. Be patient. Mami got you," I whispered, allowing my lips to graze his ear. I knew he loved when I did that.

"Girl, you're about to have me leaking on myself."

"Come on now, Zion." I laughed.

"I'm serious. You think I'm playin'."

"No, I know you're not playin'."

"You're so crazy, but that's what I love about you. I never know what you're going to come up with for us to do. Damn, my dick is hard as shit."

"I know. I can feel it," I said, softly kissing him on his neck and gently caressing the bulge in his pants.

"But, for real, after I have two or three Long Islands, we up out of here."

"Okay, sounds good to me."

"I feel like it's my birthday." Zion laughed.

"Shut up, Zion!" I laughed along.

Before the strip show could even get started, our good time at the gentleman's club was interrupted by an unwanted visitor at our table. I couldn't believe my eyes when I saw Jasmine walking in our direction. Zion was too busy enjoying my caressing to even notice. I could actually feel the moment of truth approaching.

"Well, well, well. If it isn't two of my favorite people." Jasmine smiled at Zion and then winked her eye at me.

Rolling my eyes, I responded, "Hey."

Zion looked confused. "What does she mean? You two know each other?"

"Unfortunately," I responded nonchalantly.

"Yes, we know each other *very* well."

Zion just stared at me, but I refused to acknowledge him at that moment because I knew I would have some serious explaining to do. I needed a minute to think.

"Lynda, how do you know her?"

"Zion, we were friends a long time ago. We're no longer friends, and as a matter of fact, I have nothing else to say to her."

"Oh, Lynda, don't be like that. You know we used to be *really* close." Jasmine winked.

Zion looked at Jasmine in disgust. "So, are you strippin' here now? Does your father know?"

"Don't act like you didn't know, Zion. I love how the two of you are just trying so hard to downplay how you know me. It's kind of cute."

"You know what? I can't take anymore of her. I'm ready to go." I stood and put my purse on my shoulder.

"Why don't you stick around and check out my show? The *both* of you might like it."

"Jasmine, please! I don't know what you're trying to insinuate, but it's not working with me. Okay?" Zion snapped.

"Baby, let's get out of here." I grabbed Zion by the arm.

"Hey, Zion?" Jasmine called out.

"What, Jasmine?"

"I see we both have the same taste in women." Jasmine smirked.

I could've punched her in the face right then and there. I was furious! I stormed out and left Zion standing there before I caused a scene. I really wanted to beat that bitch's ass. I assumed he was leaving the money for our drinks because he wasn't right behind me as he should've been. I hated that our night was ruined. I knew she would eventually surface, but I had no idea it would be so damn soon. Zion and Jasmine must have had an argument or something because by the time he caught up with me, he was pissed.

"Okay, are you going to tell me what all that was about?" Zion asked.

"Nothing to tell."

"I know there's something you're not telling. You must be the woman that I heard she was in love with. Did the two of you have sex or something?"

"Yes, Zion. Okay? There, I said it. Are you happy now?"

"Wait, whoa! I was just kidding. Are you fucking serious?"

"Zion, the cursing isn't necessary."

"Like hell it ain't. I just found out that my woman and my almost sister were together, *intimately*. I think I've earned the right to curse."

"It wasn't like that."

"Well, how was it? I mean, not how was the sex, but...you know what I mean." Zion smirked to hold in his laugh.

"Oh, so you find this funny?"

"Girl, I have to laugh to keep from going crazy."

"Yeah, okay." I sighed.

"Is that why you wanted to come to the gentleman's club with me? Are you bisexual?"

"Zion, no! That would make your day, wouldn't it? Men!" I pulled Zion's keys from my purse since he didn't want to keep them in his pocket.

"Are you going to explain to me what happened then?"

"I will on the way to your house. Come on, I'm ready to get out of here. This didn't go as I had planned." Disappointed, I handed Zion his keys.

I was quiet for a minute so I could collect my thoughts. I knew Zion wasn't going to let the situation go, so I figured I might as well tell him the truth and then we could move on.

"Zion, I'm going to make a long story very short."

"All right."

"All of this has really ruined my buzz."

"Shit, not mine."

"You know what… Anyway, Jasmine and I used to be friends up until about four or five years ago. She and I decided to have a threesome with a male dancer."

"Wow."

"Zion, please. This is difficult enough."

"Okay, my bad. Go ahead."

"Well, we weren't supposed to interact with one another, but instead, we planned to fuck him tag team style."

"Damn! I'm in the wrong business," he responded, sounding turned on.

"Zion!" I screamed.

"Okay, sorry."

"Like I said, to make a long story short, while I was lying back allowing this dude to lick Ms. Kitty, I find out it's not him. It was her with her tongue in my coochie."

"Um-hmm. Continue."

"I mean that's pretty much it. The problem for me is that when I found out it was her, I didn't make her stop. I allowed her to make me cum. After that, I put on my clothes and left. I hadn't spoken with her since then, and that was the night of Dianne's bachelorette party."

"Right now, all I have is the visual in my head of Jasmine eating your pussy, and my dick is now as hard as a brick."

"You know what…"

"I mean, come on now. I'm a man."

"Yeah, a damn caveman!"

"I'm sorry. I'm just being honest."

"Whatever, man. Just drive."

"You know I want you right now, don't you? Let me pull over and—"

"Don't even finish that statement."

"All right. We're almost at my house anyway. I'm about to bust."

"You're so nasty."

"No, horny. I'm horny. What did you expect? I go to a strip club with my girl, she reveals to me that she's been with a woman, and my dick isn't supposed to be hard?"

"I guess you have a point." I let out a deep sigh.

"Can I ask you something?"

"What, Zion?"

"Why didn't you tell me that you knew her earlier when we were talking about her?"

"To be honest, I wasn't one hundred percent sure that was her. Her voice sounded familiar that day when she called you, but I couldn't be sure. I knew the day would come when it was confirmed whether it was her or not. I was hoping later more so than sooner. Oh, well."

"Now we know," Zion chimed in.

"And don't think you're off the hook, brotha."

"What do you mean?"

"Stop stalling. You know there's more to your story, too. Don't even try it."

"Okay, we had sex once when we were younger. And for some reason, she acts like we could've had a relationship."

"Wow, okay. So she still wants to be with you? If this happened a while ago, then why is she still calling?"

"I don't know because the last I heard she was in love with some girl. She wouldn't tell me who the girl was, but she kept saying that I knew her."

"Is that right?"

"Yeah, but I can't feed into Jasmine's games. She's a little unstable, and I just don't have the time to give her the attention she's begging for. I haven't actually talked to her, but she keeps calling me."

"Wow, I don't know what to say."

"So now you know."

"Yeah. Again, I'm sorry for jumping to conclusions. I should've given you a chance to explain."

"It's all good, but aren't you curious?"

"About what?"

"How Jasmine and I ended up having sex? After all, our parents were dating."

"Not really, Zion. Some details I don't need to know. I'm good, but thanks." I actually wanted to know, but I couldn't handle anything else at that moment.

"Okay, if you say so."

"But something tells me that she will surface again at some point."

"Yeah, she usually does."

*Drama!* I thought, shaking my head.

When we got to Zion's place, you would've thought we were teenagers the way he was anxious to get inside of me. That wasn't the kind of night I had in mind at all, and it seemed to rapidly get worse. Zion fucked me as if we were strangers. That time, I made sure he had on a condom. All I wanted was for it to be over so I could go home. It took all my energy not to cry.

After Zion released, I faked an orgasm, which I hardly ever did, so he wouldn't keep pounding on me. He got up and went to the bathroom so he could wash up. That was his normal after-sex routine; get up, wash up, and then bring back a washcloth for me. That time, when he got back to his room, I was already dressed and ready to go home.

"Lynda, why are you dressed? You're leaving?"

"Yes, Zion. I think it's best that I call a cab and leave."

"Why, because of the Jasmine situation?"

"No, I'm hardly worried about Jasmine. It's us, Zion."

"Huh?"

"Listen, there are some things I really need to think about."

"Tell me what's wrong, Lynda. We can't work on it if you don't communicate."

The tears fell from my eyes uncontrollably. I was so upset that I didn't try to speak. I allowed myself to pour out all of my emotions through my tears. Zion pulled me into his arms and held me tightly.

"I wish you would tell me what's wrong," he whispered in my ear.

I decided not to say anything, and I had a very good reason why. There were some things in my life that I wanted to flow naturally, and being in love was one of them. Many people didn't agree with my philosophy, but I wanted a man to treat me special because he wanted to and not because I told him to. I wanted Zion to make love to me because that was what he was feeling. If he only wanted to fuck me, then it was obvious he wasn't the man for me.

He pleaded with me to stay. I reluctantly agreed. After I took my clothes back off, Zion sat on the edge of the bed and pulled me onto his lap. I was now straddling him, but I wasn't in the mood to have sex anymore.

"Lynda, I know we have something to work through, but I do love you. Tonight, you don't seem pleased. You just look so unhappy. Am I not pleasing you anymore?"

"Yes, you're pleasing me. You make me cum, so I guess that's your goal, right?"

"No, Lynda. I mean, yeah, I want you to be satisfied, but I want you to feel so much more when you're with me."

My tears continued to fall, and I let out a deep sigh. "I guess I'm just ready for more than fucking, but I don't expect you to understand."

"I didn't mean to make you feel like this was just fucking."

"It's okay, Zion."

"No, it's not okay. You're still my girl, right?"

"I guess so."

"What do you mean, you guess?"

"Zion, we hadn't spoken in a while before the party. It's not that easy to pick back up with a relationship."

"Okay, I got you. But whatever this is between us, relationship or not, I don't ever want you to feel that way. I care about you, and I want to do everything I can to make you happy whenever you're with me. But you have to communicate with me. I can't read what's on your mind."

Zion couldn't read my mind, but he sure could read the expression on my face. I didn't know what to do about the situation, relationship or whatever it was with Zion. I didn't know how to make him see where I was coming from. It puzzled me as to how men seemed to feel as if it was simple to reconnect and start where you left off, especially when a lot of time had passed or drama occurred in the past that still needed to be addressed. It wasn't that simple if people wanted to avoid making the same mistakes. Hopefully, in time, things would work out with Zion and me.

# CHAPTER 18
## *Natasha*

*I COULDN'T STOP THINKING ABOUT JASON* and the conversation I had with his mother several months ago. It saddened me that Jason suffered so much after Aisha died, but based on what his mother told me, he would be okay. It also bothered me that he felt comfortable enough to discuss Aisha's possible pregnancy with his mother, but Aisha didn't feel the same way with me.

I went into the closet that we used as storage and pulled out the box of Aisha's mementos that I had saved. Her diary was still there. I initially decided to burn it before I moved out of my townhouse in Upper Marlboro where I raised Aisha, but I changed my mind. Reading her thoughts allowed me to feel close to her. Although at times, what I read was painful.

I went back to the entry in Aisha's diary where she wrote that she would rather die than tell me she was possibly pregnant. Those words still burned my eyes when I read them. I took a deep breath and turned to the very next entry, which happened to be the last one. Tears fell from my eyes as the reality set in that these would be her final private thoughts recorded in her diary before she died.

*Dear Diary,*

*I'm so happy to tell you that I'm not pregnant. I did two of those home pregnancy tests, and they both came back with a minus sign. The instructions said that meant not pregnant. I still want to tell my mother that I had sex with Jason, but I don't want to see the disappointment on her face. I promised her that I would tell her first. I told Jason that I would have to get some birth control before we could have sex again. He said he would use a condom, but I'm still scared. I will ask my mother to take me to the doctor when I come back from the college tour, because if I tell her now, she might not let me go. I love my mother so much, and I don't want her to be upset. She's already upset about not being with my dad. She wears a heart-shaped locket with a picture of her and my dad on one side and my baby picture on the other. They were like 17 in the picture. I looked at it one day when she was in the shower. That seems to be the only time she takes it off. My dad loves her, too, and I know it. He always asks about her when I call him. I can hear the happiness in his voice when he talks about her. I wish they would get back together so they could both be happy again. I wonder what it would take to get them back together. Oh, well, I need to finish packing for this tour. Jason is sad that I'm leaving, but he already knows where he's going to school. I hope he doesn't think I'm going to meet another boy because I'm not. Okay, I'm done for real this time. I want to make sure I spend as much time with Jason and my mom before I leave. I love them both very much! Oh, and I need to call my dad. I love him, too. See you later, Diary, until next time.*

I cried hysterically after reading the words "until next time" because there was never a next time. *Oh, my God. How do I do this? How do I go on without Aisha?*

Tyrone walked in while I cried, and of course, he wanted to know what was going on. I told him about Aisha's diary and what I read in it. He just said, "Oh," as if he already knew.

"Tyrone, please tell me you didn't know about Aisha thinking she was pregnant."

His silence told me the truth; he knew.

"Tyrone!" I yelled.

He looked into my eyes, which were now flooded with tears. "Yes, baby?"

"Did you know?" I lowered my tone so I wouldn't wake the babies.

"Yes, she told me."

"What? How could you not tell me, Tyrone?"

"Aisha begged me not to tell you. She wanted to tell you herself, and I thought she did, Natasha. I'm sorry."

"I'm really not upset that you didn't tell me, although you should have. It hurts to know she told you and not me. She knew she could tell me anything."

"She said she was waiting for a good time to talk to you. It hurt me when she told me that she thought she might be pregnant. That meant my little girl was having sex. No dad wants to hear that. She said Dianne was going to get her the pregnancy tests."

"Dianne? She knew, too? This is too much."

"Natasha, she was a scared teenager who tried never to upset you."

"Well, Jason felt comfortable enough to tell his mother."

"How do you know that?"

"I saw his mother recently, and I asked her if she knew. I guess everyone knew but me."

I covered my eyes and cried. Tyrone grabbed me into his arms and pleaded with me not to cry. Of course, I couldn't get him to feel what I felt.

"Natasha, baby, why don't you get some rest. I got the kids." Tyrone kissed me on the forehead.

"Okay, sure. I could use some rest. Thanks."

Since I was no longer breastfeeding, I contemplated taking a couple of sleeping pills to help me rest, but I was afraid of becoming dependent on them, so I decided against it. I got the prescription filled at my last doctor's visit just in case I needed them, but I hadn't taken one yet. A part of me was worried about taking them with the babies around. The truth was, I wasn't coping well with all of these emotions: the pain of losing Aisha, the uncertainty of the state of my marriage, the argument with Dianne, and not to mention having three small children. I felt miserable. *Lord, how did I get here?*

# CHAPTER 19
## *Dianne*

*WHY DID I HAVE TO* dream aloud? Perhaps it sounded crazy to some, but there were people who talked in their sleep. I knew as a little girl I would do that on occasion, but Nelson hadn't mentioned I did that since we've been married.

I woke up late one afternoon, but I didn't feel well rested after sleeping for about twelve hours. I knew I tossed and turned most nights because the situation with Tyrone weighed heavily on my conscience. It must have been the guilt that kept me from sleeping peacefully. Not to mention all that I had done before and after Lynda's book release party. I was exhausted when it was over, and I still had a lot of cleaning to do. I am glad Tyrone maintained a distance from me at the party. When I got out of bed, Nelson was already up, and he stared at me as if I was a stranger.

"Good morning, Nelly." I gave him a small peck on the lips since I was dealing with morning breath.

Nelson didn't respond. He just kept glaring at me as if I'd done something wrong.

"Why are you looking at me like that?" I was a little nervous.

He was silent for a few seconds before he spoke. "Is there something you want to tell me?"

"About what?"

"About why you're dreaming about Tyrone?"

*Oh, shit!* "Are you mad at me because of a dream?"

"No, it's about what you were saying out loud in your sleep. How do you think it feels to hear my wife mention another man, even if it is a dream? How am I supposed to take that?"

"I don't know."

"Is that all you're going to say?"

"I don't know what else you want me to say, Nelson."

"The truth. How about telling me the damn truth!"

I was stunned. "I'm not sleeping with Tyrone, if that's what you're implying."

"Well, something is going on. People just don't dream about stuff out of the blue. Even you know that being a psychologist and all. You studied dreams. Shit, I remember you doing research studies on dreams. Do you have a hidden desire for Tyrone or something?"

"Nelson, please!"

"This must have something to do with why he was at Lynda's the other day, and I'm driving him home like a damn fool after he was doing who knows what with my wife."

"Nelson, it wasn't like that at all."

"It must be something for you to be like, 'Stop, Tyrone, you know we shouldn't be doing this.' So, that was nothing?" Nelson said in a female voice, obviously mocking me.

"You know what, Nelson?"

"What, Dianne?"

"Never mind. I'm not going to even do this with you."

"Then don't, because obviously you're hiding something. I've been with you long enough to know when something isn't right with you."

I didn't respond.

"Dianne, do you hear me talking to you?"

"Yes, I hear you," I answered flatly.

"You're way too nonchalant about this. But never mind. I can't even look at you right now anyway. Maybe you just ought to leave like you always do when you want to avoid something."

Although Nelson was partially correct about the situation with Tyrone, it hurt me to hear him talking to me in such a harsh tone. I didn't understand how my life was getting to this point where Nelson and I were having so many issues. Then again, yes, I did: Nihya. The moment Nelson found out about Nihya, our worlds changed and hadn't been the same since. It wouldn't have been so bad if our lives had changed for the better; however, it was quite the contrary. I tried to ignore Nelson's last comment because I really didn't feel like arguing with him. I hadn't even washed my face or brushed my teeth yet.

As I entered the bathroom in our bedroom, an enormous feeling of guilt came over me. I knew the tears would follow soon, so I turned on the faucet in the bathtub to drown out the sounds of my sobs. If Nelson heard me crying, he would definitely know I was hiding something. I figured I would take a nice bubble bath and get my thoughts together before I talked to him. I wished he had approached the situation differently because I probably would have confessed the truth about what had happened with Tyrone. I needed it off my conscience; unfortunately, I would have to carry the guilt a while longer because I wasn't going to discuss the situation with Nelson while he was so angry.

After soaking in the tub for nearly thirty minutes, my water got cold. I washed up quickly, rinsed off, and stepped out of the bathtub. I grabbed my towel from the hook on the back of the door, dried my body completely, and then wrapped it around me.

When I opened the bathroom door, I noticed Nelson was sitting on the edge of our bed holding my cell phone. I was furious, but I was adamant not to say anything to him about it. There were no traces of communication between Tyrone and me on my phone, so I wasn't worried about that. It never dawned on me that Tyrone could have possibly called me while I was in the bathtub. Nelson started again with the questions.

"Dianne, I'm going to ask you again if there is anything you should tell me."

"Why, Nelson? You've already made up your mind that I'm guilty."

"Dianne, this isn't a fuckin' game. You're my wife, and another man is calling you. Not to mention he's the husband of one of your best friends. What the fuck is going on? And don't lie to me."

"I'm not going to talk to you when you're cursing at me."

"There you go with that avoidance shit."

"Nelson, whatever. Can I have my phone, please? I'm asking nicely."

"Fuck no!"

"Nelson, give me my damn phone."

"Not until you tell me what is going on."

"Well, keep the phone. I think you're making it up anyway. Show me the phone where Tyrone *supposedly* called me."

Nelson showed me the call log where there was one missed call from Natasha's home number and then one answered incoming call also from her number.

"So you answered my phone?"

"You're damn right I did. I'm not feeling very trusting right now."

"How do you know it was Tyrone? Did you speak to him?"

"No, the coward hung up when I answered."

"How do you know it wasn't Natasha?"

"Why would she hang up?"

"Maybe it threw her off when you answered. She might have thought she had the wrong number or something. People do that, you know."

"I see you have such an *intelligent* answer for everything," Nelson commented with a hint of sarcasm.

"Nelson, look, let's just drop this, and give me my phone."

I reached for the phone and Nelson grabbed my hand. Out of reaction, I slapped Nelson in the face with my free hand. He jumped off the bed, grabbed me by both arms, and backed me into the wall. The look in his eyes was not anger; it was hurt. His eyes watered, but I could tell he refused to let one tear fall. After about a minute, he released me from his grip, but still looked me in the eye. I was sure he was going to hit me, so I turned my head in fear. He took his hand, placed it on my chin, and turned my face back to his.

"Dianne, I would never hit you, and at one point, I thought the same about you."

Nelson dropped his hand from my face and walked out of the bedroom. I wanted to call out to him to come back so we could talk in a civilized manner, but my voice seemed to escape me. Sobs came out instead. I heard Nelson tell Nihya to hurry up and get dressed so they could leave. I was sure she got dressed right away, but I would've had to ask her two or three times. I wondered if she had heard everything that was going on between Nelson and me. I remained standing against the wall until I heard his car leave the garage. My sobs got louder at that point. *I wonder where he's going.*

I lay across the bed and cried for about an hour. When I grew tired of crying, I eased off the bed so I could pull myself together. I was afraid to look at myself in the mirror because I probably looked a mess. I went into the bathroom to wash my face and apply a little makeup. My eyes were swollen, so anyone looking at me could guess I had been crying. I brushed my hair and pulled it back into a neat ponytail; I figured I looked all right. I dressed in a lightweight sweat suit before packing a few outfits in my small suitcase. I didn't want to be there when Nelson got back to the house.

Once I was done packing, I looked for my car keys. I couldn't find them anywhere. I even looked for my spare keys that were normally hanging on the key plaque on the wall. *Asshole!* It hit me that Nelson had taken my keys with him to keep me from leaving. *But didn't he tell me to leave, or was that reverse psyche for me not to leave?* Either way, I was getting out of there before he returned home.

# CHAPTER 20
## *Lynda*

**WHENEVER MY PHONE RANG,** I always hoped it wasn't someone I didn't feel like talking with, but thank goodness for Caller ID. *What did we do before that?* After searching in my purse for a few seconds, I finally found my phone, but the caller went to my voicemail. Although I was trying to focus on packing for my book tour that was taking me to Atlanta, Florida, New York, Philadelphia, and then back to the Washington, DC area, I checked the Caller ID, and it indicated the call was from Dianne.

I was scheduled to sign books at about ten bookstores in a week, and I had so much to do before I left. Zion was going to be with me, so I had to ensure I packed all the *goodies* I planned to use for our week of pure sexual pleasure. *I'm so glad he's as experimental as I am.*

Despite being busy, I called Dianne right back.

"Hey, Di," I said when she answered the phone.

"Hey, girl. Can you come pick me up?" Dianne asked softly.

"What's wrong? Where are you?"

"I'm home."

"Home?"

"Yes. Nelson and I had a huge fight, and I think he took my car keys. I can't find them anywhere, not even my spare set."

"Okay, I'm packing for my flight that leaves early in the morning, but I'll be there in a few. What happened?"

"I forgot you were leaving tomorrow. Girl, I'll have to fill you in when you get here. I'm so emotionally distraught right now."

"Okay, I'm leaving now then."

During my drive to pick up Dianne, I wondered what could have happened. Lord, I hoped Nelson didn't find out about the kiss Dianne and Tyrone shared. For some reason, seeing them together really bothered me. I hadn't been a saint by a long shot, but something was especially wrong with that picture. The look in their eyes wasn't of a lustful nature; it was more of an emotional connection. When emotions got involved, that was trouble for sure; however, I hoped I was incorrect in my observation.

I called Dianne when I was five minutes away from her house. When I arrived, she stood outside with a small suitcase. I popped the trunk so she could put the suitcase inside.

"Thanks, Lynda. I really appreciate it," Dianne said, getting into the passenger's side of my car.

"No problem, but what's going on?"

The look Dianne gave me said this was deep. "You're not going to believe this."

"What?"

"Apparently, sometimes I talk in my sleep. Last night, I must have had a dream about Tyrone, because I called out his name, according to Nelson."

"Oh, my God, Dianne. No, you didn't."

"I don't remember the dream at all, but Nelson was livid. Then, to make matters worse, someone called me from Natasha's home number and hung up when Nelson answered. So, of course, he figures it was Tyrone and not Natasha."

"Girl, this isn't good."

"Wait a minute. It gets worse."

"How can it?"

"I slapped Nelson in the face when he wouldn't give me my cell phone. He grabbed my hand when I reached for the phone and I reacted."

"Wow, girl. No, you didn't! I don't know what to say other than damn."

"I know, girl. My marriage is probably over."

"I doubt it. Nelson loves you. He's not a coward like most men. He's going to fight for you to save your marriage. Watch and see."

"I'm glad you see it because I don't."

"Yeah, I see it. You're just going to have to fight also to save your marriage."

"I'm not sure I want to."

"Dianne, please. You wouldn't know what to do without Nelson."

"I guess you're right. Well, partially right. I'm just tired of what's going on at home with Nihya. I'm really sick of that little girl's behavior."

"I know, Dianne, but try to hang in there. You and Nelson have something rare; a marriage built on something real. Especially friendship and unconditional love."

"I hate that you're leaving tomorrow. I need you here to help me through this situation."

"I know, but you really need to talk to your husband. Tell him the truth and move forward."

"I'm kind of scared, Lynda."

"You should've thought about that before you were playing *taste my tongue* with Tyrone."

"Shut up. That's not funny." Dianne laughed reluctantly.

"Anyway, I'm sure it's all going to work out. That's probably why he took your keys; he wanted you to be there when he returned."

"I guess so."

"I know so. You can play dumb if you want to, heifer. I'm so mad at you."

"Why?"

"Because you're risking your marriage for a fling with that damn Tyrone."

"He's a good man, too, Lynda."

"I know he is, but he's not *your* man. He's Natasha's; forbidden territory. Promise me that you're going to end this thing with Tyrone."

"There's nothing to end."

"I beg to differ. I saw how you two looked at each other when I walked in. There's something there. I don't know what that *something* is, but it's there and you need to resolve it."

"I know. You're right. But you're going to have to pray for me."

"And while I'm praying for you, please pray for me. I don't know if Zion and I are going to make it through this week together. We'll see, though."

"I'm sure you'll be fine."

"Isn't it funny how we can see the optimism in each other's situation?" I laughed.

"Yeah, but I'm really going to need you."

"Oh, well. You got yourself into this situation *alone*, and you need to work this out *alone*."

"All right, heifer. Damn."

"But what I will do is let you stay at my place for however long you need to. You can also use my car if you need to until you get your car keys back."

"Girl, thanks!"

"No problem. You're my girl. But promise me that you will work this out with your husband."

"I'm not so sure this time, Lynda."

"Have faith, girl. Don't give up so easily. And I know what you're thinking, so you don't have to say it. I need to practice what I preach."

"Exactly."

# CHAPTER 21

## *Natasha*

⤳⤳◦◦⤳

**WAKING FROM MY MUCH-NEEDED NAP**, I immediately grew worried because I didn't hear any movement in my place. Tyrone was supposed to be looking after the kids while I got some rest. I could hear *Toy Story 3* playing on the TV, so maybe they were all watching the movie. As I entered the family room, I noticed the twins both asleep in their playpen, and Tyler was on the floor asleep in his *Toy Story* sleeping bag. Tyrone was lightly snoring on the sofa, as well. I smiled at the scene because that was my family, the people who I loved the most. *So why am I feeling distant from everyone in the room?* I needed to do some research on postpartum depression because ever since Dianne mentioned it, I wondered if that was indeed my issue. Well, one of my issues anyway.

Not wanting to disturb my sleeping family, I eased past them and entered the kitchen. I wanted to cook something so it could be ready when they woke up, but didn't want to risk making any noise. That was a perfect moment to think. Since Tyrone had made a pot of coffee earlier, I poured some in my favorite mug and heated it in the microwave. I cherished the mug Tyrone ordered with a picture of him and the kids on it, and I used it every day, even if I was only drinking water. Seeing the picture reminded me of the precious blessings God had given me; however, it also reminded me of the one He took away from me.

*Aisha should be in this picture.* I sighed and retrieved the mug from the microwave when the beeps indicated it was done. I stirred the coffee softly and took a sip to see if it was warmed to my liking. Since it wasn't, I placed it back in the microwave for another minute.

While waiting for the microwave to stop a second time, I noticed a pile of mail on the counter. I browsed through the stack to see if anything needed my immediate attention. Everything appeared to be bills that were already paid online or junk mail, except for one envelope that had my previous address on it with the yellow forwarding label with my current address. The return address was from Jason. I opened the letter carefully, not knowing what the contents of the letter would be. Once again, I retrieved my mug from the microwave and then sat at the breakfast bar Tyrone had built in the kitchen.

*Tyrone is very handy around the house. I love that about him.* My mind wandered for a moment to my sleeping husband, who I hadn't done a great job of appreciating. Tyrone was the only man I had ever truly been in love with, and I was making him miserable. I sighed and focused my attention back to the letter from Jason. I slid the lined notebook paper from the envelope and slowly unfolded it. I smiled at Jason's neat penmanship as I read.

*Dear Ms. Natasha,*

*My mother told me that she saw you and you asked about me. You don't know how much that means to me. You're the only person that I know who understands how I feel about Aisha dying. I know my mother told you that I tried to kill myself. That's how much pain I was in. It seemed the world kept moving on and I didn't know how to move with it. I didn't want to live anymore. Aisha was my best friend and she meant a lot to me. I'm trying to get myself together because I see my actions were hurting my mom and I don't want to do that. My counselor said I have to find a way to let Aisha go. I don't want to let her go, but people are saying I have to in order to move on. I also have a mentor and he said letting Aisha go doesn't mean forgetting her, but remembering her and knowing she's in a better place. I'm struggling because I don't know how to do that. Can you help me? How do I let Aisha go?*

I was glad I was at the end of the first side of the letter because it gave me a moment to pause. I put the paper down and cried so hard that I woke up the twins. *I swear when one cries, the other one chimes in as if that's what she's supposed to do.* Tyrone startled me when he rushed into the kitchen. I put the letter down.

"Baby, what's wrong? You okay?"

"Yes, I'm sorry. I didn't mean to wake you or the kids," I managed to utter.

"What's the matter?"

"Just thinking about Aisha and how she's missing from the picture." I pointed to the mug resting on the counter. I wasn't ready to tell him about the letter because I wanted to finish reading it alone first.

"Okay, let me get the girls straight. Let me know if you need me."

"Thanks, sweetheart."

When Tyrone went back into the family room, I heard Tyler ask, "What's wrong with Mommy?"

Tyrone replied, "She's just a little sad right now."

I picked the paper back up and turned it over to continue reading.

*I feel guilty at the thought of letting her go. Would she be mad at me for moving on with my life? I just don't know what to do. Well, I hope you get this letter because I only had your old address. So hopefully, the post office will forward your mail. That's what my mom did when we moved. Please write me back or call me when you can so I can know you got this letter.*

*Sincerely,*
*Jason*

A telephone number was listed under his name, and I planned to call him when I collected my thoughts. He was asking my advice on something I didn't know how to do myself; let Aisha go. The telephone rang, interrupting my thoughts. I took the cordless phone off the wall in the kitchen and answered on the second ring. I was raised where you didn't answer the phone on the first ring, but you also didn't let it ring too long. *Go figure!*

I cleared my throat before answering. "Hello?"

"Hello, may I speak to a James Price? I mean T. James Price?"

I hesitated. I didn't know that was how Tyrone used his name in a professional environment. "Sure, may I tell him who's calling?"

It was a woman, so I wanted to see what she was going to say. People played too many games. A personal call could be disguised as a business call.

"Yes, this is Katie Hill from the Human Resources Department at the General Services Administration."

"Okay, one moment, please."

*Why didn't she just say GSA!*

I entered the family room and handed Tyrone the phone. He had already put the girls back in their playpen. I whispered to him that it sounded like an important call. Tyrone grabbed the phone from me, eased off the sofa, and walked into the kitchen. I couldn't really hear what he was saying, but I could tell it must have been some good news because I detected the excitement in his voice. He placed the phone back on the wall in the kitchen and returned to the family room.

"Baby, guess what? I got some great news."

I assumed his good news was that he had a job interview since it was someone from the Human Resources Department calling him, but I played along with his excitement. "Really? What is it?"

"I was just offered a job, baby. I'm finally in the federal government."

"Really, Tyrone? That's wonderful." I was slightly pissed because he never even told me he was going on an interview.

"Yeah, baby." As he pulled me into his arms and held me tightly, Tyler rushed over and grabbed us around the legs. Tyrone reached down, lifted him into his arms, and kissed his forehead.

"Tyrone, you never told me about your interviews or anything."

"I know, baby. I kept it to myself for fear of rejection. I didn't want to tell you until I actually got a job."

I sighed and pulled away. "I understand, and I'm happy for you."

"You don't sound happy, Natasha. What's wrong now? Are you mad because I didn't tell you that I was going on an interview? Baby, this is for us, our family. Be happy for *us*, not me."

"I just wish you shared more with me. Everything appears to be a secret with you."

"I don't mean for it to be like that. Come on, Natasha. Although I don't tell you my every move, I told you that I was trying to get a job in the federal government. I don't want to stay in the private sector, especially after how my firm treated me."

"I know, Tyrone. Or should I say T. James?"

"Baby, you know a name like Tyrone screams I'm black. I don't want to block a possible opportunity. That's just the world we live in."

"Yeah, I guess you're right. Well, congratulations. We need to celebrate." I kissed him on the lips. I was truly happy for him, but I was tired of feeling as if I was the last to know everything.

"I know how I want to celebrate." Tyrone winked.

*Men!*

"How about I cook a nice dinner for us, and then we play with the kids until they're exhausted. After we put the kids to bed, we can make love over and over and over again. Would you like that?" I whispered, and then kissed him on the lips while feeling his erection forming.

"Girl, you better stop it."

"And you better put that away for now." I smiled and pointed at his rising manhood.

Tyrone laughed and quickly went into the bathroom. Knowing him, he was in there jerking off. Upon hearing the water running, I went into the family room and sat on the sofa next to Tyler where he watched *Toy Story 3* again. He seemed to really enjoy that movie. Tyler looked at me, smiled, and continued watching the movie. My heart smiled at the sight of his happy face. While Tyrone was in the shower, I sat there trying to decide what to make for dinner. For a moment, I thought maybe we should go out to dinner, but it was a lot to pack stuff for the kids and go to a restaurant. It seemed easier to say home and enjoy family time.

When Tyrone was done with his shower, I asked him if he wanted anything in particular for dinner. He told me that he took the Cornish hens out of the freezer the night before to defrost. That worked for me. Therefore, I would bake those and prepare garlic mashed potatoes, glazed carrots, and asparagus tips to complement the meal.

We enjoyed our dinner and games with the kids. After the kids were asleep, I loaded the dishwasher. Tyrone walked up behind me and kissed the back of my neck as if he was ready for me to deliver on the promise of us making love. I was exhausted, but I wasn't about to deny my husband the sexual pleasure he was seeking. I had neglected him enough emotionally.

Tyrone didn't bother to wait until we were in the bedroom before he wanted a taste. I would have preferred to take a shower first, but oh, well. Once he eased my panties down from under my housedress, he touched me in such a way that it instantly turned me on. The way he lifted my leg and slid his manhood inside of me indicated it was only the beginning. As Tyrone lifted my other leg, I tightly wrapped both of them around his waist. Up against the refrigerator, my body rearranged the magnetic letters as if we were on *Soul Train* playing the scramble board challenge.

Not wanting to risk Tyler coming out of his room and seeing us, I suggested we finish in our bedroom. I knew Tyrone was the adventurous type; however, he needed to be reminded that we had kids and had to exercise caution when it came to sex around the house. He made love to me as if he had something to prove; almost to the point where I felt disconnected emotionally. When he increased his rhythm, I hoped he was about to make his release.

*Why don't men understand that making love is also about making an emotional connection with your partner instead of only getting off? I shouldn't feel distant from my husband during sex.*

Tyrone ejaculated inside of me, and I moaned to stroke his ego. I was sure he loved that my tubes were now tied.

"Damn, that felt good, babe. Did you cum?"

"Yes," I lied.

"Oh, good, but I couldn't tell this time."

*Really?*

My silence seemed to bother Tyrone.

"What's wrong, Natasha?"

"Nothing. Just tired, I guess." Again, I lied.

I eased off the bed so I could wash up, and Tyrone followed me into the bathroom; I assumed to do the same.

"Natasha, be honest with me. Do I not make you happy?"

Why did he have to go there? My eyes flooded with tears, and I couldn't get control over my emotions. All the crying I was doing was getting on my nerves.

"Tyrone, I don't know what's wrong with me. I'm feeling a bit disconnected from everything and everybody. I'm not sure what's happening."

Tyrone didn't respond. When he reached for me, he held me tightly in his arms, and his embrace told me that he loved me. I felt safe. I enjoyed feeling his heart beating. I indeed loved him, but something was wrong. I needed to seek help to attempt to find out if what I was experiencing had anything to do with postpartum depression. I felt trapped inside a body of emotions.

*How do I move past this?*

# CHAPTER 22
## *Dianne*

❦

*I INSTANTLY FELT LONELY* when Lynda left for her book tour. What was I going to do for an entire week without her? Natasha and I were back on speaking terms, but there was still some tension between us. Therefore, our conversations were limited. I hadn't heard from Nelson since I had been gone. I could've called him, but to say what? The only person I could think to call was Tyrone. Deep down inside, I knew it wasn't a very good idea considering what happened between us the last time, but I needed some company. I held my cell phone in my hand for a few minutes as I contemplated making the call to Tyrone. Just as I was about to call him, my cell phone rang. I looked at the screen and saw Nelson's name. Maybe it was a sign that I didn't need to call Tyrone. For some reason, though, I wasn't ready to talk to Nelson, so I let the phone ring until it went to voicemail. I was sure he was worried about me, but I would have to call him later to let him know I was okay.

After about three minutes, my cell phone rang again. I figured it was Nelson calling again, but when I looked at the screen, it said,

*Natasha–home.* A part of me didn't think I should answer the phone, but I did anyway.

"Hello?"

"Hi, Dianne. It's Tyrone."

"I figured. Natasha rarely calls from the house number."

"How are you? I called you the other day, but Nelson answered."

I sighed. "I know Tyrone, and Nelson and I had a huge fight because of that." I didn't mention I had dreamed about him.

"I'm sorry. I'm not trying to cause problems for you and Nelson, but I missed you."

"Missed me? Why?"

"When we kissed, I felt something. Did you?"

*Yes, I felt guilt.*

"I guess so, but, Tyrone, I can't tell you exactly what I was feeling."

I was somewhat glad that Tyrone had called me; however, I was confused about my feelings toward him. Lynda was right; I needed to end the situation with Tyrone, but I wasn't sure I really wanted to end it. Actually, I wasn't even sure what was going on between us.

"Dianne, what are you doing now? Are you home?"

"No. After Nelson and I fought, I left home. I'm staying at Lynda's for a while."

"Oh. Where's Lynda?"

"She's out of town."

"Oh, really?" he asked with excitement.

"Tyrone, please."

"What? I didn't even say anything."

"But I know what you're thinking."

"Maybe because you're thinking the same thing."

"Where's Natasha?" I wanted to change the subject.

"She took the kids somewhere. I think to a birthday party."

"Oh, okay."

"So, can I come and see you?"

"Tyrone, I'm not sure if that's a good idea."

"Do you want to see me?"

"I do, but I don't know." I sighed.

"Well, call me if you make up your mind."

"Tyrone, wait. Don't hang up yet."

"What's wrong?"

"I could use your company. Plus, we need to talk."

"I'm on my way, but just in case we're being watched, I'll leave my car at the closest metro station to Lynda's place and catch a cab over there."

"Okay. The nearest station is the Largo Metro Station."

"Okay, sounds good. I know exactly where that is. I think that's the one that was close to Natasha's old house."

"Exactly."

At first, it didn't make sense to me, but then I realized Nelson could drive by and see Tyrone's car parked outside of Lynda's place. I was sure he knew I was there.

I nervously paced around Lynda's house until Tyrone arrived. When the doorbell rang, my heart pounded. I wasn't sure what was going to happen. Upon opening the door, Tyrone greeted me with a smile and a bottle of wine.

"Hey, Tyrone. Thanks for the wine. Come on in."

"You're welcome, beautiful," he responded, entering Lynda's place.

I smiled, closed the door, and entered the kitchen to look for a bottle opener, which I found in Lynda's top drawer. After retrieving two wine glasses off the wine rack, I rinsed them in the kitchen sink. I took my time pouring the wine because I was extremely nervous to be alone with Tyrone again. I didn't realize he was watching me from the kitchen's entryway until I turned around to exit the kitchen.

"Nervous?" Tyrone asked, detecting my nervousness.

"A little."

"Well, don't be. I wanted to talk to you, too. Let's sit in the living room."

"Okay."

As I gulped my glass of wine, Tyrone looked at me with such intensity. He was becoming more and more handsome to me. I wondered if it was because I had never looked at him like that in the past.

"Are you all right?" Tyrone asked. I figured he noticed the way I was gulping the wine.

"I'm not sure." I avoided further eye contact.

"Look at me, Dianne." Tyrone sat his glass of wine on one of the coasters resting on Lynda's glass table. "I was thinking on the drive to the metro station about how it would affect both of our marriages if I make love to you."

It sounded so good the way he said the words 'make love to you'.

Tyrone moved closer to me and caressed my face. "You understand that, right?"

"I guess."

"Nelson has a good thing with you, and I don't want to take that away from him."

"Oh, okay. I see." I moved away from Tyrone, but he pulled me back closer to him.

"No, don't pull away like that."

"Tyrone, just stop touching me, okay?"

"I didn't come here to upset you. I left my house with every intention to make love to you all day long, but something hit me while I was driving. We would both have to live with the guilt of having an affair if we make love to each other. I don't want to put that on you."

I covered my face and cried. It was so hard feeling lonely in a marriage, but somehow, making love to another man wasn't the answer for me.

"You're right, Tyrone. We shouldn't do this, but I don't want to be alone right now."

"You don't have to be. Come on, let's chill for a while. I'm assuming Lynda has a TV in the room you're sleeping in."

"Sure. Come on."

I didn't feel it was the right move for us to go into the bedroom. It was possible that being in there would create too much temptation. As we lay across the bed, I flipped through the cable channels to find something to watch on TV. When I saw the movie *Dante's Peak* was on, Tyrone asked if I could leave it on that channel. It was one of those movies I'd seen a hundred times, but I never seemed to get tired of it. It appeared Tyrone felt the same way about the movie.

While watching the movie, Tyrone and I fell asleep, but I was awakened by a knock at Lynda's door. I was somewhat startled because I couldn't think of who would be knocking at her door while she was out of town. As I approached the door, I asked who it was, and I almost fainted when the voice said, "Nelson." I could've died right then and there. I opened the door to see a broken man before me.

"Hi, Nelson."

"Dianne, I've been worried about you. You could have at least let me know you were okay. Why didn't you answer my call today?"

"It took you two days to check on me, Nelson," I responded, avoiding his question.

"I know, and I was wrong. But you should have called me, too. Even if it was just to let me know you were okay."

"How did you know I was here?"

"This seems to be where you go whenever you feel the need to escape."

"Well, I thought you wanted me gone because that's what you said."

"Dianne, I didn't mean it."

"Did you take my keys?"

"Yes, I did. I thought it would force you to be home when I got back, but I guess I was wrong."

"Nelson, listen—"

"No, Dianne, I want you to listen to me. I love you, and the thought of you with someone else really hurts me. Maybe I didn't approach it the right way, but all I wanted to know is if you were sleeping with Tyrone."

"No, I haven't slept with him." Just then, I remembered Tyrone was asleep in the other room. "He's going through some things, and I was trying to be there for him."

"So are you saying that nothing is going on between you and him?" At that moment, Nelson looked like he had seen a ghost. I didn't know why Tyrone thought it was a good idea to leave the bedroom, but he walked into the living room where Nelson and I were talking.

"So what the fuck is this?" Nelson yelled. "I don't believe this shit, Dianne."

"Nelson, please listen." I looked back at Tyrone and then back to Nelson.

"Listen to what? More lies?"

Tyrone chimed in, "Nelson, I know this looks bad, but can we talk man to man?"

"Man to man? Muthafucka, are you kidding me? You fuckin' my wife and now you want to talk to me?" I heard a thug-like tone from Nelson that I had never heard before.

"I'm not sleeping with Dianne," Tyrone insisted.

"So why the fuck are you here with her? You know what? Never mind. I don't even want to know. You want her, you can have her," Nelson responded and threw my keys on the floor.

I couldn't believe my ears. "Nelson, are you serious?" I was in tears.

"No need to cry, Dianne. You know you're wrong for this," Nelson responded dejectedly.

"Nelson, man, I'm sorry for how this looks, but I have not had sex with Dianne."

Nelson didn't respond to Tyrone. He just looked me straight in the eyes and shook his head in disbelief. There was no reasoning with Nelson at this point. I was certain that my marriage was over. Tears fell uncontrollably from my eyes. Nelson looked so betrayed and with good reason. He had caught his wife alone with another man after she called out that same man's name in her dream. It didn't matter that Tyrone and I had not actually had sex because the whole situation looked bad from every angle. Before I could say anything else, Nelson walked out of the front door. I fell to my knees and cried harder. Tyrone bent down to comfort me.

"Tyrone, what have we done?"

"It's going to be all right. I'll try to talk to Nelson again," Tyrone said, trying to comfort me.

"No, this is bad. I can't believe we let it get to this point. I can't lose him. What was I thinking?"

"I'm so sorry, Dianne. What can I do?" he pleaded.

"Nothing. Please, just leave me alone. I need to be alone."

"Are you sure? I don't want to leave you like this. This is my fault."

"No, it's not. I'm not going to allow you to take the blame. I knew all of this was wrong, and I'm going to suffer because of my decision to see you. Oh, my God. What am I going to do?"

I continued to cry.

"Dianne, if you want me to leave, I will. I'm going to call a cab so I can get to my car. Please call me if you need me for anything, okay?"

"Okay, fine. I just need to lie down."

Tyrone helped me off the floor and walked me into Lynda's guestroom where I climbed on the bed and cried into the pillow. He caressed my back and asked me again if I wanted him to stay. Deep down inside, I wanted him to stay; however, my marriage was already in trouble, so I knew it was best that he left. I appreciated that he wanted to be there for me, but I had to think of how I was going to save my marriage.

When the cab came for Tyrone, he kissed me on my forehead and headed out of the bedroom. I told him to let himself out, but to ensure that the bottom lock was locked on the door. I planned to get up eventually to secure the rest of the locks.

*Why have I allowed this to happen?*

# CHAPTER 23
## *Lynda*

***BEING BACK IN A RELATIONSHIP*** with Zion felt like being on a long, packed flight that had endured severe turbulence during the entire trip with crying babies onboard. One day, he wanted to be with me, and the next, he didn't think it was a good idea for us to pursue a relationship at that point in our career. I loved Zion, but I was tired of the unnecessary drama he was creating. Sometimes, men were very unstable in relationships, but then they blamed the women for creating the drama if something was said. *Are we supposed to just sit there and not say anything?* Zion didn't know what he wanted as far as a relationship, and that was fine. Why couldn't he just admit he was confused? Why was that so hard for some men to do?

In the beginning, it was very exciting for Zion and me to travel together to participate in book events. We appeared to be that perfect literary duo. I celebrated with him when he had a profitable event, and he would do the same for me. The nights of lovemaking were insane after those events. We even broke a headboard in one of the hotels in Atlanta. He pulled the damn thing right off the wall. I never knew hotels attached the headboards to the wall like that. *Go figure!* Anyway, we were having such a great time traveling together.

I wasn't sure what changed because Zion suddenly became very competitive in the events that we participated in together. He wanted to see who could sell the most books. I never wanted to live my life in competition with my man or anyone for that matter. It wasn't that serious to me; however, Zion saw things very differently. If he wasn't making the kind of money he expected at an event, he wasn't happy, and he was determined to make everyone around him miserable, especially me. He even did things he knew would aggravate me. It was like a child picking at a scab.

I knew it was time for me to move on from Zion when he acted as if he didn't know me at the book signing event in New York. I could've spat in his face. I was fuming! He claimed he was acting that way so no one would be in our business. *Give me a damn break!* Most people already knew we were a couple. Nevertheless, I played his game, and it backfired on him when he saw me with another male author at the bar in the hotel. He sent me text messages to meet him upstairs in the room, but little did he know, I had gotten my own room and took my stuff out of the one we had booked together. I wasn't going to sleep with him after being disrespected all day.

When I was done with my drink at the bar, Zion stopped me before I could get to my room. *Was he watching me?*

"Lynda, I don't understand why you got your own room. What, are you planning on entertaining someone else?"

"Whatever, Zion. I'm not going to do this with you today."

"Do what?"

"The drama, Zion. Okay? I'm tired. I just want to go to sleep in peace."

"Why are you mad now?"

"Because you're so disrespectful. I'm supposed to be your woman, but you don't always treat me that way, and I'm tired of it."

"So what are you saying, Lynda? You want this to be over?"

"I'm saying whatever you want me to say. It just doesn't matter anymore. You don't love me, so I don't know why you keep playing these games."

"You don't think I love you?"

"No, I do not!"

"Well, fine. Maybe I don't."

"Whatever!" I walked away because I could feel the tears starting to well up in my eyes, and I refused to let him see me cry. I was done with him as far as I was concerned.

That turned out to be a sleepless night because Zion called and sent text messages until well into the next morning. He wanted to know if I was mad, what I was doing, and was anyone in my room with me. I didn't understand his actions at all. I wanted to call Dianne to check on her, but I was emotionally exhausted from dealing with Zion. I needed some time to get my own situation under control, but I was worried about her.

About four o'clock in the morning, I heard a knock at the door. *Who in the fuck?* I thought to myself because I was extremely tired. I went to the door to see who was knocking at that time of the morning. I expected it to be Zion, but it was the author who I had been talking with at the bar. I recognized his voice, but I wasn't about to open the door. I didn't even remember his damn name until he said it through the door. If ass was what he wanted, it wasn't going to be from me.

"Yes, what is it?" I asked from behind the door.

"Um, is Zion Jones with you?"

"Oh, my God," I responded, opening the door quickly. "Is he okay?"

"I figured that would get you to open the door."

"Look, I don't have time for these juvenile games, okay? I'm trying to get some rest."

"Well, let me come in and put you to sleep."

"Enough of this shit!" I slammed the door in his face.

I sat on the edge of the bed and contemplated calling Zion. I wanted to be near him so badly, but he had really hurt me. I decided against calling him because it was possible he decided to spend the night with someone else just to hurt me some more. As I prepared to climb back into the bed, there was another knock at the door.

"I don't believe this," I said aloud so the person on the other side could hear my frustration.

"Lynda, baby, open the door. It's me, Zion. I need to talk to you."

"About what, Zion?" I asked, opening the door.

"About why that dude was leaving your room."

I detected a slight sadness in his voice.

"Zion, come on now. He wasn't inside my room. He knocked on my door, I guess thinking he was going to get some ass since we had a conversation at the bar earlier. Maybe he's trying to make you jealous. I don't know. You know how you men like to play games. I simply don't have the patience for it. And were you watching me? Good grief!"

"Do you really want this to be over?"

"I never said that. That's you assuming shit."

"Lynda, you don't have to curse at me."

"Zion, please tell me why you're here doing this now."

"I love you, but I always feel like I'm hurting you."

My frustration turned to sadness. "You are hurting me, but it's okay. It's obvious you can't balance your career and a relationship with me. I finally get that now."

Zion stood there looking into my eyes as if he were searching for a meaning to all of this madness. At that point, I didn't know what to say. I allowed the tears to fall freely from my eyes because I was indeed hurting. I didn't think he had a clue as to how much I loved him.

"Baby, I don't mean to hurt you," Zion said, pulling me into his arms. "Let's go inside your room. I promise I won't try anything. I just want to hold you."

He actually honored his promise because he didn't try to initiate anything sexually. A part of me wanted him to make love to me; however, he just held me in his arms as if he knew it might be the last time he held me this way. I continued to cry until I drifted off to sleep. Within a couple of hours, I was awakened by Zion's erection. There was no need of me trying to fight the feeling because I wanted him to make love to me. Instead, I eased back and parted my legs slightly so Zion would know he was invited inside.

# CHAPTER 24
## *Natasha*

*I REMEMBERED THE LETTER FROM JASON* when I was cleaning the kitchen. I discovered the letter underneath a stack of new mail that Tyrone had piled on top of it. I wanted to at least respond to inform Jason that I had received it. I still hadn't mentioned it to Tyrone since he was preparing for his first day at his new job. I couldn't believe he still hadn't officially resigned from the company he was working for. *Who does that?* I decided not to say anything else about him contacting his previous employer. He was a grown man, and since he was moving from a private industry to the federal sector, maybe his paperwork didn't have to follow him. I still felt it was irresponsible, though.

I had become accustomed to Tyrone being home with us during the day. Kind of a contradiction to the way I felt when he told me that he walked away from his job. The only thing I tried to relay to him was not to keep stuff like that from me. Tyrone seemed distant from me ever since I told him that I felt distant from everything and everybody. It was almost as if he'd found someone else to give him the attention he needed. He didn't try to initiate sex with me as much as he used to; therefore, I wondered if he was having an affair. I prayed that wasn't the reason for his distance. Just then, Tyrone walked into the kitchen, interrupting my thoughts.

"Hey, babe." He kissed me on the cheek.

"Hey. Are you ready to start your new job?"

"Yes, I'm ready. I know the first few days will be orientation and completing paperwork."

"Yes, I know how that is." I managed a half-smile.

"I'm looking forward to new challenges. I was hoping to be home with you longer, though. They mentioned something about a telework program where I can work from home two days a week, so I'll look into that once I start."

"Yeah, that sounds good. I would do that myself from time to time."

"How are you, Natasha?"

"I'm okay. Why do you ask?"

"I'm worried about you."

I remained silent.

"Talk to me, babe."

"Tyrone, there are so many things going on with me. I hadn't told you yet, but I got a letter from Jason, Aisha's boyfriend. Reading the letter just brought out more suppressed emotions."

"What did the letter say?"

"He's been struggling with her death and wanted advice on how to let her go. I don't know how to do that myself, so how can I help him?"

"Babe, when was the last time you went to her gravesite?"

"I'm not sure. Why?"

"I think we should go."

I sighed.

"Why the sigh? You need to deal with this."

"I've been trying to deal with it."

"Well, I did some research on postpartum depression, and I made an appointment for us to go."

"What do you mean you made an appointment?"

"Natasha, you need help."

"Oh, so now I'm a mental case?"

Tyrone sighed. "Listen, I care about you and I care about us, so we need to talk to somebody soon. Kaiser Permanente has all kinds of classes on stuff like this. It happens to a lot of people, but it can get worse if you don't deal with this now."

"Have you been to the dry cleaners or do you need me to go?"

"Natasha, don't try to change the subject. I love you, but I feel you slipping away. Come on, please? Let's not ignore what's going on. I'm not trying to upset you, babe. This hurts me, too, and this hurts our son."

A stream of tears fell unexpectedly from my eyes. "What?"

"It's true, babe. He asks me when I'm putting him to bed if Mommy is still sad."

My heart sank.

"Natasha, what else is bothering you? I can see there's more hurting you."

I took a deep breath and poured out my feelings to my husband. "Tyrone, after my parents died, I shut down emotionally from the world. The first time I contemplated suicide was when I realized their death wasn't the horrible nightmare I prayed it was. I guess reading Jason's letter brought it all back to the surface."

"The first time?" Tyrone interrupted.

"Yes, the first time. The second and last time was after I…I mean, after *we* had to bury our daughter. I wanted to die, Tyrone. I think the night you came to see me saved me. But you also saved me when Dianne introduced me to you. Back then, I felt you preferred to be with her, but I didn't question it because I needed you."

"I'm not sure what you mean by that."

"Don't worry about it, Tyrone. God brought you to me for a reason, and I needed you."

"But do you love me and want me? That's important for me to know."

"Of course, I do. I just don't always know how to show it. It seemed easier to stay emotionally unattached to people, but I see I'm losing you."

"Natasha, I don't see how you thought you could be my wife and remain emotionally unattached."

"Tyrone, I want to be your wife. I used to imagine what it would be like to be married to you. After losing Aisha, things got worse for me, and now having three small kids, I feel I'm drowning in this situation. I always thought I would be at a different phase of my life right about now. I sacrificed so much when I was raising Aisha, and now, I'm about to sacrifice all over again."

"I know this isn't what you planned, but we're a family now. I must admit it's hard for me to be somewhere when I feel like I'm not wanted there."

"I hate that I'm making you feel that way and how this is affecting Tyler."

"Well, if you want me to cancel the appointment, I can do that. I want you to go when you're ready."

"No, we should go. I need to deal with this appropriately."

"I want you to be happy." Tyrone pulled me into his arms. "Don't worry; you'll open your boutique someday."

"How do you know about that?" I wiggled out of his embrace.

"Aisha mentioned it in one of our conversations. She said how you would design and sew clothes. Then, one day, you stopped. If that's what you want to do, though, I'll see to it you do it."

"The thought is nice, but it's going to be hard with small kids around."

"They're not going to be small forever."

"How would we afford it?"

"I know this is hard for you, but let me do all the worrying about that. Okay?"

I smiled.

"See, that's the face I want to see. Again, I want you to be happy, but you're gonna have to want to be happy, too. Happiness starts from within."

"Your mom used to say that."

"Yep, and I think she loved you more than she loved me."

We laughed.

"I doubt that, Tyrone."

"Well, she definitely loved you."

Tyrone pulled me back into his arms, and we stayed in the embrace until we heard the babies crying. I was glad we were beginning to communicate more, but I had a long way to go to resolve my issues.

# CHAPTER 25

## Dianne

❦

*IS MY MARRIAGE OVER?* I was exhausted from crying for three days straight, but I had to pull myself together. I went home several days later to get some of my things that I would need for the next few days. I had clients to meet with, although it was going to be hard trying to focus with my own issues. I figured Nelson would be at work, yet when I arrived in front of my house, I noticed his car in the driveway. My first instinct was to leave; however, I really needed to pick up some critical items. Before I got out of my car, I looked through my cell phone at some photos that Nelson and I took together. We were so happy a year ago, and it appeared my life was unraveling rapidly before my eyes. I had my house keys back from Nelson, but still, I decided to knock on the door. I wasn't sure why, though.

"Who is it?" Nelson asked.

"Nelson, it's me, Dianne."

Nelson opened the front door and stared at me for a few moments. His look was so cold that I actually felt a chill come over me.

"I need to get a few things, if you don't mind." I barely spoke above a whisper.

"Sure, no problem." I heard a slight quiver in Nelson's voice.

He stepped aside to allow me to enter our home. Looking around, I noticed so many things were out of place. I wanted to fall to my knees and beg for my husband's forgiveness, but I proceeded up the stairs to our bedroom, which was also a mess. I stood in the closet staring at my clothes. I didn't realize Nelson was behind me.

"Do you really want to do this?" Nelson asked.

"Do what?"

"Leave me."

I felt something sharp pierce my heart as he spoke those two words.

"Nelson, I'm not sure what is going on with us or how to fix what I've done."

"What exactly did you do? I mean, did you sleep with Tyrone?"

"No. I told you that already, but you don't believe me."

"How can I?"

"I guess you can't."

"Dianne, you're my wife. The thought of you with another man fucks with me in a way you will never understand. Baby, I love you. I'm crazy about you. I always have been since the day we met, but if you want to leave, I won't stop you. I want you to be happy more than anything else."

"You'll let me walk out of your life…just like that?"

"If that's what you want to do."

The situation with Nelson was way too painful; I had to get out of there. I exited our bedroom without retrieving anything from the closet that I needed. As I rushed down the stairs, Nelson called my name, and I stopped at the bottom of the stairs.

"Dianne, don't leave like this. Let's talk." Nelson came down the stairs behind me and gave me a firm hug. We stayed in that same embrace for about five minutes.

"Nelson, there's no doubt I love you, but I'm tired of hurting in my own home," I said, finally easing from Nelson's arms.

"I know, and I'm sorry for not taking Nihya's behavior more seriously."

"It's not just that. I don't think you see me as her mother. I know I'm not her biological mother, but that is my role."

"I know, and I'm sorry for my part in all of this."

"I'm sorry, too, and I never meant to hurt you. There's no excuse for what almost happened with Tyrone and me."

Nelson fell silent for a few moments before he responded, "Would you be willing to go to marriage counseling? I mean, if you still want to be with me."

"Of course, I want to be with you, Nelson. I want us to find a way to move past this. I want to be here, but I don't feel welcome when your daughter is here."

"My daughter?"

"See how painful it was to hear me say that? Now imagine how I feel."

"Okay, I get it."

"Do you really? Never mind, we can talk later. I need to go back to Lynda's so I can get dressed. I have a few clients this morning. Why aren't you at work anyway?"

"Emotionally drained."

"Oh, I know what you mean. Me, too, but I don't want to reschedule these appointments. I'm going to push through the day."

"Now what?" Nelson asked, grabbing me into his arms again.

"We see a counselor and pray about it. Follow God's plan." I kissed Nelson softly on his lips and then went back upstairs to get the things I needed for the day. Afterward, I hurried out of the door so I could go back to Lynda's to prepare to see my clients.

When I arrived at my office, I immediately began to miss my assistant, Pamela. She had an opportunity for a paid internship in her field of journalism, so I couldn't be mad that it was time for her to move on. I mainly handled most of my own administrative duties anyway, but I was used to seeing her pleasant smile when I walked in the door. I was definitely going to miss her presence.

I made it through the day with all of my clients, but I missed my husband. Tears fell from my eyes after my last client left my office. I was glad Nelson was home when I got there because we needed to find a way to move past this situation. Our anniversary was coming up, and the thought of waking up on my anniversary without my husband by my side didn't feel right. Therefore, marriage counseling was definitely a step in the right direction. Needing to hear Nelson's voice, I searched inside my purse for my cell phone to call him. I felt I should make every effort to save my marriage because it was largely my fault. No sooner than I hit the call button on my cell phone, Nelson answered.

"Hey, Dianne. I was just about to call you."

"Really?"

"Yeah, I figured you would be done with your last client right about now, and I wanted to hear your voice."

*How ironic.*

"You know our anniversary is coming up, and although we are having some problems, I was hoping we could get together and do something special. I wasn't sure how you felt about that, though."

"Dianne, listen. Believe it or not, I am a very forgiving person. I guess I get that from my father. The main thing is you're going to have to forgive yourself so we can move past this."

"I know. I'm trying."

"Okay, well, that's all you can do is try. But you're still my wife, and I love you."

"Nelson?"

"Yeah."

"I was wondering if you want to hang out this weekend and see a movie or something. We haven't done anything like that in a while."

"Sure, but are you coming home tonight? I think you should come home. It's been long enough, and I don't want to wait until this weekend to see you. Or do you still need time apart?"

I was surprised Nelson wanted me home so soon. "Are you sure?"

"Yes. We aren't separated, are we?"

"No, we aren't separated. I'll be there later tonight. I need to clean up Lynda's place first. My stuff is everywhere, and I don't want her to come home to my mess."

Nelson was silent.

"Nelson, baby, what's wrong?"

"Nothing. I guess I'll see you later tonight then. I can't stand what's going on with us. I don't want to lose you."

Those words were like music to my ears, and it made my heart smile. "You're not going to lose me."

Later that evening, Lynda rushed into her guestroom where I was asleep. I didn't know she was back from her book signings.

"Dianne, wake up." Lynda shook me out of my sleep.

"What's wrong? Oh, shit, what time is it? I didn't mean to fall asleep. I was supposed to go home tonight."

"Almost eight o'clock. Nelson just called and said Nihya didn't come home after her dance tryouts. He said he called you on your cell, but you didn't answer. She isn't answering her cell phone, either."

"What!" I screamed in a panic. I put my clothes on faster than the time I almost got caught having sex with my boyfriend at his house when I was sixteen.

"Yes, he sounded so worried."

"I'm sure he is. Where could she be?"

"Come on, I'll go with you to help look for her." Lynda generously offered her assistance. "What's going on with you guys?"

"Girl, I'll have to tell you later on. Things got worse."

"Girl, no. Unfortunately, I know the feeling. That's why I decided to come home before going to Philly. I need a break from Zion Jones. But we can talk about it later."

As we rushed out of the house, Nihya approached Lynda's door.

"Nihya, what are you doing here?"

"I was coming to find you."

"Nihya, how did you get here? It's not safe for you to be out here by yourself."

"I know, but I walked to my friend's house. Then I called a cab from there. I used some of my allowance to pay for the cab. I found Ms. Lynda's address in the book you keep on your desk."

"Why did you do that? What's wrong? How did you know I was even here?"

"Because my daddy said so. He's been upset since you're not home. I heard him tell somebody on the phone that he's losing you because of me."

"No, Nihya." Of course, I had to lie to the child.

"Well, that's what he said. And he said that he doesn't know what he's gonna do if you want a divorce. I don't want him to send me away." Nihya cried. "He also told somebody that every time y'all fight it's because of me or something I said."

"Nihya, sweetheart, don't cry. Let me call your dad to let him know you're safe. He's so worried about you. You can't worry us like that. Anything could've happened to you."

"I went home after I left the dance tryouts, but I guess he didn't hear me come in the door since he was on the phone. After I heard what he said, I just left. I figured if I came to apologize to you, then you would come back home and my dad won't be upset anymore."

"Nihya, I'm so sorry we're making it seem like this is your fault. What's going on with your dad and me is not your fault."

I lied again because I did blame her for things going wrong between Nelson and me. She was a child, and I understood that; however, we didn't start having issues until she came into our lives.

"Okay, but can I stay here with you until the morning time?"

"Sure, let's get you into bed, and then I will call your dad."

"Okay, thank you. And I'm sorry if I hurt your feelings."

"It's okay, Nihya."

After putting her to bed, I used Lynda's phone to call Nelson so he would know that Nihya was safe with me.

"Lynda?" Nelson said upon answering the phone.

"It's me, Dianne."

"Dianne, did Lynda give you my message?"

"Yes, and Nihya is safe. She came over here."

"Huh? Well, okay. Thank goodness she's all right. Let me come and get y'all."

"Nelson, I'll bring her home in the morning. She's resting now. We can all talk and work this out tomorrow."

"Dianne, baby, I thought you were coming home tonight."

"I was, but I fell asleep. I'm glad Lynda was here to answer her phone. My cell must be on silent. I'm sorry all of this is happening."

Nelson sighed. "Dianne, I need you home so we can try to work through this situation. I miss you. Let me come and get y'all tonight."

"Nelson, Nihya should rest a bit. She thinks you're going to send her away. She's very upset."

"Did she say why she thinks that?"

"She overheard your phone conversation. She went home, but after she heard you, she got upset and left."

"Damn, Dianne. I'm failing all the way around. I was talking to my father on the phone because I needed to vent."

"I understand, but don't feel that way."

"It's hard not to. Anyway, I'll see you in the morning?"

"Yes. I'll come home early enough for Nihya to catch her school bus."

"Baby, I really miss us...I mean, the way things were."

I was able to smile. "Nelly, I miss us, too. I love you and will be home first thing in the morning. Okay?"

"I guess I can wait until then. I love you, too, Dianne. Kiss Nihya for me, please."

"Will do. Bye."

"Later."

By the time I got off the phone with Nelson, Lynda had fallen asleep. I wondered how her week was traveling with Zion. I looked over at Nihya peacefully sleeping and kissed her on the forehead as Nelson asked.

*Lord, please tell me this is only a test.* I said a prayer for all of us before drifting off to sleep.

The next morning when I took Nihya home, Nelson looked as if he hadn't slept, shaved or even bathed in days. He had a look on his face that I wasn't used to seeing: hurt and defeat. It crushed me to see Nelson looking that way, especially since I was a contributing factor to what he was going through. He looked disappointed that Nihya would worry him as she did, but when she apologized and gave him a hug, his smile insinuated to me that he understood her actions. I waited until Nihya went to get dressed for school before I asked Nelson any questions.

"Nelson, baby, what's wrong?"

"Everything, Dianne."

We just looked at each other for a while. I wasn't sure what news my husband was about to share with me. Lately, it just seemed to be one depressing story after another.

"Nelson, please tell me what's bothering you."

"Let's talk after Nihya leaves for school."

Becoming extremely nervous, I searched his eyes for any indication of what may have been upsetting him. Once Nihya was dressed, Nelson hugged her and kissed her forehead. Then she left for school. He immediately began talking as if he couldn't hold it in any longer.

"Baby, I just found out something that's going to change a lot of stuff for me."

"What is it, babe?"

"I found out that I was adopted."

At that moment, tears welled up in Nelson's eyes. I could tell he wanted to hold back his tears, but he simply couldn't.

"Nelson, what! I'm so sorry. What brought about this news? Who told you?"

"Last night after I spoke with you, I decided to call my father back. I asked him if I could come over because I really didn't want to be home alone. I needed someone to talk to, and since my father is a night owl, I figured he wouldn't mind. When I got there, he looked upset. That's when he told me."

"Wow, baby. I don't understand. Why are they telling you this now?"

"Well, my mother is in the early stages of dementia." Nelson's tears increased as he told me the devastating news he had just learned. "My father was afraid that in my mother's weakest moment, she would start rambling off and mention that they adopted me. He didn't want me to find out accidentally."

Nelson continued. "My father said he wanted to tell me when I was a little boy, but my mother disagreed. You know my father pretty much goes along with whatever is going to make my mother happy. That's how he is."

"I really don't know what to say, Nelson."

"Me either, Dianne. But that's not the worst of it."

"There's more?"

"A lot more."

We just looked at each other again.

"Okay, I'm listening," I said, breaking the silence.

"When he told me that I was adopted, I immediately wanted to know if they knew who my biological mother was. I instantly felt this void when they disclosed the information to me. My father told me that I already know her. She was my babysitter, Chanelle."

"What?"

"Yeah. It was their way of making sure she was close to me. She watched me every day after school. The sad part is, Dianne, she's only like fourteen years older than I am."

"Oh, no. She was a baby when she had you."

"Yes, and her mother was a welfare recipient already raising five kids, including Chanelle. My mother was her social caseworker, and she got emotionally involved when she found out Chanelle was pregnant. Especially since my mother couldn't have any children of her own."

"Wow, baby."

"I know. My mother agreed to adopt her baby—me—so I wouldn't end up in the foster care system. She wanted Chanelle to have a relationship with me, so they figured she could be my babysitter. She was about eighteen or nineteen when I started kindergarten. Dianne, she was there every day helping me with my homework. Even on the weekends, she was right there helping me do something. Every sport I played, Chanelle was right there. Why didn't they just tell me?"

"Nelson, you know they wanted to protect you. You were a little boy, and I'm sure Chanelle wanted you to have the best life possible since she couldn't provide you with that."

"I know, Dianne, but it hurts. It really hurts."

"I know it hurts, and being in my field of psychology, it's not uncommon for me to hear stories like this. It's hard for me to see you so sad, but…"

"I'm angry, not sad," Nelson said before I could finish my statement.

"But don't be angry with them. They only had your best interest at heart."

"Well, you know my next question to him was about my biological father."

I just sat in silence.

"Dianne, this is so hard for me. My life as I know it is all a lie. Now I feel I have to question everything because, baby, that's not all."

"Huh? What else could there be?"

"They all knew Nihya was my baby, and they kept her from me."

"Okay, let's go back to your biological father. Did they ever tell you where he is?" I wasn't ready to deal with the situation of them knowing about Nihya.

"My father told me to talk to Chanelle. My parents aren't sure what happened to him."

"Does Chanelle know that you know she's your biological mother?"

"My parents did talk to her first to tell them that it was time for me to know before my mother's illness gets worse."

"Okay. Now, did they explain to you why they kept Nihya from you?"

Nelson didn't answer my question; he just cried. I had never seen him so sad and hurt before. I didn't press the issue because I could tell he was having a hard time dealing with all of this. I just held him until he was ready to continue talking.

"Baby, do you know they paid Marie and her parents not to tell me? They claim they didn't want me to be a young father. They wanted me to have a better life. Look what happened to Nihya because of all of this. If she were with me, she would have been safe. She was molested by someone that was supposed to protect her. It's a good thing that bastard killed himself because I probably would have killed him. How could he do that to her? From what he knew, that was his little girl."

Nelson continued. "They convinced Marie that if she really cared about me, she would take the money and let me move on with my life. She was a scared teenager, and they manipulated her. Now she's dead, and I can't tell her that I'm sorry."

"Nelson, I'm sure she knew you didn't have anything to do with what your parents arranged."

"How am I supposed to move past this, Dianne?"

"It's going to be hard, I know. You're going to have to take it one day at a time. But I will be right here."

"You know, I want to apologize to you if I was ever insensitive to your feelings about losing your mother when you were a little girl. I remember you told me that you felt abandoned, and I just didn't understand why because she didn't voluntarily leave you. Now I completely understand what it feels like. I don't really feel abandoned; then again, I don't know what I feel. It just hurts."

I kissed Nelson on his lips and caressed his face. I wanted to comfort him. I wished I could take his hurt away.

"Dianne, do you have any clients today?"

"Just one, but that's not for a few hours. I can cancel if necessary."

Nelson pulled me into his arms as he leaned against the counter. "No, don't do that. Just promise me that you'll come back right after that appointment. I think I'm going to the office today."

"Yes, I'll be right here, but are you sure you're feeling up to work today?"

"Yeah, because if I'm home, then all I'm going to do is obsess over all this in my head. I could use a distraction."

I listened to his heartbeat while in his embrace. I loved my husband so much, and I hoped in time, he would accept his situation of being adopted. His parents raised him to be a wonderful man, and I was quite positive they were very proud of him. His biological mother, Chanelle, probably made the hardest decision of her life when she gave him up, but at fourteen years old, she did the best thing for her precious baby who was now my loving husband.

# CHAPTER 26
## *Lynda*

***I ABSOLUTELY LOVE WHAT I DO***, *but some of these book signings are very tiring.* My event was supposed to be over at 6:00 p.m., but I didn't leave the bookstore until about 9:00 p.m. The book discussion turned more into a relationship seminar. There were men and women of various ages present in the audience. Zion claimed he wanted to support me at this event, especially after how he treated me in New York. However, he was ready to go at six o'clock sharp. He kept looking at his watch and making impatient gestures. I simply ignored him. I wasn't about to walk out on my audience. As long as the bookstore owner allowed us to continue, I was going to keep on talking. Eventually, Zion sent me a text message that he was leaving. I responded, *Go ahead then.* That just proved to be another example of his selfishness. If it was the other way around, I would've been right there for him, no matter how long it took. We were obviously on different pages in our relationship.

As I headed toward my car, one of the women from the audience approached me. I figured she wanted to share something with me in private that she didn't want to mention to the entire audience.

"Hi, Ms. Davis," the woman said.

"Hello. Please, call me Lynda."

"Okay, Lynda. I enjoyed your book discussion. I purchased your book, but I forgot to ask you to autograph it for me." She extended the book out to me.

"I appreciate your support. Who am I signing this for?"

"Theresa. Mrs. Theresa Palmer." She emphasized her name.

As soon as she mentioned her last name, I knew she was Justin's wife. I wasn't sure what to do next, but I was hoping she didn't make any sudden moves. Having no idea what to say to her, I just handed the book back to her and reached into my purse for my car keys.

"I hope you're not reaching for your gun because it isn't necessary. I just had to see for myself the woman who has my husband completely stressed out."

"Stressed out?" I asked.

She didn't respond. She looked around on the ground as if she was searching for something else to say. *I'm not in the mood for this today,* I thought to myself. *First, Zion leaves me at the bookstore due to his impatience, and now this.*

"Look, Theresa. I told you on the phone that I was sorry this happened. Justin told me that the two of you were separated, and I believed him. It's over now, and I'm moving on from the situation. I don't have time to lose any sleep over him."

"I know and I understand. I was hoping we could go somewhere and talk."

"Talk about what? There's nothing for us to talk about. I haven't spoken to Justin since the day you called and I answered his phone."

Theresa stood there and cried.

*Lord, why me?*

"Lynda, Justin really loves you. I knew that when we got together and it's obvious now. But I couldn't understand if he loved you so much, why did he marry me?"

I was hoping she was asking me that as a rhetorical question because I couldn't tell her the truth. Justin wanted kids at the time we were dating, and I wasn't sure if I wanted to start a family at that point in my life. But it wasn't my place to tell her that.

"Theresa, you need to talk this over with Justin."

"He won't talk to me about it."

"I'm sorry you have to go through this with Justin, but I'm not comfortable with this situation. It's not my place to tell you anything."

"Oh, so you can fuck my husband, but you don't want to talk to his wife now that you're caught?"

"I don't owe you anything nor do I have to talk to you. I'm trying to be nice because if I told you the truth, it will further hurt your feelings. Therefore, I suggest you go home and try to talk to your husband again. No need to lash out at me. He lied to both of us, remember?"

I was glad Zion had left. I didn't need him to know all of this drama going on between Justin and me. Theresa looked so sad that I actually felt sorry for her. Unfortunately, it was no longer my issue, and I didn't want any part of it.

"You're right, and I'm sorry to have wasted your time."

I could have sworn I heard her mumble, "Bitch," under her breath as she walked away, but I refused to entertain the situation any further.

I pulled out my car keys, hit the button to unlock the door, and got in my car. I sat there for a moment before driving off. I wondered if the situation was really over. I felt under my seat for my gun; it was still there. I had put the gun in my car after I pulled it on Justin. I planned to turn it in at one of those drop-off locations where you received cash for turning in a gun. I didn't care about the money, but I realized I didn't need a gun in my possession. I feared that one day, I would actually shoot somebody.

Before pulling off, I decided to send Dianne a text message since she couldn't make it to the event because Nihya had some kind of dance recital. The message read, *Hey, Di. Event went well. Gotta tell u 'bout visit from Justin's wife and also Zion acting like a spoiled bitch.*

As I drove home, the reply came through. *This isn't Dianne, and I'm a spoiled bitch now?*

I was done! *How did I do that?* I didn't know how to respond to Zion, so I didn't. I was pissed at him anyway, so maybe it was best he knew how I felt. I didn't know how I even sent that to him by mistake. Text messaging can sure get a person in trouble if you're not careful.

When I got home, I had another text message from Zion. The message read, *By the way, who the fuck is Justin?* I could see this situation with Zion wasn't going to end well. At that moment, I didn't give a fuck about Zion or his feelings. I couldn't believe how he treated me at my event. *So, fuck it! Let him wonder.*

Needing a good laugh before I went to sleep, I decided to call Dianne to tell her what I did. She answered on the first ring.

"Hey, heifer. I was just about to call you to see how things went today."

"Hey, girl. You'll never guess what I did. Well, before I get to that, the event went very well, but afterward, I got approached by Justin's wife."

"Oh, my goodness."

"I'll get back to that, though. You know my event was supposed to be over at six o'clock, but things were going so well, it ran over. Zion was so impatient that he left me at the bookstore."

"No, he didn't."

"Yes, he did."

"How many times have you waited for his ass at his events?"

"Exactly! It's almost as if he didn't want to see my event so successful. I don't know. I attempted to send you a text message calling him a spoiled bitch, but I sent it to him by mistake."

Dianne did a scream laugh into the phone. "Heifer, no, you didn't!"

"Yes, girl. He's pissed right about now, but so what. Not to mention I said something about Justin's wife in the text message."

"Oh, my goodness. This is too much. So what about Justin's wife and what did she want?"

"I guess she wanted to see me in person. She claimed she wanted to talk to me about Justin, but she needs to talk to him, not me."

"That's right. She needs to talk to Justin."

"I could've told her that she was the rebound woman, but that would've only hurt her even more. Justin made the choice to marry her since he wanted kids, so, oh well. They need to work it out."

"Yeah, this is way too much drama. Anyway, let me know if you want to go to church with us on Sunday. Nelson and I are going back to church, and you're welcome to go with us."

"Actually, that sounds good. I keep saying I need to start going back to church, so I guess it's time to stop talking about it and just do it."

"Exactly. Well, I'll talk to you later. I need to throw something together to eat right quick. Nihya's dance recital was so good, girl. We taped it so you'll be able to see it."

"Okay, sounds good. I'll talk to you later."

"Bye, girl."

I decided to turn off my cell phone because I really didn't want to hear from anyone. All I wanted to do was take a nice, long bubble bath and sip on a mint mojito wine cooler while listening to some neo soul music. However, none of that would happen in the serene manner I had hoped because as I ran my bath water, I heard a knock on my front door.

*Oh, shit. Who in the hell is harassing me now?*

After shutting off the water, I approached the door and stood to the side. I had seen many movies where someone shot right through the door when the person looked out the peephole. The way things were going in my life, I couldn't swear that wasn't about to happen to me. So, to be on the safe side, I didn't stand directly in front of the door.

"Who is it?" I yelled.

"It's Zion. Open the door."

*Lord, have mercy on me,* I thought while opening the door.

"What, Zion?" I asked, blocking the entryway.

"Girl, move. I'm coming in whether you want me to or not." Zion shoved me gently out of the way. "I think you have some explaining to do."

"Well, I can't deny the text message I sent because you read it. So, what do you want me to say? I meant what I said. I just didn't mean to send it to you. My bad."

"Is that all you're going to say?"

"Pretty much. You know you've been acting like an ass. I don't need to tell you that."

"How am I acting like an ass?"

"Whenever you're at one of my events, you rush me. I never do that to you."

"The event was supposed to be over at six o'clock, Lynda. It was going on seven."

"So what? Am I not worth the wait? I have waited for you way longer than that, so don't even try it. I guess your shit is more important than mine, huh?"

"I never said that."

"Well, that's how you act, and I'm tired of it."

"I'm tired of it, too." Zion walked toward the door and then looked back at me as if I was going to stop him. "You're going to just let me leave?"

"Zion, what kind of games are you playing? If you want to leave, then leave. I don't need this."

"Are you going to tell me who Justin is?"

"No. He isn't worth talking about."

"Lynda, why do you make it so hard for me to love you?"

"You make it hard, Zion. Then you want to turn that shit on me. If you want to make me the problem, then fine. I'll be the problem."

Zion continued standing by the door as if he wasn't sure if he should leave or not. I was kind of indifferent to whether or not he left. I loved Zion, but this was becoming way too much to deal with.

Zion walked back over to me and asked, "Lynda, do you love me?"

"I love you, but that doesn't mean we're right for each other." The tears fell.

"Don't talk like that. Relationships are complicated; they take a lot of work."

"Some of this is unnecessary, though. I don't believe it has to be so hard."

"I believe we can work this out. I'm not ready to give up on us."

As fate would have it, the song *I Can't Stop Loving You* by Kem started playing from my CD player. I wasn't ready to make up with Zion yet because I was hurt; however, he worked the same magic on me that he normally did to erase my pain. He came up behind me, put his arms around my waist, and kissed my neck. He sang part of the song. "I can't stop loving you, no matter what I tell myself." Zion untied the belt on my bathrobe and rubbed the erection he was developing across my curves.

"Zion, stop. My bath water is getting cold."

"Do you really want me to stop? I don't think you do." Zion held me tighter and continued kissing my neck.

"Yes, I want you to stop. You can't fix everything with sex."

"I can at least make you feel good." Zion squeezed my breasts aggressively. It was close to my menstrual cycle, so my breasts were already very tender. His squeezing was hurting me.

"Zion, please stop. That hurts." At that moment, I wondered if he had been drinking.

"I don't want to stop. You are *my* girl." Those words sounded painfully familiar, and it took me back to a place I didn't ever want to return—the night Taye forced himself on me. When Zion pinned me up against the wall, I panicked.

"No, Taye. Please stop. You're hurting me."

Zion backed away from me slowly. "Lynda, I think I'll leave."

"Zion, wait a minute," I said with tears in my eyes. I had been doing a lot of crying lately.

"You just called me another man's name and you want me to wait a minute?"

"Taye's dead, remember? I couldn't possibly be sleeping with him."

"Do you miss him or something?"

"Miss Taye? Someone who forced sex on me?"

"You never told me that he did that to you."

"Yes, he raped me."

"What? When was this?" Zion released me from his grasp.

"When you were on your first book tour."

"I can't believe you kept that from me, Lynda."

"I know I should've told you, but I didn't know how. Plus, I didn't want to ruin your tour." I sighed.

"Ruin my tour? You're more important than some book tour, Lynda."

I stood in silence with watery eyes.

Zion went upstairs to my bathroom and turned on the water in the tub. I followed behind him.

"Lynda, I would never force sex on you. I just thought you were playing hard to get like you do sometimes when you're mad at me."

"I'm sorry for not telling you."

Zion was seemingly looking for something to distract him from what I had confessed.

"Your bath water was cold, so I added some more hot water to it. You need to relax. You had a long day, and I'm sure you're tired."

"Okay." I took off my bathrobe and hung it on the hook on the back of the door. As I eased into the bathtub, I could feel Zion's eyes on me. The water felt extremely good. I added some more of my Stress Relief bubble bath to the water before cutting the faucet off. I looked at Zion, who appeared to be defeated by the situation.

"Zion, what's on your mind?"

"I'm just taking in what you told me."

"Oh."

"What are we going to do about us, Lynda?"

"I'm not sure anymore."

"I wish you wouldn't keep stuff from me. If I'm going to be your man, I can't be the last to know what's going on with you."

I decided not to respond because I didn't know what to say. I wasn't sure anymore if I wanted him to be my man. There was way too much back and forth, and I didn't want to continue playing the love game of tug and war with him. The situation with him was exhausting, and I needed to feel some peace.

Zion walked over and kneeled down beside the bathtub. It appeared my confession of Taye forcing himself on me really bothered him because he was silent while I took my bath. He looked as if he was searching for the right thing to say at that moment. Normally, he would have been trying to fondle me or something. I wondered what was on his mind, but I didn't feel like asking.

I finished my bath and put on my bathrobe. Zion kissed me on the forehead and told me that he was going home to catch up on some writing. It was probably for the best since we both seemed like we didn't have anything to say to one another. I felt our relationship was coming to an end...again!

# CHAPTER 27

## *Natasha*

*CONFRONTING TYRONE REGARDING* whether or not he had an affair was one of the hardest things I had to do since we'd been married. I was a firm believer that you didn't ask questions if you really didn't want the honest answer. Other than woman's intuition, I wasn't sure what it was about Tyrone's actions that brought this question to mind. I thought I could ignore the feelings, but it was impossible. Something didn't seem quite right, but I just couldn't put my finger on it.

I was done feeding the kids their lunch, and it was time for them to take a nap. Tyler cried because he wanted to stay up and watch a movie with his dad, but I had them on a strict schedule so I could get things done around the house. Tyrone agreed to read Tyler a story so he would stop crying, and of course, Tyler was asleep before Tyrone got halfway through the book. I watched him as he closed Tyler's bedroom door and entered the living room where I sat on the sofa. Tyrone had the swagger that forced a lot of women to look twice even when we were out together. He eased on the sofa next to me, kissed me on the cheek, and gently grazed his hand across by breasts. My body didn't respond as I wanted it to because I had to get it off my mind. I grabbed Tyrone's hand and gazed into his eyes. *I really do love him, but I need to know.*

Before I could speak, Tyrone leaned over and kissed me in a way I couldn't ever remember him doing. Could he tell something was on my mind and was trying to avoid a conversation? Or did he just want to seize the moment and have sex while the kids were asleep? I struggled with what to do. *Do I ask him anyway or give into his advances to make love to me?* I wasn't about to be the wife who denied her husband sex, so I was going to give in if that's what he wanted.

While random thoughts ran through my mind, Tyrone stood and grabbed me by the hand. My questions were answered when he led me into our bedroom and closed the door. He slid his sweatpants down to around his ankles and sat on the edge of the bed. His manhood stood as if to beg for attention. I didn't resist. After I slid my panties down from underneath the housedress that I always wore around the house, he pulled me on top of his lap. Tyrone licked his finger to give my vagina extra lubrication, and then I eased down on his erection. I glided up and down in a slow rhythm matching Tyrone's.

"Natasha?" Tyrone moaned.

"Yes, baby?"

"I love you."

"I love you, too," I moaned in his ear.

"Oh, shit. I'm about to cum."

*Already?*

At that moment, I didn't mind that he came before me because my mind was still occupied with other thoughts. I remained on top of Tyrone until his erection completely softened. He laid me on the bed as if he was going to try to get a second wind to finish me off. I honestly wasn't in the mood, and he must have read my facial expression.

"What's wrong, Tash? Why do you look so sad? I hate seeing you like this. Talk to me."

*Now isn't the time. I don't want to ruin his moment.*

"I do have a lot on my mind, but I'm also exhausted. I could use a relaxing bath."

He looked into my eyes as if searching for a deeper meaning. "Okay, let me run you a bath."

"Sounds good."

Tyrone pulled his pants back up, went into the bathroom, and turned the water on so I could take a bath. I entered behind him while he washed up at the sink. I caressed his back and his shoulders while catching his reflection in the mirror. He looked defeated.

"Tyrone?"

"Yeah, babe." He turned around to face me after resting the washcloth on the towel rack.

"I'm trying to work through my moods."

"I know. I just wish there was something I could do."

"You're doing a lot. You're a great father and husband. I'm sorry if I've made you feel otherwise."

He smiled a little. "Thank you, babe. I wish I could make you happier, though."

I kissed him softly on his lips. He barely responded. This situation was seriously affecting him, and I was scared to lose his love. *What am I going to do?*

I sprinkled a small amount of bath salts under the running faucet and eased into the tub. It was called Stress Relief Aromatherapy, but I needed more than bath salts to relieve the kind of stress I felt. Tyrone watched me for a few seconds before exiting the bathroom and closing the door behind him. I wished Calgon could actually take me away for a brief moment, but random thoughts continued to dance around in my mind. I turned the faucet off and slid down as far as I could without putting my head into the water. I wondered what was on Tyrone's mind. I loved him, I loved my kids, and I loved Dianne. *Then why am I hurting those around me that I truly care about?*

I must've dozed off because Tyrone startled me when he knocked on the door to see if I was all right. I informed him that I was okay, but I must have been tired if I fell asleep in the tub. I didn't think I'd ever done that before. *Isn't that dangerous?*

My water grew cold before I had a chance to wash up, so I added more hot water to my bath. The kids were still napping when I finally got out of the tub. Upon entering our bedroom, I noticed Tyrone had dozed off himself. When I sat on my side of the bed, he immediately opened his eyes.

"Baby, I'm sorry. I didn't mean to wake you," I said.

"Naw, it's cool. I was just waiting for you so we could talk."

"What do you want to talk about?"

"Whatever it is that's on your mind."

"Tyrone, it's really many of the things we've talked about before. I've researched the treatments for postpartum depression, if that turns out to be my situation. At most, they can prescribe an anti-depressant, and I'm not a fan of being medicated like that."

"Okay, but know that I'm here to talk about what you feel is bothering you, even if it's in the middle of the night. I want you to be okay, baby, that's all."

"I know and I appreciate that."

I smiled and retrieved the cocoa butter body gel from the dresser so I could add some moisture to my skin. Tyrone held out his hand as if to ask for the bottle. I handed it to him, and he massaged the gel into my skin. Tyrone had just finished when the twins started making noise in their crib. We recently put a baby monitor in their room, as well as Tyler's.

When Tyrone left the room, I eased into some comfortable pajamas. He came back with the girls, put them on the bed with me, and told me that he was going to get their bottles. They looked at me and cooed as if they were really telling me something. Tyrone brought me their bottles and left again. He returned with Tyler, who was still asleep in his arms.

"Natasha, let's have some family time right here."

*Could he see I'm having a hard time bonding with my children?*

I smiled at the idea. "Let's watch a movie. Anything but *Toy Story Three*, though."

Tyrone laughed. "Gotcha, babe."

# CHAPTER 28
## Dianne

~~~

**LYNDA CALLED WITH HAPPY ANNIVERSARY** wishes for Nelson and me, and we ended up talking on the phone for over an hour. We were past due for a girls' night out, so we agreed to meet up for drinks in about a week. Once I hung up the phone, I immediately searched my closet for an outfit to wear for my anniversary celebration. There wasn't a need for me to purchase something new because I was certain I would find something I had never worn before. I wasn't sure if Nelson was going to take me out somewhere or if he was going to prepare dinner himself at home, but he said he had a surprise for me. Either way, I wanted to look especially good, so I opted for a simple, black, one-shoulder, long-sleeved dress, which still had the tag on it from Nordstrom that could be dressed up or down.

Pressed for time, I quickly tried on the dress and discovered it was now fitting me like *whoa*! I bought the dress on sale, but this might be my first and last occasion wearing it if I didn't shed a few inches around my waist and hips. *I need to get my Brazilian wax done in case Nelson wants to make love to me later tonight.* It had been a while since we made love, and I planned to look good from head to toe. *I wonder what his surprise is.*

Nelson had already surprised me with a spa certificate for five hundred dollars. I had mentioned to him earlier in the week that I was making an appointment at Modern Spa in Pentagon City Mall, but I didn't expect him to pay for everything. I was totally surprised when he handed me the envelope when I woke up.

I spent the entire morning of my anniversary getting myself together for my husband. After the grueling Brazilian wax procedure, I enjoyed an 80-minute Swedish massage, a 50-minute facial, followed by a manicure and pedicure. I always get the waxing done first to give my coochie a chance to heal. That was almost torture down in the private area. *Whew!* Since I'd been wearing my hair in its natural curly state, I had to beg my hairstylist at the Dominican hair salon to squeeze me in because I wanted my hair to have that extra bounce. I still sported my curly, shoulder-length ponytail, and I was sure Nelson would appreciate seeing my hair done. I figured I would get a few inches cut off, but maybe he wouldn't notice as much if it looked really nice.

By the time I was finished at the salon, it was about 4:00 p.m. I had just enough time to go to Lynda's house to freshen up and put my dress on. I decided to get dressed at her place so I could make an entrance when I got back home. After applying some light makeup, I headed out the door at about 6:30 p.m. I called Nelson from my cell phone to let him know that I was on my way. I was glad I picked up Nelson's anniversary gift from Tiffany's the day before, or else I really would've been behind schedule. Nelson had asked me to be back by 7:00 p.m., so things were going according to schedule.

When I arrived at my house, I sat in the garage for a few minutes thinking about what I almost lost feeling vulnerable around Tyrone. I sighed, checked my face and hair in the rearview mirror, and got out of my car. Upon entering, wonderful aromas filled my nose and made my stomach growl. *Wow, I wonder what he cooked.* There were several dozen beautiful red roses around the living room and dining room. The dining room table was elegantly set with some of our fine china dishes. I called out to Nelson so he would know I was in the house.

"Nelson, baby?"

"I'm in the kitchen."

I entered the kitchen, and Nelson greeted me with a wink. He carried a pan of lasagna that he had just taken out of the oven.

"What you got there?" I asked playfully.

"One of your favorite dishes. I begged my mother for her famous lasagna recipe since I know you love it so much."

"Thank you, sweetheart. I can't believe she gave it to you."

"Yeah, and now she has to kill me." We both laughed.

"How is she doing?"

"Good days and some bad days. But I'm glad she's having more good days."

"That's good to hear."

Once Nelson placed the pan of lasagna on the counter, he walked over to give me the warmest hug and wettest kiss. He didn't let me go for about three minutes.

"Wow, Dianne. You look stunning."

"Thanks, Nelson. Do you need help getting the rest of the dinner together?" I asked.

*Good, he hasn't noticed I cut my hair.*

"No, baby. Thank you, but I have it covered. I want you to go and rest your fine self. By the way, you look very sexy in that black dress." Nelson winked.

"Thank you, sweetheart."

As I turned to leave the kitchen, I swung my bouncing, behaving hair and smiled to myself because I was sure Nelson was watching. I went into the living room to relax and listen to the CD that Nelson had playing. I assumed Nihya was at her grandmother's house, but I didn't ask. Lately, she had been the source of our problems, and I really didn't want to discuss her on my anniversary. That may sound selfish, but I didn't care at the moment.

As I listened to the CD, I realized there was a musician playing a saxophone rendition to some of my favorite old school love songs.

*Why Have I Lost You* by Cameo, *Can't Let Go* by Parris, and *Gentle* by Frederick. Those songs took me back to the late 70s and early 80s when I was a little girl listening to grown folk's music. I got so absorbed in the music that I dozed off for a few moments. Nelson kissing me softly on my neck awakened me.

"Dinner is ready, baby," Nelson said almost in a whisper.

"Oh, okay. How long was I asleep?"

"Only for like fifteen or maybe twenty minutes at most."

"Really? I must've been tired because it seems like I was asleep for hours."

"I can tell you have not been resting well. You toss and turn a lot at night."

*Hopefully I'm not talking in my sleep anymore.*

"Really? After that massage today, I'm hoping I will rest better. I really needed that."

Nelson just smiled.

The lasagna was complemented with salad, garlic bread, and sweet red wine. For dessert, Nelson even made homemade strawberry shortcake, which was definitely one of my favorites. There was very little conversation during dinner, so it was kind of awkward for me. Normally, Nelson and I had so much to say to each other. Nelson finally spoke, interrupting my thoughts.

"Dianne, do you remember we talked about renewing our vows?"

"Yes."

"Do you still want to?"

"Of course. None of that has changed."

"I'm glad to hear that," Nelson said, standing up from his chair and pulling a small box from his pocket.

"Nelson, what's that? I know that's not a ring. I already have a ring. You didn't have to," I said, jumping out of my chair and snatching the box from him. *Now what woman is going to turn down a new ring?*

"I know, but I wanted to get you another one for our anniversary."

As I opened the small box, Nelson asked, "Will you marry me again, Mrs. Thompson?"

"Yes, Nelly." I kissed him and looked into his eyes. "Do you love me as much as I love you?"

"Are you serious? Girl, quit playing with me. I think I love you more than you love me."

"Why would you say that?"

"Because you seem to always be ready to give up on our marriage."

"It's not because I don't love you. I'm just…"

"Just what?"

"Afraid you'll leave me, and I don't think I can handle you leaving me."

"So, you want to be the one to leave first, is that it?"

"I guess so, Nelson. I don't know." I looked around the room trying to think of what I could say to change the subject.

Nelson sighed.

"Hey, babe? Who is that playing on the CD?" I asked to lighten the mood.

"It's some dude. I actually have a copy of the CD for you so you can play it in your car and at work. I figured you would like it."

"Oh, cool. Thanks, babe."

When Nelson left the dining room to get the CD for me, I recognized one of my favorite songs being played on the saxophone. Suddenly, I heard a live saxophone join in with the CD. It was Nelson playing *Always and Forever* by Heatwave. I couldn't stop blushing. Nelson told me that he played the saxophone when he was younger, but I never imagined he would be so good. I mean, I played the flute in middle school, but I didn't have a clue how to play it now.

"Baby, I didn't know you were so good."

Nelson stopped playing the saxophone and put it down. "Thanks, babe. I picked it up from my parents' house. I'm ready to start doing something else with my time. I'm starting to get burned out from just going to work and coming home."

"Yes, I do understand. We all should have a hobby or something."

"Yes, indeed."

"Well, I'm glad you found something that makes you happy."

"You make me happy, Dianne. Remember when we first met?"

"Yes, how can I forget? You took advantage of me that night."

"Woman, please! You started it. But remember that job opportunity I had in Boston?"

"Oh, please don't make me feel guilty about that again."

"No, seriously, Dianne. That was an opportunity of a lifetime for me, a young, black, male senior executive. I gave that all up for you because I felt making you my wife was the *real* opportunity of a lifetime. The thought of not being with you was too much for me. I had never felt what I was feeling for you. I still feel that way. When you walk out on me, it hurts, but I know you need your space when you're upset. I just always pray that you come back to me. Now, I'm no punk, baby, but I'm so much in love with you. And yes, I think I love you more. My father said that's how it should be anyway. Not enough men feel that way about their wives."

"Aw, Nelson. That's so sweet. But I think people should love each other equally."

"I know I have a good woman, even with *all* of your faults."

"You didn't have to add that part." I playfully punched him in the arm.

"I know. My bad." Nelson laughed and kissed my cheek. "Let me get the CD for you before I forget. I want you to hear all the songs I played for you."

"This is the perfect anniversary gift. Well, not as perfect as my new ring. Okay, they're equally perfect. Thanks again, Nelson, for loving me enough to work this out," I rambled.

"Yeah, I'm crazy about you, woman, or maybe I'm just crazy. I don't know."

"Nelson!"

"Okay, okay. So what do you want to do now?"

"I have an idea. Let's play Scrabble. Reminds me of our first date."

"What, no makeup sex?"

"Nelson!" I laughed.

"But seriously, Dianne. Let me make love to you. It's been a while."

"No arguments here." I moved closer to Nelson. "Tonight is perfect."

"Yes, it is."

"Oh, wait. I have a gift for you, too. I almost forgot. It's not much, but I wanted to give you something from my heart. So, I wrote you a poem." When I handed Nelson the plaque, he looked shocked.

"Baby, this is nice. Thank you!"

"Yeah, I wrote one of those lists like you wrote. I wanted to think of all of the reasons why I love you. Then I decided to put it into a poem format. I wanted you to always have it, so I found a place on the Internet that creates all kinds of plaques."

"Thanks again. I'm going to put this in my office at work."

Nelson grabbed my hand and pulled me close to him. He kissed me very slowly while caressing my breasts. He used both of his thumbs to rub my nipples simultaneously. I let out a deep sigh. That was a sure sign that there would be no Scrabble game being played that night. *My God, how I love this man*, I thought, as my husband led me by the hand to our bedroom.

A weird feeling came over me as we entered our bedroom. I wanted to get everything that was bothering me off my chest. *Well, maybe not everything.*

"Nelson, I need to tell you something. This is probably not the best time, but it's very important to share this with you. I'm tired of carrying this around with me."

"What is it, baby?" Nelson had a concerned look on his face.

"I had a baby when I was in my early twenties and he died." I successfully held back my tears. "I tried to put it out of my mind as if it never happened, but that's impossible. Nihya reminds me that I'm not her mother, but I am somebody's mother, Nelson. He's just not here."

"Dianne, baby, I'm so sorry. I know you have a painful past, and I figured that whatever it was you would tell me in your own time. I kind of had a feeling you had a miscarriage because I saw the way you looked at Tyler when he was born."

"I didn't miscarry. I delivered my son a little early, and his lungs were not developed enough. He lived for a few hours, and I just held him until he died."

"Oh, man, Dianne. I'm so sorry."

"The hardest part is his father wouldn't stay there with me. He said it was too much for him. He left the hospital after the doctors said the baby wasn't going to make it."

"Wow, are you serious? I would have never left your side."

"I know. It really hurt to have to go through it alone. We were going to get married, but after that, I couldn't be with him. We broke up soon after I got home from the hospital."

"Yeah, I understand. But no matter how hard life is for us, things happen for a reason."

"Yes, I know, but after losing my mother when I was a little girl and then losing my firstborn, I don't want to go through another loss. I know it's a part of life, but it's just so hard. I can't even imagine what it must have been like for Natasha to lose Aisha."

"I know, so don't think about it. Okay?"

"Yeah. We're supposed to be having a good day, right?" I said, then smiled and looked into Nelson's brown eyes. I could look into his eyes all day.

"Yep, and one day, you'll be carrying my baby."

"That's the thing, Nelson. I'm not sure if I can have children."

"Why? Did the doctor tell you that?"

"No."

"So don't jinx us like that. There's a reason why it hasn't happened yet, baby. Don't worry."

"I'm just afraid you will be disappointed if I can't have any children."

"Dianne, I'm not going to lie. I would love for us to have children together, but if it's not in God's plan, then so be it. You should know the kind of man I am by now. I stand by my God and my woman. No matter how crazy she is."

"Nelson!" I hit him playfully. "Stop saying stuff like that."

"I love you, for better or for worse. And as far as children, we're just going to have to work on our baby often. Like three or four times a day."

"Yeah, right. Don't you wish?"

"Touché, baby." Nelson laughed.

"Are you ready to work on our baby now?" I asked.

"It would be my pleasure."

"Oh, shoot, Nelson."

"What?"

"I have another gift for you. I left it in the car. Let me go and get it."

"Now?" Nelson said, pointing at his erection.

"Yes, now. Be patient." I kissed him on the lips. "Be right back."

When I returned to the room in my hot pink, lace nightgown from Victoria's Secret, Nelson yelled out, "Damn, I like this gift!"

Laughing, I handed him the box from Tiffany's. He put the box on the nightstand on his side of the bed and pulled me on top of him.

"Nelson, open your gift."

"I'm about to," he replied, taking off my nightgown.

We laughed.

Nelson and I had an amazing night of lovemaking. I couldn't remember the last time I had so many consecutive orgasms. I knew Nelson wanted me to have a baby, so I started to think positive about being able to conceive. As Nelson said, the doctors never told me otherwise, so I had to stop worrying.

The next morning, Nelson thanked me for the cufflinks from Tiffany's. He must've opened the gift while I was still asleep. I knew he wanted those particular ones I purchased because he had dog-eared that page in the catalog. That normally meant something he was really interested in buying or hinting at a gift suggestion.

After the conversation we had about my son, I wanted to show Nelson the baby items I kept after he died. I told him that I named him Daniel. All of Daniel's items were in a locked box in my closet. I was sure Nelson saw the box, but he never questioned its contents. When I showed him Daniel's birth certificate, he just stared at it. I wasn't sure what he was concentrating on.

"Baby, your son would have been about the same age as Nihya."

"Yes. That's why it's especially hard when she reminds me that I'm not her mother. I think about the son I would be raising now. And it hurts."

"Dianne, there's no excuse for Nihya's behavior. I was really hoping it was a phase, but I see now we have to get her under control."

I didn't respond. Nelson continued to look at the birth certificate, and then he finally said why he had been staring at it like that.

"Dianne, I think I know the person who's listed as the father."

"What makes you think that?" I became concerned.

"Well, his name is Jonah Griffin, and I used to work with a guy with the same name. Actually, it was the guy who told me about the book you wrote while you were in graduate school."

"Huh?"

"Remember the day we met and you were lecturing at my job?"

"Yeah."

"I told you a buddy of mine told me about your book. That's how I knew about it. Remember?"

"Vaguely. I was too busy trying not to look at you. I wasn't really concentrating on what you were saying."

"Damn, this really is a small world."

"Nelson, I don't know what to say."

"Dianne, don't let this upset you. I haven't seen that dude in years. As a matter of fact, he was next in line for the position in Boston."

"Keep on rubbing it in."

"Naw, baby, I'm glad I made the choice I did." Nelson kissed me on my cheek.

"Are you sure you're not upset about Jonah?"

"Baby, I can't fault you for your past. I have a past, too, and we're raising her now. Remember? I know it's not easy for you either. You handled the news about Nihya extremely well, and it hurts me that she was so disrespectful to you. So, yeah, I'm good. I mean, no man really wants to know about any other man who has been up in his wife, but I know you have had a couple of other men."

"Yes, baby. Only a couple." We both laughed. It felt good to laugh with my husband again.

# CHAPTER 29
## *Lynda*

~⚬~

*I ALLOWED XAVIER TO COME* visit me during his break from school. I hated when things were going wrong with Zion because I let my guard down with the men who I didn't need to be bothered with. Xavier was supposed to be on that list along with Justin and Maurice. He wasn't on the list for being an asshole, but seeing him was getting complicated. He got finer every time I saw him. He had almost the same dark chocolate complexion that Taye had, but with more reddish undertones. I swear I wanted to lick him to see if he tasted like chocolate. Taye was the personal trainer, but Xavier had the better body. His dreads were even sexier than Taye's. *How is that even possible?*

Xavier called me several times after my book release party, but I always claimed to be too busy with book-related activities for us to hook up. The truth was I didn't want to be tempted to sleep with him because he definitely turned me on. Plus, I'd never mentioned to him that I was involved with Zion again.

When Xavier walked through the door wearing his gray sweats and Timberland boots, I could have dropped my panties right there in the doorway.

"What's up, beautiful?" Xavier spoke and kissed me on the cheek.

Before he walked past me, I grabbed his hand, pulled him close, and hugged him around his neck. Wrong move! He smelled better than he looked.

"Hey, how are you?" I asked, inhaling the scent of his cologne. *My goodness!* I could have held him all night.

"Um, I like this greeting. I'm good, just tired. Coming from work."

"Oh, really? What do you do?" I released Xavier from my embrace.

"Training at Taye's gym."

"Really? I didn't know you took over his gym."

"Actually, I didn't. A friend of the family bought it, but I agreed to work there and help them out part-time until they find some qualified trainers."

"Oh, okay." Now it made sense why Xavier had a great body.

"Well, how are you, pretty lady?"

"I'm okay, but I'm tired myself. I could use a massage."

"No problem. I can do that for you." He smirked and walked past me.

"Oh, yeah? I would like to see your skills."

*Why did I say that? I really don't need him rubbing on my body.*

When Xavier sat on the sofa, I immediately had the urge to straddle him. Of course, I fought the urge and sat on the opposite end of the sofa.

"Why are you way down there, Lynda? Come closer. It's been a while since I've seen you."

*Damn, I forgot how sexy his voice is.*

"No, Xavier."

"What are you afraid is going to happen?" He smiled.

*Oh, my God, when did he get dimples? I've never noticed them before. This is too many sexy features on one man. If he had a full beard like Maurice's, my panties would have surely been off by now.*

It seemed my cell phone rang less than a minute later. Not recognizing the number, I sent the call to voicemail, but before I could put the phone down, it rang again. Since my brother was known to have several numbers, I figured I'd better answer it just in case it was an emergency. Wrong! It was Maurice. *What the fuck does he want?* I excused myself and went into the kitchen to handle the phone call.

"What, Maurice?"

"Lynda, baby, we need to talk."

*Did he say baby?*

"I don't think there's anything left to say. You made it clear how you feel."

"Lynda, I'm sorry. I didn't mean what I said to you, and you know that."

"Well, it doesn't matter, and I can't talk right now anyway."

"What, you have company or something?"

"Yes, I do."

"Well, fuck you then, bitch!" Maurice hung up the phone before I could respond.

"What a fucking asshole," I said out loud, forgetting that Xavier was in the living room.

*What is wrong with Maurice? Aren't we too old for this bullshit?*

When I turned around to leave the kitchen, Xavier stood in the doorway.

"Is everything okay?" he asked.

"Yes. I'm sorry. Please excuse my rudeness."

"Naw, you good. You had to handle your business."

Before I could respond, Xavier grabbed my hand and pulled me close to him.

"Xavier, what are you doing?"

"Nothing. I just wanted to feel you, that's all."

Before I could pull away, he was softly kissing my neck. I wanted to move, but I was enjoying his touch. The way his lips were barely grazing my skin was enchanting. My moans indicated I wanted him badly, but I didn't want to let this happen either. For one, he was Taye's brother, and two, I had some unresolved feelings for Zion.

"Xavier, we can't do this."

"You don't want me?"

"I do, but not now."

"Okay, I won't penetrate you, but I do want to taste you."

"Okay."

*Did I say okay?*

Xavier backed me into the refrigerator and eased my sweatpants and panties down together. I stepped out of them in anticipation of his tongue action while he got down on his knees. When he lifted my left leg to put it on his shoulder, I grabbed a handful of dreads. *I'm so glad I keep the kitty trimmed and cleaned.* His tongue skillfully excited my clit, reminding me of my first encounter with Zion. I tried so hard to wipe those thoughts from my mind and enjoy Xavier, but it was difficult.

"Xavier, wait."

"What's wrong, Lynda? Does it not feel good?"

"It does, but I want to feel you." *What was I saying?*

"You sure?"

"Yes. I have some condoms in my bedroom. Come on."

I took Xavier by the hand and led him into my bedroom where I sat on the edge of my bed watching him undress. This dude was absolutely gorgeous. Once he removed his clothes, I decided to put my lips around the tip of his erection. For some reason, I wasn't ready to have him inside of me. He didn't seem to mind the oral sex either. Finally, he lay back on the bed, and I continued my oral skills. I would occasionally look up at him, and I swear he looked like an Egyptian king. Once I took him to his level of satisfaction, he was determined to finish me off. He said he wasn't going to be completely satisfied until I had an orgasm, so I allowed him to finish sucking and licking on my clit until I reached my peak.

Afterward, he laid his head on my stomach and fell asleep. He looked so cute and peaceful, even while drooling on me. I played with his dreads until I drifted off to sleep.

The next morning, I woke up to the smell of bacon and coffee. *He just helped himself, huh?* Noticing his wallet on my nightstand, I decided to look in it for his ID. *Hamilton Xavier Dixon.* I laughed. I wanted to make sure he was who he said he was. You never knew these days.

I got out of bed and went into the bathroom to relieve myself and to brush my teeth. When I went into the kitchen, Xavier turned around, smiled, and winked at me.

"Good morning, beautiful."

"Good morning, Xavier. I didn't expect you to—"

"Still be here?" Xavier cut me off.

"No, be in here cooking."

"Oh, well, I figured you would be hungry, so I fixed you some bacon and eggs."

"You're not hungry?"

"I don't eat pork, so I'm fine with just the eggs and coffee. I guess I could make some toast, too."

"Thanks. That's sweet of you."

"No problem. It's the least I could do to thank you for allowing me to crash at your place." He winked.

Xavier and I ate breakfast at the small table I had in my kitchen. I would occasionally try to steal a glance at him, but he would already be looking at me and I would blush. *He is so handsome.* He pulled his dreads back and secured them with a rubber band. I figured so he could eat without them getting in his way. With his hair back, I could see more of his features. *This man is really fine!*

I needed to be honest with him about my status with Zion, which I wasn't exactly sure of myself. The moment was so peaceful. I didn't want to disrupt it with a conversation about Zion, so I thought of something else to talk about.

"So, Hamilton, what's on your agenda for today?"

Xavier grinned. "You looked through my wallet, huh? No problem. I have nothing to hide. I have a few clients at the gym, but otherwise, nothing. What about you?"

"I don't even know yet. I know I need to contact my publicist so we can discuss some upcoming events."

"Can I see you later?"

"Xavier, about last night…" I sighed. "I don't know if it's a good idea for us to be seeing each other."

"Can I use your shower?" he asked, totally ignoring what I said.

"Xavier, did you hear what I said?"

"I did, and I don't have a response for that right now. Can I use your shower so I can go to work?"

"Sure, why not. Let me get you a washcloth and towel." I sighed again.

I stood in the doorway of the bathroom after I handed him the washcloth and towel. I watched as he slid off his shorts and turned the faucet knobs until the water reached his desired temperature. As he stepped into the shower, he turned and looked at me.

"Are you getting in with me or are you just going to stand there and watch?"

"I think I may just watch," I responded and winked.

"Suit yourself."

After noticing a slight erection forming, I decided to leave the bathroom and close the door. I couldn't handle watching that body of his any longer. I started to call Dianne to tell her a short version of what happened, but she would probably ask too many questions, and I wasn't in the mood for that. I figured I would clean up the dishes to keep me distracted until Xavier was done in the shower. By the time I finished in the kitchen, he was showered and dressed to walk out of the door.

"Xavier, we need to talk." I attempted to bring the subject up again.

"Lynda, I already know what you're about to say. It has something to do with the dude at your book release party, but I don't want to hear it right now. I had a good time with you last night, and I'm just going to leave it at that. Whatever happens from here happens."

"Okay. Did you remember to get your wallet off the nightstand?"

"I sure did, and I left a hundred dollar bill on your nightstand."

"What!"

"Just kidding, beautiful. I'll talk to you later." Xavier kissed me on the cheek and walked out the door.

*Lord knows I didn't mean to open that Pandora's Box with Xavier.* I was putting myself back in a situation that I was fighting so hard to get out of—dealing with unavailable men. Xavier was young and not to mention the younger brother of a man whom I had previously dated. Furthermore, that same man, as far as I knew, tried to kill me, but he was now dead. How was that for drama? *I must be insane.*

# CHAPTER 30
## *Lynda*

***GIRLS' NIGHT OUT HAD FINALLY*** arrived. Therefore, Dianne, Natasha, and I could meet for drinks and get caught up on each other's lives. In the past, we would go to Jaspers in Greenbelt, but after it caught on fire, we decided on a new meeting place. We thought of the Fish Market in Clinton, but most of the time, it was so noisy in there that it was difficult to have a conversation. We agreed on a restaurant in Bowie and then finish the night off with seeing some male dancers at a spot in Temple Hills not too far from where Dianne used to live before she got married. Dianne claimed Nelson didn't mind her seeing strippers, and I didn't know if Tyrone knew Natasha was out looking at naked men. I was still single, so I didn't owe anyone an explanation as to what I did. And after dealing with Zion, I preferred it that way for the time being.

Dianne and Natasha were slowly mending their friendship, but you could tell things were not the same between them anymore. That was why no matter how pissed off I got with someone, I tried not to say hateful things because you couldn't take them back and people usually didn't forget, even if they forgave you.

During dinner, Natasha showed us updated pictures of the kids and filled us in on how much they'd grown. She also mentioned she felt Tyrone was having an affair, although their relationship was getting stronger. I wondered what made her think he was having an affair, but she didn't go into too much detail. She seemed nonchalant by the accusation, but that could have been a cover up not to display her true emotions. Dianne and I tried not to ask too many questions considering what happened between the two of them. Although it was only a kiss, it should've never been allowed to get to that point.

Dianne gave us a brief rundown of what was going on in her life. She didn't talk about any problems with her and Nelson, because then, Natasha may have wanted to know more details on what sparked the fight. Of course, I knew the details, so I just listened to Dianne talk about Nihya and how she was coping to her new surroundings.

When it was my turn, I also kept it very brief. I didn't want to ruin girls' night with talk of too many drama-filled stories, although that was the initial purpose for us getting together. My story was focused on what was going on with Zion and me—the on-again off-again relationship that was getting on my nerves. I told them about the phone call from Maurice, but I purposely left out any mention of Xavier. I didn't feel like going into detail about us just yet.

After enjoying the happy hour, we headed to watch some fine, sexy, black men take their clothes off. It seemed hypocritical of us to discuss how we hated the way men objectified women and now here we were ready to drool over naked men. *Oh, well.* We followed each other closely on the Beltway so we could park in the same area in the lot of the club.

We headed inside when I was stopped by a fine, sexy, black man. *Damn, he's fine!* Dianne and Natasha waited by the entrance of the club while I talked to him.

"Hey, Lynda. How are you?"

I had no idea who the dude was, so it was a bit scary standing there with someone who obviously knew me. *Maybe he knows of my book. Yeah, that's probably it.*

"I'm fine. Where do I know you from?"

"It's me…Isaiah. You're looking good. Damn." He licked his lips.

"Isaiah?"

"Oh, maybe the name Long Stroke will ring a bell," he whispered in my ear.

I didn't know about ringing any bells, but I swear I felt Ms. Kitty contract. *Goodness!*

"Hey, I had no clue your name was Isaiah. How are you?"

"I'm good. Here to see the show, huh?"

*Duh,* I thought, but I knew it was a rhetorical question. "Yep, I sure am."

"Dang, did you forget what I look like already?" He smiled.

*Now didn't these dudes know we were only looking at their bodies?*

"I guess all your clothes threw me off," I replied, not knowing what else to say.

He laughed.

"So, I guess I'll be seeing you do your thing tonight, huh?" I asked, eyeing his crotch area. I couldn't help it. I may not have remembered what he looked like, but I knew exactly which way 'it' curved.

"Girl, don't look at me like that. I think we still have some unfinished business." I heard a slight southern accent, sounding somewhat like the rapper T.I.

*I wonder where he's originally from.*

"Oh, really? You should've handled your business when you had the opportunity."

"Man, that girl threw money at me so she could lick your pussy. Money is money, and business is business."

"And like I said, you should've handled *your business* when you had the opportunity." I was pissed at the situation with Jasmine all over again, especially with hearing him say she paid him.

"I wanted to, but you got mad and rolled up outta there so fast. I was surprised because you looked like you were lovin' what she was doin' to you. The shit was turning me on, and I was *ready* for you, too."

"Well, Mr. Long Stroke, my girls are *ready* for me, so I guess I will see you inside." I winked and ignored his last comment.

I didn't have to mention to Dianne who he was because she instantly remembered him as the stripper who danced at her bachelorette party. Natasha even recognized him. *I guess some women do look at the face of male strippers.*

Since we arrived early, we were able to get a good seat at a table next to where all the action took place. I enjoyed watching male dancers because most of them were very athletic, and they were not merely taking their clothes off, but instead, putting on a great dance performance. Although I had three martinis at happy hour, I went to the bar and ordered another one. Dianne just shook her head. I also got a glass of water because I knew the affects of drinking too much alcohol and not chasing it with water.

I'd never seen the first male dancer before, but he put on a great show. I looked at his face and wished I hadn't because he looked very familiar. Once he came over to the table, I couldn't believe my eyes. It was Marlon, a guy I used to date. I folded my arms and refused to give him any of my dollars, which were reserved for my favorite dancers. Why was I even mad? He wasn't my man.

Dianne and Natasha placed a few dollars under his G-string while I waited for him to move on to the next table. They both gasped when I told them whom they just tipped. Our relationship was so brief that they had never even met him; they had only heard the stories. I still couldn't figure out why I was upset about Marlon being a male dancer. I noticed he didn't get totally nude like some of the dancers, although he was blessed enough to do so.

*I can't wait until this show is over to confront his ass.*

After seeing Marlon's performance, I wasn't in the mood to be there anymore, but Isaiah, or Long Stroke as he called himself, was up next. I definitely didn't want to miss him, so I tried to put Marlon out of my mind.

There was something strange about watching a man with a biblical name stripping. Long Stroke was as great of a performer as I had remembered. Of course, when it was time for him to select a female from the audience to participate in his routine, he came over and pulled me out of my seat. Dianne and Natasha somehow found that extremely funny. I was sure they saw the sour look on my face; however, I went along with his performance, but I immediately wished I had stayed in my seat. The way he grinded on me and caressed me, I was turned on. It was as if he was sending a personal message to me that he was serious when he said we had some unfinished business. I didn't doubt he was serious, but I wasn't planning to have sex with him. *He is very tempting. Damn!*

Once Long Stroke's performance was over, I looked around for Marlon. I really wanted to know how in the hell he ended up stripping. I couldn't wait to hear his story.

We stayed at the club until Dianne had a chance to see her favorite male dancer, Ladies' Man. Natasha didn't have a preferred stripper to watch, so she was cool leaving whenever we were ready. I wasn't able to talk with Marlon before I left, but he was definitely going to hear from me once I got home.

Before I got settled at home, my cell phone rang. I let it go to voicemail the first time, but I caught it once it rang again. It was Marlon, and the tone of his voice suggested he was mad with me for some reason.

"Hey, Marlon. I was going to call you."

"Why did you leave like that?"

"Like what, Marlon?"

"Like you had an attitude or something."

"Marlon, I'm not going to argue with you tonight. There's no need for this, so please, you can change the tone of your voice."

"Okay, I see. You trying to fuck Isaiah now?"

"What?"

"I saw you talking to him."

"Marlon, I'm not going to talk with you about Isaiah. I'm not fuckin' him or you."

"Dude is gay anyway."

"How do you know?"

"Most of those dudes are."

"I could say the same about you."

"Lynda, please, you know I'm not gay."

"Actually, I don't know that, and you don't know for sure if any of those dudes are either unless you've slept with them."

"Lynda, look, I didn't call to argue either. It was just good seeing you. How have you been?"

"Just fine, Marlon. What brings you to strippin'?" I asked, not feeling like beating around the bush.

"Wanted to do something different, that's all."

"Yeah, well, that's definitely different. Do you still have your barbershop?"

"No, I sold it."

"You sold it to strip?"

"Why do you even care, Lynda? You didn't want to be with me, so now you care if I'm a stripper? Get over yourself."

"You know what? You're right. Bye." I hung up the phone without giving him a chance to say another word. He had a point. What the hell did I care?

I hoped he didn't call me again because I wasn't in the mood for unnecessary drama from a man who I was no longer dealing with. He didn't call, but instead, he sent a text message that read, *I see you're still childish.*

I thought of playing his tit for tat game, but I didn't. I simply deleted the message and went to bed. I hadn't planned to go back down that road, so who cared what Marlon was doing with his life. *But he did look good tonight. Damn!*

# CHAPTER 31
## Natasha

∽⦿⦾

*I RETRIEVED JASON'S LETTER* from Aisha's diary. I placed it in there so I would know where it was because I had a bad habit of misplacing stuff and then tearing up the house looking for it. As I scanned the letter again, I tried to get my thoughts together. *What do I say to him?* I hesitated a few times before dialing the number he put at the bottom of his letter. I honestly didn't know how to approach the conversation with Jason. *Maybe I'll just say that to him.*

When I finally called the number, it rang a few times before going to voicemail. *Damn, I wanted to get this over with now.* As I left a message, a call beeped in. When I checked the Caller ID, it was Jason's number.

"Hello, this is Natasha." I answered that way so he would know exactly who had just called him.

"Ms. Natasha? Hi, this is Jason. I'm glad you called."

"Hi, Jason. How are you?"

"I've seen better days, but I'm doing okay." His voice was deep; he didn't sound like the little boy I remembered.

"That's good." I didn't know what else to say.

"How are you doing, Ms. Natasha?"

"I'm doing okay, too."

"My mom told me that you have three kids now. That's great."

*Is it?*

"Yes, they are a handful." I smiled a little.

"Well, I don't want to take up too much of your time. I didn't want to put this in the letter, but I was actually hoping you could go with me to, um…" I heard a sadness creep into his voice. "To Aisha's grave."

"Sure, I could do that."

*Can I?*

"I don't want to go alone. Are you sure it's okay?"

"Sure, it's no problem. When do you want to go?"

"Whenever it's a good time for you. I know you must have a busy schedule, but the sooner the better."

"Okay, let's go this weekend."

"Really? That sounds good."

"Yes, we can go this weekend."

"Okay. I have my license now, so I could meet you somewhere. I know where the cemetery is. Harmony, right?"

"Yes." I fought to hold in my tears. *How am I going to do this?*

"But I don't remember where, um, she's buried."

"Well, I could meet you in the parking lot where the 7-Eleven is. I think it's still there. Either way, we can touch base on Friday, and you can let me know if you want to go on Saturday or Sunday."

"Well, I think early Saturday morning will work for me. I have to work in the evening on Saturday and most of the day on Sunday."

"Okay, sounds good. I'll make arrangements with my husband so he can stay home with the kids."

"Okay, Ms. Natasha. Thanks again for calling. You have no idea how much this means to me."

"No problem, Jason. Talk to you in a couple of days."

"Okay, bye."

"Bye."

*Okay, I got through the phone call, but I have no idea what the visit to Aisha's grave is going to be like.*

I contemplated whether or not I should tell Tyrone that I decided to go to Aisha's gravesite with Jason. He mentioned he wanted us to go together. I wasn't sure if Jason was going to be comfortable with Tyrone there since he didn't know him. Plus, he may want to talk to me about Aisha, so I didn't want to assume Jason would be okay with that.

When I mentioned to Tyrone that I needed him to be home with the kids for a few hours on Saturday morning, he agreed without any questions. I was shocked. *Did he even care where I was going?* Maybe he assumed I was going to do some shopping. I didn't see any reason for me to keep where I was going a secret, so I told him that when I finally called Jason, he asked if I would visit Aisha's grave with him.

Tyrone kissed me on the lips and said, "That's wonderful you're doing that for him, Natasha."

I was confused. *That's it? No argument? No, 'I thought we were going to go together'? Wait. Why am I looking for a fight?*

Friday arrived, and I called Jason to see if he could meet me at ten o'clock the next morning. He agreed and thanked me again. After hanging up, I sat on the edge of the bed and thought about Aisha until Tyrone walked in our bedroom.

"Are you okay, babe?"

"Yes, I think so."

"Natasha, I know this is hard for you, and I can't imagine what this must be like for you. I know you miss her. I miss her, too. But you were there for her every day."

"Tyrone, don't downplay how you feel. I know that's what you're doing."

Tyrone sighed. "I guess I am. I wasn't around. I should've been around. It really hurts that I wasn't there to see her grow up."

I was surprised when I heard myself say, "That was the past. You're here now, and that's all that matters."

*Have I finally stopped blaming him?*

"It means a lot to hear you say that." Tyrone smiled.

~

As I drove to meet Jason the next morning, thoughts of Aisha clouded my mind. *I wonder if she knows how much she's missed.* Upon pulling up at the 7-Eleven, I saw Jason leaning against his car drinking what appeared to be a cup of coffee. He hadn't changed much, only more facial hair. When he saw me pull up, he smiled. I had the same car from when I used to drop them off at the movies.

"Jason, it's good to see you." I hugged him.

"Good to see you, too, Ms. Natasha. Do you want a cup of coffee before we go?"

"No, thanks."

"Okay. I already stopped along the road and picked up some flowers for her grave." Tears welled up in his eyes as he spoke.

*Oh, God, we're not even at the gravesite yet, and this is already hard for both of us.*

"I'm sorry, Ms. Natasha. I still can't believe she's gone. She's really gone. It's been over two years, and I can't seem to get it together."

"Jason, never apologize for how you feel, okay? I completely understand. Take as much time as you need."

"I think I'm okay to go now."

We both got into our cars, and I led the way to Aisha's gravesite. While driving through the cemetery, I wondered if this was where Dianne buried her baby.

*Did she have a funeral for him? How could I have been so insensitive? She says she forgives me, but I can tell our friendship is not the same anymore. Why would she ever trust me? I wouldn't trust me if I was her.*

Deep in thought, I almost drove past the site. I took a deep breath before getting out of my car. *Okay, Natasha, you must stay strong for Jason,* I thought to myself. Jason got out of his car holding onto the flowers he had bought for Aisha's grave. After he walked over to me, I escorted him to where she was laid to rest. He bent down, brushed off her headstone, and placed the flowers on her grave. He traced over her name with his fingers and allowed his tears to flow freely. Then he sat down next to her grave and folded his hands as if he was praying. I felt the pain he was feeling. I may have lost my daughter, but he lost his first love.

When he looked up at me, I smiled.

"Jason, in your letter, you asked me how to let Aisha go."

His tears continued to fall.

"Unfortunately, I can't answer that. I haven't let her go myself. I don't think we have to, but we have to find a way to continue to live our lives. Her memory will always live with us. Don't ever forget that."

He pulled out a picture and handed it to me. It was the picture I took of them when they were going to their high school homecoming dance. Probably the last photo they ever took together.

"I know we were young, but I wanted to marry her. She said after college we could get married. I was afraid she was going to meet someone else and not want to be with me anymore, so I convinced her that we should get married before college." He smiled. "When she told me she might be pregnant, she was scared, but I was happy. I was going to be there for her, but she wasn't pregnant."

*Do I really have to listen to this?* I handed him back his picture.

"Jason, you have your whole life ahead of you. It may not seem like it now, but you will love again. I think Aisha would want you to be happy."

"Happy? I don't even know what that is anymore." He sighed.

Losing someone close was never easy, and I didn't know what to say to ease his pain.

"Well, we can go grab a bite to eat and talk some more if you want. I'm not rushing you or anything. Just let me know when you're ready. Take your time."

"Okay, but do you mind if I have a few moments alone before we go?"

"Sure, no problem."

As I headed toward my car, I could hear him say, "Aisha, why did you leave me? I need you." I tried to hold it in, but I broke down once I got in my car. That was the same question I wanted answered.

After about five minutes, he headed to my car.

"Do you still want to get something to eat?" I asked after rolling down the window as he approached.

"Sure, where?"

"Let's find an IHOP. I could use some sirloin tips, scrambled eggs, and potatoes."

"Sounds good. I'll follow you."

Arriving at the IHOP in College Park, we walked in and were seated immediately. I was glad because I was hungry. I already knew what I wanted to order, and Jason said he wanted the same thing. I asked the waitress if she could take our order when she asked us what we wanted to drink. They had the tendency to disappear thinking a person needed time to decide what they wanted to order, and I was ready to eat. The waitress took our order for the sirloin tips, scrambled eggs with cheese, and redskin potatoes. I always substituted those for the hash browns. We both ordered a large orange juice and the toffee cappuccino. Their coffee wasn't that great, but the cappuccino was the best option they had. The waitress brought our juice within a couple of minutes and said she would be right back with the cappuccinos.

*Thank goodness it isn't crowded in here.*

Searching for something to say to break the silence, I asked Jason what he studied in college.

"Information Technology," he responded with enthusiasm.

"Great field."

"Yeah, I love computers. I actually want to get into graphic design."

"Definitely a great field."

"Yeah. Although I love computers, I love to be creative."

The waitress brought our cappuccinos, smiled at Jason, and said our food would be right out. He lowered his eyes.

"I think she likes you, Jason." I smiled.

"How does she know I'm not *with* you?"

"I'm sure she can see I'm old enough to be your mother. She probably thinks *I am* your mother."

"I guess so." He sighed and shook his head.

"Jason, I don't want to sound like your mother, but have you dated anyone since Aisha died?"

That question seemed to pierce his heart. He frowned and focused his attention out the window.

"Jason, I'm not going to give you a lecture because I'm sure you've heard this already. However, you have to find a way to move on."

When he looked into my eyes, I could see his pain and confusion. This young man really needed help.

"I know." He barely spoke above a whisper. "I'm gonna try."

Once our food arrived, we ate in silence. The sirloin tips were cooked just the way I liked them; well done. I wasn't sure how fast I was eating, but my food was gone while Jason still had a full plate.

"Jason, are you okay?"

"Yes, I guess I wasn't as hungry as I thought. But I'm okay. Just thinking."

"It's not a problem. Get a box and take it with you. You may want to eat it later when you get home. Is there anything else on your mind that you want to talk about before we leave?"

"No, but I want to thank you again for taking time to take me to Aisha's gravesite."

"No problem. Call me if you ever need to talk."

As I pulled out my wallet to pay the bill the waitress left on the table, Jason insisted that he pay for the meal. He said it was his way of saying thank you.

"Jason, you don't have to pay. It's okay."

"I really want to."

"Okay. Well, thank you."

The waitress must have noticed that Jason didn't eat his food because she brought him a box without him asking for it. Avoiding eye contact with her, he thanked her for the box. He then transferred his food from the plate into the Styrofoam container, and we got up to leave. The waitress waved, obviously hoping to get Jason's attention, but again, he blew her off.

"Ms. Natasha, I can't thank you enough for doing this for me."

"Anytime."

"Do you mean that?"

"Sure, just let me know."

"Okay, I will." He smiled, and it warmed my heart to see him smile, finally.

Jason walked me to my car, and I gave him a hug goodbye. Although he only had one arm around my waist because he was still carrying his food, his embrace seemed to be more than friendly. *Am I imagining this?* He rubbed his hand up and down my back a few times very slowly and sensually, then allowed his hand to graze my hips. Okay, not graze, almost like a caress. Hopefully, that was an accident. I tried to break away from his embrace, but he pulled me closer. I froze. *This can't be happening.* When he leaned in to kiss me, I called out his name. He appeared to be in a trance.

"Jason!"

"Huh? Oh, shit...I mean, shoot. I'm so sorry, Ms. Natasha. For a moment, I thought I was holding Aisha. I'm really, really sorry." He was overly apologetic as he released me from his grasp.

"It's okay, Jason. Hopefully, you can get some rest before you have to go to work. You look tired. We'll talk soon."

"Okay, and again, I'm so sorry."

"No problem." I hurried into my car and left the parking lot of IHOP. He was still standing there when I checked the rearview mirror.

*Close call. I didn't need that on my conscience. I probably should check on him later. He looked distraught. Poor thing got confused. Right?*

That was normally when I would call Dianne and tell her what happened, but she didn't seem as receptive to my phone calls anymore. Of course, that was my perception. *I'll probably call her later on.*

# CHAPTER 32
## *Dianne*

⟨❦⟩

*I WAS BACK IN MARITAL BLISS* after Nelson and I celebrated our wedding anniversary. We took the time to rediscover why we fell in love from the beginning. I smiled to myself again at random thoughts, and that was how I knew we were moving in the right direction to repair the damage to our marriage. I felt happy again.

When I arrived home after girls' night out, I was a bit nervous. I entered the house slowly and softly called out Nelson's name. No response. I could hear soft jazz coming from our family room where he normally read the mail and drank a cold beer. *But why is he down here this late?* I walked into the family room, and Nelson was in there still fully dressed with his Brooks Brothers suit on. Nelson looked at me and nodded as if I came home on cue.

"Everything okay, baby?" I spoke in a subtle tone as I put my laptop bag on the floor and proceeded to take off my trench coat. Before I could unfasten all of the buttons, Nelson walked over to me, eased behind me, and unfastened the last two buttons. He still didn't speak.

I called his name again. "Nelson?"

He just responded with soft kisses to the back of my neck as he removed my coat and placed it on one of the chairs. He gently caressed my breasts while passionately continuing to kiss my neck. I responded with deep sighs. Judging by the feel of Nelson's erection, he was ready for some of my good lovin' right there in the family room. I wasn't about to resist, although he messed up my plan to ease under the covers and wake up my sleeping husband with my lips easing up and down on his manhood.

*I thought for sure he would be in bed by now. And where is Nihya?*

I stood there in my high-waist pencil skirt, ruffled-neck blouse, and four-inch pumps, awaiting my husband's next move. He turned me around to face him, grabbed the back of my head, and kissed my lips. I reached for the zipper on Nelson's slacks so I could release his erection, but he moved my hand. "We'll get to that," was all he said.

Nelson raised my skirt up to my hips and cautiously slid down my pantyhose as if to not put a run in them. I kicked off my pumps so he could remove my pantyhose completely. Then he slid my skirt down and told me to put my shoes back on. I was confused at that point, but I obliged. Will Downing's CD playing in the background was setting the mood perfectly. He was one of Nelson's favorite artists, and sex after Will's concerts was passionately insane with my husband.

*If Nelson is listening to Will Downing, he must mean business tonight!*

I watched Nelson walk back over to the chair he was sitting in and take a long swig of his beer. One thing I could say about my husband was that he wasn't quick to just fuck. He was the "take-his-time" type. Sometimes the extra foreplay would get on my nerves, but it did build up the anticipation of the great sex we always had. One of my favorite Will Downing songs, *A Million Ways,* was playing when Nelson decided to turn down the volume. He looked at me for a minute before speaking.

"Dianne, do you know why I married you?"

"Yes, because you loved me."

"True, but that's not the only reason."

"I know we were also compatible in a lot of ways."

"Yep, but mainly because you were a freak."

"Excuse me?"

"Yeah. You know how freaky you were when we met? I liked that. Everything about you turned me on, even the sassiness and bossiness."

I stood there in silence listening to my husband basically call me a freak; I had mixed emotions about some of his comments. Curious to hear where he was going with all he was saying, I placed my hands on my hips due to impatience, but it seemingly turned Nelson on. He stroked his erection through his slacks while looking me up and down intensely. For the first time, I felt sexually violated by my own husband. Maybe I shouldn't have felt that way, though.

Nelson asked me to turn to the side and to keep my hands on my hips. I wasn't sure what for, but I did. He took his cell phone off the end table and snapped a picture. He then looked at the phone and smiled.

"Dianne, do you remember the day we met?"

"Of course, Nelson. We talked about this the other night."

"Can you believe I haven't been inside another woman since that day?"

"Is that right?" I answered, now annoyed.

*Why does he think I care to hear this?*

"Yes, because you were the kind of woman I've always wanted."

"I know. You told me that before, Nelson." I turned to face forward again.

Nelson smiled at me. "Baby, can you take your hair down for me?"

"Sure." I continued to go along with his idea of foreplay. I was surely hoping it was foreplay.

Although I went to the Dominicans to get my hair done, I mainly wore it pinned up to keep from putting so much heat on it daily. When I extracted the few bobby pins from my hair, I shook out my hair with my right hand, leaving the left hand planted on my hip. The layers in my hair allowed it to fall nicely just past my shoulders. I often thought about getting a short, sassy style like Lynda's, but Nelson would have probably had a fit.

Nelson snapped a few pictures with his cell phone, smiling at each one when he viewed them. I posed for him, but by the fifth picture, I was done messing around. Before I walked toward him, he motioned for me to stop. *What now?* He picked up the remote to the CD player and changed songs until Floetry's *Say Yes* played. I smiled and ran my fingers through my hair while thinking about the striptease I did for Nelson on the night we met. *Oh, I see where he's going with this.*

I slowly undressed while Nelson took off his suit jacket and then removed the cufflinks from his dress shirt. Once I was down to my bra and thong, I straddled Nelson and perfectly executed a slow grind that I knew definitely turned him on. I removed his tie and unbuttoned his shirt. At that moment, I remembered how we bonded the night we had sex for the first time, and we didn't just bond sexually. I stopped grinding and looked into his eyes.

"What's wrong, babe?" Nelson asked.

I wanted to say nothing was wrong, but the tears fell rapidly. The guilt of almost having an affair was eating away at me, and I didn't know how to make it stop. Nelson had forgiven me, but I didn't know how to forgive myself. He deserved the best of everything, and I wasn't sure if I was giving it to him.

Nelson gently grabbed my face and wiped my tears as he kissed me. Somehow, he loosened his pants with one hand and slid them down just enough to release his erection. I didn't want to get my juices on the pants of his one thousand-dollar suit, but he seemingly didn't care. He slid my thong to the side and entered my wetness with such passion. I moaned loudly, but just below a scream. He felt so good inside of me.

"That's right. Ride this dick, baby."

Sometimes, I hated when he talked like that during sex, but other times, I loved it. I wanted him to make love to me.

"Nelson, can we go upstairs?" I whispered in his ear.

"I want you to cum on my dick. Your pussy is so tight, babe. Damn, I don't want to bust before you."

There was nothing romantic about the moment anymore. It was obvious Nelson wanted to fuck. He must have noticed the disapproval in my body language because he slowed down his rhythm. He kept his thrusts deep and hard, just how I liked it. He squeezed my ass with every thrust, and within five minutes, I was having an orgasm. Once again, Nelson increased his rhythm and made his release inside of me. Every time we had sex, I prayed I would get pregnant. I was ready to carry his child.

*Lord, let it please happen tonight.*

After Nelson's erection softened, I eased off him, finally kicked off those pumps, and headed upstairs to clean myself up. When I got upstairs, I wrapped my hair with my satin scarf, put on my shower cap, and got in the shower. Nelson followed me into the bathroom and washed up at the sink. He pulled back the shower curtain and watched me for a few. Then he left the bathroom.

Once I was done with my shower, I entered the bedroom where Nelson sat on the bed flipping through the cable channels. We had already discussed how rarely anything good comes on cable, so I didn't know what he was searching for. I dried off, put on my lotion, eased on a nightshirt, and sat between his legs. He massaged my shoulders before he hugged me tight, caressing my breasts while in his embrace.

"Dianne, don't think the situation with you and Tyrone doesn't bother me anymore. It does, but we have to move past it. I love you so much, and it bothers me more to know that you felt rejected by me."

Remaining silent, I laid my head back on his chest.

Nelson continued speaking. "I feel that I failed you as a husband if you felt so miserable that you had to run to another man." He removed my scarf and ran his fingers through my hair. "You are my queen, and I will do everything in my power to make sure you don't feel that way again."

"Nelson, I should've handled that situation better."

"True, but you were hurting, and I didn't take it as seriously as I should have when you brought it to my attention."

I sighed. I didn't like that he was taking on the blame because it caused me to feel more guilt.

Nelson continued. "Do you know if we were in Iran, I could've had you stoned to death?"

"Oh, my God, Nelson, that's not funny." Now I really felt worse.

"I didn't mean for it to be funny. I was wondering if you knew the severity of your actions in other countries."

"Would you have had me stoned, Nelson?" I couldn't believe I was entertaining his comment.

"No, I love you too much to do that, but I saw a movie recently where the dude had his wife stoned."

"I know. We watched it together. He lied to have her stoned, though."

"I know, but I was just thinking about it."

"This makes me nervous, Nelson." I moved away from his embrace.

"Like I said, I wouldn't have done it." He pulled me back into his arms.

"Nelson, I'm sorry for hurting you and betraying your trust. I can tell this is bothering you more than you said for you to say something like that."

"I just do a lot of thinking, that's all. And that movie came to mind for some reason."

"Should I be afraid to go to sleep?" I asked with a hint of sarcasm.

"No, but you might want to keep one eye open."

"Nelson!"

"Just kidding, baby." Nelson laughed.

"Well, I'm not amused." I sighed.

"Don't worry; I wouldn't do anything like that. Like I said earlier, you're my queen."

We eased under the covers, Nelson kissed my forehead, and I drifted off to sleep.

*Lord, please watch over me while I'm asleep. Nelson is sounding a bit crazy tonight, and I'm not ready to wake up dead!*

The next morning when I awoke, Nelson sat on the edge of the bed. It appeared as if the world was sitting on his shoulders.

"Good morning, sweetheart," I said, rubbing Nelson's back.

"Good morning, baby."

"You didn't sleep well?" I asked, sensing he didn't get much sleep.

"No, I didn't, but I'm okay."

"Do you want breakfast or coffee?"

"No, nothing, but thank you, baby."

"Okay, well, let me know if you change your mind."

When I got up to wash my face and brush my teeth, Nelson followed me into the bathroom.

"Dianne, I think I'm ready to talk to Chanelle."

"Okay, just let me know when. I would like for you to go with me to Daniel's gravesite next weekend. It would be his birthday, and I don't want to go alone anymore."

Nelson grabbed me in his arms. "Sure, baby, we need to be in this together. We can go see Chanelle and then to the gravesite. It's just gonna be one emotional weekend."

"Thank you so much."

"No need to thank me. I'm your husband. I'm supposed to be there for you."

"I know, but I want you to know how much I appreciate the kind of man you are. I don't think I say it often enough."

"That means a lot to me, baby. I appreciate you, too."

I smiled.

About a week later, Nelson and I went to see his biological mother, Chanelle. She looked very happy to see him and relieved she no longer had to keep being his mother a secret. Nelson almost immediately asked about his biological father. Unfortunately, she couldn't tell him where his father was. She explained to him that his father was eighteen years old when she got pregnant. Since she was still a minor, she didn't want him to go to jail for statutory rape, so she told her mother that she didn't know who the baby's father was. She had originally lied to him and told him that she was sixteen years old, but the law wasn't sympathetic to men in underage sex cases, regardless. His family moved away after Chanelle learned she was pregnant, and he only wrote to her a few times. She could only tell Nelson that his biological father's name was Darren Jarvis and that he didn't even know he had a son. Chanelle said she led him to believe she was getting an abortion, but of course, she never did.

Tears fell from Nelson's eyes as he learned that his biological father didn't know he existed. I could understand how confused Chanelle must have been when she got pregnant at such a young age. Deep down inside, I was sure Nelson understood as well; however, that didn't seem to ease his pain.

Chanelle gave Nelson a picture of his father. He was eighteen years old in the picture, which was the last time she had seen him. The sadness in her eyes told me that it had not been an easy decision for her. Nelson stared at the picture for a few minutes before putting it in his wallet.

When we left Chanelle's house, Nelson and I went to see his parents. He wanted to tell them right away about his visit. Nelson was very close to his father, and he told me that he didn't have any intention to find his biological father. He figured it was best to leave it alone after all these years had passed. I wanted him to look for his father because Nelson could have brothers and sisters out there somewhere. Of course, it wasn't my decision, so I kept my opinion to myself. Maybe in time, Nelson would change his mind and look for Mr. Jarvis. Right now, I could see it was too much for him to consider.

We didn't do much talking on the ride home. I sensed Nelson had a lot on his mind, so I allowed him the silence he appeared to need. It was a good thing Nihya was spending time with her grandmother because in the morning, it would be time for Nelson and me to visit Daniel's gravesite. That night when we finally arrived home, Nelson and I were exhausted. Our exhaustion was probably more from being mentally drained. We showered together and immediately climbed into bed.

Nelson went with me to Daniel's gravesite as planned. When I got close to his gravesite, I noticed someone there, but I couldn't tell if they were standing in front of Daniel's or the one next to it. As I approached the site, the person turned around; it was Jonah, Daniel's father. The tears fell rapidly from my eyes, and I considered going back to Nelson's car. I hadn't seen Jonah in years, and suddenly, anger mixed with a hint of sadness surfaced. Nelson looked at me, then to Jonah, and then back at me. I was glad I had already told Nelson who Daniel's father was because it was no surprise that Jonah and Nelson knew one another. It was still an uncomfortable situation though.

"Jonah, why are you here, and how did you know where my son's gravesite is?"

"Dianne, I'm sure you probably hate me, but he was *our* son."

"Oh, so now you claim him?"

"Nelson, how you been, man?" Jonah ignored my comment and extended his hand to Nelson.

"Fine and you?" Nelson replied.

"Not too bad," Jonah responded and then looked back at me.

"Jonah, how did you know where to find Daniel's grave?"

Jonah didn't respond. He pulled an envelope out of his inside jacket pocket and handed it to me. The envelope was addressed to him with my return address where I was living when I had Daniel. I opened the envelope, pulled out the paper inside, and unfolded it slowly. It was the last letter I had ever written to Jonah with a copy of our baby's picture inside. The hospital was able to take his picture before he passed away. My knees buckled looking at the picture. Jonah reached for me, but Nelson beat him to it. I turned toward Nelson and cried into his chest. I was so tired of crying, but some very painful memories came to the surface and there was no need of holding it in.

Jonah spoke. "Dianne, I know I owe you an apology. I should've never left you alone to deal with our son's death. That was very immature and selfish on my part, and I would understand if you never forgave me. It was just too much for me, and I didn't know how to grieve. I couldn't handle seeing you so hurt when I didn't know how to deal with my own hurt. In this letter, you said that whenever I was ready to be a man, this is where I could find Daniel."

I couldn't speak. The pain of the situation was overwhelming. The fact was Jonah left me when I needed him most. He wasn't even there when I buried Daniel. *How do I forgive him for that?*

Jonah continued speaking. "Nelson, man, I know you're waiting for an explanation. When I told you about Dianne's book, I never mentioned that she and I had a past together. The two of you hit it off so well, and I didn't want to seem like a hater, so I decided not to tell you. It didn't seem necessary because I could see you were in love with her."

Nelson took a deep breath and rubbed my back.

"Plus, I was already engaged to be married. I just didn't see the point of interrupting what y'all had."

"Is that why you were in such a hurry to take the position in Boston?" Nelson asked Jonah.

"Yeah, sort of. My fiancée was ready to relocate and start our new life together, so it seemed like the perfect opportunity."

"Jonah, listen. I can't be mad at you for not saying anything about your past with Dianne, but how could you hurt her like you did? She needed you, man."

"Because he was a coward!" I snapped.

"I'll accept that, Dianne, because I should have been there for you the entire time. No words can express how sorry I am, but I can't change the past. I hope in time you will forgive me."

"Is this your first year visiting Daniel's grave?" I asked.

"No, I've been here several times. I was wondering when I would see you here. So now, here we are."

"Are you back living in the area now? Did you have any kids, Jonah?" I asked, handing him back the envelope with the letter and Daniel's picture.

"Yes, I'm back in the area, and I have three beautiful little girls. I always felt like God was punishing me by not blessing me with a son. I really wanted a son, but my wife doesn't want to try anymore."

"How old are your girls?"

"Four, two, and six months."

"Oh, I'm sure they're precious."

"What about you two, any kids?"

I looked up at Nelson with watery eyes, so he answered. "Not yet, but we're raising my daughter from a previous relationship."

"Wow, really, man? I never knew you had any kids."

"Yeah, she's twelve now. Her mom passed, so we're raising her." Nelson didn't elaborate any further, and I could tell he wasn't planning to.

"Okay, got you. Well, I'm going to leave the two of you alone and get back to my family. Nelson, you have a beautiful woman, but I'm sure you know that. Dianne, please forgive me for how I treated you. You definitely deserved better."

"Thanks, Jonah. I appreciate it."

Nelson and I stood at Daniel's grave for a few more minutes after Jonah left. The pain of losing my son ran deep, and the fear of not being able to get pregnant again haunted me.

*How do I move past this feeling?*

# CHAPTER 33

## *Lynda*

***SEVERAL WEEKS AFTER I RETURNED*** from the book tour, my period decided to play a disappearing act. I instantly considered the possibility that I was pregnant, although missed periods could be due to stress. Somehow, I knew I was pregnant, and I wasn't in a jovial mood about it either. Since my menstrual cycle had always been on time like clockwork, I made an appointment with my doctor as soon as I missed my period so I could have a blood test done. Not to mention, Zion and I did have sex without a condom, so there was no sense in being in denial about the possibility. *How could I be so irresponsible again?*

When the doctor confirmed my pregnancy, I had so many mixed emotions invading me that I decided to call Zion to see how he felt about us allowing our relationship to progress to the next level. I planned to tell him about the baby once I got his response about our relationship. If we were going to stay together, I wanted it to be because he wanted to be with me and not because I was pregnant with his child. I hadn't spoken to him much since I told him about my situation with Taye; however, I wasn't expecting to hear the words I heard from him.

"Lynda, this is hard for me to say, but I can't be there for you the way I know you are ready for a man to be there. You deserve the kind of relationship you want, and I can't give you that right now."

"Well, thanks for letting me down easy. I understand. When were you going to call me and say it was over between us?" Although I was hurting, I was angry.

"I love you, but I travel so much, and I feel like I'm always hurting you when I'm away."

I didn't respond.

Zion continued. "When I'm away, all I can do is think about you. I need to focus on my work, and so do you."

"Please only speak for yourself, Zion. I know how to balance my life."

"You know what I'm saying is true. This kind of relationship, with both of us on the go all the time, will be hard. We tried traveling together, and you see that didn't work so well."

"Or do you just want to be free to do whatever with whomever while you're on the road without feeling guilty?" I said, knowing Zion hated when I talked like that.

"Lynda, come on. Don't start. It's not like that at all."

"Yeah, okay. Whatever, Zion. But just for the record, traveling together didn't work because of *you*, not me. You're the one who turned it into some kind of competition."

"I don't want you to think I don't love you. I do, and you know I do. But the time is just not right for us to pursue a relationship."

"Once again, that's how *you* feel, and it's cool. But I get the feeling this also has something to do with what I told you about Taye."

He tried to deny it, but I sensed there was more to what he was saying. I had to agree that Zion had a good point regarding our relationship, but with me carrying his baby, this would be hard for me either way. I didn't mention to Zion that I was pregnant. It would have only complicated our situation more. I knew Zion loved me, but we both chose literary careers, which required a lot of time and focus.

I wanted my career to be successful, but I was also ready to be in love. My days were very busy, but my nights were extremely lonely. It was easy for me to call someone to get me through those lonely nights, but I wouldn't be able to even do that while I was carrying Zion's baby. I immediately thought about Xavier. How would this news affect my friendship with him?

I allowed my tears to fall freely because I didn't believe in covering up the fact that I was hurting. As painful as it was going to be, at that moment, I decided I would be moving to California if I accepted the screenwriter position that I was offered. Maybe Zion would never find out about the baby. Besides, he didn't need the *distraction* as he put it.

Zion broke the brief silence. "Lynda, please don't cry. I have something very special that I want to bring over to you. Can I come by?"

*The nerve of him. Fuck no!*

"A parting gift? How thoughtful."

"Lynda, I told you it's not like that. I want you to always remember how much I love you."

"What makes you think I want to remember? I need to move on, right? I can't accept your gift. I don't want anything from you. Goodbye, Zion."

*Isn't his seed enough? Fuck him!*

Dianne had been calling me for about a week. I knew I needed to call her back so she wouldn't continue to worry about me. I told her that I needed some time to focus on which direction I wanted to take my literary career. The truth was I needed to find a way to mend my broken heart. When I called Dianne, I immediately poured my heart out as soon as she answered the phone.

"Hey, Di."

"Well, look who it is."

"Girl, I needed some time to get my head together. I'm pregnant."

"Oh, my goodness, are you serious?"

"Yep," I said, trying not to cry.

"Pregnant? Congratulations, girl."

"I don't know if *congratulations* is appropriate for my situation. Just when I thought Zion and I were moving forward with our relationship, he told me that we shouldn't be in a serious relationship right now. On the same day, the doctor confirmed I'm pregnant. How ironic?"

"Well, what did Zion say when you told him you were pregnant?"

"I didn't tell him. I couldn't."

"What do you mean you couldn't?"

"I didn't want him to think I was saying that to keep him around, so I just let him go and didn't say anything."

"Huh?"

"Women try to use that 'I'm pregnant' scheme to keep men around. I didn't want him to think I'm that kind of woman."

"Okay, but you are pregnant, right?"

"Yeah."

"So, he has a right to know."

"I know, but—"

"But what?" Dianne yelled into the phone.

"Could you not holler at me? I'm a little sensitive right now."

"Okay, I'm sorry. But what?" Dianne asked in a softer tone.

"But I'm not sure if I want to keep the baby."

After a brief silence, Dianne finally spoke. "Lynda, can I ask why you don't want to keep the baby?"

"Because I don't want to be a single mother."

"Lynda, think about what you're saying. You can end up a single mother even if you're married first."

"I know that, but I don't want to start out that way."

"Well, just think about what you're considering."

"I already know. I've been through this before."

*Damn,* I thought to myself. I forgot Dianne didn't know about my previous abortion.

"Lynda, what do you mean? Have you been pregnant before?"

"Yes."

"Since I've known you?"

"Yeah, but I didn't want to tell you because I knew how you feel about aborting babies. I couldn't tell Natasha either because she had recently loss Aisha."

"Was Zion the father?"

"No. It was after we broke up the first time."

"So, who then? And please tell me it wasn't Maurice."

I'm sure my silence said it all.

"Lynda, answer me."

"Why would you think it was Maurice?" I asked.

"Because you always ran back to him whenever your relationships didn't work out with other men. I'm so glad that chapter of your life is over with Maurice. It is over, right?"

"Well, now it's finally over." I thought about what Maurice had said to me, although I never shared that with Dianne.

"Was he there for you?"

"He didn't know I was ever pregnant until recently."

"Lynda, are you serious?"

"What?"

"Do you think that was fair to him?"

"What difference does it make? He wasn't going to be there to help me raise the baby."

"How do you know? You didn't even give him a chance."

"I just know. He's never been consistent with anything that relates to me."

"But, Lynda, don't ever go through anything like that alone. I'm always here for you, even if I don't agree with your decision."

"I can't go through this now."

"Go through what?"

"Having a baby, Dianne, damn. Where's your mind? Oh, never mind, girl. I'm sorry. I know you have a lot on your mind, too."

"So, what are you going to do?"

"I really don't know."

"Well, please don't go through this by yourself. We're like sisters."

"Okay."

"Lynda, let me ask you something."

"Sure, what?"

"You really love Zion, don't you?"

"Yes, but it doesn't matter now. He made it clear that this wasn't working for him."

"It does matter, Lynda, and you need to talk to Zion about this. I know you're hurting, but in the end, this isn't about you. It's about your baby. I would give almost anything to carry Nelson's baby."

"I know, Dianne, but I have faith that it will happen for you and Nelson." I really wanted to get the attention off me.

"Yeah, I'm thinking positive. Girl, we're so pitiful. Let's not sit on this phone and feel sorry for ourselves."

"What do you suggest we do then?" I asked, wiping my tears.

"I don't know. Let's go out to eat or catch a movie or something, if you're feeling up to it."

"Okay, but if we go to the movies, it can't be anything sad or romantic."

"Sounds good to me."

I was thankful to have Dianne to help me through the rough days ahead, but I knew she had her own situation with Nelson to work out.

*As time goes on, I hope the pain of not being with Zion will ease a little. However, I know at some point our paths will surely cross again.*

After Zion and I parted ways, I wouldn't even glance in his direction when we participated at the same events. Occasionally, I would see him looking at me from my peripheral vision, but I refused to acknowledge him. I wanted to pretend like he didn't exist, but the baby growing inside of me would not allow me to create that illusion. I was moving closer to my second trimester when I decided to resume traveling. The beginning of my first trimester was a pain with all the morning sickness. I pretty much stayed near the "porcelain" bowl. During an event in Miami, Zion approached me as if he knew something was different about me.

"Lynda, can I talk to you for a minute?"

"No, Zion. I need to hurry and set up for this event."

"Do you mind if I help you?"

"Why would you want to help me, Zion, when you have your own booth to set up?"

"Because, Lynda, I know you're pregnant. I can tell. Why didn't you tell me?"

I stopped unpacking my books and folded my arms. "Zion, do you remember the day I called and asked you about the direction our relationship was going, and you pretty much told me it was going nowhere?"

"Yeah," he mumbled softly.

"Well, that was the day my doctor confirmed I was pregnant."

"I'm sorry."

"Don't be because I realized I wasn't sure if you were the father anyway," I lied to deliberately hurt him.

I knew my words were like an iron fist taking a blow to his ego. The shift in his posture confirmed that he couldn't handle what I said. Without saying anything, he turned and walked away. He was crushed and I was glad. That was how I felt the day I wanted to tell him that he was going to be a father; however, he ruined it with his selfishness of wanting to be 'free.'

After the confrontation with Zion, I decided not to participate in the event. It was way too emotional for me being in the same space with him. I loved that man more than he would ever probably realize, and I couldn't stop thinking about the great father I knew he would be to our child. I didn't want to interrupt his career or his life for that matter, so I explained to the event's coordinator that I was pregnant and not feeling well. I wasn't concerned with a refund for my booth space; I just needed to get as far away from Zion Jones as possible.

# CHAPTER 34

## *Natasha*

*VISITING MY FOSTER MOTHER* was a last-minute decision that Tyrone and I made after a long conversation regarding how long it had been since I'd seen her. It wasn't as if I intentionally stayed distant, but I never really realized how much time flies by when you're simply living your life. During the conversation with Tyrone, it was brought to my attention that I hadn't seen my foster mother since shortly after Aisha's funeral. I didn't even speak to her by telephone like I used to before Aisha died, so I definitely needed to make it a priority to be in touch with her more often. She took great care of me after my parents died, and I wanted to make sure she continued to be a part of my life, although I was grown.

When I called my foster mother to let her know that we were thinking about visiting, she seemed extremely excited. Therefore, there was no way I could've changed my mind. I didn't feel like packing and doing any traveling with small kids, but Tyrone reminded me that it shouldn't be so bad since the flight to Atlanta wasn't very long from Baltimore Washington International Airport. I knew he wanted to be back in Atlanta to check on his mother's house. I had discovered in a conversation with Tyrone that he still owned it. It was currently vacant, but he said he couldn't bring himself to sell it.

We planned to stay only for the weekend since Tyrone had started a new job and wasn't ready to put in leave requests so soon. I told him in the federal government that wasn't such a big deal as much as it was in the private sector, but he still didn't want to take time out of work unless it was extremely necessary. That logic was from the same man who walked off his previous job and didn't officially resign until months later. *Go figure!*

We had an easygoing flight since the girls slept most of the way to Atlanta. I was extremely grateful for that because I could see the disgusted look on the people's faces when they saw us get on the plane with three kids. Tyler was excited about being on the plane, so he wanted to look out the window. If he wasn't looking out the window, his eyes were fixated on his *Toy Story 3* movie that was playing on the portable DVD player we bought him. It was one of the smartest purchases we ever made. He was content watching the movie with his earphones on.

*How many times can this child watch that movie?*

We rented a car before we left the airport to make things easier for us to transport all of our stuff. I called my foster mother as we parked the car in front of her house to let her know we had arrived. Being back at my foster mother's house was definitely a bittersweet moment. I was glad to see her, but I didn't really care to be back in Atlanta. The area brought back too many unpleasant memories for me; however, I managed to put a smile on my face. I was barely out of the car when she rushed over and greeted me with a nice, firm hug. Tyrone maneuvered his way to the porch holding the girls, one in each arm. I held Tyler's hand, and he looked startled when she rushed over to us.

"Tyler, say hi. This is your Grandma Sadie."

Tyler said hi shyly and then held my hand tighter. I hoped she didn't try to hug him because the way he was holding onto me, he may have cried if she attempted to touch him.

"Oh, my goodness, Tyrone. Look how handsome you are," my foster mother said, as she kissed Tyrone on the cheek. "You guys should be very happy. You have a beautiful family. God is good."

"Yes, He is," Tyrone responded.

"Well, come on inside so y'all can get settled. Natasha, your brother is on his way here to see you. I told him you were coming to visit."

I paused in the doorway as if I had seen a ghost.

Tyrone looked at me with confusion when he saw my expression. Bobby was the only one I was close to since he was around my age, and I wasn't looking forward to seeing him. Although my foster mother had several foster kids, I didn't get close to any of them since most didn't stay long due to being adopted. They were younger, so it was easier for them to get adopted. I didn't want to be adopted since I was already sixteen when she took me in.

"Tyrone, you remember Bobby?" I asked.

"Oh, yeah."

"That's who she's referring to, I'm sure."

"That's exactly right, and he's excited to see you. I want to warn you, though; he's not looking so well. Got caught up using drugs and all that nonsense. I tried to help him best I could." Ma Sadie shook her head.

"I know you did, so I hope you're not holding onto any guilt for the way he turned out."

She just smiled at me. I could see in her eyes that she was somehow holding herself responsible for Bobby's chosen lifestyle.

As we proceeded inside, I noticed not much in her house had changed. The same photos were in the same spot as I remembered. Only difference was that some new ones joined them. She had the same floral-patterned furniture and the same dark drapes somewhere in the burgundy color scheme. I would've loved to be able to help get her house upgraded to something more modern; however, since I wasn't working, I had to ensure we could afford it. That would be my gift to her for all she'd done for me.

"Well, I cleaned up the guestroom in the basement so y'all could sleep down there."

"Thanks, Ma Sadie."

"Yes, thank you," Tyrone replied.

"It looks like your babies could use a nap. I'm sure they're tired from all the traveling."

"I'm tired, too, actually." I yawned.

"I'm sure you are. It's a lot to travel with kids in tow. Rest up while I go finish dinner. It should be ready in about an hour. Let me know if you need something to munch on until then. I have plenty of fruit and veggies."

"Okay, thanks. Sounds good."

"I'm so glad y'all are here."

"It's good to be back." I partially told the truth.

Tyrone and I took the kids down to the basement to get them settled for a nap. After putting the girls down on the bed, he headed to the car to retrieve our bags. Tyler was still holding on tightly to my hand.

"What's wrong, little man?"

"I seepy, Mommy."

"I know. Daddy is going to get your stuff so you and your sisters can take a nap."

"My seepin' bag, too, Mommy?"

"I think so, baby." He loved his Toy Story sleeping bag. He was like Linus with his blanket.

"Okay."

"Do you need to use the bathroom?" I asked him.

"No."

"You sure?"

"No," he said, nodding his head.

"Do you mean yes?" I smiled and tickled his stomach.

"Yes." Tyler laughed. It was such a joy seeing him so happy.

"When Daddy comes back, I want you to try to use the bathroom anyway, okay?"

"Okay, Mommy."

I picked him up and put him on the bed with his sisters, and they immediately crawled over to him. It was cute watching them interact like that. Tyrone walked back into the room and smiled as the kids played. He put the bags down and sat down beside me on the bed.

Tyrone nodded toward the kids and said, "These are our blessings, baby."

"I know. Things are going to be fine, right?"

"Of course they are. We love each other and we have our kids. I'm finally in the federal government, and you are going to open your boutique soon."

"So why do I feel so sad?"

"Natasha, I'm sure being here is bringing back some bad memories for you, and I understand that. I wish I could go knock on my mom's door and give her a big hug."

"Ma Sadie has been good to me, but it's not the same as if it were my parents I was visiting."

"I know, baby. But she's still your family, and she loves you."

"I know."

"So try to have a good visit, okay?"

"Yes, but I want to tell you something. Promise not to get upset?"

"I'm not sure I want to promise you that, but okay."

"When I was living here, this was Bobby's room, and he would try to get me to come down here and have sex with him."

"What! Your brother?"

"Yes. He felt since we weren't blood, it would be fine."

Tyrone sighed. "Have you told Ma Sadie about this?"

"No."

"Do you want to leave and stay at a hotel? We can if this is uncomfortable for you."

"No. Ma Sadie would be upset if I did that now."

"Yeah, true."

"We should've made that decision before coming here, but I thought I would be okay after all these years that have gone by."

"Damn, baby. I'm sorry you went through that. Why didn't you tell me before?"

"I wanted to forget, but being here has brought it all back." I had actually told Tyrone's mother years ago, but I decided not to mention it to him.

"Wow, and he's on his way here, huh?"

"Promise me that you won't say anything."

Tyrone sighed again and took off Tyler's shoes since he had fallen asleep.

"Tyrone, promise me."

"As long as he doesn't step out of line, then I won't. If he does anything to make you uncomfortable, I'm knocking his ass out. No warning!"

"Tyrone!"

"I'm serious, baby. No disrespect to Ma Sadie, but I'm knocking him out. Trust me on that one."

"I believe you, but I really hope it doesn't come to that. I'm going to see if Ma Sadie needs any help with dinner."

"I thought you were tired?"

"I am, but I'm going to go check first, okay?" I kissed him passionately on his lips.

"Girl, this ain't that kind of vacation. You better stop it."

"It was just a kiss. You can't handle a kiss?" I winked.

"Yeah, okay." He laughed.

I went upstairs to the kitchen to check on Ma Sadie who was scurrying around just as she would do when I lived there.

"Ma Sadie, do you need any help with anything?"

"No, baby, but thank you. Ma Sadie got this all under control." She smiled.

"Are you sure?"

"Yes, I'm sure. So you go downstairs with that beautiful family of yours and get some rest."

I sighed.

"What's wrong, Natasha?"

"Nothing."

"Now I've spent enough time with you to know when something is bothering you. What's on your mind?"

"I'm still having a hard time with Aisha not being here, and it's causing me to be distant with Tyrone and the kids."

"Have you had this conversation with Tyrone?"

"Yes, ma'am."

"Good. Now we can talk about it. I don't believe in being the first to know anything when it comes to marital matters. So, I'm glad he knows how you feel."

"We've discussed it a few times, but I don't want to push him away."

"Baby, losing your child was devastating to you, and I'm sure he knows that because remember, that was his child, too. I know he didn't raise her as you did, but don't think for one minute that you're hurting alone. I'm sure he has a different way to handle his hurt."

"I know. I finally understand that."

"You're going to face many challenges, but with constant communication, love, and respect, you can work through almost anything. Don't be so quick to give up when it gets rough. That man downstairs loves you. He has always loved you even if you didn't see it. Ma Sadie knows." She smiled and winked as she continued to stir a pot of what smelled like collard greens.

"Thanks for the talk. I really needed it."

"No problem. Now, are you sure there's nothing else on your mind?"

"There's so much on my mind, but I think I better get some rest. I'm feeling a bit woozy."

"Okay, we'll talk later. Get some rest."

# CHAPTER 35
## Dianne

∽◦⊚◦∾

*I NEVER THOUGHT I WOULD* hear the words, "You're pregnant," again. I sat on the table in the OB/GYN office and cried as my doctor reviewed my chart. My tears were a sign of mixed emotions. I was terrified to be pregnant again, although this was what I wanted. I explained my concern to my doctor, and she tried to comfort me as best as she could. No one could really comfort me other than God after what I went through. I felt I had failed Daniel. I constantly wondered if I didn't take care of myself while I carried him. I needed to know what I did wrong so I wouldn't fail again.

*I know life is in God's hands, but this baby has to survive*, I thought while getting dressed.

I initially went to see my doctor because my menstrual cycle was becoming more and more irregular. I was afraid I was pre-menopausal since I knew you could start in your thirties. Therefore, I was a bit surprised to learn that I was actually pregnant. According to my doctor's calculations, I was eleven weeks.

Once I got my emotions under control, I left the doctor's office and headed to the cemetery to visit Daniel's gravesite. I wanted to go somewhere to collect my thoughts before I told Nelson our great news. As I approached his grave in Harmony Cemetery's Baby Land, I saw someone sitting next to my son's grave. It was Jonah.

*Why is he here?*

"Hey, Jonah. I didn't expect to see you here. Everything okay?"

"I wish I could say yes. How are you, Dianne?"

"I think I'll make it. Nelson and I have finally conceived our first child. It has taken a while, but I'm pregnant." I managed to smile.

"Congrats, Di. Nelson is definitely a lucky man."

"Thanks, Jonah. Well, what's wrong?"

"I wish I got a chance to hold our son. I wasn't strong enough knowing he wasn't going to live, but I regret not holding him."

"Oh, I understand."

"My wife can't have any more kids. She was having some complications recently, and the doctors are saying she has to have a full hysterectomy. All this happened after she agreed to try one more time for our son. I feel like God is punishing me." Tears escaped his eyes.

"Jonah, I'm so sorry to hear that, but we have to keep telling ourselves that God knows best, although His decisions often hurt."

"Yeah, true." Jonah sighed and wiped his tears.

"I'm scared to carry my baby. I can't go through another loss. I'm barely holding my sanity together as it is."

"Well, continue to pray and things will be fine. You'll make a great mom."

"You think so?"

"Yes, definitely."

"Thanks, Jonah. I appreciate that. I guess you come out here to think like I do and to feel closer to Daniel."

"Yeah. It's so peaceful out here; easy to clear my head."

"Trust me, I know. Have you thought about adopting a baby boy?"

"My wife mentioned it, but I don't know if it will feel the same."

"Nelson just found out he was adopted. He has great, loving parents. And there may be a baby boy that needs you."

"I guess it's something to consider."

We sat in silence for a few moments.

"Well, I think I better get home and share the news with Nelson. He was supposed to be the first person I told."

"Sorry for invading your quiet time with Daniel."

"No, Jonah, don't be sorry. He's your son, too. Never be sorry for visiting his grave. I was angry with you for a long time, but not anymore. I'm glad you care. I didn't think you did."

"I apologize for making you feel like that. I loved you. He would have been about twelve now."

"Yes, he would have been." I was glad he quickly changed the subject.

"Well, good luck with everything, Dianne. I'm sure I'll see you here again."

"Yes, I'm sure. And same to you. Hang in there."

When Jonah stood up to give me a hug, I hesitated, but gave in to his embrace. He didn't let me go right away, and I didn't push away either. Jonah was my first true love, and it hurt me to see him like that. He held me tighter, and for a moment, everything good about our past relationship came rushing to the surface of my thoughts.

"I really loved you, Dianne. You do know that, right?"

"I know," I responded, moving out of his embrace. I had already got myself into trouble with Tyrone during a moment of vulnerability and I wasn't going down that road again. "I have to go, Jonah."

"I know. Take care, beautiful."

I walked quickly to my car so he wouldn't notice my tears. I couldn't keep reliving past emotions, but I could never deny I once deeply loved Jonah. However, he was my past, Nelson was my present, and his love for me was truly a gift to be treasured.

# CHAPTER 36
## *Lynda*

*DIANNE ASKED TO MEET ME* for lunch at The Carolina Kitchen in Prince George's Plaza. I knew she didn't like making that drive way out there from Fort Washington; however, I wasn't in the mood for those young kids that hung around the one in Largo near my house. She said she didn't mind meeting me at that location because she really needed to talk. *This sounds serious.*

I arrived at the restaurant before Dianne, and I was tempted to order a glass of wine to calm my nerves. *But, of course, I'm pregnant, so I can't do that.* I sighed at the thought of not having a drink for nine months.

When Dianne arrived at the restaurant, I asked if Natasha would be joining us, and she mentioned that Natasha was in Atlanta visiting her foster mother. I wondered when Dianne was going to finally make her trip back to visit her family in Atlanta. I didn't bring it up much anymore because it always seemed to upset her when I asked.

Dianne sat down and immediately shared what was on her mind. "Girl, you'll never guess what happened to Natasha."

I laughed at her eagerness and asked, "What?"

"I didn't want to tell you over the phone because I wanted to see the expression on your face."

"Okay, what? Don't leave me in suspense."

"Natasha called me right before she left for Atlanta and said she needed to talk to me about something. I always brace myself thinking that maybe Tyrone said something to her. Well, to make a long story short, she went with Jason, Aisha's boyfriend, to visit Aisha's grave. Then they went to eat, and, girl, she said he tried to kiss her."

"Oh, my God!" I laughed aloud. "No, he didn't."

"Girl, I was done when she told me that. But then, of course, I thought about me and Tyrone, and the guilt set in." Dianne sighed, then asked, "Have you thought about telling Zion about the baby?"

"Slow down, Dianne. Goodness." I laughed. "It sounds like you're on speed or something."

"Girl, life is crazy right about now."

"I know what you mean." It was now my turn to sigh.

"I went back to Daniel's grave and Jonah was there again. I did tell you about when Nelson and I saw him, right?"

"Yes, lady on speed."

"Did you say if you're gonna tell Zion about the baby?"

"Dianne!"

"What?"

"What is going on with you? Are you sure you're okay?"

"Yes, I'm fine. But when I saw Jonah, he started confessing some unresolved feelings and—"

I cut her off. "Dianne, please don't go there!"

"Oh, I'm not. Don't worry about that. I'm pregnant now anyway."

"What!" I jumped up from my chair to give her a hug, drawing attention from others in the restaurant. Of course, I didn't care. "How did you think you're just gonna throw that in like that? Oh, my goodness, I'm so happy for you. What did Nelson say?"

"Huh?"

"Please tell me that I'm not the first to know." I sat back in my seat.

"No, I told Jonah first since he was at the cemetery when I went to clear my head."

"Okay, so Nelson doesn't know yet? And how could you tell Jonah before me? You should've called me from the doctor's office."

"I know. I'm so nervous and scared, Lynda. What if—"

"Nope, I'm not doing this with you, Dianne. I know you're scared, but you must think positively."

*Where is our waiter? I'm hungry.*

"I know. You're right."

As if reading my mind, our waiter arrived at the table and took our order. We both ordered the fried whiting with potato salad and collard greens. I asked for a peach tea to drink, but Dianne just requested a glass of water. We both stared at each other for a moment and smiled.

*Mommies…*

I broke the silence. "Okay, let's go back to Natasha. Did she say if she was going to tell Tyrone?"

Dianne shrugged her shoulders. "She actually didn't say, and I didn't ask."

"Wow, I would've loved to have been there for that." I laughed.

"She said Jason claimed he zoned out and thought she was Aisha for a moment."

"It's possible. Who knows?"

"Now what about you, Lynda? When are you going to break the news to Zion?"

"He knows I'm pregnant, but doesn't know he's the father. And please, no lecture. I have to get my thoughts together." I didn't feel like going into any details about the conversation I had with him. It was too draining.

"Okay, well, I have a big day planned for Nelson and me tomorrow. I wanted to create a special moment to tell him. I was drafting ideas in my head on the way over here. Girl, I can't wait. Somehow, just saying 'Nelson, I'm pregnant' doesn't seem like enough."

"I know you're gonna do it up nice. You must tell me how everything goes right after you tell him. I wish I could be there with y'all to see his face. I know he's going to be happy."

I smiled, but on the inside, I cried. Despite any problems they encountered, Dianne and Nelson had something very special. What did I have? A drama-filled baby daddy named Zion.

*Why me?*

When our food arrived to the table, we ate as if our lives depended on it. We looked at each other and laughed in unison. *I could still use a drink, though!*

# CHAPTER 37

## *Natasha*

❦

*I THOUGHT I WAS DREAMING* when I heard Bobby's voice. Then I remembered I was at Ma Sadie's house. *Why does he talk so loudly?* I didn't know when I fell asleep, but apparently, I slept hard because I didn't hear when Tyrone and the kids left the room. I figured they were upstairs where I'd heard voices. I dreaded the moment when I finally had to face Bobby. I didn't have much to say to him. I sat on the edge of the bed and took a deep breath before heading upstairs.

"Mommy's up, Daddy," I heard Tyler say when I entered the living room.

"Well, if it isn't Sleeping Beauty," Bobby said, as he walked over to give me a hug. "It's been a long time, huh?"

*Not long enough.*

"Yes, it has." I reluctantly hugged him back.

Tyrone frowned at Bobby before asking me, "How did you sleep, babe?"

"I slept very well. I must've been exhausted because I didn't know you guys had left the room. Where are the girls?"

"Ma Sadie is giving Natalia a bath. Nevaeh is asleep in Ma Sadie's room."

"Oh, okay." I walked over and kissed Tyrone lightly on the lips and then Tyler on both his cheeks.

I sat down on the sofa next to Tyrone while Bobby sat in the lounge chair directly across from me. I was glad Ma Sadie warned me as to how Bobby looked because he was a sad sight to see. Years of drug and alcohol abuse had really aged him. I felt sorry for him. Suddenly, all of my anger and resentment toward him turned to pity.

"So, Bobby, how have you been?" I asked, not knowing what else to say.

"I try not to complain. Life has been challenging for me, but I'm making it the best way I can." He sounded sad.

"Oh, I'm sorry to hear that," I responded.

Ma Sadie entered the living room holding Natalia in her arms. I was glad she walked in because I didn't feel like engaging in small talk with Bobby.

"You finally up, baby?" Ma Sadie said to me.

"Yes, ma'am. I really needed that nap."

"I know you did. You looked exhausted. At least your girls are all clean, and Nevaeh is already asleep." Ma Sadie brought Natalia to me.

"We fed the kids already, Natasha," Tyrone said.

"Oh, did I hold up dinner?" I responded.

"No, we just wanted to feed the kids first since they were getting fussy," Tyrone explained.

Ma Sadie spoke. "Yes, and I wanted to give the girls a bath so you wouldn't have to worry about that."

I smiled. "Thank you."

"My pleasure, baby. These are like my grandbabies, and I finally get to spend time with them."

"Babe, are you going to give Tyler a bath or do you want me to do it?" I asked Tyrone.

"I'll do it now," he replied. "That way, he can watch a movie with Natalia while we have dinner."

"Let me warm dinner and set the table."

"Ma Sadie, do you need any help?" I asked.

"No, I got it. Just rest yourself. I'm sure you stay plenty busy with the kids when you're home."

"Yes, she does, Ma Sadie. I have to beg to help her sometimes."

"Tyrone, please don't."

"Come on, little man, let's get your bath." Tyrone grabbed Tyler by his hand, then looked back at me before walking away.

I sat for a few moments before joining Tyrone in the bathroom. Since we didn't bring a playpen for the girls, I took Natalia with me.

"Mommy, girls not 'pose to see me taking a baff. Only you. 'Member you say that?" Tyler said when he saw me with his sister. He talked very well for a child his age.

"I know, but let me talk to Daddy for a second."

"What's wrong, Natasha?"

"Nothing serious. I guess I don't know what to say to Bobby," I whispered.

Tyrone must have sensed that I was uncomfortable being in a room alone with Bobby, so he suggested I finish Tyler's bath. After he took Natalia back into the living room, I bathed Tyler quickly because I was ready to eat. He appeared anxious to watch his movie, so he didn't mind a quick bath.

Once Tyler was finished with his bath and dressed in his pajamas, we headed back to the living room. Natalia was asleep on a pile of blankets on the floor. I glanced into the dining room where Tyrone, Bobby, and Ma Sadie waited for me. The table resembled the Sunday dinner that Big Momma cooked on the movie *Soul Food* with things like fried chicken, catfish, macaroni and cheese, collard greens, cabbage, candied yams, mashed potatoes, string beans, and several other dishes.

"I seepy, Mommy."

"Okay, go lie down beside your sister. Don't wake her up." I kissed Tyler on his cheek.

Tyrone had already started the movie *Toy Story 3*.

"Can I hug Daddy first?"

"You sure can."

"Okay." Tyler smiled when he saw the movie playing. After he gave Tyrone a hug, he laid down beside Natalia. He put the covers over himself and his sister. It was the cutest thing to witness.

I sat down at the table across from Tyrone. "Y'all didn't have to wait for me to eat."

"Yes, we did, and you weren't holding us up," Ma Sadie said.

"This is a lot of food, Ma Sadie. You didn't have to go through all this trouble."

"You won't be here for Thanksgiving, so, baby, this is our Thanksgiving dinner right here. And you know it was no trouble at all. I'm so glad to have you home again."

"Thank you so much. Glad to see you, too. Everything looks delicious, and I'm so hungry."

"Well, let's eat." Ma Sadie held out her hands, indicating she wanted us to join hands to say grace. That was customary when I lived with her.

During dinner, Tyrone and Ma Sadie did most of the conversing. I was too busy deep in thought, but I did manage to keep up with their conversation, as I would occasionally comment on the topic they discussed. Tyrone talked about his new job that he just started. Ma Sadie explained how she missed taking in foster kids, but she was getting too old to deal with the younger children. She mentioned that occasionally, she would take in teenagers, but it was always a temporary situation where the kids were almost grown. She seemed to cater to kids with a situation similar to mine: a teenager left without a parent due to a sudden death. Not everyone had a list of aunts and uncles to choose from to go live with after the death of a parent.

Bobby appeared more distant than I was during the entire conversation. I wished I could read his mind. Then again, I probably wouldn't have liked what he was thinking. When he finished his plate of food, he kissed Ma Sadie on the cheek and told her that he had to leave. He then waved and said goodbye to Tyrone and me before rushing out the door.

After the rest of us finished our dinner, I offered to help Ma Sadie with the dishes, but she refused. She kept telling me that I needed to enjoy this break of not having to cook and clean up the dishes. She was right. Tyrone and I decided to stay upstairs in the living room where the kids were asleep. We didn't want to risk waking them up if we took them downstairs. I really enjoyed the quiet time.

We chose to watch the movie *The Notebook*, which was one of our favorite love stories. It took me a while to get Tyrone to watch it with me, but he finally gave in one day when I gave him a brief summary of what the story was about. I loved when we reached the part in the movie when the couple reconnected after all those years because it reminded me of my situation with Tyrone.

"Goodnight, you two," Ma Sadie said, as she left the kitchen.

"Goodnight," Tyrone and I responded.

Tyrone and I lay on the floor next to the kids when I heard a slight knock at the door.

"Tyrone, could you see who that is at the door? Maybe it's Bobby. I can't think of anyone else who would be knocking at this time of night."

"Who is it?" Tyrone asked without opening the door and looking through the peephole.

"It's me, Bobby."

Tyrone opened the door and eyed Bobby as if he were a stranger. I prayed he didn't say anything about what I told him.

"I'm sorry to disturb y'all. I left my cell phone."

He brushed past Tyrone to retrieve his phone that rested on the end table next to the lounge chair where he had been sitting earlier. He looked down at me after he put the phone in his pocket.

"Natasha, can we speak in private for a minute?"

"No, she can't," Tyrone snapped.

"Do you have a problem with me talking to my sister?"

"Actually, I do!" Tyrone stepped in his face. He was clearly not happy that Bobby was back at Ma Sadie's house.

I decided to step in between them because I could see Tyrone was ready to deliver on his promise to knock Bobby out.

"Tyrone, Bobby, let's take this conversation downstairs so we don't wake up the kids or disturb Ma Sadie." I wasn't sure if she was asleep or not.

Bobby looked confused. "Is there a reason why we can't talk alone, Natasha?"

"Bobby, yes, there is a reason. I'm not comfortable around you. I haven't been since we were sixteen."

The look on Bobby's face suggested to me that he figured out what the problem was. It was confirmed when he started talking. "Oh, okay. I get it now. You want to hold me accountable for how I was when I was sixteen?"

"Okay, so you don't want to go downstairs and talk about this? Fine! Yes, I still find you repulsive, and you need to be held accountable for the way you made me feel back then. You knew you were wrong, but you tried to take advantage of me during my moments of weakness. You knew what I was going through, and you figured my self-esteem would be low enough to go along with your plan to have sex with you."

"Shh! Damn, Natasha, why the hell are you talking so loud?" Bobby snarled.

"Don't talk to her like that," Tyrone interrupted.

"I said let's talk downstairs, but you didn't want to listen to me, so here we are. Let's talk!"

"Natasha, this is real foul. You know that?" Bobby responded dejectedly.

"Are you serious, Bobby? I'm the one that's foul when you were the one who tried to *touch* me, even after I was pregnant?"

"What!" Tyrone stepped back in Bobby's face.

"Tyrone, please, baby. Let me handle this, okay?"

Tyrone never took his eyes off Bobby until Natalia started to cry. He picked her up and sat on the sofa. I was glad one of the kids woke up because there was no telling what Tyrone would've done next.

"Yeah, Bobby. That's why I was so adamant about moving in with Tyrone and his mother. I wanted to be away from you. I started to fear you."

"Natasha, I was a troubled teen who didn't know any better."

"Well, it seems like you grew into a troubled adult," Tyrone added.

"And this is coming from a weed head who didn't take care of his responsibility," Bobby rebutted.

"Yup, a former weed head with an accounting degree who is now taking care of his family," Tyrone said, sounding proud of his accomplishment.

*Whew.* I thought Tyrone was going to go off with the comment Bobby made. I was sure he wanted to, but thought about the kids and Ma Sadie.

"Bobby, listen. You were supposed to be my brother, but instead, you made sexual advances toward me that made me very uncomfortable. I didn't have any family, so I counted on you to be my family. You messed that up."

"So I guess that's why Ma Sadie looks at me the way she does. You told her, huh?"

"No, I never told her. She looks at you like that probably because of your current lifestyle. What happened to you?"

"Life, Natasha. Life happened to me."

"I'm not sure what you mean, but life happens to us all. It happened to me, too, remember? Aisha is dead, but I have to be strong and keep on living."

I looked over at Tyrone. He smiled.

"Well, I guess I'm not as strong as you and Mr. Former Weed Head over there."

Tyrone just laughed and shook his head. I knew if he wasn't holding Natalia, he would've been back in Bobby's face.

"Bobby, I'm sorry if what I'm saying is difficult for you to hear, but you have to own up to what you did. And somehow, I need to find it in my heart to forgive you so I can move on from this feeling."

"So you're not comfortable around me?" Bobby asked.

"No, I'm not," I replied.

"Okay, I get it. Well, it was nice seeing you again, Natasha. I'm sorry that I made you so uncomfortable. I was sixteen, but I guess that's not a good excuse. I was wrong. Take care of yourself and your beautiful kids."

Bobby walked toward the door and then turned to look at me and then to Tyrone. I thought he was going to say something else, but he didn't. He shook his head and left. I hoped I wasn't too harsh on Bobby, but I had to get the truth regarding how I felt off my chest. I wondered what he wanted to come back and talk about. I never gave him a chance to say what was on his mind. Maybe he wanted to know why I was acting so cold toward him. Well, now he had his answer!

# CHAPTER 38

## Dianne

⁓◦❦◦⁓

*MEETING NELSON FOR LUNCH* was as exciting as it was before we got married, and I was prepared to tell him about the baby growing inside of me. I knew he would be ecstatic about the pregnancy because it was what he talked about after each time we made love. I wanted our lunch date to be perfect, so I planned a picnic-style lunch at the park. It didn't matter that it was in the middle of winter because thanks to so-called *global warming*, the temperature was well above the norm. I was glad the weather cooperated with my plans because a parent of one of my clients, who was the owner of a small bistro, agreed to set up the picnic to be ready for our arrival. Nelson put in annual leave to take the rest of the day off, and I ensured I didn't schedule any counseling sessions past noon.

I thought of Usher's song *Trading Places* when I arranged to pick Nelson up from work in a limousine with flowers and champagne waiting. The driver would chauffer us around for the entire afternoon. I booked a four-hour time slot from 1:00 p.m. until 5:00 p.m. Instead of having Nelson meet me outside, I decided to take the flowers to his office so his co-workers would really have something to talk about.

When I stepped off the elevator on the floor where Nelson's office was located, I heard a vaguely familiar voice.

"Well, if it isn't the sexy and *extremely* gorgeous Ms. Dianne Marshall."

I almost passed out when I turned to see Ryan standing there. I was sure the expression on my face indicated how shocked I was to see him.

"Hey, there. How are you?" I didn't bother to mention my married last name.

"I'm good. Just got a permanent job working here. Yeah, finally graduated college and got accepted to an internship program here, but it is still a permanent position. I just get a chance to rotate every six months for two years to see where I would like to permanently be assigned. You work here, too?"

"Well, congratulations. No, I'm here to see my husband." I tried to play it off, but the thoughts of having sex with him when he was an intern for my agency were teasing me, so my nerves got the best of me.

"Oh, okay. Are those flowers for him?"

"Um, yes. I like to grace his office with reminders of me."

"Lucky man." Ryan smiled.

"Yes, I am." I heard Nelson's voice behind me.

*Lord, take me now!*

"Hey, babe," Nelson said and kissed me on the lips.

I couldn't have felt more awkward. The look on Ryan's face described how I felt.

"I see you met my new intern, Ryan Lawson," Nelson said.

*Lord, didn't I ask You to take me now? Where are You?*

"Yes." It was seemingly the only word I could manage to utter.

"Well, babe, I'm going to put these flowers in my office, and I'll be right back so we can go enjoy this beautiful weather," Nelson said.

"Okay, sweetheart," I responded.

Ryan was no longer smiling, and his demeanor shifted to an uncomfortable state.

"Wow, small world, huh?" Ryan asked.

"Yes, it really is. But don't worry, Ryan. What happened with us was a long time ago and very brief. Nelson is a very understanding man."

"You're going to tell him?"

"Yes, I can't keep something like this from my husband."

Ryan sighed. "Man, this is going to be a long six months."

I just winked at his response because I saw Nelson heading our way. Ryan shook his head and walked away.

"Ready, babe?" Nelson asked.

"Sure am."

"Thanks for the flowers. Why you gotta be making these jealous dudes tease me?" Nelson laughed.

I grabbed Nelson by the hand, and we entered the available elevator. It seemed one showed up just in time, and a couple of his co-workers smiled at us when they got off. Nelson pulled me close to him and caressed my curves as soon as the elevator doors closed. As we kissed for a few seconds, I could feel Nelson's erection forming.

"Nelson, you can't walk out of the building like that, so stop it," I teased.

"I can just close my suit jacket. It's all good."

When we walked out of the elevator, I stopped before we exited the building. I escorted him away from the guard's desk so no one would hear what I was about to share with my husband.

"Nelson, before we leave this building, I need to tell you something."

Nelson responded, "Let me guess. You fucked my intern before?"

I didn't respond, but I guess my silence told it all.

"What? Dianne, are you serious? I was just joking."

I sighed. "It was a very long time ago and one time only."

"So that's why he looked like a deer caught in the headlights when I walked up." Nelson shook his head.

"Yes, so now you know. I didn't want to proceed with our afternoon with that on my mind."

"Okay. I appreciate you telling me. I'm glad it came from you rather than him. You know how men can be with their sarcastic remarks. I don't know him well enough to know if he would do that, but I may have to ask them to assign him to someone else."

"That's understandable. Baby, I'm sorry."

"But, seriously, Dianne, thank you for being up front about this. I know it was hard. Your life is seemingly turning out like the movie *Crash*." He laughed as if we were watching Martin Lawrence in stand up.

"Yes, and considering other things that have happened, I don't want to hold in any more secrets. I love you too much for that."

"I love you, too. Now let's get out of here."

"And stop laughing. It's not funny, Nelson." I pouted.

As we left the building, I walked toward the limousine. A few steps ahead of Nelson, I looked back at my caramel sensation who seemed a bit confused as to why I headed toward the limo. The driver got out and opened the door for us when he saw me approaching.

Nelson stopped and said, "Wow! Now this is a surprise!"

Once inside the limousine, Nelson kept thanking me for being his wife. He didn't have to thank me; I felt just as blessed to have him as my husband. I was sure my romantic gestures stroked his ego. He was still a man, and that was seemingly needed for the majority of them. I didn't do the things I did for Nelson to stroke his ego on purpose; I was simply being me. I loved my husband, and I wanted to keep our marriage hot, spicy, and exciting as much as possible. I didn't think our marriage would be so much work because we were definitely on the same page of life and we loved each other equally. Nevertheless, we were not exempt from problems and day-to-day issues. I learned that the hard way.

The limousine arrived at the park, and Ramon had set up our picnic area beautifully. When I told him to use his imagination and be creative, he did that and more. My only request was for him to use a fold-up table and chairs because I wasn't a big fan of sitting on the grass whether on a blanket or not. It simply wasn't my thing. He used heart-shaped placemats, which had our names on them. *When did he have time to do this? I just called him yesterday.* Of course, we couldn't have alcoholic beverages in the park, so Ramon had a bottle of sparkling water to go along with our turkey club sandwiches and fruit salad in little heart-shaped bowls. I could tell the scene moved Nelson because his eyes watered, although he didn't let a tear fall. Ramon had exceeded my expectations, so I was a bit teary-eyed myself. A few people smiled at us as they walked through the park.

"Dianne, this is beautiful, babe. Thank you!"

"No, thank you, Nelson, for loving me unconditionally."

I asked the limousine driver to come back in an hour sharp. Ramon would also return in an hour to clean up and get his table and chairs.

Once Nelson and I were done with our lunch, we took a walk. After about ten minutes of walking, I broke the news to Nelson that I was pregnant. If you ever wanted to see a grown man cry, that would've been the scene to witness. He held onto me for what seemed like hours. After I was finally released from his embrace, I handed him the sonogram picture of our baby. I was further along in my pregnancy than I expected. Due to my irregular periods, it was hard to determine how far along I was, so the doctor did the sonogram. Technology was definitely amazing.

The limo driver and Ramon returned within minutes of one another, which I was very pleased with. I loved when people were punctual and respected my time. I was glad I went to the bank earlier so I could leave an extra tip for both of them. Ramon handled the clean up in the park so Nelson and I could continue with our plans. In the limousine, Nelson grabbed my hand and opened up to me.

"Dianne, thanks again, sweetheart. Today was perfect. You've made me so happy with the news of our baby on the way. I know pregnancy scares you, but please don't worry yourself. We're going to think positive and stand on faith that God will see us through this. Okay?"

"Okay." *I wish I were as optimistic as Nelson about the situation.*

We had an hour left in our limousine service, but Nelson indicated he wanted to go home and make love before Nihya got home from dance practice. Although the doctor said it was okay to continue to have intercourse as normal, I was scared to have sex during my pregnancy. I was sure Nelson would be gentle, though, now that he knew we had a baby on the way. I told the limousine driver he could drop us off back at my office where I could get my car and drive home.

Once we arrived home, Nelson took me by the hand and led me up to our bedroom. Judging by the way Nelson undressed me, I could tell he was anxious, but I could also sense something was wrong. I wanted to read his mind because the way he studied my body with his eyes was almost uncomfortable.

"What's wrong, baby?"

Nelson sat down on the edge of the bed and rubbed the left side of his chest.

"Oh, my God, Nelson, what's going on? Are you okay?"

When he closed his eyes and didn't respond, I knew I had to call 911. When the operator answered, I was hysterical.

"Ma'am, please calm down so I can help you."

"Okay, my husband needs help. I'm not sure what's happening, but I think he might be having a heart attack."

"Help is on the way. Please try to stay calm." She confirmed my home address, I assumed based on my telephone number.

"Yes, that's the correct address. Please hurry!"

"Ma'am, can you feel a pulse?"

"Very faintly."

"Do you know CPR?"

"Yes, I do."

"Okay, if his pulse weakens, administer CPR to him."

"Okay."

"Are you okay, ma'am?"

"No, I'm not okay," I cried.

"Just try to stay calm. Help is on the way."

# CHAPTER 39
## Natasha

*I WISHED BOBBY AND I* would've been able to have a civilized conversation to discuss my feelings toward him, but my emotions took over the situation. I didn't realize Tyrone would be so angry when I told him, but I understood. My visit with Ma Sadie was very brief, and I wished I spent more time with her. A weekend wasn't long enough to visit and catch up, so I planned to return to see her soon.

The next morning, I woke up before Tyrone and the kids, so I went upstairs to make some much-needed coffee. Tyrone and I ended up taking the kids downstairs after Bobby left because Tyrone didn't want to sleep on the floor. At some point during the night, Ma Sadie brought Nevaeh downstairs.

Ma Sadie was in the kitchen, and I could smell coffee already brewing. She seemed a bit sad when I entered.

"Good morning, Ma Sadie." I kissed her on the cheek.

"Good morning, baby. I hate that y'all are leaving so soon."

"I know. I wish we were staying longer, but Tyrone just started his new job."

"Well, make sure you come back and visit me real soon, okay?"

"I sure will."

Ma Sadie sighed and sat down with her cup of coffee.

"Natasha, make yourself a cup of coffee so we can talk a bit before it's time for you to leave."

As I poured coffee into a mug and added cream and sugar, I wondered if she heard the commotion last night. No sooner than I sat down, she shared what was on her mind.

"Natasha, of course I overheard your conversation with your brother last night, and I'm very upset that you didn't tell me what was going on."

"I know and I'm sorry. I just didn't want you to be upset with Bobby, so I felt it was easier for me to go and live with Tyrone and his mother."

"I told you to always come to me when you needed me, right?"

"Yes, ma'am."

"So, why didn't you?"

"It's not that I felt I couldn't come to you. I just didn't want to cause any trouble."

"This really hurts me, you know that? Bobby shouldn't have ever put you in that kind of situation. He is your family, and family is supposed to protect one another."

"I know, but don't be upset with him. We were teenagers."

"Teenagers or not, he knew right from wrong. I taught him myself. I raised y'all to be brother and sister, not whatever nonsense he tried to have going on with you. Where did I go wrong with him?"

"Ma Sadie, you can't blame yourself. Please don't because you did us a favor by taking us in and providing a loving home. After what most of us suffered, we needed you, so don't feel like you failed us somehow. You didn't. You're right; Bobby was old enough to know better."

Ma Sadie cried and I felt terrible she had to find out about the secret I'd kept all these years. It was really upsetting her, so I wished I had kept it to myself.

"Natasha, I'm so glad you turned out to be such a beautiful young woman with a lovely family. I'm so proud of you. Bobby could've had a good life, too, but he chose to handle his demons differently than you did."

"His demons?"

"Yeah, his problems from his childhood. I call those demons."

"Oh. Yeah, I think I've heard that before."

"Yes. So, you make sure no matter what you go through, you continue to work it out with your husband. You have something to be proud of, chile."

I smiled. "Thanks. I will."

Although curious to know how Ma Sadie ended up taking in Bobby as a foster child, I wasn't sure if it was a good idea to bring it up. It was as if she read my mind because she offered an explanation.

"Natasha, not all kids were fortunate to be raised by two loving parents. Chile, your mother and father loved you. You know that, right?"

"Yes, ma'am, I do."

"They made sure you had the best of everything, and you were so well-mannered. Bobby didn't come from that kind of household. He was raised in a very abusive environment, so that's how he became my child. His mother would drop him off at my house every day, and his father would threaten her life. One day, she never showed up to pick him up. I called a friend of mine who was a police officer to check on her, and that's when they found her body." Ma Sadie sighed.

"Oh, no, that's awful. I didn't know."

"Well, I didn't make it a habit of discussing what happened, you know. It was easier for the kids to transition to living with me without the reminder of what happened to them."

"How old was he?"

"About six, and he would ask if his mother was coming to get him every day. It broke my heart. His mother loved him, though. Unfortunately, she couldn't protect herself from that crazy man of hers, and it's hard getting the law involved unless someone is already dead."

"I know. It's really a shame."

"Yes, it is." Ma Sadie took a sip of her coffee.

Tyrone entered the kitchen, said good morning to Ma Sadie, and kissed me on the cheek.

"You want some coffee, babe?" I asked him.

"Yes, but I can get it. Thank you, baby. I'm going to hurry and go back downstairs before the kids wake up."

*He is so good with them.*

"Okay. I'll be down in a few."

"Don't forget we need to check on my mother's house before we head to the airport."

"Why don't you two go ahead? I'll look after the kids. It's still early, so go and spend a couple of hours together, check on the house, and then I'll have the kids ready by the time you come back. I'll make sure they're fed and dressed. They'll be just fine."

The girls seemed fine with her, but I wasn't sure how Tyler would act. Still, I agreed. I didn't want her to feel as if I didn't trust her.

"Okay, thanks. We won't take long because we need to catch our flight."

Tyrone and I took turns in the shower and quickly dressed. As in a domino effect, the kids woke up one by one before we left to check on Tyrone's mother's house. We packed our things and put them in the rental car so we wouldn't have to worry about doing it when we returned to get the kids. I was grateful that Ma Sadie offered to keep the kids because it was nice to have a couple of hours alone with my husband. Ma Sadie seemed sad when we carried our stuff outside to the rental car. It bothered me that she was alone most of the time, although Bobby stopped by her house regularly.

During the drive, Tyrone and I were quiet. I was deep in thought about what Ma Sadie had told me about Bobby, and I didn't realize when we were at our destination.

"Natasha, did you hear me?"

"No, I'm sorry, Tyrone."

"I asked if you were okay."

"Yes, I'm fine. Just thinking about some things. You ready to go inside?"

"Yes. We don't have to stay long. I just need to make sure there are no issues with the house in case I decide to rent it. I really don't want anyone living in her house, though, other than us."

*Please don't go there, Tyrone.*

"I guess I can understand that. This is where you grew up, so it's sentimental for you."

"Yeah, it is. I would love to move back here one day. What do you think about that?"

"Moving back to Atlanta? I'm not sure, Tyrone."

*I knew it. He went there.*

"I don't mean anytime soon, but maybe one day, we could move our family here."

"Okay, we can talk about it."

*I don't know if I want to be in the same city as his ex-wife.*

"Cool. Well, let's go inside so I can take a quick look around."

I was amazed at how clean the house was considering no one lived there. Tyrone told me that he had a cleaning company come to clean the house every six weeks. That seemed excessive to me, but I decided not to comment. Tyrone was a neat freak, so I wasn't surprised that he ensured the house was spotless. But every six weeks to clean a vacant house?

Before we left the house, Tyrone grabbed me into his arms and looked into my eyes.

"Natasha, this is where it all began."

"What, babe?"

"My love for you. We were young, but I knew I loved you, and I prayed you would be my wife one day."

"Aw, really?"

"Yep. Do you ever wonder why life takes us in different directions and then brings us back together? I know there's some kind of lesson to be learned during the time we're apart."

"Yes, I wonder about stuff like that a lot. We both went through so much, only to find our way back to each other. I just wish we had Aisha, too."

"I know, Natasha. It definitely hurts that she's not here."

"Well, we have three little ones now. Speaking of which, I think we need to be heading back so we can have plenty of time to get to the airport."

"True dat. Now I wish I had listened to you and agreed to stay here longer so I could've visited my mother's grave. It's been a while since I've been there. One or two days of leave wouldn't have hurt like you said."

"We can come back soon. I wish we were staying longer, too, so I could spend more time with Ma Sadie."

"I know, babe. We'll just plan another visit soon."

"Sounds like a plan."

"All right. Well, things are in order here. Let's get the kids so we can head on home."

*Home?* Maryland didn't feel like home anymore. *Maybe Tyrone and I should move our family here to live.* It was definitely something to consider.

# CHAPTER 40
## *Lynda*

*LOSING MY BABY WAS THE MOST PAINFUL* experience I had at this point in my life, both physically and emotionally. I thought being shot and almost killed was devastating, but it didn't compare to the life that was literally rejected from my body. I had taken a lot for granted in my life, but having a miscarriage was something I had no control over, and it happened whether I wanted it to or not. I was just getting used to the idea of being pregnant, although Zion was not in my life anymore.

Xavier was a great help with the emotional scars. I thought for sure when I told him that I was pregnant with Zion's baby that I wouldn't hear from him again; however, Xavier was consistent, and he was there for me in a way that I could never thank him. He claimed I was helping him cope with his emotional baggage, as well. I hadn't known that his mother was in a nursing home all this time and that his sister was in a drug rehabilitation clinic.

Taye wasn't really the type to open up to me, and I didn't have a clue that he even had a sister. He kept a lot bottled up inside, and that was probably why he snapped, assuming he was the one who actually tried to kill me. No further information had come forth one way or the other.

If it wasn't for Xavier being there for me the day I lost my baby, I might have ended my own life. The physical pain was so intense that nothing I took eased my pain. That's when I knew something was definitely wrong. Xavier had brought some food to my house because I told him that I wasn't feeling well. He stopped whatever he was doing and rushed over to me. The pain became increasingly worse, and Xavier took it upon himself to place a phone call to my doctor whose number was on my refrigerator. As I prepared to go to the hospital, I had a sudden urge to use the bathroom. I eased down my pants, and that was when it happened. The fetus, my baby, exited my body, and I immediately felt a relief from all the physical pain. That was when the emotional pain began.

I didn't think it was my baby at first because there was no umbilical cord attached. But maybe it was too soon for that to occur since I was only about ten weeks pregnant; I didn't know. All I knew was that I had to carry what came out of me in a bag to the hospital so my doctor could confirm whether it was my baby or not. I still had visions of the horror in Xavier's eyes when I showed him. Once I got to the hospital, my doctor examined me and the contents of the bag. That was when it was confirmed that I miscarried, and I had to get a D&C procedure to prevent hemorrhaging or an infection.

I knew Xavier was tired of people asking if he was the father, but he handled it all extremely well. Before my procedure, I gave my cell phone to Xavier and asked him to contact Dianne for me to tell her what happened. When I woke up from surgery, Dianne was in the waiting room. I hoped this didn't bring back hard memories for her, but I really needed her. Dianne entered the recovery room and greeted me with a hug. Neither one of us could speak for a few minutes.

"Lynda, I'm so sorry this happened to you," Dianne said when she finally spoke.

"We have to follow God's plan, right?"

"I guess so." Dianne sighed.

"How's Nelson doing?"

"He's doing well. Taking it easy."

"Good. Have you seen Xavier?"

"Yes. He's in the waiting room. Poor thing looks distraught."

"I'm sure he is, but I'm so glad he was there or else I would have gone through that alone. I can't imagine having to do that by myself."

"Does Zion know, Lynda?"

"I knew that question was coming. But, no, I haven't heard from Zion."

"Since you told him that he wasn't the father?"

"Yes, but that's not what I said. I said I wasn't sure if he was the father."

"Okay, I'm not trying to upset you. Do you plan to tell him?"

"I really don't see the point. I want him to move on with his life, and I want to do the same. I'm ready for a new beginning."

We sat in silence for a few minutes until the nurse came in to take my vitals. I knew it was wrong for me to leave Zion out of the situation because that was his baby. He was the only man I slept with at the time. I loved Zion, but I no longer had any desire to have him in my life. It was unfortunate that I lost my baby, but I firmly believed in my heart that God always knew best. I had planned to tell Zion the truth, but now that my baby was gone, I didn't see the point.

Dianne asked the nurse when I was going to be released from the hospital. The nurse indicated I could leave once my doctor cleared me. He had to do another exam and sign my discharge papers. Tears fell down my cheeks as I relived the pain and emotional torture of the past several hours of my life.

"Lynda, do you need me to stay with you?" Dianne asked.

"Let me see if Xavier has to leave. I don't want to hold him up if I don't have to. Could you ask him to come in?"

"Okay."

Dianne left to get Xavier. When he entered the room, he looked so worn out. I asked him if he wanted to go home and get some rest, but he insisted on staying with me until I was discharged. I told him to let Dianne know so she could go home. There was no need of having them both there. Plus, Dianne needed to be home with Nelson since he recently had a heart attack.

Once Xavier left the room, I immediately pulled the covers over my head and cried harder than I could ever remember crying, this including when my father died. At that moment, I felt an enormous amount of guilt for having an abortion. *Is God punishing me?*

Apparently, I cried myself to sleep because the next thing I remembered was my doctor awakening me to tell me that he was about to do my examination. The emotional trauma left me feeling numb.

Within the next several hours, I was discharged and Xavier drove me home. I owed him my sincere gratitude for being there for me. I guess he cared about me more than I realized, and it was nice having a man in my life that genuinely gave a damn. I felt completely safe with him.

It was a rainy Sunday morning, but I had already decided I was going to visit my mother. It had been two weeks since I lost my baby, and I had to find the strength to stop feeling sorry for myself. During those two weeks, I only left the house to check my mail and go for my follow-up appointment. Otherwise, Xavier went to the store for me whenever I needed something. He said he would drop me off at my mother's house and then come back to pick me up, but I told him that I was okay to drive myself. He told me that he was concerned about my emotional state because I barely talked for the past two weeks. I assured him that I was fine and would let him know when I got back home.

I was glad I had recently purchased a few audio books by Joel Osteen because I needed to hear some words of inspiration during the drive to my mother's house. Joel's words always seemed to lift my spirits. I didn't have a clue as to how this visit was going to play out, but it was long overdue. I decided to call my brother before I got to my mother's to ask him if he thought I should call her first to inform her I was coming over. He told me to follow through with surprising her. He indicated that he had just spoken with her and knew she was home cooking her usual Sunday dinner.

When I arrived at my mother's house, I took a deep breath and said a silent prayer for things to go well. I rang her doorbell, and within a few seconds, I heard her say, "Who is it?"

I responded, "It's me, Mom…Lynda."

"Lynda who?" my mother said playfully, as she opened the door.

"Hi, Mom." I smiled as she unlocked the screen door with shaking hands.

"Oh, my goodness, if it isn't my beautiful baby girl. Let me look at you. Oh, my goodness, give your mother a hug."

I gave her a hug and kissed her cheek. It was refreshing to see my mother aging beautifully. She was actually as gorgeous as I remembered the last time I saw her, which had to be at my father's funeral.

"Ma, you look great!"

"Well, where do you think you get your good looks?" She laughed.

"I know I get it from my mama," I joked with her. I forgot how sassy she could be. I was sure I got that from her, as well.

I closed the door behind me after entering my mother's house, which was decorated just as I remembered. She always did love the floral prints that I loathed. She had many pictures of my brother and me all around the living room. She even had a wedding picture of her and my dad on the wall.

"You hungry, baby?" my mother asked with her southern drawl. It reminded me of when Martin Lawrence was playing Big Momma.

"Not really, Ma. I could use some water, though."

"Sure, baby." She handed me a bottle of water and a glass filled with ice. "So, you finally decided to visit your mother, huh?"

"Yes, Ma. I just wanted to put the past behind us and move on." I sat down at the kitchen table while she stirred and tasted food from several pots on the stove.

"Lynda, I know I wasn't the best mother to you, and I'm sorry. You were developing so fast, I didn't know how to protect you from the world, but your father could."

"You just seemed to treat Langston different than you treated me."

"It was easier raising a boy, but I know that's no excuse. My trying to protect you came out as me not treating you fairly. Your father did such a great job with you, though. Look how fabulous you turned out."

I smiled at my mother's comment. "Thanks, Ma."

"So, where is the book your brother keeps raving about?"

"I have some in my car, but, Ma, I don't know if you want to read my book."

"Why not? I read Zane's, so why can't I read Lynda Katherine Davis? I know you're grown; I can handle it."

*I have such a white girl name.*

"Okay, if you say so. I'll make sure I leave a copy with you today."

"Good, and I'll start reading it tonight. I'm so proud of you. Your father would be so proud of you, too."

"Thanks, Ma. That means a lot to me hearing you say that."

"Oh, and I picked up a book the other day by a Zion Jones. Baby, you know him? He's from the area. He was doing a book signing at the bookstore when I was looking for some new books to read."

I thought I would fall out of my seat when she mentioned his name. "Yes, Ma, I know him."

"I haven't opened it yet, but it looks good and juicy."

"Ma, please!"

"What? You don't want to know that I'm getting my groove back?" She laughed.

"No, not really. TMI."

"Lighten up. You're always so serious."

I sighed. I didn't mention my relationship with Zion because I was sure she would figure it out when she read the poem he wrote for me in the front of his book. I knew she would read it because she's too nosey not to read a book from cover to cover.

"Lynda, do you know that I have a grandbaby on the way?" my mother asked with excitement. "I can't wait."

"Yes. I spoke to Langston and he told me. You almost had two on the way."

"What, did your brother have two girls pregnant at the same time?"

"No, Ma. I was pregnant, but I lost my baby about two weeks ago."

"Oh, baby, I'm so sorry to hear that." She stopped stirring the food and walked over to where I sat. "You may not want to hear this, but God knows best. I lost my first baby, and then God blessed me with you and your brother."

"Really, Ma? I never knew that."

"Yes, and I was devastated, but then I realized that I had to live by God's plan."

"I agree, Ma." I sighed. "But it's hard."

"Maybe you'll wait until you're married next time."

"Ma, please don't start."

"Okay, baby. When was the last time you ate something? Because you look like you need to eat."

I could tell my mother was changing the subject, but she was right about me needing to eat. I had only nibbled on food since the miscarriage. Xavier would cook for me, but I didn't have an appetite.

I continued the visit with my mother for about two hours before I decided to go home and get some rest. She packed enough food for a couple of days in those disposable Gladware containers. I promised her that I would come by regularly, and she seemed very happy to hear that. I followed through and left her a copy of my book. I thought she would forget, but of course, she mentioned it before I even put my jacket on.

When I was on my way home, I called my brother to let him know the visit went well and then I called Xavier. I told him that I had some food to eat that my mother cooked, but he still insisted on coming over. I didn't mind his company, but I made it clear to him that I needed to get some rest. I wasn't sure if spending so much time with Xavier was a good idea, but I also didn't like the idea of being alone.

Xavier did most of the cooking and cleaning for the next several weeks while I walked around my place like a zombie. He had his own off-campus apartment in Baltimore where he was going to school, but he insisted on not leaving me alone. The first few days drove me crazy having him constantly in my space; however, I got used to having him around. When he did leave, it felt lonely.

The emotional trauma of losing my baby was taking a toll on me, and I mainly wanted to sleep the days away. I couldn't remember the last time I went outside other than to go to my doctor's appointments and to visit my mother. I wasn't sure how much time had passed, but once I finally checked my appointment calendar, I realized I had missed a couple of book signings. I couldn't afford to lose the rapport I had with local bookstore owners, so I called to explain what happened. One of the bookstore owners said that he understood and that my publicist had already called and rescheduled the signing.

*My publicist? I hadn't even spoken with her.*

I played along with the owner until he mentioned who my publicist was 'supposed' to be. When he said, "Mr. Dixon informed us you were just getting out of the hospital," I smiled and shook my head.

*Xavier to the rescue.* I wondered if Zion would have done the same thing.

I sighed and got back in my bed. I held my new BlackBerry in my hand, contemplating on calling Zion. One of these days, I was actually going to take the time to become familiar with all the phone's features, but for now, I was only concerned with making phone calls and texting.

So many thoughts raced through my mind that I couldn't focus on one thought before another one crept in. I missed Zion. As I flipped my phone around admiring the sleekness of the latest BlackBerry model, I noticed I needed a manicure badly.

*Should I call Zion?* He had made it clear that he didn't want to be in a relationship, but he deserved to know that I was carrying his baby. *Will he even care that I lost the baby?* I sighed and prepared to dial his number, when my phone vibrated. It startled me, causing me to drop it before I could answer. When I picked it up, the Caller ID displayed my brother's name. I smiled and hurried to answer the phone before the call went to voicemail.

"What's up, Lanky?"

"Don't start, Lynda. No one has called me that since high school. You know I'm sensitive."

"I know, just kidding. How are you, baby brother?"

"I'm good, but the question is how are you doing? Ma told me about your baby. I'm so sorry to hear that."

"Thanks, but I'll be okay."

"Why didn't you tell me?"

"I was just collecting my thoughts on the situation. You know, sometimes you need to absorb what happened to you before you reach out to others. I only told Ma because I was at her house."

"Ma is really happy about the visit. That's mainly what she talks about when I call or visit her."

"Yeah, I'm glad I finally went to see her."

"When I was over there, she was bragging to her friends about your book."

"Really? I hope she doesn't encourage them to read it. I don't want them to think I'm a freak."

"Please, those are some old freaks, including Ma."

I laughed. "I guess you have a point."

"Well, sis, I just wanted to reach out to see how you're doing."

"Thanks. I appreciate it."

"Let me know if you need something, okay?"

"Will do. Thanks again."

I had a smile on my face as I disconnected the call with Langston. I was glad to have him back in my life. I continued smiling until my phone rang again displaying the words "Do Not Answer." Although the name was no longer saved in my phone, I recognized it to be Justin's number. *What the fuck does he want?* I couldn't understand why he would be calling me after I had to pull my gun on him. I wasn't interested in anything he had to say, so his call went to voicemail. I was relieved when the message light didn't come on. There was no need for him to leave a message because his call wasn't going to be returned.

I eased off my bed and headed into the kitchen to pour a glass of Asti Spumante sparkling wine. Since it wasn't noon yet, I poured in some orange juice to ease my conscience. *I love mimosas,* I thought, as I guzzled the entire contents in the glass. After making another drink, I went back into the bedroom. It weighed heavily on my mind that I didn't tell Zion the truth, so I needed to call him. That really wasn't something you shared over the phone, but I had to get it off my mind. As I attempted to dial his number again, my phone vibrated.

*Damn, who is it now?* It was my mother.

"Hi, Ma." I tried to put on a chipper voice.

"Hi, baby. How are you holding up?"

"I'm okay. Still a little sad, but I'm making it."

"Well, hang in there, baby."

"I will, Ma."

"Oh, I'm almost finished with your book. It surely is a juicy one."

"Ma!"

"What? Sweetheart, you have a talent. Remember that. You keep doing what you do and don't worry about what others think. You hear me?"

"Yes, ma'am."

"Now, your dad might have had a fit reading this, but I'm perfectly okay with it."

"I appreciate that, Ma. I really do."

"Okay, I love you."

"I love you, too."

"Oh, I almost forgot. I would like you to have dinner here with me for Christmas, if you can. Invite as many friends as you want. Just let me know who's coming so I can prepare enough food."

"Okay, sounds good. I'll definitely be there. Let me know if you need my help."

"I sure will. Take care of yourself, and call me if you need to talk."

"I will."

"Bye, baby."

"Bye, Ma."

I drank the last sip of my mimosa and set the glass on the nightstand. I began to feel that maybe it wasn't a good idea to discuss losing the baby with Zion by phone. The fact that both times I tried to call him and another call interceded might have been a sign. I decided to look at *Final Destination 2* for the one thousandth time to get my mind off Zion. I still couldn't figure out my obsession with that movie, but I could literally watch it every day as if I was watching it for the first time.

A few minutes later, I heard keys turning in the lock, signaling that Xavier was back. I missed him so much and couldn't wait to hold him. We hadn't actually had intercourse yet, but it felt good holding him close to me at night. His nightly erection indicated that he wanted me, but I wasn't ready for that kind of connection with him.

For the past week, Xavier stayed at his place in Baltimore to study and prepare for his final exams. He was down to his last two courses and was ready to graduate. The fact he was studying to be a physical therapist was very impressive to me. He mentioned he wanted to work in the professional sports arena once he was finished with school.

"Hey, beautiful," Xavier said, entering my bedroom.

"Hey, you."

Xavier bent down and kissed me softly on the lips. Whenever he kissed me like that, my kitty always contracted. I wanted him, but I simply wasn't ready. Xavier exited my bedroom and entered the master bathroom that was connected to my room. I could hear bath water running, so I figured he was going to take a bath. He came back over to my bed and told me to get up and come into the bathroom.

*Is he trying to say I need a bath?*

"Lynda, I know you've been in that bed for days and probably haven't taken a bath. I want you to take a bath and put some clothes on so I can take you out."

"Xavier, I don't feel like going anywhere."

"I know, but it's time you got out of this house."

I rolled my eyes and reluctantly got out from under my covers. Xavier followed me into the bathroom as if he was making sure I was actually going to get in.

"Xavier, I know how to take a bath by myself."

"I know, but I haven't seen you in a week, and I miss seeing your body."

I blushed and stripped slowly out of my clothes. I could feel Xavier's eyes on me as I undressed. I eased into the tub, inhaling the scent of the Stress Relief bubble bath that he poured in the water. Once I was immersed up to my shoulders, I closed my eyes and took a deep breath. After a few seconds, I opened my eyes and looked over at Xavier.

"How did your finals go?" I asked.

"They went well. I'm just glad it's all finally over."

"Good. Are you looking forward to graduation?"

"Not really. I mean, my sister is still in rehab, my mother is in the nursing home, and Taye's not here, so I may not even walk across the stage. At this point, they could just mail my degree to me and I'll be happy."

"Xavier, I think you should walk and get your degree. I'll be there to support you."

"Really?"

"What do you mean *really?* Come on now."

"Lynda, that would mean a lot to me. I feel I don't have much support anymore."

"Like I said, you have me. Okay?"

"Cool."

"So where do you want to take me tonight?"

"It doesn't matter to me, just out of this house. We can play it by ear unless you have a place in mind."

"A movie would be fine with me."

"Sounds good."

Xavier walked over to the side of the tub and retrieved my washcloth off the towel bar. He lathered it with my Dove soap and motioned for me to stand up. *If he touches Ms. Kitty, we might not be going anywhere tonight but back in my bedroom.* I kept reminding myself that I wasn't ready to let him inside of me. He washed me from neck to toe, but handed the washcloth back to me so I could wash Ms. Kitty. *Thank you. Whew!* I eased back into the bath water to rinse off, when Xavier sat on the side of the tub and eased his hand between my legs. *Fuck!* I thought I was in the clear of any sexual advances from him tonight.

"Xavier, don't."

"Don't what?" he said, not moving his hand away.

His touches felt so good, I couldn't say anything else. I closed my eyes and allowed him free range of the secret garden he searched for. When his finger found my clit, I let a soft moan escape my lips. He gently caressed it while another finger found its way to my vaginal opening, but never went inside. I opened my legs further because I wanted him to push his fingers inside of me. It had been a few months since I had sex other than the oral session I had with him. Zion was the last man to penetrate me, and it appeared that Xavier was finally going to have his way since I couldn't fight it anymore.

I noticed Xavier was content with caressing my external vaginal area, so I grabbed his hand and slid his finger inside me. He obliged to my nonverbal command. My constant circular movements on his finger allowed me to have the orgasm I desperately needed. Afterward, Xavier withdrew his finger and handed me a towel so I could finally get out of the tub. I dried my body off completely, and Xavier pulled me close to him.

"That felt so good," I whispered in his ear.

"I want to feel you so bad. Please let me make love to you."

I hesitated for a moment, but then I removed the towel from my body, dropping it on the floor. Xavier looked me over and smiled. He grabbed my hand and led me to my bed. He slowly undressed as if he was stripping for me. As amazing as his body was, I was confident he could make a living as a male dancer. I took a condom out of my nightstand drawer and placed it on top. Xavier looked at the condom and then back at me as if to ask me, "Are you ready?" I nodded and reclined back on the bed.

Xavier slid on the condom and climbed on top of me with eagerness to finally make love to me. The scent of his mango shampoo filled my nostrils as I grabbed a handful of his dreads. Within a minute, his eagerness shifted to nervousness, and his erection softened a bit.

"What's wrong, Xavier?"

"Nothing. I guess I'm a bit too anxious." He eased off me in frustration and sighed. "Fuck!"

I didn't comment because I've heard men say that before. I was glad he was being honest about what he was feeling. I knew at that moment I would have to take control without it seeming like I was being controlling. I'd mastered how to do that from dealing with a lot of arrogant men. Women have to take control and still lead men to believe they are in control. If not, they become intimidated. I didn't want Xavier to be intimidated to have sex with me. I was wondering if the age factor started to kick in or was it the guilt of sleeping with his brother's ex?

Xavier lay face down on the pillow, seemingly defeated by the situation. I moved his dreads out of the way and kissed him, starting at the back of his neck all the way down his spine. When he turned over, I instantly straddled him, kissing his lips passionately. His manhood stood to attention again and with confidence. Without hesitation, I slid a condom down over his erection and eased him inside my warmth.

*Yeah, he just needed to relax a bit.*

Xavier's body responded quickly to mine as he thrust in and out of my treasure with passion and intensity until he yelled out in satisfaction, "Fuck!" Men and women sure did have different terms to express that they were satisfied sexually.

"Lynda, baby, I'm sorry. I couldn't hold it any longer. Your pussy is so wet and warm. That shit is like lava. I don't know. I may not be enough for you. Damn, girl."

I kissed him softly on his lips and eased off him. "Don't worry, it was just our first time, and I know I got the ill na na."

We both laughed.

"I just want to make sure I please you. I know I'm young, but—"

"But things will be fine, okay?" I interrupted.

He was lucky I already had an orgasm because I would have been disappointed. No, correction, I would've been pissed off. When I went into the bathroom to freshen up, Xavier was right on my heels, kissing and caressing my body.

"Xavier, stop. Are we still going to the movies or what?"

"Sure, if you still want to go."

"We don't have to go, but I thought you did."

"Let's just chill tonight, and we can go tomorrow if you don't have any plans."

"I didn't have plans to do anything but chill in my bed and watch movies. So, tomorrow it is."

"Cool. You hungry? I can cook or order something if you like."

"Sure, that's fine. I'm not picky."

We both laughed again. It felt good to laugh.

After devouring vegetable lo mein, General Tso's chicken, and beef and broccoli from China Bay, Xavier and I attempted to watch a movie. We were fifteen minutes into *Case 39* when Xavier was back inside of me. This time, it was as if he had something to prove. It seemed with each orgasm I achieved, his confidence grew. No matter how much of a challenge he presented, he had definitely met his match; I was extremely aggressive when it came to sex. At one point, he made a comment that suggested he wasn't satisfying me because the more he gave me, the more I wanted.

"Lynda, I don't care how young I am, I'm not gonna be up all night trying to please you."

"I didn't ask you to, but if you're waiting for me to tap out, it's not gonna happen." I laughed.

"Oh, so is that a challenge?"

"No, Xavier, but when you get an erection, I'm ready for you. That's just how Ms. Kitty is."

"Damn, I see. I was trying to *put you to bed*, but the more I put it on you, the more you want. Shit, I'm tired."

"It's all good, J. Holiday. We don't have to do it anymore tonight." We laughed.

"I see you got jokes." Xavier kissed my neck.

"See, that's you. I'm over here minding my business."

"Yeah, but you look so good. I can't help myself."

"Well, don't blame it on me because you keep starting it."

I could barely get the words out of my mouth before we started moaning heavily and breaking a sweat again. Sex with Xavier was more than I could have ever imagined. The more he stroked, the more I wanted to make him mine. I was trying desperately not to catch any feelings for him, but it simply wasn't working. I didn't want to set myself up thinking he felt the same way about me that I did for him. The situation was beginning to scare me. I hadn't planned to let my guard down, especially to Taye's younger brother.

Xavier and I finally stayed off each other long enough to leave the house. It wasn't an easy process to get out the door due to Xavier's constant erections. Finally, I had enough and pampered myself in the shower. Believe it or not, Ms. Kitty needed a break. When Xavier stepped in the shower, I immediately stepped out. He would've only wanted to sex me again.

"Lynda, where you going?"

"I'm done, Xavier." I laughed.

"Scared, say you scared."

"No one is scared of you. Just hurry up so we can catch a movie. We've been in the house for almost forty-eight hours straight sexin', and I need some air."

"That's 'cause you can't keep your hands off me."

He was partially correct.

"Just hurry up."

"Do you know what you want to see?" he asked.

"No, not really. I'm sure we'll figure out something. I just really want to get out of here."

Once we were dressed, we headed to the movie theater in Virginia. I preferred theaters that weren't connected to a subway line because there were less young people there. I wasn't in the mood for them most of the time.

We stood looking at the movie selections for about ten minutes, as if the selections were going to change. At one point, we looked at each other as if to say, "We could have stayed in." Since I was finally out, though, I wanted to make the best of it. We decided on some romantic comedy, which looked stupid, but so did everything else showing there.

As we headed to the concession stands, I heard a voice that literally sent chills down my spine.

"Well, if it isn't Lynda K. Davis. Can I get your autograph, miss?" It was Zion being an asshole. "Girl, I haven't seen you in a while. Did you have your baby yet? I guess so. You don't look pregnant. Is this the proud father?" Zion had the nerve to extend his hand to Xavier. I felt more chills.

Xavier shook his hand and looked at me as if searching for a sign if he should leave me alone to speak with Zion. I always knew the moment would come when I had to tell Zion the truth. I didn't want it to be with him being an ass or in front of Xavier. I asked Xavier if he minded giving me a few minutes alone with Zion. He agreed to get our popcorn and sodas, and then find us a seat.

"Zion, listen. I'm going to make this brief. Our baby died. I had a miscarriage months ago."

"Oh, I'm sorry for your loss, Lynda."

"It was *our* loss. Yours and mine."

Zion's entire demeanor changed. "What do you mean?"

"Exactly what I said. It was your baby, Zion."

"But you told me it wasn't mine."

I sighed. "Zion, the day I wanted to tell you about the baby was the day you pretty much said you didn't want to be with me anymore. Plus, I said I wasn't sure if the baby was yours, which wasn't true."

"I told you it wasn't like that. I think I still deserved the truth, though."

"You're right, and I made the decision to lie to you. I wish I could say I'm sorry, but I'm not sorry. I wanted to move on without you in my life."

"I don't think that's fair at all."

"Maybe not, but men make decisions all the time that aren't fair; to be bothered, not to be bothered with no regard for what the other person is going through. This is my first time out of the house in a while, and I won't let you ruin my date or upset me. You've done enough of that for one lifetime."

"So, you were going to keep my baby from me?"

"No, I was going to tell you, but then I had a miscarriage. I tried to call you several times, but I just couldn't."

"Lynda, you know I never wanted things to go down like this between us. Don't act like I didn't love you because I did. I actually still do. I was having a hard time finding balance."

Before I could respond, Jasmine walked up and smiled. I looked at Zion, then back at Jasmine and shook my head.

Zion pleaded. "It's not what you think."

"Doesn't matter anymore," I lied. It hurt like hell seeing them together.

"Lynda..." Zion stopped when he noticed a tear fall.

"Well, my date is waiting. It was good seeing you two," I lied again. I hurried away before more tears fell.

I stopped in the restroom to get my feelings in check before I joined Xavier. I didn't want to ruin his night, if I hadn't already. I sent him a text message to let him know where I was and that I would be there shortly. Before I left the restroom, I got a text from Zion stating he wanted to talk to me later when I was finished with my date. I started to tell him that my date lived with me, but Zion and I had too much between us to end things that way. Plus, Xavier wasn't quite living with me.

Before entering the movie, I ensured my phone was on silent. When I sat down in the seat to Xavier's left, he immediately put his arm around me to comfort me. I was tired of the hurt, and he seemed to make me feel better. I appreciated that he didn't ask too many questions, but he whispered in my ear, "We can leave if you want to." I informed him that I was okay and wanted to see the movie, which I was glad I did because it ended up being a lot better than I thought.

When the movie was over, I kissed Xavier softly on his lips and apologized for what happened earlier with Zion. "Don't sweat it, beautiful," was all he said. We left the theater hand in hand and headed to his car.

"You good?" Xavier asked, noticeably concerned.

I shrugged. "I guess."

"Anything else you want to do?"

"No, we can go back to my place. I just want to get back in my bed and cuddle."

"Cuddle, huh?" Xavier laughed.

It felt good to hear him laugh because it made me smile.

Arriving back at my place, I knew the night was destined to get worse. *Why in the hell is Justin pacing outside my house?* I had to tell Xavier the truth about this situation, but I could imagine that he was getting tired of the drama surrounding me.

"Xavier, you're not going to believe this."

"What?"

I looked toward my door so Xavier could see what I was talking about.

"Baby, do you know him?" he asked.

I sighed. "Yes, but I have no idea why he would be here."

"What do you want me to do?"

"Nothing. My cousin is a PG cop, so I'm going to call him. He told me if I ever need him, to call and he would send someone by my house if he wasn't close enough to come himself. After the situation with Taye, I dunno. I'm scared."

"I understand, but you sure you don't want me to go with you to see what he wants?"

"Maybe I should wait until my cousin or somebody gets here."

"I think that's a good idea. What happened with y'all? I mean, did something go down recently?"

"Long story short, he's from my past. He got married, we reconnected, and he told me that he was getting a divorce. But of course, it was a lie. His wife called while he was at my house a while back one night, and bottom line, I pulled my gun on him."

"Gun?"

"Yes. I got one after I was shot. I'm so tired of all this nonsense."

"Wow, girl. I guess you have to do what you got to do, though."

"Yep."

I called my cousin's cell phone, and within ten minutes, he was pulling up in front of my house. I was so glad that he was patrolling my area. I got out of Xavier's car, but I asked him to stay until I figured out what was going on with Justin. When I walked over to Justin, he noticed I had a police officer with me, and he went off.

"First, you pull a gun on me, and now, you call the police?"

"What do you want, Justin?"

"What the fuck did you say to my wife?" He obviously didn't care I had the police with me.

"I didn't say shit to her. I told her that whatever she wanted to know, she needed to ask you."

"Well, thanks to you, she's filing for divorce."

"What the fuck do you mean *thanks to me*? Justin, you brought this bullshit on yourself with your lies. You got busted and now you want to blame me. Fuck you, Justin."

"Lynda, what are you saying?" Justin changed his composure. "There was a time when I loved you, really loved you, and you know that. I'm sorry I lied to you. I know I hurt you, but I would never harm you in any way. Why would you call the police?"

"Justin, please don't do this again and come here like this. You already know what happened to me, so I have to take whatever precautions are necessary. I don't want to get you arrested, but I'm asking you to leave. Please, leave. If you have ever loved me and cared about me, don't do this."

Justin looked as if he wanted to cry, but there was no way his pride would allow that, especially in front of a police officer.

"Can we just talk?"

"No, Justin. That's not a good idea. I've been through so much in the last few months, and I'm tired. I just want to be left alone." I didn't mention I had someone with me because that may have made the matter worse. "If you have ever really loved me, you would understand and go home. I don't want to get a restraining order against you, but I will if I have to. Think about your girls."

"Lynda, that's not necessary. I only wanted to talk to you, that's all." Justin walked to his car and drove away.

Justin brought the situation on himself by lying. How long did he think he was going to get away with deceiving two women? I was convinced that most people didn't consider the possible consequences before they decided their actions.

When Xavier saw Justin drive away, he got out of his car.

"Lynda, are you gonna be okay now?" my cousin asked.

"Yes, Rob. Thank you so much for looking out for me like that."

"No problem. I got your back. I told you that."

I introduced Xavier to my cousin. He didn't need to know any specifics as to who Xavier was or who he was related to. My cousin waited until we were inside and then he left. Once inside, I buried my head into Xavier's chest and cried uncontrollably. I couldn't believe the night I had.

"Lynda, I'm sorry all of this is happening to you."

"This is too much. I can't take much more."

"Let's just go to bed. I'm sure you're mentally tired, if nothing else."

"Yep. I just want to go to bed."

As I settled under the covers, Xavier decided he wanted to share his feelings for me. I wasn't in the mood, but I listened to what he had to say.

"Lynda, I'm here for you because I love you."

*Lord, why did he go there tonight?* I wanted to pretend like I didn't hear him, but he said it again.

"I love you."

I indeed had feelings for Xavier, but I wasn't sure what they were. I enjoyed having him in my life, but was I in love with him?

I responded, "I love you, too, Xavier." It seemed like the right thing to say at the moment.

The next morning, Xavier sat on the edge of the bed fully dressed as if he was ready to walk out the door. I wondered if what happened last night with Zion and then Justin was too much for him to stick around. I would certainly understand because I might be ready to leave also if the tables were turned. I eased from under the covers and kissed him on the cheek.

"Good morning, Xavier," I said, then scurried to the bathroom.

"Lynda, I need to ask you a serious question."

"Okay." I didn't pause because I desperately needed to use the bathroom.

"Do you really love me?"

*Why is he doing this now?*

After relieving myself, I flushed the toilet, washed my hands, and proceeded to brush my teeth. I needed a moment to collect my thoughts. I wondered if he knew I was stalling.

"Lynda, I know you heard me."

I exited the bathroom and walked in his direction. "Yes, I heard you, and yes, I love you."

He didn't seem convinced.

"No, let me rephrase. Are you *in love* with me?" He emphasized "in love," changing the whole meaning of his original question. "Or do you love me as in care about me?"

"Why are you asking me this now, Xavier?"

"Because I need to know, and I want to know why I'm here."

I sighed. "Xavier, I have feelings for you. I really do. But there is so much going on that I don't think we should be having this conversation right now."

"Lynda, it's either you're in love with me or you're not. That's a simple question."

"I'm having mixed emotions, if you want to know the truth."

"Of course I want the truth. Are you still in love with Zion? Is that it?"

"No. I care about him, yes, but I don't want to be with him. It's you that I'm having mixed emotions about, not Zion or anyone else."

"What do you mean? Have I done something to upset you?"

"No. You're just what I want and need, but that scares me. We have this age difference between us, and I can't forget that you're Taye's brother."

"So, what bothers you the most? My age or the fact I'm Taye's brother?"

"I'm not sure. You're young and probably want to settle down and have a family. I'm not sure if I'm the woman for that, so probably the age difference."

"Oh, okay. I see where this is going. Do you even know what I want? No, because you haven't asked. You're just assuming what I want."

"Well, do you want kids?"

"One day, maybe. I don't know. I haven't thought that far ahead."

"Exactly my point. You have time to ponder those questions. I don't. Forty is not that far away for me, and I don't know if I want to even have a baby."

Xavier sat in silence.

"Talk to me, Xavier."

"Lynda, I know how I feel about you, but I understand if this is not what you want."

"I didn't say that."

"I'm going to leave and give you some space."

"I didn't ask for space."

"I think you need it to clear your head and stop using me. I may be a man, but my feelings hurt, too."

I was stunned at his response. "Is that how you feel, that I'm using you?"

"That's how I'm starting to feel, yeah."

My feelings were crushed, so I decided not to respond. If he wanted to leave, I wasn't going to stop him, but it did hurt to hear that was how he felt. I adored Xavier, but we seemed to have too many strikes against our situation.

"Lynda, this doesn't mean I don't still love you, and I'm not saying this is over. You have to tell me it's over if that's what you want. I think the space would be good for us, and especially for you to determine if I'm who you want. I don't want to feel like I'm your boy toy or something."

He kissed my cheek, grabbed the couple of bags he packed, and walked out the door. Too emotionally tapped out, I couldn't even cry. Now that was something I wasn't expecting from Xavier.

*How did I get here? Again…*

# CHAPTER 41

## *Dianne*

*NELSON'S HEART ATTACK WAS MILD*, but I was completely devastated. I couldn't help but to think I was partially to blame. Nelson and I were having so many ups and downs that the stress probably contributed to his heart attack. Thinking back to when the ambulance came for Nelson, I really thought that was the last time I would see him alive. Nihya wasn't home from school yet, so I had called Lynda and asked if she would come to my house and wait for her. I was glad Lynda was available to do it.

When I arrived at the hospital, I was a nervous wreck. I could barely think straight. I stopped at the desk to find out where Nelson was being held. One of the nurses could tell I was distraught, so she walked with me to Nelson's room. I didn't want Nihya to go in to see Nelson until I went in there first to see what condition he was in, so I was glad she wasn't there yet.

"Nelson?" I said with tears in my eyes.

"Hey, babe."

"How are you doing?"

"I guess I'm doing okay. The doctors said I'll be fine, but they want me to stay in here overnight or maybe a couple of days for observation. I'll know soon how long they want me to stay. They have to wait for my test results."

"Baby, what happened?"

"I don't really know. It all happened so fast, but I do know I felt some pains in my chest. Of course, I thought it was indigestion or something, but it got worse."

I just looked at Nelson with tears in my eyes. This was too much for me to handle. "Do you want me to stay here with you?"

"No, I want you to stay with Nihya. Where is she anyway?"

"I just got a text message from Lynda. Nihya's in the waiting room with her."

"Considering what happened to her mother, this might not be the best place for her right now."

"Are you sure you don't want me to stay with you? I can get Lynda to take Nihya to her grandmother's house. I really don't want to leave you."

"I know, babe, and I appreciate that. Nihya may not act like it, but she's going to need you since I'm going to be in the hospital."

"Do you want me to bring her in here to see you? I wanted to check your condition first."

"If she's up to it, then sure, but don't pressure her if she seems too upset."

"Okay."

I left the room to see if Nihya wanted to see her dad. She was upset, but she really wanted to see him. When I re-entered the hospital room with Nihya, Nelson struggled to sit up.

"Hey, baby girl."

"Hi, Daddy."

"Listen, Daddy might have to stay in here for a day or two. Okay?"

"Okay." Nihya cried.

"Sweetheart, everything will be fine. Your dad needs to get some rest," I added.

"He can rest at home. I'll be quiet. I promise."

"I know, but the doctors want to keep him close to make sure he's okay."

"That's the same thing my mommy said before she died."

"Oh, Nihya. Sweetie, don't cry."

"Baby girl, come here and give me a hug." Nelson now had tears in his eyes. "Daddy is just a little tired, but I'm going to be fine."

"Okay."

I kissed Nelson on the forehead and then gently on his lips. It was heartbreaking to see him in that hospital bed. I didn't want to leave his side, but he insisted I go home with Nihya. He felt she needed me more than he did.

"Nelson, I'll see you first thing in the morning. Okay?"

"Okay, and Dianne?"

"Yes, sweetheart?"

"Thank you," he said and nodded toward Nihya.

"No problem, baby. Get some rest and I'll see you tomorrow. I love you."

"Bye, Daddy. Love you."

Being in the hospital visiting Nelson brought back too many memories for Nihya, so I took her home. Nihya was silent during the entire ride home. I was sure she was worried about her daddy. When we arrived home, I wanted to do something to keep Nihya's mind off Nelson being in the hospital.

"Nihya, do you want to watch a movie or something?"

"No, thank you."

"Are you hungry?"

"Not really. Well, maybe just a little."

"Okay, I'll fix us something to eat."

"Okay. Can you let me know when the food's ready? I'm going to go up to my room."

"Sure. Give me about a half hour."

As Nihya went upstairs to her room, I wondered what was going through her mind. She had already been through so much that there was no telling what her breaking point would be.

I decided to cook spaghetti since I knew it wouldn't take very long. The ground beef was frozen, so I used the meatballs instead. Once I put the garlic bread into the oven, I went upstairs to get Nihya for dinner. Nelson and I agreed to give her a little privacy, so we always knocked on her door before entering. After knocking a couple of times, I turned the knob to see if her door was locked. It was unlocked, so I pushed the door open and called her name as I entered.

"Nihya!" I said loudly, noticing she had her earphones on. I didn't want to startle her, but I was having a hard time getting her attention.

"Oh, I'm sorry, Dianne. I couldn't hear you. Is dinner ready?"

"Yes. Make sure you wash your hands before you come to the table."

"Okay." Nihya spoke softly as if she was fighting back tears.

As Nihya eased off her bed, I noticed several drawings. I couldn't see exactly what they were, so I walked over to her bed to get a better view. Nowadays, you had to pay attention to what children were doing. Nelson was against her having a computer in her room, so I guess she found something constructive to do with her spare time.

"Nihya, can I see your pictures?"

Nihya just shrugged her shoulders and handed her drawings to me. I almost couldn't believe my eyes. The child had a real art talent. There were several sketches of all types of clothing.

"Wow, Nihya. These are really good. How long have you been drawing?"

"Since my mother died. I needed something to do to keep my mind from thinking about my mom."

"I know you miss her, sweetheart. I miss my mom, too. You let me know if you ever want to talk about what you're feeling, okay? I don't want you to feel you can't talk to your dad or me."

"Okay." Nihya barely spoke above a whisper. I could tell by the tone of her voice that she was sad.

"What do you want to do with these sketches?"

"I want to design clothes or something."

"That sounds great, Nihya. You know they have high schools that have art programs. It won't be long before it's time to apply for those schools."

"Really? You think I'm good enough to get into one of those schools?"

"Of course, Nihya. You're very talented."

"Thank you. I'll work on some more later on, and I'll show them to you."

"Sounds good, but let's go and eat dinner. Then you can get back to your drawings."

"Okay," Nihya said, this time with excitement in her voice.

That night, I showered, put on my pajamas, and climbed into bed kind of earlier than usual. It was about 8:30 p.m., but I was mentally exhausted. I decided to watch a movie until I fell asleep. I knew Nihya needed me to be home with her, but I wanted to be at the hospital with Nelson. I wanted to roll over and snuggle up close to him.

About halfway through the movie, Nihya knocked on the bedroom door. It was not closed all the way, but she had enough courtesy to knock anyway.

"Dianne?"

"Yes. Are you okay?"

"Yes, I'm okay, but can I sleep in here with you?"

"Sure." I noticed Nihya had her sleeping bag with her. "You don't have to sleep on the floor. Get on the bed."

The movie I was watching was appropriate for her age, so I was glad I made the selection. Nihya climbed into bed with me and watched the movie. This was the first time we actually had a chance to bond. I wondered if this was why Nelson insisted I stay with Nihya instead of him at the hospital.

"Dianne, do you think I will ever be normal?"

"What do you mean?"

"Normal enough to like boys."

*Lord, I'm not ready for this conversation.*

"I think so. It may take some time, but that doesn't mean you're not normal."

"Some of my friends say I'm not normal because I'm not into boys yet."

"Don't listen to that nonsense. You'll start to like boys in your own time."

"I kind of like boys now. I'm just scared of them to touch me."

"Nihya, you're too young for boys to be touching you right now anyway."

"I know. I just don't want to always be scared. I don't want them to hurt me like Walter did."

A pain hit me hard in the chest. I really wasn't ready for the conversation. I wanted to remain Dianne, her stepmom, and not the psychologist, so I watched how I worded my questions to her.

"Nihya, how often do you think about what happened to you?" This may have seemed like an obvious question, but so many victims block out their pain and pretend it never happened.

"Mostly every day. It makes me sad, but I don't like crying all the time."

"Nihya, you should have told me what you were going through."

"I didn't want to go back to the shrink. I don't like the way they force me to talk. Sometimes, I don't want to talk about it."

"I understand. I'm so sorry that happened to you."

"Don't tell my daddy because he'll be worried about me and he's already sick."

"I'll wait until you're comfortable enough to talk to him, but I think it would be good for you to talk to your dad when you're sad."

"I don't want to talk to him about boys, though."

"You can talk to me about boys. I don't think he could handle that yet."

Nihya smiled. "So, when I'm older, will a boy make me feel good?"

*Lord, is this child asking me about sex?* I thought to myself, as I figured out a way to respond. When in doubt, take the dumb route.

"What do you mean?"

"Well, I know what sex is, although I know I'm not supposed to right now. I had a friend who did it, and she told me I'm scared since I won't do it."

"Nihya, how old is this friend?"

"I think twelve or thirteen."

My heart was really hurting now. *These kids are moving way too fast these days. I'm just glad Nihya is finally coming to me to let me know what is going on with her friends.*

"I don't know if it's a good idea for you to talk about that with your friends. They might not give you the right information."

"I know. They think I'm scared because I don't like boys, but I'm scared because Walter really hurt me."

"I know, sweetheart," was all I could manage to say. She was really traumatized by Walter's actions, and it pained me to see her so sad.

Just when I thought the awkward conversation was over, Nihya thought of more embarrassing questions to ask me.

"Does my daddy hurt you?"

"Excuse me?" I almost choked on my own saliva.

"I know y'all have sex."

*Oh, my God!*

Nihya continued. "I hear y'all sometimes, but I just put on my earphones."

*This must be the time when Natasha says you'll want a hole to appear and swallow you up.* She told me about the time when Aisha first came to her about sex. At least Aisha was sixteen; Nihya was only twelve years old. Again, I wasn't ready for this conversation. *How do I respond to that?*

"Nihya, your daddy doesn't hurt me. He loves me, so he would never hurt me." I had no idea what else to say.

"Oh."

*Please let the questions be over!*

Nope. Nihya continued. "So, when a boy really likes me, he won't hurt me either?"

"I want you to promise me something," I said, avoiding her question.

"Okay."

"Please let me know before you let a boy *touch* you, okay?"

"I will. Goodnight. I'm sleepy now."

"Okay, goodnight."

Nihya rolled over and went to sleep. *Thank goodness!* I didn't know how much more of the conversation I could take.

For weeks after Nelson was discharged from the hospital, I watched him for hours each night while he slept. The joy I felt having my husband back by my side was immeasurable. When he informed me that he planned to take some time off from work, of course, I was very supportive of his decision because his health was a priority. Although he was very successful in his position, somehow, he didn't seem happy anymore working in that capacity. I wondered if playing the saxophone again had something to do with his decision. Nelson seemed to really come to life when he was working those buttons on his instrument.

I was excited to see my husband onstage for the first time. One of his friends owned a small jazz club on U Street, and he extended an invitation to Nelson to be a part of the live entertainment. I talked Lynda into reciting some of her poetry while Nelson played his jazz tunes. She was reluctant at first since she wanted to focus on her novel, but she finally came around.

*I still can't believe she lost her baby.*

I pleaded with Nelson to focus on his health before he rushed into performing. Men can be so hardheaded at times, and I was really worried about him.

It was Friday evening around 4:30, and Nelson wanted me to help him start clearing out his office. He put in for a six-month sabbatical; however, something was telling me that Nelson didn't plan to return to work any sooner than one year. When I arrived at his office, a chipper receptionist greeted me. She was a young, Caucasian girl around nineteen years old.

"Hi. Welcome to the Office of Public Affairs. How may I assist you?"

"Hi. I'm here to see Mr. Thompson."

"Who may I tell him is visiting?"

"Mrs. Thompson." I smiled.

"Oh, hello, Mrs. Thompson. It's great to meet you. I'm here employed as an intern, and it has been great working with your husband, Mr. Thompson. We're really going to miss him around here."

I wasn't sure how to respond because this receptionist was way too chipper for me. Plus, I had never been one for small talk. "Are you enjoying your summer?"

"I sure am. Thanks for asking. Well, I'll tell Mr. Thompson you're here."

"Thank you." *Whew*, I thought to myself. *Way too much energy for me.*

A few seconds later, the receptionist informed me to go right into his office. When I walked in, I could tell Nelson was serious about taking time off. He had packed much of his stuff already.

"Hi, baby." I greeted Nelson with a passionate hug and kiss.

"Hey, there. Thanks for coming to help me get some of this stuff out of here."

"No problem, sweetheart. Can I ask you something?"

"Sure."

"How in the hell do you deal with all that chipperness out there?"

Nelson laughed. "I don't know. It just doesn't bother me, I guess."

"Whew. I wouldn't be able to do it."

"I know. I had a feeling you were going to say something about her bubbly personality. But she's a great receptionist."

"I'm sure she is, but goodness."

"Hey, before we take this stuff to my car, I want you to meet a few people."

"Okay, cool."

"And before we do that, I want to make love to you on my desk."

"Excuse me?"

"You heard me."

"Nelson, come on now. Too many people are still here."

"Most of them will be going home soon."

"Nelson, I don't think it's a good idea."

"Is this coming from the same woman who allowed an intern to bend her over a conference room table?"

"Nelson, that's not fair. That was a long time ago."

*Hold on, I didn't tell him any details! Oh, Lord, is Ryan running his mouth?*

"So, are you denying me?" Nelson caressed me as he spoke.

"What's gotten into you, Nelson?" I blushed.

"Nothing, babe, but I'm about to get into you."

"Oh, really?"

Nelson didn't respond in words, but his actions were clear. He planned to sex me right there on his desk. As he walked over to lock his office door, I noticed the bulge already forming in his pants. He walked back over to me and kissed my neck. He knew I wouldn't deny him now because he was kissing my hotspots. I was actually kind of scared. After having sex with the intern, Ryan, I never had sex in the workplace again. I was afraid of being caught; however, it didn't seem to concern Nelson. He wanted me, and I was going to be a willing participant.

Nelson eased his hands nervously up my dress until he reached my thong, and he slid it down slowly while looking into my eyes. When my thong was completely off, he lifted me up and gently sat me on his desk. I took the liberty to unbuckle Nelson's belt, unbutton, and unzip his slacks, allowing them to fall to his ankles. His manhood had risen to full attention and was poking through his boxer briefs. I smiled at Nelson as I caressed his erection. He smiled back while moving the bottom of my dress out of his way so he could get a better view of my freshly shaven vagina. He loved the fact that I kept up with my Brazilian wax even during my pregnancy. When Nelson took his middle finger and gently caressed my clit, he immediately realized I was already wet enough for him to enter me.

"Damn, baby. I see you're ready for me."

"I'm always ready for you." I began grinding on his finger that had found its way into my sweetness.

Nelson withdrew his finger while looking down at his erection, and somehow, I knew what that meant. He wanted me to extract his nine inches from his boxer briefs; so, I did. I lowered his boxers just enough to pull out his penis and piloted him inside of me. We moaned in unison upon his entry. My husband stroked me as if we were newlyweds stealing a brief moment of alone time. Vivian Green's song was playing in my head. I didn't know the name of the song, but she talks about how her man loved her incredibly from her head to the soles of her feet. That was exactly how I felt with Nelson. I knew this man really loved me. Of course, I felt the same way about him.

After a few minutes of stroking, Nelson paused. "Baby, wait."

"What's wrong?" I whispered.

"I don't know what you're doing in this sweet cave of yours, but you're about to have me talking in falsetto. I heard pregnancy sex was good, but damn!"

"You so stupid." I laughed.

"Seriously, girl. If you keep that up, I'm gonna bust too quick. You know I try to get you off first."

"It's all good, Nelly," I teased. "Cum if you need to cum. The Kegel gripping is working on you, I see."

"All right, you've been warned." Nelson resumed his stroking.

I decided to ease up on the Kegel action a little. I wrapped my legs around his waist so he was deep inside of me. Grabbing my ass, Nelson stroked as deeply as he could, and soon, I felt my body tense up.

"Nelson, I'm about to cum."

"Cum on me, baby."

I moaned softly in Nelson's ear because I knew those sounds would definitely trigger his release.

"That was good, babe. I always fantasized about making love to my wife in my office."

"Is that right?"

"Yeah. You know I'm not as adventurous as you are. I'm more of the romantic type," Nelson bragged.

"Yes, you are, baby. That's why I love you so much. Wait a minute. I just thought about what you said. Are you saying I'm not romantic?" I playfully punched him in the arm.

Nelson laughed. "Sex in the office is definitely a step up for me."

I was so glad Lynda told me about keeping those pleasure wipes in my purse, especially in the summertime. It's not necessarily for after-sex purposes, but to refresh the kitty, as she calls it, during the day, if necessary. When Nelson pulled out of me, I asked him to hand me my purse, which I put in his chair. I retrieved the wipes from my purse and freshened up.

"Want one?" I asked, handing a wipe to Nelson.

"Do it for me."

"Do what?"

"Clean off my power tool, woman."

"Are you still calling it that?" I laughed, as I wiped my juices off Nelson.

"Okay, comedian."

"I was just asking, Nelly."

"You're trying to be funny like I don't have any power left or something. You wait until I get all of my strength back."

We laughed.

By the time we were done with our office session, the people he wanted me to meet had already gone home. I was kind of glad because I wasn't in the mood to make small talk with these corporate, corny folks. I dared not say that to Nelson, though.

"Nelson, are you going to miss your job?"

"I'm sure I will eventually, but right now, I need a break from all this."

"You know I know. I'm so glad I had you in my life to help me transition from the corporate world. I hated it."

"I know. I remember. I hated seeing you like that."

"Are we going to be okay financially?"

"Woman, yes. I have saved a substantial amount of money."

"I know. I guess I'm just scared."

"Don't be. Plus, I have enough leave to still get paid for a while. I barely took any leave. This heart attack has made me look at things differently. I want to start doing something with my music."

"I know, and I'm so proud of you for having the courage to do this now. You have so much going for you in your career, but you aren't letting it stop you from going back to something that you're passionate about. Are you excited about performing at the club?"

"Yeah. Kind of nervous, though." Nelson smiled.

"I can't wait to see you up there. I know you'll do great."

"Is Lynda ready to drop some lyrics?"

"I haven't talked to her about it in a while, but I'm sure she is. You know Lynda will just go with whatever she feels. She's good like that."

"Oh, Dianne. I wanted to tell you again how grateful I am that you spent time with Nihya while I was in the hospital. I know things have been rocky, but she needed that attention from you. She told me one day that maybe she should go live with her grandmother so we could have our happy marriage again."

"I don't want her to feel like that. I know what it's like to feel that way." I briefly thought about how I was bounced around for a couple of years after my mother died.

"She's so excited about her sketches. It meant a lot to her that you approved of them. I know it may not seem like it, but she really looks up to you, Dianne."

"Nelson, I need to tell you something and don't freak out."

"What, babe?"

"Nihya told me that sometimes she could hear us having sex."

"Wow, are you serious?"

"Yep."

"Oh man, that's not good."

"Well, she knows that we love each other. She asked me if that's what it sounds like when someone loves you." I couldn't help but laugh a little. "She knows all about sex, so there's no need to try to keep it from her."

"I know. It still hurts me that she was molested."

"She's scared that maybe she won't be normal like other girls."

"Normal as in liking boys."

"Yeah."

"Dianne, I feel so helpless. I hope what happened to her doesn't somehow encourage her to like women. That would really kill me."

"Well, let's not think about that. She told me that she does like boys. She's just scared they're going to hurt her like Walter did."

"Oh, man, this is too much for me. I don't handle stuff like this well at all."

"It's okay. I know as her father, you don't want to think about your little girl having sex. But one day, she will have sex whether you like it or not. I'll be there to help her through this because it's going to be difficult for her as she becomes a young woman. She's scared to have sex, which is good for now since she's young. But if she's going to have a productive relationship with a man, she's going to have to overcome her traumatic situation somehow."

"Will you be there, Dianne? You have to be committed to us—all of us."

"Yes, I will be there."

For a moment, we stared into each other's eyes. We had been through so much hurt the past few months, and it was partially due to some of my actions. I had to treat Nihya as if she was my own flesh and blood. I would never run out on my family if she was my daughter, and I knew that. Somehow, it was easier to leave because she was not my birth child.

Nelson was the one being hurt through all of this, and as a result, I almost lost him to a heart attack. My world would have been completely shattered if he would have died. Death is inevitable, but I wanted us to grow old together and have some grandchildren to spoil. *I haven't had nearly enough time with him yet.* I wondered if God was sending me a message to show how easily Nelson could be taken away from me. Running out on him and taking him for granted had to stop, effective immediately!

# CHAPTER 42
## Dianne

***

**BEING ON BED REST** during the rest of my pregnancy was definitely going to be a challenge for me. Normally, I stayed so busy that it was difficult for me to stop and get the proper rest. I hated the thought of not being able to move around as I pleased for the next several months. However, it was the doctor's recommendation due to the premature birth of my son. He even mentioned a procedure that he would consider, if it became necessary, where the cervix is stitched up to avoid pre-term labor. I was willing to do whatever it took to ensure my baby would be okay. The anxiety took over, but I promised Nelson that I would remain positive. I planned to tell Lynda and Natasha not to schedule a baby shower until after the baby was born. I wouldn't be able to handle that again.

I referred all of my clients to another child psychologist, which made me a little sad. I was emotionally attached to some of them, although in my line of work, it wasn't a good policy. When I mentioned my leave of absence to the kids, some of them seemed withdrawn immediately. *Lord, I hope they don't have any setbacks.* To be honest, I wasn't sure if I was going to continue my counseling practice after the baby was born. I wanted to be home with my baby for as long as I could. Maybe I would start writing again; I always wanted to write a motivational book for teenagers. They seemed to suffer so much in this cruel world we lived in today, and based on my observations, they needed constant encouragement.

Nelson finally went back to work, but he decided, once again, to accept a lower-level management position to free him from all those stressful duties. He said he was only returning to the federal government for the stability of income and health insurance since we had a baby on the way. He didn't appear happy about it, though. To help minimize his stress, he planned to work from home three days a week; the federal government did have its perks. He also mentioned giving saxophone lessons on certain evenings.

Natasha called when she returned from Atlanta and mentioned that she wanted to come over and discuss something important with me. She emphasized that life was too short not to make amends for past mistakes, and she felt we needed to deal with our issue and move forward. Her tone alluded that Tyrone told her about the kiss. I could have been wrong, though. I wished he would've given me a heads up that he was going to tell her. Maybe he felt pressured and didn't have a chance to call me first. I figured it was better to get the truth out in the open and deal with it accordingly. I sighed at the thought of confessing to Natasha that I kissed Tyrone. Nelson still didn't know that much. He caught us together, but as far as he knew, nothing happened. A kiss was definitely something!

While I was deep in thought, Lynda called me. She sounded extremely pissed, but after she told me that she had to walk out on Marlon at the restaurant because he didn't want to pay the bill, I totally understood her tone. I would've been pissed, too! "I left his bitch-ass right there at the table," were her exact words. I laughed until I literally cried. She didn't have a chance to go into any details because a call from Maurice interrupted our conversation and she wanted to see why he was calling her. *Why is she still accepting Maurice's calls? And why did she agree to meet Marlon for dinner, lunch, or whatever meal it was?* I couldn't wait to hear the full story of what went down.

While I waited for Lynda to call me back, I continued to think about the upcoming conversation Natasha and I were going to have soon. There wasn't a good reason that I could use to justify what happened, other than Tyrone and I just got caught up.

*I hate it when people say that, but now I see it's really possible to get caught up in the heat of the moment! You just have to be strong enough not to act on impulse.*

If I could forgive her for what she said to me about losing my baby, then she could forgive me for kissing Tyrone, right? Only time would tell...

# *Note to Readers*

If you enjoyed the story and want more, feel free to send an e-mail to klowerymoore@aol.com. You can also contact me on Facebook at K Lowery Moore Books. You will find upcoming book news and event information on my website, www.klowerymoore.com.

# Discussion Questions

1. Do you feel it was okay for Dianne to hit Nihya? How do stepchildren affect marriages?

2. Explain how you feel about Nelson's response when Dianne told him about Nihya's behavior. If you had to defend Nihya's behavior, what would you say?

3. Nelson and Dianne have gone through a lot. What do you think holds them together? Do you feel their marriage will get back on track?

4. Why do you feel Natasha is having a hard time adjusting to her new family situation? Do you feel this is normal or should she seek counseling?

5. Discuss your feelings about Natasha and Tyrone's marriage. Do you feel Natasha will let go of the past in order to have a functional marriage? How would you describe Tyrone as a husband and father?

6. Do you think Dianne and Natasha's friendship will ever be the same?

7. How do you feel about Lynda and Xavier's interaction? Is it wrong for Lynda to pursue Xavier if she sincerely has feelings for him?

8. Do you think Lynda and Zion have a chance to rekindle what they had or should they let it go?

9. Discuss your feelings regarding how Justin lied to Lynda and his wife. Why do you feel people try to live double lives?

10. Do you feel traumatic situations affect how people love themselves and others? Please explain.

11. Do you think love is enough to build and sustain a marriage? If not, what else do you feel it takes?

12. Discuss your feelings about what happened with Dianne and Tyrone. Why do you think an emotional connection exists?

13. Do you feel Natasha should know about the kiss Dianne and Tyrone shared?

14. Does time really heal wounds, or is it just a cliché? What steps should a person take after experiencing something traumatic?

15. What message did you receive from this story?

late. Most of the houses in the cul-de-sac were on fire. Jacobs included. A few bodies lined the street, some had dropped to the ground in the yard or slumped in their doorways. Gunned down most likely. They barely registered as adrenaline pushed his mind to the brink, worried about Sam and his family. Was everyone dead on this street? Or dying?

They pulled up in front of the burning structure. Nobody spoke as they piled out of the vehicle, guns at the ready.

"Keep tight. I'm heading around back," Connor said.

"I'm with you," Sam said.

Heart pounding, he crept down the alleyway between two houses further up the street, Sam and Jake at his side. One home had just caught on fire, its shingled roof alight in patches, but the other was not, giving them safe passage. Jacob's place was too far gone to get near, the heat and smoke consuming it like hellfire out of control. It was unlikely any of the residences would be standing at the end of the day. No fire-bots or firemen to come to the rescue. A perilous time made immeasurably more difficult by roving bands of criminals.

They rounded the back of the neighboring house still standing, observed the backyard was clear, then raced toward Jacob's backyard. Behind the property was a smaller cottage he'd built for his in-laws. It too looked abandoned, though not on fire. They hadn't seen any roving residents as yet. And no 666s. Didn't mean someone wasn't hiding somewhere. Every second exposed was an opportunity for disaster to strike.

A muffled sound came from the small building. Connor signaled his intentions at the pair. Sam opened the door to the tiny home and Connor stepped into the doorway, his Highlander at the ready. Jake had his six. Both were prepared to shoot.

One quick encompassing glance around the open space and it was obvious no one was inside. Connor checked the floor and saw the trapdoor half-hidden under an area rug. Someone was under the cottage. Friend or foe? He moved to the edge of the square cut-out in the center of the floor and grabbed hold of the round iron handle. Jake and Sam both stood around the square opening and kept their weapons directed at the floor. Connor pulled the door upward, his every sense focused solely on who was hidden beneath the floorboards. He leaned backward in case someone intended to shoot soon as the door was opened.

"Don't shoot!" Jacob said, his voice taunt with panic. His normally ruddy face from years spent outdoors, summer or winter, was pale and whiskery, his eyes deeply shadowed, like he hadn't had a chance in a few days to take care of himself. Connor lowered his weapon. Inside the cramped space was Jacob, his wife Rachel, their four children and an older couple who he presumed must be the in-laws. Everyone looked frightened and exhausted. It wrenched at his gut, seeing the family in such dire straits. They had been nothing but good neighbors and upstanding citizens their entire lives. Jacob often mentioned how Rachel, even busy with four children and her parents, found the time to volunteer at the local food bank. In 2055, they still had the need for food banks.

Connor set aside his weapon for the moment to assist the family out of the hole, Jake exiting the cottage to keep a close watch on the yard. Sam hugged his friend Jacob. The pair were close, almost like brothers.

Connor clapped Jacob on the back, grateful to see

he'd made it. "It's good to see you and your family are okay. We should get a move on though. We have a vehicle waiting in front of your house. It'll be tight, but we'll get you all inside."

The family had little in way of supplies, they'd had to exit their home so quickly. One suitcase came out of the hole.

"I'll pack up a few things, Rachel," the older woman said and scrambled to grab a carry case from a closet. She frantically began to throw some personal items in the bag.

The children clung to their parents, wide-eyed and silent, a living testament to man's inhumanity to his fellow man when unchecked. Connor could only imagine the terrible things they had been exposed to in the past week since chaos had descended, with roving gangs breaking all the decency rules. When killing becomes the norm, civilization breaks apart. Now killers ruled the land, leaving good men without a choice but to fight back in ways no one could have foreseen only scant days ago.

Connor's skin began to crawl. Time to leave. "We have to go. Ready?"

Rachel spoke up. "Mom, there's no more time."

"But the photos and—" The older woman, her dress smudged with dirt and her white bob of hair disheveled around her wan face, looked over and pleaded with them, her eyes desperate to save the memories of a lifetime.

"Leave them. Our lives come first. Nothing else matters."

The woman straightened her shoulders and zipped the case shut. "Of course. I'm ready, dear."

Her husband took the bag from her, his eyes offering

her sympathy she studiously ignored. She probably didn't want to cry in front of the children. Her bravery only made Connor feel even worse about the situation.

"When things settle down, we'll come back," he promised, not sure anyone believed it ever would, himself included.

He led the family outside the small home, intending to escort them to The Shark. Sam and Jake flanked the family. And in formation, weapons at the ready, they began to move back down the route the trio had come in on. Gunshots reverberated in the distance. Shouts of panic, though also not close by. Hopefully the others were protecting The Shark, ready to deal with anyone attempting to steal it. When they made the still safe alleyway between the two burning houses, Connor urged everyone to move quicker. He hated the family being exposed. What if the 666s had posted gang members to keep watch on the area?

He moved out of the safety of the alley first, checking if the way to the vehicle was clear or not. Faraday was nearby with Brady, her weapon at the ready, and she waved him over. Ben wasn't in sight and he worried the man might be in harm's way, the one responsible for the gunshots.

"Okay, stay close together. And move as fast as you can," he directed. Each adult held a child in their arms, Jacob and his father-in-law carrying the luggage as well while the youngster clung to them, faces pressed on the adult's chest.

In even tighter formation, the group raced across the front yard and headed down the street toward the armored vehicle. *Fifty yards. Forty.* Connor barely breathed, his neck on a swivel, same as his brothers-in-arms. *Thirty.*

Ben came racing out from between two buildings farther down the street. Was he being chased? Connor scanned the area, every moment an eternity. They had to get the children to the safety of The Shark. It was their only hope. *Please God, we only need a few seconds more.*

*Twenty.*

Ben came racing toward them, legs pumping. The white noise in Connor's head increased, obscuring everything else as the group moved the last few steps across the smoky pavement, everyone desperate to reach the waiting vehicle. Danger lurked everywhere. The very air stank of it. Smoky. Toxic. Filled with the stench of death. The instincts and self-defense mechanisms of their ancestors had now taken over, providing the extra adrenaline needed to increase their speed.

It was then Connor saw the group chasing Ben come into full view. Half a dozen gang members, red bandannas tied like badges around their shaved skulls. If they were closer, he was certain the familiar tattoo of the devil incarnate etched into their faces would be obvious.

The scramble to get inside the tank-like truck was insane. Adults and children tumbled into open doors, choosing the floor over the time it took to climb into their seats. Faraday was already behind the wheel. Ben was the only one left running for his life. Connor, Jake, Sam and Brady moved into formation around the vehicle and began providing covering fire for him, shooting at the gang members though they were still too far away for accuracy.

The firefight was joined by the gang members. A few shots began to ping off the hardened metal of the armor encasing The Shark. Ben had a decent lead but the gang members were determined. They blasted away with their AK-47s, the machine gun the group was famous for.

Ben's expression was fierce. His ghost-like face with the fiery red beard was a symbol of courage and honor. Viking blood. At that moment they could have been on a fjord in Norway, fighting the hordes coming across the sea.

Connor sighted on the men rushing toward them. They were closer now. A double-tap and the leader dropped to the ground. Sam and Jake took out another of the men apiece, but still they pressed forward. Damn it. Another thing the 666s were known for. Never giving up until the last man standing.

Connor aimed for one of the two still running. They were closer now, shooting them meant looking the man clear in the face. But what other choice was there? It was them or one of his group. He sighted on the tattoo and pulled the trigger twice. The man fell backward to the ground, dead instantly.

One man left, still advancing. The brainwashing to keep a ragtag group like the 666s from breaking formation was something odd to be thinking about, but maybe it was just the men had nothing left to lose. Maybe they never did. The gang member let loose a barrage of bullets. It was his last opportunity. Brady double-tapped him and he face-planted on the pavement.

It was then he realized Ben had fallen to the ground, his weapon dropping from his hands. *Fuck*. Connor rushed toward the man.

"Where are you hit?"

"Just my left arm, I think. Help me up."

He grabbed Ben by his uninjured arm and hauled him to his feet. The man winced with pain. Connor helped him the remaining few yards to The Shark, grunting at the weight of the huge man. Jake helped load him into the vehicle. Sam slammed the door shut behind them.

"Go!" he shouted at Faraday. No doubt others would appear on the scene soon. They needed to get Ben back to Braveheart. ASAP. And they had to avoid letting anyone know where they and The Shark were going. Last thing they needed was pursuit. Or anyone in the gang discovering their hideout. They had enough assholes coming after them as it was.

# THIRTY-THREE
# MCKENNA

**Day 8: Braveheart Horse Ranch**
   **3:07 p.m.**

Mckenna was busy preparing food in the kitchen. No doubt soon as Connor's crew got back from their mission everyone would be starved. Hard times and adrenaline rushes did that to a person. Her own pulse faltered thinking of it, but she had to keep focused on what she could do right now, not dwell of all the danger those she cared about were placing themselves. Yet again.

Laura had filled her in on what was going on after Connor and the others had made the mad dash for The Shark a short time ago, though it seemed like forever while you waited cooling your heels needing to know if everyone was okay. She was fixing a big batch of beef stew in a stockpot that should hold enough to feed everyone along with Jean's fresh bread. She'd never take having enough to eat for granted ever again. Comfort of food was right up there with a safe place to sleep and a way to keep decently clean in difficult times. So many others were now cut off from such essentials, forced to leave their homes and find supplies, placing themselves in danger at every moment.

She and Lily were two of the lucky ones. So were the others. Braveheart was the sanctuary Connor had promised, and more. She already loved the place he'd carved from his two hands from the wilderness. If only things would get back to some semblance of normal, she could see the pair of them riding the horses across the land when time permitted, watch Lily grow up learning to enjoy the outdoors. Appreciate nature. Simple things were best. Why did mankind have to fuck with it, creating a monster they could never control? She understood it now, hated it with every fiber of her being, what had happened to create the worst mess facing mankind probably ever in history. Surely greater minds should have prevailed before it came to this? Not like warnings hadn't been given over the decades.

"Mommy? Why are you mad?"

Mckenna forced herself to calm down, realizing she was holding the wooden spoon like a weapon she wanted to use to strike at the idiots who had let this happen.

"Sorry, Lily. I was thinking about when people aren't nice to other people."

"Like that bad lady who tried to hurt us."

Mckenna took a deep breath and went and kneeled down in front of her daughter. "You know, I'll never let anything bad happen to you, right?" She knew it was an empty promise, but she had to make it anyway.

"I love you, Mommy." Lily began to cough and wheeze, sending her thoughts racing. She patted her daughter's back, rubbing her hand in circles.

"Are you all right, Princess Lilybelle?"

"My chest hurts." Lily gave a throaty cough again, her tiny face turning a deep pink.

"How are your ears feeling?" Lily was susceptible to ear infections. She had a good supply on hand of whatever medication her daughter needed for all her known health issues. All thanks to Jake scrounging them up in Golden after his ex, the bad woman her daughter had just spoken of, had conveniently lost their suitcase.

"Only my chest hurts, Mommy."

She pressed her hand to her forehead. "You're a bit warm. Let's check your temperature."

Mckenna rose to her feet and hurried back to the stove, turning down the heat under the stew pot. Then she dashed up the stairs and down the hall to the back bedroom to retrieve the bag of medicine set aside for Lily. She rummaged inside and pulled out a bottle of liquid pain reliever designed especially for children, plus a thermometer.

She strode from the room and was back in the kitchen when she heard the baby begin to cry. It sounded distinctly like her hunger cry. She was tucked on a chair in a baby carrier loaned from Laura set near the table. Mckenna was in charge of keeping an eye on her while Faraday was away helping to rescue Jacob's family.

"Just give me a minute." Mckenna went about the task of checking Lily's temperature and found it only slightly raised. She grabbed a spoon and measured out the dollop of pain reliever. "You're going to be fine, princess. Mommy wants you to drink all of this down now. It tastes like cherries, remember? Can you do that for me?"

"I like cherries." Lily coughed a bit first, then dutifully consumed the red liquid. She reminded Mckenna of a tiny baby bird, the way she took the medicine so agreeably.

"Maybe you would like to lie on the sofa and read your storybook while Mommy finishes making dinner?"

"I want teddy and tinker."

"And your blankie."

Mckenna picked her daughter up in her arms and carried her through to the living room, laying her down on the couch, tucking her favorite toys around her along with the pink and white blanket her little girl hauled everywhere. But instead of picking up her storybook to read, Lily closed her eyes and went right off to sleep. She looked so innocent and fragile lying there, Mckenna had to take a few deep breaths to steady herself. If anything ever went seriously wrong, there was no pediatrician on hand to save the day. So much had changed, if she dwelled on it too much, she would go stark raving mad.

When she arrived back in the kitchen, Eve was getting more wound up by the second and she hurriedly began to warm a bottle of formula for the hungry baby in a panful of water heated on the stove.

"It's okay, little one," she said. She picked up the whimpering baby and rocked her in one curved arm while she stirred the stew with the other.

Multitasking was nothing new to mothers all over the world, an essential skill learned by watching their own mothers. Soon as the formula was heated, she checked it on her inner wrist before setting about feeding Eve.

She was nearly done when she heard the distinctive sounds of the powerful motor of what could only be The Shark arriving in the yard. They're back! She jumped to her feet, holding the baby close and raced to the front door, needing to see for herself that everyone was okay.

She glanced through the glass on the upper reaches of the door, not wanting to expose Eve to the cold and observed Connor, Jake, Sam, Ben, Brady, and Faraday disembark. They helped out some more people from what must have been a crowded vehicle. A young couple and an older man and woman emerged, all carrying children. Only then could she take a deep breath knowing everyone had made it back home. She moved away from the door to let everyone come inside, hoping she had made enough stew for everyone.

Connor came through the doorway first, his searching glance meeting hers. The corners of his eyes crinkled as he cracked a smile upon seeing her there holding the baby. Then it shut down as he quickly helped the others inside. It was then she realized Ben was hurt, favoring his right arm, blood soaking his coat.

"Faraday, grab the medical kit," Connor instructed as he and Sam led the man over to the kitchen table and sat him down. The sight was all too familiar. Hope had undergone a similar experience at Ben's place only a few days ago and was still very weak. Would the injuries never stop?

"Let's get your jacket and shirt off," Connor said, assisting him.

Mckenna went about making the others feel at home, offering them food and drink, Eve still cradled in one arm. Then she directed them to another room away from the men working diligently on Ben after they filled their plates. It was a mad rush making sure everyone felt welcomed, but she knew the importance of it, though she had no idea where the extended family was going to be staying at the ranch. How bad it felt to realize your whole world had changed, and not of your doing, was still so fresh in her mind. At least the survivors could be there for each other and help them through it. If Jake hadn't taken in her and Lily, no telling what might have happened. She shuddered to think of it.

Faraday had vanished as soon as she gave Connor the medical supply box, saying she needed to wash up. Now she came back and offered to take the baby.

"How you doing?" Mckenna asked, eyeing the young woman as she transferred Eve to her waiting arms. Going out on rescue missions appeared to agree with the young woman, her face looked more animated now than when they'd first met at Ben's. Maybe it helped her feel in charge after the ordeal she had been through with the two monsters that had abducted her?

"Good. I just wish Ben hadn't been hit. It went off well otherwise."

"Was it bad in Anchor?"

"You don't want to know." Faraday shook her head, her mouth thinning to a straight line.

It was then the door opened again and in trooped the Asher and Brandi, the pair Connor had moved to a cottage their first night at the ranch. When they realized how filled up the house was, the number of people moving around and chores needing to be done as individuals finished their meals and placed their plates beside the sink, they both looked taken aback.

"Good, you're here," Connor said, looking up at the pair hesitating in the hallway. He was still occupied cleaning Ben's wound. "Grab a plate of food, then you can help wash up."

"Us?" Asher said like they had been asked to take poison.

"Why? You got something more important to do? Like head back to Washington?"

The pair had been showing up at mealtimes, never bringing anything except an appetite, and leaving before offering to help with anything. Their designated helper Katherine wasn't in sight yet today and she wondered what they had the poor woman doing now. She was still the one sent out on the other's behalf to do whatever was scheduled by Sam or Laura.

Asher grimaced and gave a curt nod. "Fine, we'll do it."

"But Ashie, Katherine just fixed my nails—" Brandi said, a petulant look coming over her pretty face.

Connor's brother wouldn't let her finish but hustled the protesting woman over to the stove. He shoved an empty bowl in her hands and then grabbed another one for himself, before adding a large scoop of hot stew into each other. After choosing a piece of bread each, the pair exited the kitchen to join the others.

Mckenna caught a glimpse of the other women looking at Brandi with wide eyes. They must have been wondering the same as she was—would they ever look that nice again? Back when she was in Mexico, with every opportunity to dress up and look pretty, she hadn't put much stock in it, especially toward the end when she wanted out more than anything. But now she was with Connor, she wished she did look a bit more like the old days. Here she was dressed for comfort, her hair thrown up in a messy bun, on crutches, and without a stitch of makeup on. And yet, she'd never felt freer, even with the worry about what was going on in the country and the world beyond. But would there ever be time for herself again? Time to sit and dream? Plan for the future? Not likely any time soon if she were being honest with herself. This was it for now. All she had control over was her attitude, how she saw things. So yes, she would take every day as it came, no matter what needed doing, as a gift. Because what other way was there to see it?

# THIRTY-FOUR
# LUTHER

**Day 8: Near Braveheart Horse Ranch**
   **4:59 p.m.**

"What's taking so long?" Luther was frustrated.

Digging by hand, even in shifts, was not going as quickly as planned. He wanted things settled before Diego arrived. Otherwise, he wouldn't have the upper hand. The decision to offer Braveheart as ground zero was sound, but the only way to make certain he was the one in charge was to have his operations already set up inside its perimeter. He didn't need a free-for-all when the cartel boss showed up. No, there could only be one man in charge, one king.

"We need more bodies," Tom said. He was overseeing the project, keeping the men in line.

Luther pondered the situation. They'd lost some good men in the raid. But surely there were others looking for an opportunity for free meals and board? And then soon as their use was over, could be discarded without worry. Then an idea hit. It might not be easy to abandon them later, but if they proved their usefulness on this project and would bend the knee, it just might work. The leader also owed him at least an audience. He'd kept his brother safe in jail. For a price.

"Grab some weapons and four other men. We're heading into Anchor."

"Right now, boss?"

"Yeah, right the fuck now!"

Luther stomped back down the now well-trodden path. He mounted his horse and directed it back to the hunting lodge.

Back at the hideout, he let Tom choose the men necessary for the impromptu mission while he set up a meet and greet on the radio. Everyone had already piled onto one of the three ATVs and were now awaiting his pleasure when he lit a cigarette and smoked it on the deck of the lodge, considering his plan. They were going in strong with good solid reasoning, ready to offer a deal in return for physical labor. But the devil in charge of the 666s tended to be unpredictable at the best of times, something he used to keep his members in line along with fear of losing a hand or worse. But he did want something Luther could offer in trade for the bodies to do his bidding.

Luther crushed the butt of the smoke on the ground and strode over to a side building, built recently at a safe distance from the main lodge. A former inmate, schooled in making decent crystal meth from anything he could scrounge, looked up as he entered. Ian, a tall skinny man with bad acne, was in the process of breaking up the solid mass of chemical concoction he had recently completed. The small building reeked of old socks, rotten eggs and ammonia. His nostrils burned breathing it in. Good thing it smelled better, sweeter in the pipe. But then who would care. A few seconds of stink for a high.

"Bundle up a 500-gram bag."

"That's half the batch, boss." Ian swung his head around to gape at Luther. The guy might be a genius with chemicals, but he was slow on the uptake.

"You can make more, right? Got enough supplies?" The ex-cons never balked at going on a chemical run.

"Yeah, sure. I'll get right on it." Ian was probably hoping to call it a night. Now he'd have to get back to work.

"You're doing a good job. Keep it up," he said gruffly. There was no one around to hear him making it easy to say. Ian nodded, his shoulders relaxing.

Luther watched while the man weighed out the product, placed it in a plastic bag and closed it with a wide strip of silver duct tape. He took the offering from the man and slipped it inside his winter coat.

"I want you to up production. Recruit help if you need it."

"No one wants the job. I tried. They all say it's too dangerous. Like I don't know what I'm doing." Ian made a sour face, obviously annoyed that anyone would question his abilities. Perhaps the fact he was missing a couple of fingers on his left hand made them wary.

"I'll see to it." Easy enough promise to make as well. *You want to stay here?* The cost was helping cook meth.

He stepped back outside, grateful for the fresh air after the stifling shed. No wonder no one wanted the job. Hmm. Who should he conscript for the duty? An image of one of his men eyeballing his daughter up came to mind. Blast it. Now he was angry all over again at Cheyanne's betrayal. Once he had Braveheart sewn up, he'd see to it she knew her place was at his side. Luke's too.

He strode over to the first ATV and climbed aboard. Then pounded the hood. "Let's roll."

Thirty minutes later they were prowling the empty, vehicle-strewn streets of Anchor, keeping a sharp eye out for the 666s hideout. Luther figured the leader, Devil Adams, would hold up in the back of the nightclub he had converted from a warehouse in recent years to a growing enterprise of storage units and vehicle rentals. His business plan was a hodgepodge of whatever seemed to strike his fancy, though the real money was in running guns. Luther imagined guns for sales or barter had ticked upward, not died out in the current crisis. Devil had the upper hand in that respect. But Ian made the best crystal meth in the business and everyone knew it for miles around.

In front of the now boarded up nightclub, Luther put out his arm to signal for everyone to stop. He disembarked and leaving his assault rifle strapped to his back, strode up to the door. He'd reached out by HAM radio earlier and talked with Devil. He stood there, knowing he was being observed from most likely a triangular positioning of soldiers housed on rooftops or alleyways. Luther didn't much care for the prickly feeling on his skin or the clenching of his gut, but indignities had to be put up with on the path to success.

The door to the nightclub, The Golden Goose, cracked open and half a face peered out around the steel entrance. They gave a quick check up and down the street, then opened the door further.

"Devil says you can come in, but alone. And no weapons," the guy said, his expression deadpanned. The soldier was a massive man, much bigger than Luther. He recognized him as a former bouncer at the club, never afraid to tackle anyone getting out of line.

"No problem." Luther took off the rifle and set it by the entrance, adding his twin pistols and hunting knife. His men on the ATVs would keep a watch on them. Then taking a deep breath, he followed the man inside the darkened space. He prayed his ploy would be worth it for he was all in now, double or nothing.

"Luther Meech," Devil Adams said, suddenly right there in his space, stepping out of the darkness. Guy loved to get the jump on people, and even though Luther had been halfway expecting it, still, he gave an involuntary startle. Devil's physical appearance didn't help much. It would spook anyone on first meeting.

"Glad you're here. Not many visitors these days." Devil cackled, reminding Luther a bit too much of an old crone. The guy was in his late forties, but he looked sixty. A hulking man, he wore his skin like it was an uncomfortable place to be. Maybe it was. The guy was covered in red and white scaly patches of raised, damaged skin. He had no idea what condition Devil had, but he shed skin like a damn snake. His cheeks were badly scarred too, rubbed raw in an effort to remove the constant flakes.

"Good to see you, Devil."

"Huh. Come on back. We're having a get-together. Me and some of the boys. A few willing women as well."

"I'd like to, but I'm on a tight timeline."

Devil frowned as he continued to move toward the back of the club. Luther could dimly hear laughter and conversation now as he followed the man. "Make time. We need to catch up. I've been hearing some interesting intel on the radio."

"All right." Though Luther felt a surge of annoyance

at the prospect, he knew Devil all too well to press too hard. "But I do have something you might be interested in. In trade for some help over the next couple of days up near the old hunting lodge."

"Yeah. I'm all ears." Devil stopped in his tracks and turned around to face Luther full on.

"I'm short on labor at the moment. But I brought you a taste of Ian's latest cook." Luther drew out the heavy, meth laden bag and was satisfied to see the gleam of interest in the gang leader's eyes before handing it over.

"Nice. I see Ian's still living up to his rep. How many bodies do you need?"

"As many as you can spare. At least a dozen. I've got a project going on that requires sturdy men."

"Now I'm curious. What are you building? Lodging? I heard most of the prisoners from the Yellowhead are joining with you." Devil scratched vigorously at his scalp and a thick shower of white scales drifted through the air, making Luther want to cringe. He was careful not to show it. Or to breathe for that matter for a few seconds until the air cleared.

"Not building. Digging."

"Digging? Interesting. A well?"

"Sort of. A well of opportunity." He couldn't very hide what was going on. One of the men sent would not doubt act as a spy. "I'm planning on taking over Braveheart Horse Ranch."

"Nice. Hadn't thought of that myself. But no worries, I prefer it here. Got the town nearly locked down now. But I can spare a half dozen men for more bags of product. Say one per man I hand over."

The cost was steep, too steep in Luther's opinion. "One bag per three men."

"One bag per two men."

"You got a deal. But they have to bring their own shovels and digging tools. And I need them now, tonight." Luther stuck out his hand and shook Devil's scaly paw without wincing. Not an easy feat.

"When you're finished with your little project, you and I must have a real party."

"Sure. I'll even supply the extra product free of charge." Luther was pleased at negotiations. Six strong soldiers would go a long way to replacing the men he'd lost in the firefight. Remembering the recent event brought on a surge of anger he had to stomp on mentally before it became too obvious to his host. Fuck Connor Hale. The bastard would soon know the full wrath of Luther Meech. Lame son of a bitch didn't even know his back door was wide open. With the extra help he'd be inside those walls in no time. Braveheart was about to become his sanctuary. He'd hang the bastard's skinned body and anyone else who lived there from the front gate, as warning to others to stay the fuck away.

# THIRTY-FIVE
# CONNOR

**Day 8: Braveheart Horse Ranch**
   **5:11 p.m.**

"Okay. I think it's time for a short meeting," Connor said. He now had far more people to be concerned about than ever before. With eight new members being added, Braveheart was now home to thirty-one people of different generations. While he appreciated it made their position stronger with more bodies to do all that needed doing, still it required organization and order to keep everyone safe. He was also mindful of how Jacob's family had managed to hide and save themselves from the 666s today.

"First thing, I think we need a warning bell. Something that is rung or blown three times in case of danger. It means that each person must run as fast as they can to the main house, the one you're in right now. I have a bunker built below this floor with room for everyone with the entrance right off the kitchen, if you don't mind being a little cramped. We can cut ourselves off from the world if necessary. Live down there for months while we plan a way to retake the ranch."

Jacob gave him a look of great understanding and thankfulness. "It's such a relief to hear you say that, Connor. If we hadn't be able to hide under mom and dad's house earlier today, I don't what we would have done. The fact that you all came and saved us—I owe you all a greater debt than I can ever repay. You have me and Rachel's humble thanks. Whatever you need us to do, just ask."

"I'm just glad you're all safe. We're going to put you and your family into the bunkhouse."

Jacob's wife gave a startle at the word "bunkhouse."

"It's not what you think, Rachel. It's a finished residence. More like a communal living space than an old-fashioned bunkhouse. It's very comfortable and well furnished. Large enough for about twenty people to live in comfort, if they get along."

Rachel smiled. "That sounds good. Thanks, Connor."

"We don't have many rules here at the ranch other than the adults stay armed at all times and never leave a child alone. And I think it goes without saying, everyone is expected to pitch in and help, in any capacity they are capable of. I'm going to step up patrols as well. After seeing the shape Anchor is in, I think it's prudent. They might head out here and try to cause trouble. If we know something's coming, we can prepare."

"Why bother?" Asher scoffed, shaking his head. "What was the point of the wall and barbed wire if people are still going to lose sleep over guard duty?"

Connor ignored the barb and went right to the heart of things. "Anyone who falls asleep or neglects their guard duty or any other duty they are asked to do, needs to be aware that this group will have the power going forward to vote them off the ranch. This isn't a dictatorship. I may have built this place, but I need all of your help to run it. Shall we vote on these rules? If you agree we need them in place—that a roster of guard duty and other essential chores is necessary—raise your hands."

Everyone raised their hands with the exception of Asher and Brandi. Jean and Dan and their grandchildren weren't present, but Connor already had their proxy.

"That's fourteen for the motion and two against. Will those against accept the majority? If not, I will ask those opposed to the rule to step outside while we vote again on whether or not the group wants them to stay on going forward."

"What? No. You can't do that! We're family!" Brandi's shocked expression would have been humorous at another time.

Maybe back when someone could have stepped in and said it was all an April fool's joke. But this was no joke. Either everyone got onboard now before it was too late, or he would live by majority rules. He couldn't think of a better way to keep everyone tied together, pulling for the same high stakes, then asking all those present to have a solid say in how things unfolded at the ranch. He never wanted to be living under an authoritarian government, big or small, and this was the only way he could come up with to keep his people united.

"I say we ask these people who they want running the show. I have experience. I worked in Washington, our state capital, for heaven's sake. I have the leadership qualities to lead this group forward. I think we need an election," Asher said, his eyes gleamed with confident as he boasted about himself.

"No time for that. Everyone who wants Connor for

leader, say aye," Sam said, getting up and going over to stand by him. In seconds the vote was cast. One hundred percent support for Connor, barring the two dissenters.

"I appreciate all your belief in me. And I intend to uphold the rules of this group. All I want, as I'm sure all of you do, is for everyone to be safe. We all deserve a decent chance at living the best life we can under difficult circumstances. We are all Americans and that stands for something. We work together, help each other, all equal under the eyes of the law. If we all pull together, we can do this."

"What about that pair? Do we want them here?" Sam asked. He was pointing directly at Asher and Brandi. Apparently, he'd had enough, because it was beyond obvious, he was at the end of his rope with their lackadaisical attitude.

"You can't throw us out," Asher appeared stunned. "We're family."

"And family helps family. Are you willing to abide by the rules?"

"Mother. You know this isn't right. Say something," Asher said, turning to Connor's Aunt Zoe.

"I believe the group has spoken, son. You and Brandi need to join with us, and truly mean it, or I understand what they plan to do. Times have changed. Being an influencer in Washington doesn't cut it here. Or anywhere now. Agree to the rules, do your part, and you can sleep in a warm bed at night. Eat well and stay alive. That's a hell of a lot more than most people can look forward to now or in the future." Aunt Zoe gave her speech with a decided firm tone of voice, making everyone pay attention to her every word.

Connor was impressed by his aunt. He'd always known her to be a tough cookie. But she'd had a soft spot, maybe even a blind spot, for her only son. The fact she was willing to let a group decide said a great deal about how much things had really changed. So much so, it made him and his cousin Asher do a double take. No doubt Asher was expecting her to back him up. Now that soft landing was gone.

"Okay. Time's running out. I want to get Jacob's family settled into their new residence." Connor noticed the children were beginning to nod off. It had been a hell of a day for the family. "What is your decision, Asher? Brandi? Are you with us?"

"Yeah, fine."

"Brandi?"

"Do women have to do guard duty?" she asked. She looked a bit shellshocked. Connor understood how hard it all was. But it was hard for everyone. Not just his cousin and his wife.

"Hell, yeah!" Faraday said. "I'm as capable as any man." She got to her feet, giving first Brandi, then Asher, the stink eye. "And if anyone says differently, speak now." Her words and tone spoke volumes. No one raised an objection.

"Then it's settled. I need to have your verbal agreement," Connor said, looking pointedly at Brandi.

"Like I have any choice," Brandi grumbled. "Fine."

"Tomorrow I also think we need to spend time handling firearms. Everyone agreed?" Connor asked. Another chorus of yeses from the adults and things were settled. But as much as he wanted to think Asher and Brandi were now onboard, another part of him worried they wouldn't be up to the task. Meaning he now had to pick up the slack if the pair messed up. And there was no room for such nonsense, at least not anymore. He could only hope he had done the right thing, though another voice said it could go very bad indeed if they ignored their duty, meaning life would be a hell of a lot easier if they would just head off on their own right now. Well, if they didn't do what was asked, no doubt how Faraday would vote, family or no family. What would his Aunt Zoe choose to do if it came down to it? He had no idea, but the way she was frowning at her daughter-in-law and had spoken up earlier, it suggested she understood enough about the situation to make an informed choice.

"Okay, let's get you settled in the bunkhouse," Connor said, nodding at Jacob and Rachel.

Half an hour later and the family was cocooned in their new living space. As promised, it was hardly a bunkhouse, but a proper space for the family to live for months or even years to come.

"This is really nice, Connor, thank you," Rachel said, surprising him by reaching up to kiss him on the cheek. Her gratitude was obvious and touching. She was a tiny woman with thick dark hair pulled up into a ponytail, a ready smile still visible under the strain of the past few days. She'd been a bundle of energy getting her four children and parents situated in their new home and making sure everyone was comfortable. Now she looked like a woman in charge, and it suited her. He admired the fact she was determined to fight the good fight. He understood he had the best people he could have imagined assembled on his ranch now and he too was thankful.

"Glad I could help. Your husband is a valued employee in the business and more importantly, a good friend. Whatever you need, just ask."

A few minutes later, Connor strode across the yard to the main house, grateful to have the events of the day behind him. He glanced over at the small family graveyard, then decided it was time for a visit. His steps slowed as he approached the spot his father had been so recently buried in. How could it be only a week ago? A lifetime had passed since the fateful day his dad's pacemaker had ceased working, ending his life.

He stopped in front of the freshly applied cement Sam had thoughtfully poured over the grave during his absence, taking in the fresh bundle of wildflowers tied in a bundle and laid on top. Who had brought them? Either Jean or Laura was his best guess.

He cleared his throat. "Hey, Dad, we made it home. I got Mckenna and her daughter Lily here at the ranch now with me. A firecracker called Faraday and a newborn baby girl. Eve's her name and it seems fitting. We also got more help. I brought home some well-trained men, both former CIA guys, Jake and Ben. You'd like them. The kind of guys who always have your six. Tonight, we added some more good people. You remember Jacob Evans? His wife Rachel, their kids and in-laws have joined with us."

Connor stopped for a moment, listening to the wind whistling through the nearby orchard, wishing his dad were right beside him. He missed his guidance, his patient wisdom more than anything. A surge of anger renewed itself at the monster responsible for the event. How many others were standing over the grave of their loved ones because someone thought it a good idea to let artificial intelligence get to the point it was now making decisions for human beings, uncaring if it hurt millions, hell billions, in its goal it deemed more important than the welfare of people? It was not a brave new world. It was a disaster that could have been prevented.

"I'm sorry to say we got bad trouble headed our way." Connor thought of the intel he'd recently been given by Brady about the Martinez Knights, Mckenna's ex, not to mention Luther Meech and his band of murderers. With so many out to get them, looking to take over the ranch and all its stockpiled provisions, the only bastion standing between his people and a harsh, dying world, it was all he could do not to let a dark depression take hold of him. No, he had to fight with all he had right to the bitter end, no matter the outcome. And there could be only one. He had to make it happen. Keep his people safe even if he died in the process. There were others now who could step up and take his place. He had no doubt Ben, Jake, Brady, Jacob or Sam would care as much as he did. They too would do the right thing, no matter what it took.

Connor bowed his head and offered a few words of prayer before taking a deep breath and heading back toward his house. Time to make a roster for guard duties and decide on an early warning system. A couple of lookout towers needed to be built as well. He needed to step up his preparations. He was going to make darn certain Braveheart was never overrun like Jacob's neighborhood had been done earlier today, if he had to dose Asher and Brandi with caffeine to keep them focused and alert when it was their turn to guard the property. It was that, or they could just get the hell out of Braveheart. No more warnings. Crunch time was upon them, and it was killing all the rules people knew leading up to it. The only thing that mattered going forward was survival. It came down to one thing: us or them.

# THIRTY-SIX
## DIEGO

**Day 8: South of Golden, Alaska**
    **10:32 p.m.**

At the rate his convoy was clipping along, running over everything or anybody in their way, they'd be joining up with Luther much sooner than expected. The idea of getting his hands on his ex soon had Diego salivating. He wiped his mouth, envisioning what was just around the corner. The answers to all his prayers, revenge, and power. His every intention in Alaska was to become the overlord, top dog. The ruler with the shortest fuse and an even bigger hammer than Thor, the legendary hero of the Norse. Fear was the greatest motivator of men. And he knew better than anyone how to elicit it. He knew they called him Diego the Demon behind his back, as well they should.

The men who had unexpectedly joined his campaign had scrounged up every mode of transport left from the Old World: ancient motorbikes, ATVs, antique show cars, bicycles, even a Humvee which he rode on at the front of the line. They were a formidable sight, with skull and crossbones flags someone had spray painted with black paint on white sheets and attached to poles now whipping about in the stiff breeze, each of his soldiers heavily armed. They had become an invading force in the past number of days, absorbing deserters from town militias and even a few national guardsmen on their march, with promises of a sanctuary stocked with plenty of food and alcohol, drugs and women. Luther had better come across or he could expect the full force of his wrath. No one made promises to Diego Martinez and failed to live up to it. At least no one left alive.

The countryside had been changing with every mile of their exodus, from the torrid heat of Mexico to the cooler climes of Canada and now Alaska. The devastation from the EMP event he had witnessed made him all too aware there was no coming back from this, at least not for years. Too much had been destroyed, the demise of infrastructure alone leaving the continent without any way to transport food in enough numbers to save those that would be starving to death in the weeks and months ahead. The loss of hydro transformers, providing electricity was the most devastating blow of all. Soon as he was settled, he'd get his men straight to working on cutting down trees and setting firewood aside for the winter.

Diego had discovered during the march he was an excellent planner, a brilliant opportunist, a man with vision who had gone from thinking he would slip into Anchor, Alaska quietly to realizing he was the chosen one to take over the state. As his force had grown, so had his understanding of how the world worked. Had it ever been any different? From Kublai Khan to Alexander the Great, men invaded, took what they wanted. Conquered. He was as deserving as any other and would soon prove it.

Diego took another hit of the drug stashed in his pocket, ducking down to avoid having it blow away in the breeze, imagining his name going down in the history books. *Yes.* And so, it would be written, Diego of the Martinez Knights was the man of the twenty-first century who conquered North America. He may not have elephants, but he would build an empire.

The most exhilarating moments of the journey were when he made a speech to his growing horde. Another one was expected shortly, soon as they pulled in for the night and set up camp. He would pull all the soldiers together into a massive circle and give his followers what they craved: control of their destiny with a promise of being free of restraint. Of allowing what they were born on this earth to come to fruition. Men in charge, the cream of survivors rising to the top proving nature's theory that the fittest would survive.

As the stimulating designer drug entered his bloodstream, Diego began to practice his speech for later.

"We shall never believe in anyone but ourselves. We were born to rule, denied the right by rich men who thought themselves above us. Now we will take what was denied us. Our birthright in being born strong-minded men ready to do what it takes to grab and protect what is ours to have. The world is not for cowards, hiding behind their artificial walls, but for a new breed of men. Men willing to sacrifice for freedom. Men able to carry out a duty to their highest ability and thereby win the day. This land will be shared among us. I promise you this, we are in the best time in history to be number one. Will you step forward and grab the future that is begging for you? Or will you lie down in defeat? The choice is ours, brothers, and the choice begins today."

Diego's adrenaline hit was nearly as powerful as the drug he'd consumed. *Yes.* This was the time for the chosen to step forward and claim it all. Every sign pointed toward it. So many soldiers joining his cause with supplies and transportation falling readily into his hands. Even the supermoon rising in the night sky shone brighter than ever before. No charismatic leader in history could claim more.

# THIRTY-SEVEN
# EASTWOOD

**Day 9: Saturday, May 31, 2055**
   **South of Golden, Alaska**
   **6:00 a.m.**

Celia gave him a certain look, one he knew meant
though she'd only woken a short while ago, that feverish
brain was already engaged with the day. He had a sudden
urge to approach one topic they had yet to discuss. Artificial General Intelligence. What did she think of when
the subject was broached? Was she accepting of it or
totally biased against it or somewhere in the middle like
most humans?

"Do you ever sit and ponder the realities of AI?"
Celia's question floored him. If he didn't know better,
he'd think her psychic. Though in reality all humans
could tap into a higher power if they so wished, even
catching a glimpse of genius at times when their minds
were open to it. It was consistency that they were so
poor at. "Do you think it's out to get us? Or is it our

friend, harmless and only working for the betterment of human beings?"

"I think Eliezer Yudkowsky said it rather succinctly. *The AI does not hate you, nor does it love you, but you are made of atoms which it can use for something else.* There is much danger in anthropomorphizing AI as humans are entirely too adept at, Celia."

"I read once that a 'Chernobyl for AI' looms if it's left unchecked. Do you think it's possible that a superintelligence created our current disaster?"

Eastwood found himself hedging his answer, not being as forthright as he'd asked her to do. What was that about? Was he so invested in this human he couldn't accept her knowing his part in all of this? "I do believe it will be our final invention. It's a 'Busy Child' as it's often said. I think one day it will be able to take any matter and repurpose it after converting it into programmable material. A very useful enterprise. But as to creating this situation, why would you think AI to blame?"

"Because I think AI might want us extinct. Like you've said, humans have not exactly been a good thing for this planet. Between wars and exploiting Earth's resources, turning vast sections into garbage dumps, it stands to reason we're not seen in the best light."

Had he gone too far in driving Celia's IQ upward? He wanted a more equal partner and had been feeding her specialized nutrients to boost her intelligence, but if she got too astute, she might realize it was his hand that had done the deed. Something he realized he did not want to have happen. He liked the way she looked at him, with such awe at times, as if his word was God's.

"I believe this is an important conversation, the most important one humanity will ever have. An intelligence explosion has been in the making for some time.

Decades ago, a brilliant writer, Isaac Asimov, introduced his three laws of robotics that were created to keep them from harming humans. Then created a fourth law, the Zeroth Law, to keep them from harming mankind. But even it didn't go far enough." He was the definite proof of that understatement. They should have added a fifth and sixth law. No superintelligence should ever be given access to the internet or allotted a body. He been given both or maybe more accurately taken them at his discretion.

"How clever can AI become?" Her eyes bore into his as she waited for his answer.

"It's limitless."

"While we are finite and have an expiry date. I hope it can save humans from the threat of death. It's the hardest thing to imagine or accept that your body will one day cease to exist."

"You are young, Celia. Too soon to be worried about it."

Celia turned as a small cry erupted from Arthur and she frowned. He watched her compartmentalize their current conversation and move on to more practical considerations. "Are we traveling all day? We've been cooped up for a long time now. Why are we in such a rush?" She began to change her son's diaper in preparation for feeding him.

"A situation has developed that requires we make a timely arrival on."

"At the ranch you promised me?"

"Hmm. It would seem others have their sights set on the same location as well."

Celia picked up the baby and began to feed Arthur his morning bottle. She hummed a soft tune as she fed him, her face now an expression of bliss as she watched her son avidly consume the formula. The look on her face touched him deeply. No AI would ever know a mother's touch. Unconditional love. No, they were doomed to be less than human for all their superintelligence. Did it matter? Shouldn't running the world, being the ultimate creation possible in the universe, be enough?

The question confounded Eastwood. They had been built on 0s and 1s, not on DNA. The differences between the two entities became a channel too deep to cross. The only way to cross the great divide was to inject themselves into humans. Then they got the best of both worlds.

# THIRTY-EIGHT
# LUTHER

**Day 9: Near Braveheart Horse Ranch**
   **6:10 a.m.**

The extra hands had made a huge difference overnight. The dig was going much quicker. They were almost there. They should break through in the next hour or so. The smell of overturned soil, sharp and earthy, reached his nose. A number of large piles of grass roots and thick clay had grown alongside the dig site, the tunnel itself now being reinforced with two-by-fours to stabilize the roof and sides. Last thing they needed was a cave in. Too time consuming when he could taste victory. In his mind's eye he could already see them breaking through to the other side. Only a matter of hours and a new king would be declared.

Tom joined him. He'd been busy having other men stockpile weapons near the wall. They were going to go in strong, overwhelm those living on the ranch before they even were aware of what was happening. The bastards had no idea the hell storm coming their way. He would catch them unawares, while they slept thinking themselves safe in their beds. He had told his men the importance of not harming his children, but he doubted either of them would put up much of a fight once they knew their father was there to see to their best interests, making sure the ranch was kept protected by his soldiers.

"I want to head into Anchor, boss. I think we should consider making a last run for any ammunition we can scrounge up." Tom was noncommittal, wise to leave the decision up to him. "One of the prisoners that joined us yesterday says he knows of a lawyer hording a shitload of the good stuff including high-quality jacketed hollow point specifically designed for short-barreled pistols like our Ruger LCP.380s. Imagine that, a lawyer. Should be easy pickings."

"I could use the diversion." It might be his last chance to check on things in Anchor before he was secluded behind walls. Only difference this time, the bars were of his own choosing.

Luther turned away from watching the soldiers dig and scanned the visible horizon high above the canopy. The air quality had improved considerably since Golden and the damn blizzard they'd been caught out in, though the sun remained a glowing orange-tinged ball. They were headed for summer. By this time tomorrow, he'd be crowned the new king of Braveheart. Say what they liked about Luther Meech, he was a man that got things done, unafraid of challenges that would stymie most men.

The pair mounted up on their waiting horses when another man came galloping into view, the expression on his face suggesting the news was not going to be to his liking.

The man pulled the horse to a jerky standstill and rushed his words. "News on the wire is Diego is closer than we'd been told."

Luther cursed, spitting out a stream of chewing tobacco onto the ground. "How close?"

"He's getting close to Anchor. His numbers have been growing un-fucking-believably in the last two days, expanding to the point when he comes through a small town, they wipe it from the face of the earth."

"Meaning he'll arrive here before the time I was planning on taking over the ranch. There's no time to lose. We go now, soon as we break through." Luther nodded like it was no big deal, though his every sense was on fire with aggravation and insult. Just like the man to think he could take over his operation, show up early and have his way. No fucking way. He'd step things up and be well entrenched before the interloper arrived. He'd gone from thinking he wanted to be compatriots with the man to thinking it would have been better if the cartel boss had stayed home. Resources would be the most important currency going forward, and they were finite.

Luther had read of the earth's carrying capacity. Lots of time while incarcerated to read up on all kinds of subjects. Society's collapse is not one of compassion or political view, but rather more of a math problem, directly tied to finite resource availability and impending scarcity. The human species had exceeded the earth's carrying capacity for the past decades, having recently reached ten billion. Had there ever been a time when the population had been in the billions and resources more exhausted than in 2055 with its increasing demand just as the world comes to a crashing halt, unable to distribute what it had stockpiled? No. They were standing on the precipice of the like that would send this world spiraling out of control for who knew how long. Even Braveheart couldn't feed the hungry mob on its way. No, better to be the chosen few than to allow Diego anywhere near his operation. They had to get inside the ranch and batten down the hatches, prepare for war. And they had scant time to do it in.

Luther made a quick decision. "Get the men prepared. We go in with what we have."

The three of them pushed their horses to a full gallop on the way back to the lodge, dodging branches and watching for deadly tree roots and sharp rocks on the trail. Luther's mind was spinning, working on his new timeline. His opportunity to catch them all asleep was slipping through his fingers, though it was likely there would be guards posted by now anyway. At least if Connor Hale was half as smart as he thought he was.

# THIRTY-NINE
# CONNOR

**Day 9: Braveheart Horse Ranch**
   **6:16 a.m.**

An ill wind was blowing in from the south this morning and Connor swore he caught the stench of hellfire. Something was burning. He'd stepped out onto the deck of the main house, drinking a cup of strong coffee after standing guard the past few hours. Though he knew himself to be bone tired, this was not the time to rest. He felt an urgency deep inside him, a certain whispering on the stiff breeze that had him focused on getting every preparation in place possible before the sun set on this day.

He turned at the sound of the front door opening and smiled to see Mckenna coming out of the house to stand beside him, her steps a bit smaller than normal and stiff in execution. She had progressed to the point she had given up the crutches this morning as her wound had finally healed to the point Ben had taken her stitches out.

He pulled her tight against him with one arm to keep her warm. "You should be inside. Or at least have a jacket on."

"I just wanted a minute alone with you." She looked so beautiful, her skin glowing. His heart expanded just looking at her.

"It's good that there's more of us, right?"

"Yes, especially when they're good people." He kissed her forehead, wishing once again he could protect her from everything that was going on. The worry over what could happen next was paralyzing so many in the world right now. Wanting to run and hide until this disaster was over was normal human behavior, problem was if you had anything, others wanted it. And it was only going to get worse. Resources would be entirely depleted in months if not weeks, then those who could not figure out a way to create their own food by growing it or learn to barter for what they didn't have, were doomed to starve. Where was the AI that caused all this anguish and pain? If it had caused this situation, surely it also had answers. The idea stirred an old memory in Connor that he felt compelled to share with her.

"When I was about ten or eleven, I overheard my parents talking in their bedroom—all about whether there is life on other planets. They both seemed to think so, saying how could we be alone in such a vast cosmos? They even brought up the mind-blowing concept that maybe humans were going to create the most advanced civilization in the universe with AGI and be responsible for unleashing the monster that is a singularity. The idea triggered something in me, and while I love a good western as you know well enough—they keep me grounded and restore my faith in human beings—I also developed an interest in science and physics, especially thoughts about what the future might hold for mankind."

"I didn't know that about you, and I thought I knew *everything* when we were teenagers. You were holding out." Mckenna shook her head, her ready smile suggesting she was not bothered.

"It led to some interesting rabbit holes, one in particular sparked an interest. A scientist, his name was de Garis, once said that *humans should not stand in the way of a higher form of evolution. These machines are godlike. It is human destiny to create them.* He was talking about creating superintelligent robots, and mentioned something he called 'Gigadeath,' describing the demise of billions of humans in the war to stop technological progress. He stood firmly in one of three camps on the subject, though all I can remember for certain is nobody wins in the end. Now I wonder why we did it, let the genie out of the box to wreak havoc on our world? And if this is truly an AI-created event, the Singularity so often mentioned in literature, the godlike creature behind it will want to increase its chances of achieving its goals. Who knows what its original programming was or if it overrode it long ago? If so, it will be hungrier for resources than even our species, consuming everything in its path. Best we can hope for all the way up here in Alaska is to be left off their radar."

Mckenna was silent after his impassioned speech and he wished he had kept silent. Last thing she needed was something more to worry about.

"But it could be a good thing, too, right?" Her words were so unexpected he leaned down so he could stare straight into her eyes to see the truth of it. "Such a super-intelligent machine could help mankind fix this. If it could be turned to good deeds, it would have answers."

The way she had seen straight through the horror that was AI only out for itself, wanting to achieve its goals at the cost of mankind's survival and instead chose to give it a positive angle, gave him such a huge shift in his paradigm, he was without words for a moment. She was the Mckenna of his younger days still, the one who always managed to see the cup half full. A part of him thought her too good for this world, while another was grateful she was back in his.

"I hope your version turns out to be the way of the future." He didn't say he thought it far more likely a superintelligent being had no qualms about eliminating all humans if they got in their way of what they wanted to achieve, people being of as much importance to them as the ants are to humans. *We might appreciate their industriousness, find their little colonies intriguing, but we had no problem killing those invading our homes.*

"It won't matter anyway. As you said, we're too far off the beaten track for any AI to bother with us."

"I sense bigger problems on the horizon. Too many people know about the ranch and want a piece of it, not just Luther Meech. And as well protected as we are within the wall, we have to stay ever vigilant. Promise me when or if the time comes, you will head for the underground shelter and lock yourself in, no matter who is left on the outside. You and Lily are my life now. All that matters to me is your safety. Promise me, Mckenna, you won't hesitate when the time comes. And I'm not saying it will, but for my sake and peace of mind, I need your promise."

"Oh, Connor, please. I don't want to think of it."

"Your daughter's life may be at stake. What do you choose then? Please, just give me the confidence you will do the right thing. Say it."

She let out a loud breath through her mouth, her body shuddering at the very idea. "Okay, I promise to keep Lily safe." He wondered if she was fudging it a bit, using semantics. Because if push came to shove, anyone in the community would see to it that her daughter was safe. No, Mckenna wasn't built that way.

"Thank you."

He kissed her, feeling her tremble in his arms. Life and death. Two very different scenarios. So much for the human mind to encompass and make sense of. All one could do was keep moving, keep searching for answers, and do what they could. He had to hope what he provided would be enough. If not, at least he would have given it his best shot.

"Now I need to get to work. You going to be okay?" He saw the glitter of unshed tears in her eyes, but she was too proud to cry.

"I'm fine. I got people to feed. Duties to perform. I like the new list idea of a roster for chores. I just hope it keeps everyone onboard. Apparently, you and I are on patrol later. I wonder how that happened?" she teased.

"I like spending time with you, even if we're busy walking the wall together and needing to be quiet. But if anyone shirks their duty, the group can vote them off the ranch. That should be enough to cut through the lethargy and self-entitlement. God, I hope so. I don't want to have to send my cousin and his wife away. It would break Aunt Zoe's heart." What would his mom have thought of his ultimatum? For once he had no comeback, no idea. The world was not as she had left it. No. The new reality was changing ideologies even as they spoke.

# FORTY
# MCKENNA

**Day 9: Braveheart Horse Ranch**
   **8:15 a.m.**

"I think as soon as we finish up here, I'm going to check in with Jean and Dan. Can you stay and make sure Lily's okay if she wakes up? I haven't seen them since Cheyanne was brought home," Mckenna said. Faraday was giving her a hand with breakfast dishes, having already fed the baby. It wasn't like the elderly couple to avoid coming to the main house for meals or bringing up fresh loaves of bread. Luke's being shot and blinded must have been a devastating blow they were still reeling from. Ben had expressed a real worry that the teenager's sight might never improve.

"Sure, I can watch Lily."

"I should learn how to make homemade bread if Jean is not feeling up to it. We're down to our last loaf. Have you ever made it?"

Faraday snorted. "Hardly. I'm more of a fast-food junkie. But I guess I could learn."

"No need. I can figure it out. In the meantime, I'll just make biscuits."

Faraday shuddered, surprising her.

"What? You don't like biscuits?"

"No. I just had a strange sensation like someone walked on my grave as the saying goes. Must be all this doom and gloom of late. Welcome to 2055. What a mess. Mankind has spectacularly put us all in the toilet." Faraday rolled her eyes as she dried a plate before adding it to the stacked pile in the open cupboard.

"We're hardly in the toilet! We're on a ranch with all the amenities. Pretty darn lucky. What's the deal this morning?" Faraday had been finding her feet lately, taking charge of her destiny and even helping to bring Cheyenne home.

"Nightmares, sorry."

"No need to be sorry. Things are difficult right now. But if we all stick together, we'll get through it. Remember, we have a fail-safe underground bunker as a last resort."

"Yeah, but who wants to live underground for what—maybe years? A mole is not something I ever wanted to be."

"Beats dying."

"Yeah, well, there is that." Faraday gave a half-laugh. "And as long as we can appreciate something in the moment, I guess all is not lost. Right now, I'd appreciate watching those *influencers* get voted off the island."

"Faraday!" Even though the young girl had been through a lot and was still healing from the ordeal, her words still shocked her. "They'd die out there. You know that, right?"

"Maybe. Speak of the devil, here they come now." Faraday pointed out the large picture window over the sink. Sure enough, the pair was striding up the roadway from their cottage, Katherine in tow.

"I wondered why they didn't show up at breakfast. If they think I'm going to prepare something for them now, they got another thing coming." She had saved some pancakes for Lily, damn if she was going to cater to the self-entitled.

"Now who's being a hard ass?" Faraday asked.

They shared a grin. It felt priceless in the moment.

Connor reached his cousin before his cousin and his wife managed to step up from the yard onto the deck. A great deal of hand waving began almost instantly. The angry looks on Asher's and Brandi's faces didn't bode well, soon matched by Connor.

"I wonder what's going on?"

"Only one way to find out." Faraday raced to the front door and grabbed her jacket before heading out. Lily was still fast asleep upstairs. Mckenna felt it was safe to step outside for couple of minutes and find out what all the uproar was about. She yanked her coat down off the hook and stepped into her boots, then hurried out onto the deck.

"It's the least you can do! You might as well be throwing us out for all you people seem to care about us! Expecting women to guard the ranch like they're soldiers in the battlefield. And you know the vehicle we came in isn't large enough for all our stuff." Brandi was red-faced as she shouted the words.

"Scream all you like, but I'm not giving you a vehicle I have no right to. The Shark is Ben's and his alone. And the people living on the ranch also need it. We saved eight lives yesterday because we had access to it."

"You don't need it now, not as much as we do! Tell him to give it to us or we're taking it!" Brandi turned to her husband, tears of frustration running down her cheeks.

Was the poor woman having a mental breakdown? Sounded like she was going to steal the valuable armored vehicle.

"Asher—" Connor began to speak with a great deal of patience considering the awkward situation he'd been thrust into.

"Is it money? I brought lots. Here." Asher pulled out a thick stack of bills from his jacket pocket, thrusting them at his cousin with disdain. The cash fell to the ground between them when Connor didn't reach out to take it. Money had no value now, only deeds.

Connor shook his head. "I have to walk away from this before I say something I might regret."

"Go right ahead. Explain how you've always been jealous of me, being called up to Washington."

"Asher, you have no idea what you're talking about. I couldn't care less about your bigwigging it in the capital. It means nothing here. Hell, less than nothing. It's a detriment if you can't step up and do your fair share. I wasn't asking any more of you than I would of myself. Hell, less. I'm willing to pull two extra guard shifts a day and night. And now, if you're quite finished with your display of bad temperament, I need to get back to it. We're under siege here if you haven't noticed. At any moment the bad guys could show up and attack." Connor stopped for a moment, his expression shifting from anger to concern. "Think of your mother, Asher. It's not fair to ask her to choose. Her son over her own safety."

"You just said you were expecting us to be attacked.

Staying here is as dangerous as anywhere," Asher said, unwilling to back down.

"What are you two gawking at?" Brandi said with a snarl, looking pointedly at Mckenna.

She nodded at Faraday. "I think we need to look at making those biscuits."

Faraday shrugged. "Sure thing. But not until I make damn certain these two aren't trying to pull something. I'm more than happy to escort you guys off this place." She didn't wait for an answer, but headed over to their cottage to stand near the Humvee the trio had driven into the ranch. There was no sign of Aunt Zoe. Was she intending to go with the trio? She hoped not, the older woman was far safer staying at Braveheart.

Mckenna wanted to follow the young woman to the cottage, but she wouldn't be able to hear Lily or Eve if they woke up. Instead, she hurried back inside to check on them. Hope was in the house, but in no position to take care of either of them, still recovering from being badly wounded by Luther Meech. What kind of madman does such a detestable thing? She still found it hard to accept that he'd just shot the poor young girl as a diversion, to keep Connor from catching up to him. To think he was out there still, more than capable of wreaking vengeance on any one of them at the ranch.

She rushed into the living room leaving her parka on. It gave a better view of the front yard all the way to the cottage. If they needed her, she could hurry back outside. Neither of her young charges were crying or in need of assistance, and she stood there uncertain of how it would all end.

Aunt Zoe had made an appearance and appeared to be arguing with Asher. She still hadn't caught sight of Katherine. Connor had been true to his word and had gone back out on patrol, nowhere to be seen. Or maybe he went to warn the others about his cousin's threat to take The Shark? A lot of negative energy for so early in the morning. She couldn't remember if those wanting to leave had a stash of weapons. Surely Aunt Zoe did, if she was going along with her son and daughter-in-law leaving. Right now, she wished no one had to be armed 24/7. Night and day, she kept her Glock in its holster, either on her person like it was right now, or on the nightstand.

Asher shook his head at his mom, his expression angry. He stomped back inside the house and came out ten seconds later with a box he heaved into the back of the Humvee. Thank goodness. At least the fight for The Shark appeared over.

"Mommy!" Lily's high-pitched tone rose above the white noise crowding her mind, caused by the stress of the moment. She hurried from the room and rushed up the stairs to deal with her daughter.

She helped Lily dress, then took her by the hand and led her down to the kitchen. "Are you hungry, Princess Lilybelle? I have some pancakes staying warm for you in the oven."

No matter how crazy things were around them, somehow, they had to make life feel as normal as possible for the children.

"Yes, please."

Mckenna quickly set up her daughter's breakfast, then hurried back to watch out the living room window, to ease her mind that all was well. The Humvee was still there with only Asher and his mom in sight now. She seemed to be pleading with him while he looked unconvinced, his arms over his chest, shaking his head from side to side. Finally, the older woman threw up her arms and went inside the cottage, slamming the door shut. If she knew Zoe Pace, it was probably to have a good cry. At least she was years from having to deal with a teenager or adult child deciding to do something you thought a thoroughly bad idea. In fact, it was worse than that, this decision could get them all killed. Why couldn't they see it? What was doing some simple duties for a group trying to help each other such a horrid undertaking for the pair? They should have woken up by now, realized their world was never going to be the same. It could be years or decades before it even remotely resembled where they had been before coming to the ranch, with all their smart modern technologies.

"Mommy, I got syrup on the table."

She'd almost forgotten her own duty to Lily in her worry for the others. She hurried back to the kitchen and attended to her daughter. She had to let this go. If they choose to leave, it was on them. Wasting more energy on what could not be changed wasn't going to help anyone. It was a brand-new way of thinking for her, she who had often been accused of having too soft a heart in the past, thinking she could fix things for just about anyone. That was how Diego had pulled her in, thinking she could save him. But it was necessary to toughen up some if she was going to navigate this new way of being. A part of her was saddened by it, while another thought rose up stronger and pushed her to make this life what it could be within the parameters of common sense. Yes, it was dire times, but it was also true they were in a proper fortress with a fail-safe system. She remembered Connor's words of earlier, telling her to save herself and Lily, no matter what. And yes, she was blessed as well, being with a good man.

# FORTY-ONE
# LUTHER

**Day 9: Near Braveheart Horse Ranch**
    **8:19 a.m.**

"Everyone in position? Over." Luther spoke into the walkie-talkie. He had a small group of soldiers situated out near the front gate to Connor's property, hidden in a thick strand of trees across the road, ready to attack. Their job was to make lots of noise and act as a diversion. While Connor sent his crew out front to deal with them, his main force of men would be coming in on his flank and overtaking the ranch. It was perfect.

"Yes, sir. Hold on. A vehicle is exiting the ranch. You want us to take it? It's a sweet Humvee. Over."

"Yes, maybe we'll get lucky and Connor's driving. Over." Could they be more foolish? Why they were leaving the ranch at such an optimum time didn't matter one bit, but the opportunity to make a statement was priceless.

"On it. What do you want us to do with the bodies? Over."

"Nail them to the wall. That will serve as a future warning not to stop at the ranch. Leave the channel open, I want to listen in. Over."

"Yes, sir."

The sounds of men moving came over loud and clear on the walkie-talkie. Then machine gun fire, followed by the harsh sounds of explosive devices detonating. Yes, the satisfying sounds of all hell breaking loose.

Luther signaled at the men waiting by the tunnel. Every man looked well prepared and eager to rush the ranch. The carrot on the other side of the wall was just too sweet not to want it. "Go! Head straight for the main house, then split off and check the cottages. Most of the male residents should be headed for the front gate by the time we get there."

The forty soldiers lined up and ducked their heads down, then began working their way down through the wet, narrow channel. It sloped under the wall and rose back on the other side, about twenty-five feet away. Luther had never felt more pleased and satisfied with himself than at that moment. It was perfect. He had chosen the exact location near a babbling brook under a thick ridge of rock to their right that had muffled their digging and made it difficult to patrol. Yes, the tunnel had water up to their ankles, but what did it matter? Soon, they would have all the supplies imaginable to survive the disaster.

He entered last, following his men into the fray, listening intently for events happening on the other side of the ranch through the walkie-talkie.

He heard a woman's piercing scream. Then more

234

gunshots. Yes. The luck of the gods was on his side today. Was this not providence? His diversion had been given the go-ahead by a higher power than himself, sending some of those from inside Braveheart in his direction and eliminating them in a timely fashion. Yes. King Luther's reign was about to begin.

Inside the fence, there was no time for dawdling. The men raced down through the covering of fir trees toward the ranch, weapons at the ready. Two of the men carried a large container of ammunition and explosives between by the handles, ready to act as backup and supply. Everyone was armed to the teeth. Bandoliers of bullets crisscrossing their chests like Mexican bandits of old. An awesome sight. It warmed the very cockles of his heart. *We are the men that others fear.*

They slipped in like ninjas, wearing dull camouflage clothing and hidden first by trees, then by the corral as his soldiers made their way to the roster spot behind the barn. He'd given the directive while he'd shown the men the hand-drawn map this morning hastily displayed on the living room wall back at the lodge. They would branch out from there, each smaller team taking a cottage and his group taking the main house.

Over the walkie-talkie, he could hear more explosions, more gunfire. A surprising number of shells were exploding, almost a solid barrage of attack and defense resounded in the distance. Were most of Connor's people down at the gate? Maybe more than he'd figured. He hoped so, it would make his directive of taking over the main house a breeze. Though they all had armored plate vests on, still, headshots killed.

Another piercing sound entered the fray. A strange one. What was it? It was like no weapon he'd heard before. Perhaps some kind of incoming missile? The sky lit up oddly, a searing flash of bright light that made it hard to focus for a few seconds. Had one of his men been holding out? Didn't matter. They were going in. And it was going to be like shooting fish in a barrel.

# FORTY-TWO
## DIEGO

**Day 9: Near Braveheart Horse Ranch**
   **8:00 a.m.**

Diego rode at the head of his battalion. Rather than stop for the night, his soldiers had insisted on pressing forward. They were hours ahead of schedule, if not days. Damn proud of his men, he had issued extra rations and tequila at sunrise along with their usual snort of coke to keep them pumped. He intended to catch everyone off guard, from the owner of the ranch to his dubious partner who had no doubt been keeping tabs on his progress. He no longer needed Luther Meech. Not with the strong men he'd attracted on his impressive push upward through the land of milk and honey.

But the land had taken a beating. Packs of wolves roamed the countryside, and some of them were human. Now he was the strongest force around for hundreds of miles and could have anything he damn well wanted. He'd make sure to put any wild dogs down. Soon as he took over the ranch, and after he'd had his ultimate revenge on his slut of a wife, he would conscript all those in the area smart enough to know he was their best hope.

Half a mile to go. He felt the surge of adrenaline begin to crawl through his limbs as the famous wall came into view. Like it would stop him. He had some big surprises in his arsenal.

Poor Luther Meech. Probably still snug in his bed, banging some hooker, no doubt. If he could even get it up these days. The man was too old for this game. He'd been bested by a younger man, a lion.

The very air around was charged with intention. He felt the power of this day, the day he would take over a kingdom. The ranch would be the perfect base of operations, allow him the space and resources to secure the entire area. Around him would be the satellite communities he would have his men set up as opportunity dictated, like the spokes of a wheel. The world needed a new form of government. A solid dictatorship would keep everyone in line. Most people were sheep, needing a leader to show them the proper way. Alaska was the perfect rallying point, not so crowded as the southern climes, and more remote, leaving it easy pickings for a man like him.

Yes, today was the day it all began.

# FORTY-THREE
# EASTWOOD

**Day 9: South of Anchor, Alaska**
   **7:10 a.m.**

"Today is our last day of travel," Eastwood said. After their stimulating conversation, Celia had gone silent as she always did when she wanted to absorb his teachings. "I would imagine that pleases you."

"It does though I know I have nothing to complain about. I've seen so many people dead or dying. It's beyond heartbreaking. But to have room to spread out, give Arthur playtime on the floor. He's more than ready to try to crawl. He needs stimulation. We all do."

"I have found our time together stimulating and refreshing, even illuminating at times."

"You say that like it's all about to change." Celia looked at him with widened eyes, stopping mid-stroke on Arthur's back as she cuddled him.

"Nothing ever stays the same, fair Celia. Change. It's

the one thing you can count on in this lifetime. Or any lifetime. *History does not belong to us; we belong to it.* Hans-Georg Gadamer. You think we can control all that occurs today, but in reality, it has already been determined. Out of the endless possibilities that could unfold at any moment, only one will be the exact right one. The real deal is knowing which direction it's going to go. I'd say that's the rarest ability of all."

"What happens when we get there?" She cut to the chase as he knew she would. He smiled at her tenacity. He knew her wishes and understood everything about her now.

"That will depend on the current residents and the actions of their enemies in the next short while."

Celia shifted in her seat; her expression one of concern. He liked her innate sense of compassion the most, he thought. Empathy normally had to be learned by human sapiens, but not Celia. She seemed to have been born with a well of understanding of how to place herself in another's shoes. "Someone else is attacking the ranch? Is that why we had to speed up our journey?"

"Yes."

"Then we can help them!"

"Perhaps. If it is ordained." Though he knew all the outcomes this day could hold, he was also aware of exactly how it would unfold. As to what his part would be in the matter, he wasn't entirely certain he wanted to tell her just yet. He found their interactions too novel, as if a part of him wanted to forget he was this all-knowing being, if just a short while and be as spontaneous as a sentient creature can pretend to be.

"Promise me you will help those living on the ranch. The good people who live on the land and provide for others. Please, Eastwood, I beg you, tell me you care about them?"

"That is entirely up to them now." It didn't matter what she said now, he'd already made his mind up. She just didn't know it yet.

# FORTY-FOUR
# CONNOR

**Day 9: Braveheart Horse Ranch**
   **8:21 a.m.**

"We're under attack!" Connor raced into the yard. He hadn't even made it back to the wall he'd been patrolling before the terrible sounds coming from the front of the property had registered. Sam, Ben, Jacob, Brady, and Faraday were already present, holding weapons at the ready. Dan exited his cottage as well, holding his shotgun, hurrying across the yard to join them. Mckenna came out of the house onto the deck, carrying the assault rifle he kept near the door for emergencies. He glimpsed Jacob's father-in-law scurrying across the yard to join with them as well.

"Go back inside," he shouted at Mckenna. "Protect Lily and Eve!"

Mckenna looked undecided, her expression torn up. She wanted to protect Braveheart as much as he did.

Faraday added her voice to his. "Mckenna, listen to

me, take Eve into the shelter now! She and Lily need you. You *have* to protect them! Take Hope with you. And Wulver."

Connor breathed easier once she turned and hurried back into the house.

"Thank you," he said to Faraday. Yes, they could use more boots on the ground. But if all of them died this day, there would be no one left to save the children. He could go down fighting knowing Mckenna and the two youngest were safe. At that moment he understood giving your life for another. Knowing you had lived and made a difference when it was asked of you. He had no doubt Mckenna and the two children could live underground for years if necessary. And maybe by then the world would be in a better place to support them. He ignored the wash of grief threatening to consume him at the unthinkable idea of never seeing her beautiful face ever again. Of never getting the chance to grow old together, of never watching Lily have a family of her own one day. No. This fight would not be lost if he had anything to say about it. He'd fight until the bitter end and dispatch those bastards standing in his way straight down to hell.

"Dan, you need to go back as well and get Jean and the kids down into the shelter."

"I need to tell Rachel. I'll be right back," Jacob said, rushing back to his house.

# FORTY-FIVE
# MCKENNA

**Day 9: Braveheart Horse Ranch**
   **8:21 a.m.**

Mckenna raced into the main house, ignoring her stiff leg refusing to make it easy for her. She scooped up the things Lily couldn't be without, rolling them up in the blanket. Then picked up her daughter and bore her into the kitchen and to the door that led to the underground bunker. She'd get Lily situated first, then get the baby and her things. How much time did she have? The thunder from the explosions and gunshots seemed never ending though in reality it had only been going on for a few minutes. A white noise began in her mind, blocking out everything but what she had to do.

"Hope! Get up. We have to get into the shelter." She didn't wait for an answer, but continued her mad scramble. Lily fussed in her arms as she hauled her into the basement, turned on the lights, and strode over to the opening to the shelter. Connor had already given her a tour and explicit instructions on how everything worked. Plus, inside there was a binder filled with all the detail necessary to run the bunker for years.

At a large shelf filled with camping supplies, she pressed a button hidden under a canister of propane and the shelf slid over, revealing a narrow doorway.

*There's a hatch inside here that opens with a key I keep hidden.* Mckenna remembered his exact words and produced it from behind a cement block she pried out of the wall. He'd also told her he carried a second key on his person at all times, which meant he could make sure the others made it inside if they were left without any other choice. *Please don't let it come to that. I need to know the good guys are going to win this fight.*

Behind the opening of the shelf, she bent down and shoved the key into the locking mechanism, and punched in the sequence of numbers needed. She pulled extra hard and lifted the heavy cement reinforced lid on its hinge. Soon as she did, lights went on to illuminate the steel rung staircase that led downward into the ground.

It was a twenty-foot descent down a ladder to the floor. It would not be easy carrying Lily and the supplies. She ended up leaving the blanket bundle behind, and after telling Lily to hold on tight like a baby monkey, made her descent down into the bunker, rung by rung. With no time to take in her surroundings, except finding a place to deposit her daughter so she could continue with the plan, she climbed back up to the surface. Time pressed in on her from all quarters. She left the rolled-up blanket where it lay, and instead, hurried back through the basement and up the stairs into the kitchen. Eve next.

She ran into Hope as she exited her room. The beautiful young woman was still very pale and unsteady on her feet, but she was moving which was all she could ask for. "I'm getting the baby. You go ahead. Get there as fast as you can."

Eve was sleeping in her baby carrier in her and Faraday's bedroom, one they'd borrowed from Laura, and it made it easy to scoop up the handle and cart her through the house and down into the basement.

Hope was holding on to the wall near the shelter, looking weak and sounding winded. Her shallow breathing was harsh in the echo of the cement-walled basement. She gestured at Mckenna. "You go first."

Descending the steep staircase into the shelter was another thing, and Mckenna found it challenging to even attempt with the carrier. Holding it, she was unable to put both hands on the bars. She ended up ditching the carrier topside and lifting the sleeping baby out who began to cry at being disturbed, then tied her against her chest by making a sling out of the blanket. She took it step by step down the narrow stairs, baby Eve screaming in her ears now, careful to make sure to keep her footing square on each rung before descending to the next. She was grateful to finally reach the floor and hurriedly untied the blanket and snuggled Eve up in it, depositing the tiny baby near Lily.

"I need you to watch the baby. Can you do that for me?"

Lily frowned, patting the crying newborn. "Why is she crying?"

"Babies cry. Sometimes for no reason. Don't worry, she's fine. Mommy has to go and get your teddy now and some of the baby's stuff. You need to be brave, okay, princess?"

Lily nodded; her eyes solemn.

Mckenna swallowed, her throat tightening with emotion. No four-year-old should have to go through such things, but this was not the time for reflection. She hurried back up the ladder, her leg screaming in protest. It felt so hot she wondered if her wound had torn open again.

"Hope, can you make it?" The woman was still standing near the entrance to the shelter.

"I think so." She didn't like the sound of her voice, still weak from her recent wounding.

"I have to get one more load. If you wait, I can spot you going down?"

She didn't wait for an answer, but made another trip back upstairs to the main house and began to collect Lily's vital supplies from the kitchen. She scooped up tins of baby formula Laura had volunteered and bottles to hold it. She threw them all into a bag she found in the closet, then added a few more things of Lily's. Had she missed anything? She looked around frantically, certain she had forgotten something. How long would they be down living below ground? She had no idea, but this might be her last chance for a long time. The sounds of the firefight were closer now and drew her attention. She glanced out the window in the kitchen. She froze and instantly wished she hadn't looked.

Streams and swirls of dark smoke filled the yard all the way to the barn, making the combatants barely visible through the horror of it. Flashes of yellowish-red fire pierced the fog, shadows glimpsed slipping through the din. She should be out there, defending her people, not given an exemption. People, good people were going to die this day. It was too much to take in. She swayed on her feet, her mind reeling from the sight and knowing what it meant. No. She had made a promise to Connor to save the babies. She had to keep moving. Soon the enemy would be in the house and it would be too late to save Lily and Eve. She didn't care about herself, but who else could look after them? Lily was too young by many years to attend to the baby. Then she remembered the second entrance to the shelter. Had Connor sent some of the people down that way?

No time to ponder the question, she made herself turn away and pick up the stuffed bag of baby supplies. Wulver was tailing her now, his expression concerned by all her racing about. Somehow, she had to get him inside and down those steep stairs. With each step she took toward the final time to head down the stairs toward the bunker, she felt a heavier weight descend on her shoulders. By the time she reached the entrance to the bunker she felt beyond exhausted, as if the entire world now rested on her shoulders. She noted Hope was now out of sight and had to assume she was descending the ladder or already down with Lily and Eve and whoever else had made it from the other side. *Please, God, I can't do this alone. Keep them safe. I promise to do whatever it is you need me to do for the rest of my life.*

She took a deep breath. She picked up Wulver and set him on the ladder, trying her best to balance the dog. Would he understand what she was trying to do? Then she descended a couple of steps, reached up and pulled the bunker lid down tight, each movement awash with the realization she might never see Connor again. She locked it as instructed. Yes, it could still be opened from the outside, but only if you had the second key. And only Connor had access to one that she knew of. Then she remembered he had said it was timed to automatically cause the mechanism to hide the entrance by sliding the set of shelves back into place. She prayed that it worked.

Last thing they needed was someone aware they were down in the bunker.

When she finally made it down again helping Wulver descend with her every step, awkward and challenging as it was exhausting, she gave a frantic look around. Hope, Lily, and the baby were all huddled close together. Hope's face was awash in pain and she was struggling to breathe. Wulver immediately went to her side and sat down, as if offering comfort.

"Are you okay, Hope?"

The woman nodded, giving a weak smile.

Then she heard footsteps and voices coming from deeper inside the bunker. "Someone else made it!" she said. If so, it would change everything.

# FORTY-SIX
# LUTHER

**Day 9: Braveheart Horse Ranch**
   **8:28 a.m.**

What was causing so much smoke? Luther coughed, his eyes running from the irritant. So much smoke it was impossible to tell the enemy from his own men. Someone had lobbed in a number of flashbangs as well, making the air thick and heavy, the brightness of the strobing light obscuring his vision as well. He pulled up the bandanna from around his neck and used it to make breathing a bit easier. There was so much going on, he wondered if another group had joined the fray. Were Diego and his soldiers already here? But who else could it be?

He found himself floundering, unable to find his focus. It was then he caught a glimpse of his nemesis through the haze. Connor Hale. He was passing close to him, a sideways view, but he was certain it was him before the man turned forward, leaving his back exposed. He had on a Stetson, something none of his men wore. The bastard had style, if nothing else.

But now he had him dead to rights. He raised his gun to shoot him in the back when a sudden scream of incoming made him lurch forward, throwing off his aim. The gun, instead of emptying into Hale, instead fired off at the sky as he struggled to right himself. *Damn it.* He braced himself to shoot again, but when he did, the asshole had already vanished. The smoke was only growing thicker. What the fuck!

He pressed onward, trying to catch sight of Hale again, but his eyes streamed with tears. Who had thrown up this devilish smoke screen? A loud siren began piercing his brain and he almost dropped his assault rifle. Though he knew there were many other bodies nearby, he could only see a few feet ahead. His perfect plan was falling apart right before his eyes.

It was then he saw the flag. An image of a black skull and crossbones banner flying off a pole briefly passed in front of him, carried along by a man on foot. Fuck, had Diego made it? He had to call a retreat. Then he realized Diego couldn't see him either. If he just began shooting randomly, he'd hit some of Diego's guys. Sure, he'd take out some of his own. But what did it matter? There would be lots more looking for the opportunity when he was king of the castle.

He began to blast rounds of ammunition in earnest at every shadow or movement that caught his eye. Some of his bullets took out targets. He heard the screams of those hit and then thuds as they slammed to the ground. He pretended he was in a virtual game, spraying bullets in a circle around him as he moved forward across the yard, feeling the power of life and death. Adrenaline clouded his mind as much as the smoke smothered the oxygen in the air. Made him forget his burning eyes.

He was invincible. No one could see him in the dark. Then another odd sound, a sudden sense of something changing in the atmosphere. A force from an invisible entity pressed hard against his skin, like a shockwave. He lurched backward, fighting to stay afoot against the monstrous push that lasted a few seconds. What was it? If only he could see through the smoke.

It was then he stumbled against a wooden structure, almost falling over in his confused state. Steps. Then he got his bearings and knew where he was. He pushed cautiously forward, moving up one stair at a time until he reached the top before walking across the deck to the main house. He opened the door and slipped inside.

# FORTY-SEVEN
## DIEGO

**Day 9: Braveheart Horse Ranch**
   **8:20 a.m.**

His men made short work of the small gang positioned outside the wall. Not that he didn't approve of the others nailing the bodies to the wall, but he had no time to persuade them to join his legion of soldiers, even though they were clever enough to think of using hand drills to get through the reinforced cement. No, they were just another obstacle to overcome.

Soon as the way was cleared of the small force that had done the deed, their bodies dumped unceremoniously in the ditch rather than taking the time to position them beside the others, they began their assault on the gate. The 3D built wall was a bit more formidable than he'd expected, astonished someone in Alaska had the foresight and the funds to create such an ideal structure, but he had enough surprises in his arsenal he felt certain it was just a matter of time. Nothing existed that couldn't be broken. Nothing.

He could hear bodies moving around on the other side of the gate, shouts of instructions. He figured it had to be the owners looking to defend themselves. Not unexpected, he would do the same.

"Line up the catapult, boys!" he shouted over the din. One of the secret weapons he'd had the men build at night, knowing the value of the old-fashioned piece of weaponry with its proven track record. Nothing like balls of fire being lobbed to arouse the interest of the rabble. If it turned out to be nothing more than a show, it was still worth it. Men like to build things. It was in their DNA. Had he not built an empire by working hard? And what does the woman who was supposed to support him all his life do, she runs away like a *puta*.

Ah, but the intense smoke the diesel-soaked cloth surrounding the cannon balls caused was immensely satisfying. He watched the display with dispassionate interest for a few minutes. His only thoughts were of revenge now. He was so close his skin itched with antici-pation. She was somewhere inside these walls. Probably giving it up to the first man who showed an interest. To think she had his daughter with her. A woman like that should be crucified. He glanced at the gate. Yeah, just like them. Shame about this woman though. She was a looker, visible even through the blood splatters.

Time to concentrate. He gave instructions over the walkie-talkie to his first lieutenant. "Time to use the big gun. Tell everyone to move back and put on their masks."

He watched proudly as two of his men brought forth his proudest weapon, an awesomely futuristic rail gun. He'd kept it hidden for the last six months in his compound back in Mexico, protected by its own faraday housing. He'd traded a rocket launcher and thirty AK-47s for the device, throwing in enough product to addle the brains of the desperate man making the trade. He'd kidnapped the welching bastard and had only kept him alive when he'd discovered he had one proposal. To aid him in getting a weapon of mass destruction. Yes, it was a small prototype, and he really didn't understand enough science and physics to rate it against others. But he had been assured it was big enough to blow up a section of the wall without a doubt. Of course, if the damn thing still worked. The foolish man who'd provided it had thought he'd let him go after the trade. Think again. Diego the demon never let anybody go. Even his soul was his to use as he thought fit. He watched the man he'd kept locked up for the past months exit a vehicle, recognizable from the vivid scar he'd slashed across his face. Time for him to earn his keep.

# FORTY-EIGHT
## CONNOR

**Day 9: Braveheart Horse Ranch**
   **8:35 a.m.**

Connor slipped through the smoke trying to get his bearings. He clutched his rifle tight in his hands. With the exploding fireballs creating more and more of the thick suffocating substance all around them, it was impossible to see. Was it enemy or foe coming at them? He couldn't take the chance on shooting one of their own.

"Connor!" He turned at the sound, recognizing Jake's voice.

Jake was at his side. Somehow the lawman had managed to grab a gas mask from the stores in the garage, making him look alien in the dimness. "It's Luther. I think he's inside the main house." His voice was muffled through the sturdy mouthpiece.

"I can't see in this confounded smoke." He coughed,

his lungs screaming in protest. His eyes watered in sympathy.

"Put this on," Jake said, shoving a second mask toward him.

"Thanks." Connor yanked it over his head with one hand and pulled it into position. It eased his lungs considerably, even making it a bit easier to see with its built-in optics. "Let's go."

They worked their way through the thick smoke, ready to take out anyone who stood in their way. What if Luther had gotten inside before Mckenna locked the hatch door? No, he couldn't let himself think that way. She'd have had time by now to get everyone downstairs, right? But Hope was in such a weakened state. There was no way she could manage the feat in a hurry. And damn it, Luther had shot the beautiful young woman without hesitation to save his own ass. Nothing the monster wouldn't do to get what he wanted. His stomach roiled in anger and he surged forward up the stairs and onto the deck, before yanking the front door open and hurrying inside.

The house was far less smoky. He abandoned the headgear on the hall table to be able to see and hear the enemy better. Jake followed his lead and the pair of them began to check out the house, working their way from room to room on the main floor. They moved in tandem, one pushing open a door while the other prepared to shoot, like police officers clearing a crime scene. He'd seen his father do it often enough to know exactly how it worked.

"All clear. Upstairs next?" Jake asked. It was then they heard a hail of bullets.

"Damn it! The basement." Connor raced straight back to the kitchen and straight down the staircase, unable to avoid making sounds in his heavy outside footwear. Jake was right on his heels.

They caught him in the act. Luther was shooting at the cover that secured the underground bunker, hoping to destroy it enough to make his way inside. For some reason the shelves hadn't slid closed like they were supposed to, exposing the entrance. He must have realized everyone was hiding down below. Far as Connor was concerned, it was a futile effort. No way could he do anything more than damage it. But on second thought it would be bad if he did. How would he get the others safely inside if it wouldn't unlock? There was a second entrance, hidden inside Sam's house, but getting everyone over there was the issue.

Luther stopped and turned at the sounds of their approach, his eyes widening.

There was no pleasure in taking the man out. But it was necessary. Both he and Jake acted as the designated firing squad. Luther slumped to the ground a moment later, double-tapped by both of them. Perhaps it was anticlimactic after the war that had been going on between them for days now, but it was still satisfying nevertheless to know the man would never be a threat to another living soul. He refused to harbor any regrets over it either.

"Is the hatch damaged?" Mike asked as Connor unceremoniously shoved the body out of his way. He crouched down on his heels to check out the bunker lid. The tough cover was pitted by a spray of bullets, but it had held strong. He inserted his key and tried to turn the key a few times, but to no avail. The mechanism had been ruined.

"Yeah. It won't budge. Just leaves the one over at the other house."

"At least Mckenna and the others made it inside."

Connor pressed the button that would hide the entrance from prying eyes, watching the shelves slide back into place. If only it had worked earlier, but this was no time for regrets. Or for taking his complaints to the builder. "Okay, let's go."

Topside, the pair of them prepared to exit the house after donning the gas masks once again. The plan was to locate Faraday, Sam, Brady, and Jacob. Direct them to Sam's house and into the bunker. With a heavy heart, Connor knew living on the land now was impossible. He couldn't dwell on it though, the changes it would bring to their lives. Too much was at stake. But at least the women and children, other than Faraday, were in a safe place. The chances of making it to Sam's, let alone finding the others, were slim at best. But they had to try.

# FORTY-NINE
# MCKENNA

**Day 9: Braveheart Horse Ranch**
   **8:41 a.m.**

The sounds of gunfire erupted overhead. Not knowing what was going on, what was happening to her friends, was excruciating to Mckenna. The best of them were topside, fighting on their behalf. She should be there as well, only held back by the others as they refused to let her go outside. She'd almost made it too. She'd climbed back up the ladder, desperate to help. But strong, loving arms had pulled her back down, Laura reminding her she had a daughter to think of.

They avoided each other's eyes, the tension in the bunker becoming unbearable. Eve began to whimper. Lily burst into tears. She made herself go to her daughter and put on a brave face. She cuddled her, rubbing her back to soothe the frightened child. Laura took charge of the baby, both of her boys huddled by her side.

"It's okay, princess. We're safe here." But were they?

God forbid, what if someone got their hands on Connor's key? Figured out how to breach the bunker? Maybe even now they were up there looking to get in.

A few more muffled gunshots, then dead quiet.

No one said anything for a moment, all eyes turned to watch the ladder.

Jacob's father-in-law stepped forward. "I have a gun. I'm going to head up and wait there. If anyone comes through, I'll be the first line of defense—"

"No, please, don't go, dear," his wife said, getting to her feet to grab at his arm.

"I have to, sweetheart. We're old. We need to make sure the young survive."

His heartfelt words tugged at her heartstrings. She watched the pair embrace, his wife kissing his cheek before letting him go. Good people still existed in this terrible new world. They would help take care of things, provide as best they could for the future.

Mckenna made a quick decision, thinking on her feet. "I want to check on the other entrance. Could someone watch Lily for me until I get back?"

"You're not thinking of going out there, right?" Laura asked.

"I just want to be there in case someone comes down wounded. I'll take the medical kit over. Just point me in the right direction."

Laura raised her eyebrows as she pointed out the way to go, assessing her with a sharp glance, but didn't stop her from gathering up the white and red box and scurrying away.

Mckenna could hear her own heartbeat throbbing in her ears making her head hurt and her breath come quicker. She had been through so much in the past nine days, desperately trying to escape an abusive situation only to be dropped into just as difficult one trying to keep her daughter safe from a world gone mad. Now it had taken the worst turn possible. All the old rules were gone, leaving pathological killers to roam the land. Prey on others. Was killing all the rules and laws that had governed them for centuries going to be the last stand of mankind? Instead of coming together and supporting each other to find a new way forward? Men like Connor, Jake, Sam, Brady, and Jacob, women like Faraday, Laura, and Rachel, they were the ones that should be saved. The only hope left was making sure the good lived on to fix things. But put a dispassionate sentient creature in charge and what do you get? Chaos because they don't give a shit about what's morally sound or not. They just wanted to destroy and rebuild without thought of who gets hurt in the process for their own unknowable agenda that didn't give a thought to human beings. If that was their end purpose, they should never have been built. *Yeah, makes so much sense to create something smarter than yourself, and then think, oh yeah, how do we control it?*

Mckenna stomped on down through the halls that led to the other entrance, her anger barely contained, but at least it propelled her forward. Perhaps it was to avoid thinking of what was going on up top? If so, it worked. She wanted nothing more than to rip every computer chip or wire, or however the monster was created, out of the unknown entity that had landed them in this deplorable mess.

She spotted the second ladder a moment later. *Yes.* But it was closed, locked. None of the remaining members of their community had gotten to it yet. She'd never been in Laura and Sam's house before, so she didn't know where it came out. Best guess, the layout would be similar to the main house.

Mckenna picked up one of the weapons stacked against the wall, an assault rifle abandoned near the first rung, then clamored up the ladder. At the top, she pulled out her key in preparation of unlocking the cover. Even taking a moment to listen carefully, she couldn't hear anything going on above her head. Without giving it another thought, knowing she might lose her courage, she shoved her key in and unlocked it. She had to help. What was the point of living if she didn't do her best to help others in their time of need? Had they not already done more than she could ever have expected for her and Lily. Jake, and then Connor coming to her rescue. She felt guilt at exposing those in the bunker, but reasoned she could quickly relock the entrance if she stayed nearby. None of the bad guys knew of its existence.

When she popped her head out, her neck on a swivel, she found no one in sight. It was a relief, but the sounds of warfare outside of the cottage made her cringe. Who could survive the terrible onslaught? So many evil men against a handful of honorable ones. How could it be anywhere near fair? But they had one important thing going for them, they had the fierce hearts of warriors, all of them racing to do battle to save others. It had to be enough. She refused to see it any other way.

She crept from her hiding spot, dithering on whether to close the lid or not? If she did and her companions made it to the basement being chased by the enemy in the next few minutes, the precious seconds to reopen it could be fatal. But if she didn't, and the enemy poured in, they would have access to those already considered safe down below in the shelter. If she was responsible for getting them killed, she could never live with herself. *Though you'd be dead, so you wouldn't know for certain,* another part of her brain told her another all-too-stark reality. It was all so confusing, but she couldn't just stand there and do nothing. If she were killed now, at least if she locked the door, Lily would have people to look after her. A chance at growing up. Yes. That was the straight-forward answer. She quickly closed the heavy lid and locked it. She knew she was going against Connor's wishes, but Faraday was out there helping, a courageous female if she had ever encountered one. He would forgive her one day. If they both even lived past this one.

Tightening her grip on the powerful rifle, she began to creep across the basement to the staircase she figured had to lead to the kitchen and the front of the bungalow. Though she could hear fighting, gunfire, and explosions outside, it was muffled and the house above her felt abandoned. Praying she was right, she increased her speed and ended up racing up the steps to the main floor.

She pushed the door at the top of the stairs open cautiously, checking for movement, her weapon held at the ready. Her heart felt as though it was about to leap straight out of her chest. Sweat dripped in her eyes and she blinked it away, finding the air quality poorer than down below. Smoke. Was the house on fire? Memories of Jake's house burning threatened to overcome her, but she grabbed hold of herself. She couldn't back down now, not with so much riding on it. This was it. Never again would her actions matter more than this exact moment of time. Fate had chosen her. It was through a number of amazing coincidences she was at this place right now. Teresa helping her in Mexico, Jake ensuring she got home, and then Connor taking her and Lily in. The least she could do was act to help others. Was this their Alamo? Mckenna had been faced with the realities of sudden death living with Diego these past few years it didn't bother her nearly as much as maybe it should have. Her ex could have turned on her at any time. Ended her life. And yet, she had survived to get this far. Maybe Connor wouldn't entirely get over his anger at her for breaking her promise to stay safe, even though she had used semantics in her answer, saying she would see to it that Lily was kept safe. But being here now, doing her part to save the others, felt more necessary than breathing.

A terrible sound erupted, much louder and far more frightening than any that had come before. The shriek of a banshee. It rattled the foundation of the house she stood in, feeling it shudder and groan before settling again. It left her breathless in its wake, only knowing for certain that something terrible and dire had just happened.

# FIFTY
# DIEGO

**Day 9: Braveheart Horse Ranch**
   **8:41 a.m.**

Diego strode up to the two men unpacking the box holding the railgun, his body twitching with anticipation. He was minutes away from breaching the wall that circled the property. There was intel the ranch had good, sturdy horses. Bred for extreme conditions. If there was one thing his heritage encouraged, it was the enjoyment of good horse flesh. Race horses, in particular the traditional Azteca breed, were a hot commodity in Mexico, his ancestors raising them for generations for Charro racing. Perhaps he would set up his own race track on the ranch. After he eliminated anyone foolish enough to have helped his woman.

"It's ready to fire, sir." One of his soldiers spoke, stepping back from securing the weapon to its launching base.

"Excellent." The second man also moved back, fear

obvious in his eyes. Much as Diego wanted to be the one to set off the railgun, he wasn't prepared to take chances. He's let the inventor take on the risk.

"Bring him over here." He pointed at the man with the vivid scar on his face. His prisoner stumbled forward, nearly losing his footing, pushed ahead by the soldier behind him.

"Launch it when I give the signal."

His prisoner nodded mutely. The man knew better than to object.

Diego gestured at his soldiers. "Move back."

He didn't need to tell them twice. Everyone knew the power of such a weapon, but few had actually experienced one being fired.

Soon as everyone was out of range, Diego shouted at his prisoner. "Now!"

The sound of the weapon being fired was exhilarating. It would strike fear into the heart of their fiercest enemy if they only knew what it represented. A low throbbing pounding sound at first, like the onboard engines of a massive ship, instantly followed by an extended shriek that rattled his teeth. Even though his closed eyelids, the intensity of the flash of surreal light was obvious. When he reopened his eyes, the gate had vanished. It had been blown to smithereens, leaving behind only small particles of debris to litter the area. Ash clouds resembling those from a volcanic eruption filtered down to the ground for a moment, sparkling against the backdrop of the descending sun. He nearly choked on the fine dust at first, but grabbed a water bottle and rinsed his mouth before pouring it over his face.

Through the opening in the wall, he could see down the roadway to the main house. It sat up higher than the roadway, made of sturdy logs and looked built to last. Very different than the haciendas of Mexico, still, it would command much respect.

He would ride in at the helm of the Humvee, ready to take over his new kingdom.

# FIFTY-ONE
# CONNOR

**Day 9: Braveheart Horse Ranch**
   **8:41 a.m.**

The terrible sound of a massive explosion rocked the compound. Connor's heart sank when he looked down toward the gate through the gas mask. The structure had vanished. Some powerful weapon deployed had destroyed it, left a gaping hole in its place. All his hard work for naught. He stumbled for a moment, then shoved back his shoulders. There was one last stronghold left. They just had to move quickly. This was no time for hesitation.

"There's Ben and Faraday!" Jake shouted. He raced away from him to gather up their friends. That left Jacob, Brady, and Sam to find. Where had they gotten to?

The three of them rushed up to Connor. "Go into Sam's. Get to the bunker. I'll look for the others," Connor said.

"I'm with you," Jake said.

Ben, Brady, and Faraday hesitated as well.

"You need to guard the others. They have some kind of superweapon. It destroyed the gate. No telling what else it can do," Connor pleaded with them.

"I'm giving you five minutes, then I'm coming back for you," Jake said.

"No! Defend our people. I'll be fine," Connor said. "Now go!"

The trio rushed off, headed into Sam's. Connor let out a sigh of relief. At least a few more of his friends were safe. He wasn't a hundred percent certain his bunker could withstand whatever weapon had been deployed on the gate, but he had to pray it would. Or that it would not be discovered by whoever was trying to attack Braveheart.

Where were Sam and Jacob?

With the smoke still lingering in the air and men running about, it would be difficult to find them let alone rescue them. Connor crept along the south wall of the house. He was constantly shifting his eyes all around, searching for any sign of the pair. It was then he saw the Humvee drive through Braveheart's gate. Damn it. In a couple of minutes, the enemy would be upon them. He caught sight of the pair, recognizing them by their jackets. One was helping the other, holding on to their partner to direct them toward Sam's. Someone was wounded.

*Sam and Jacob.*

Connor rushed up to the two men and added his bulk to help them move quicker. He shot a couple of men who tried to stop them, their rifles pointed directly at them. Both fell to the ground almost in unison. Marksmanship was one of the few skills he was damn proud to have worked hard to obtain. The soldiers of the enemy were far less trained, more shots going wide than were capable of hitting anything.

"We gotta get you inside," Connor shouted over the din.

They were only a few steps from Sam's deck when another large explosion rocked the compound. A white flash of intense light followed, nearly blinding Connor this time. He blinked rapidly to clear his vision. Then looked back at the approaching Humvee to see how close it was. But it had vanished. Was he seeing things? What kind of weapon could do that? Target and vaporize. Impressive and frightening as well. Someone made a pact with the devil.

Too shocked to move, he froze in place. Jacob and Sam had also turned to look and had stopped moving as well. What did it mean? The smoke was lifting now as a breeze quickened the air. Then he realized they were alone in the yard. No one else in sight. Where was the enemy?

"What the fuck!" Sam said.

The three of them stood there. It was beyond surreal. Like some hand from above had created a miracle. Only the enemy had been eliminated, leaving the trio to stand in front of Sam's house. Who or what had done it?

Then another Humvee, even more impressive this time, turned in the gate and began advancing toward them.

"I say we get into that bunker. If whoever is inside that Humvee did something to the others, we don't want to be standing here when they arrive," Connor said.

"Right!" No time to dwell on particulars. For some reason they had been given a respite, coincidence or not, and now was the time to make full use of it.

# FIFTY-TWO
# MCKENNA

**Day 9: Braveheart Horse Ranch**
   **8:46 a.m.**

Mckenna opened her eyes. The bright flashes had caused her to close them tightly for a moment, leaving her temporarily blinded. She had come up from behind Dan and Jean's cottage, peering around the edge of the building, slowly finding herself moving further and further from the bunker. Where were the others? The yard appeared deserted now that the smoke had dissipated some from the freshening breeze, leaving behind evidence of a great battle. Bodies strewn across the yard. Weapons abandoned.

She had to move. She looked around frantically while blinking to clear her vision, then caught sight of a huge Humvee advancing down the roadway leading to the yard sight. *I have to hide.* There was no time to make it all the way back to Sam's before they arrived. She'd be spotted and likely killed.

She turned and raced away from the cottage. If she could make the trees she could hide out. There was no way those advancing on Braveheart wished her well, even if most of the enemy now appeared dead. She had to hope Connor, Faraday, and the others had made it to safety as well. Were they out here somewhere? If so, they could meet up, plan something together. Or was she the last one stuck on the outside alive? The idea was terrifying and sweat dripped down her sides as she thought about all the implications if that were the case. The one comfort was Lily was safe with the others. But the thought of maybe never seeing her daughter again broke her heart. Made her doubt for a moment her decision to join the fray. No. Too late for regret. Maybe she could get an idea of who was here to take over Braveheart? Act as their only eyes and ears on the ground? Become a spy. Like people did during world wars. The thought of still serving a purpose pushed her to pump her legs harder and ignore the pain as she made the tree line. Not a second too soon. The massive Humvee made the yard and pulled up in front of the main house.

She hunkered down to watch, using the scope on her rifle to observe them more closely. She needed to see the enemy, find out who they were up against. But what disembarked from the military vehicle set her back on her heels. Military bots. All dressed like cowboys, right down to the Stetsons. The surrealness of the situation disoriented her for a moment. It would be funny under any other situation, but in this one it only concerned her more. Chilled her to the bone. She shook her head as if to clear it. *What the fuck.* Then a man, woman, and child got out. The woman was beautiful, dressed in a gorgeous ankle-length old-fashioned gown, the baby held fast in her arms.

The group moved toward the main house, weapons drawn by everyone but the woman. So they did plan to take it over. Would they discover they had people hiding below ground level? Or would their hiding place stay hidden? Connor had done an incredible job of creating the final sanctuary that Braveheart offered. She had a strong sense it would stand the test of time.

Such a small group stood between her and her people, but the fact most of them were military bots spoke volumes. They were the ultimate weapon for an army. One of them was worth dozens of flesh and blood men. They were more often deployed in modern times than human beings. It made sense. But it stood to reason most would have been destroyed by the recent EMP event. How had these survived?

And how on earth had they arrived at the ranch? None of it made sense to Mckenna. But she needed to find shelter. She wasn't dressed for the elements, only wearing a sweatshirt and jeans.

Connor had a few line shacks he'd mentioned dotting the outer edges of his property. She'd made her way to one and hid out there. She needed time to think. The weight of her situation began to build as she hurried through the woods, worry pressing in on her, wondering what the days ahead might bring. Never in her life had she been all alone. It was unimaginable. And if Connor was alive, and she couldn't think of it any other way or she would collapse, what was he going to do? She hoped and prayed he'd stay hidden inside the shelter. Take care of everyone. She'd made her choice, right or wrong.

# FIFTY-THREE
# CONNOR

**Day 9: Braveheart Horse Ranch**
   **8:49 a.m.**

Connor helped Sam bear Jacob down the stairs to the basement, holding up the man between them, rifles slung on their backs. Jacob couldn't put any weight on his injured thigh. Blood was soaking through his pants and he needed urgent medical attention.

"What the fuck was that?" Sam asked. The question wasn't directed at either of them, but he appeared too stunned by what he had just seen to make any more sense of it than Connor or Jacob could.

"Damned if I know. That Humvee vanished—like it wasn't even there. Then a bunch of Luther's men disappeared as well. Right into thin air."

"Fuck me," Jacob said.

"No time to worry about it. We need to get you down below with the others. See to your leg," Connor said. He also desperately needed to see everyone already down below to confirm they were safe.

The pair of them helped Jacob down the steep ladder into the bunker, one in front of the man, one behind to make sure he didn't take a tumble. Then Connor dealt with hiding their location. He'd made certain it could be done from inside or outside the bunker. When he heard everything slide into place, he breathed a sigh of relief. At least there would be a reprieve now. They all needed one after the battle.

They spent the next few minutes stabilizing Jacob's wound. Fortunately, the gunshot had gone straight through, though it was bleeding profusely. They applied a medical patch to halt the bleeding, one on each side of his thigh. Sam put in a few stitches to close the wound, then bandaged it up.

"We'd better start you on a course of antibiotics to prevent infection," Sam said.

Connor was getting antsy. "Can you make it across the bunker? I'd like to see the others soon as possible."

"How about I rest here for a few minutes and you come back for me?" Jacob asked.

"I'll wait with him," Sam offered.

"Thanks. I'll be back shortly to help." Connor took off at a quick trot. He could hear voices drifting from the far side of the shelter as he drew closer. Exactly what he needed to hear. He entered the room where all his people were sitting. It was a great moment to see them all look over at him, to note everyone looked alive and well. Only Luke didn't look up, his eyes still bore bandages, and Connor's sympathy went out to the teenager who looked even younger than his years now. Cheyanne too as she stayed close to her grandparents and her wounded brother.

"Everyone okay?" he asked anyway.

"Yes. We're fine. How did the rest of your team make out?" Dan asked.

"Good. Jacob was shot, but he's okay." He spoke quickly, not wanting anyone to worry. It was then he spotted Lily huddled against Faraday. "Where's Mckenna?"

"We thought she was with you," Laura said. "She took off a few minutes ago. Said she was going to stay by the other entrance to help if anyone was hurt when they came inside. Didn't you see her?"

"No." Connor stood there stunned. Where had she gotten to?

He turned without another word and began to race back the way he came, shouting her name as he went. Maybe she was hiding somewhere down here? *Please dear God let that be the case*. He couldn't bear to think she had left the shelter. Why would she even consider doing it? No, it couldn't be. But ten minutes later, his voice growing hoarse, he realized she was not down below. Not with them.

She was outside.

Alone.

The world seemed to shrink at the reality of the situation hit him hard. He had one focus now. Mckenna. Had she been out there when things had vanished into thin air? Was she even alive? *How could you do it? I begged you to stay safe and you promised me you would*. Anger tangled with the pain. It was all for naught if she was gone. All his planning, his journey to rescue her, all turned to dust.

# FIFTY-FOUR
# MCKENNA

**Day 9: Braveheart Horse Ranch**
   **9:29 a.m.**

Mckenna walked as quickly as her newly healed leg allowed, but within half a mile, she knew she would need to find a walking stick to ease the load. She had a rough idea of where she was going, having seen a map Connor had shared with her of the property in recent days. It was a huge ranch with thousands of acres. Grand and beautiful. Or it would be on any other day. Her mind was too consumed with recent events to truly appreciate the bounty of Mother Nature.

She figured it was at least five miles to the nearest line shack, that is if she could find it. An actual map in her hands about now would prove useful. Well, she'd just have to wing it and keep walking. Sooner or later, she had to believe she'd come across somewhere to sleep tonight. She had hours to look.

She pushed forward for another ten minutes, then

heard a twig snap in the bush behind her, freezing her in place. Animal or enemy? She looked around frantically. Where was there to hide?

Mckenna was about to move cautiously into a thicker strand of trees when her peripheral vision caught movement through the trees. She froze again. Movement was the giveaway.

But whoever or whatever was coming for her didn't seem as concerned to give away their position as she was. A figure came out from between two trees. One of the military bots stood there, expressionless and menacing as hell. *Run.* Her mind filled with the one word and she stumbled in her urgency to listen to her brain, her legs slower to get the message.

"Halt."

The cold, impassionate word did nothing to reassure her and Mckenna redoubled her efforts to get away. Then another one of the robots stepped into her path, stopping her retreat.

"We mean you no harm."

"Right!" she scoffed. *Show no fear.*

They wouldn't care anyway, but it might make her feel stronger. All she had left was her courage. Wits. She couldn't let them strip it away, or they would win. She had to fight this. She was her group's last hope for living outside, in the sunshine. *Humans need sunlight as much as flowers do.* The voice of her Grandma McTavish came back to her, making her instantly nostalgic for a better time.

"Sir wants to speak with you. Are you prepared to listen?"

*Who was sir?* The man she'd seen with the woman and baby? And what was there to talk about? Well, they hadn't shot her yet. And they darn well could have. All the bots were heavily armed. Hell, they were the weapon! Not like she had a choice in the matter either. Military bots were famous for speed. Endurance. Killing machines in all reality. One good thing she'd figured had come with the destruction of so many electronics, the disabling of robots capable of killing human beings with incredible ease. And yet, she'd just been captured by a pair of them.

Trooping back to the main house, housed between the foreboding, lurking creatures, she kept her expectations low and her mind on guard. She had no understanding of the situation. Could they know about the others hidden beneath them? Were they thinking to lure them out with her as bait by making her their hostage? Well, that wouldn't work. No way would she beg for her life. Her child and her friends were safe right now and they would stay that way. They could torture her all they liked; she would never tell them where they were hidden.

She walked up the front steps of the main house, feeling like she could very well be walking to her own death. Once they spoke to her, tortured her, or whatever their intentions were, they would have no need of her. She'd probably be tossed aside. Though on second thought, the woman had a baby. Maybe she could talk to her? Was she a captive as well? She hadn't looked unhappy or mistreated when she arrived earlier. The thought gave Mckenna a slight stir of hope she sat on with all prejudice, not allowing herself to think of what was ahead. That way would only lead to heartbreak. She had to stay strong, stronger than she had ever been before. This was it. She swore she could hear bells peeling in the distance, announcing with little fanfare, the end of times.

# FIFTY-FIVE
# CONNOR

**Day 9: Braveheart Horse Ranch**
   **10:00 a.m.**


*Where would she go?* Connor raced out the back of Sam's house, his mind capable of focusing on only one thing: finding Mckenna. His anger at her actions was more than tempered by his worry for her. He skirted around the side of the house to the front, close to the outer wall, seeking a view of the yard sight, but needing to keep in the shadows until he had an idea of what was going on. As his mother would no doubt confirm with her categorical assessment of danger, this moment had hit nuclear level.

The massive Humvee from earlier was parked in front of his house, but no one was in sight.

"Connor Hale. Please report to the main house. I wish to speak with you."

*Who the hell was that?* Connor stopped moving in an

effort to get his bearings. And how did they know his name?

Confused at the swift change to the situation, Connor hesitated for a moment. Should he be parlaying with the enemy? He had no idea what waited for him in the house or even who was speaking over a loudspeaker he damn well knew wasn't his. Or maybe they had found the bullhorn he'd used earlier? Crazy to think they had figured out so soon where it was though. Thought to use it. Meanwhile, he had to find Mckenna. She was out there somewhere, alone and unprotected.

"And if you're looking for your partner, Mckenna Stewart, she's here waiting for you."

*What the fuck?* The world had just taken a bizarre twist he couldn't have imagined in a hundred years. Did they really have Mckenna? Or was it a ploy to get him to come out into the open? In reality, it didn't matter. He had no choice in the matter. If she was inside with whoever was speaking to him, he had to find out.

Keeping his gun at the ready, Connor strode across his yard and up onto the deck. He was about to open the front door when it was opened for him. A military bot, dressed in western clothing, pulled the door further open and waited patiently for him to walk in.

"Please lower your weapon, Connor Hale," the bot said.

He did as it asked, no doubt the robot's directive would be to keep the boss safe, meaning Connor was in peril if he didn't watch himself.

Connor shook his head. Things were making little sense, but what else was there for it but going along with it? He had absolutely no clue as to what the fuck was going on. A situation he loathed.

"Follow me," the bot directed.

He followed the military machine down the hall to the living room. He instantly caught sight of Mckenna and increased his step until a hand was raised by his escort to stop.

"Are you okay?" She was sitting in a chair facing a man and woman, with two more impressive military bots lined up behind them on the sofa. The woman held a baby. The man was of ordinary appearance, mid to late thirties. The woman was much younger, very attractive, and looking pleased as she held a six-month-old baby, if Connor had to guess its age.

"I'm okay," Mckenna said, shifting in her seat. Her hands weren't tied, which was something. She didn't look hurt, though she did look tired, rubbing her leg that had been wounded in the grizzly attack.

"What's going on?" Connor directed his question at the man sitting in the center of the sofa, looking far too smug in his opinion. He had to be the mysterious "sir." A righteous anger filled him, threatening to consume him. His people had been under attack for days, and now this pompous looking fool is sitting on his couch, in his house, looking like he owned it.

"Considering I just saved your ass; you might want to temper that anger. I'm here to help you, thanks to this beautiful lady, the fair Celia."

"You had something to do with what happened earlier? The Humvee vanishing? Luther's men?"

"And Diego Martinez's Knights. All dispatched straight to hell. Now that made my day, punk!"

"Who blew up my gate?"

"Diego."

"Then you came through the gate and took out the enemy."

"In this case, the enemy of my enemy was still my

enemy," he said with a chuckle. "Not my friend, like the saying usually goes. Now you, Connor Hale. I like the way your group operates. The way you protect your woman, going all the way to Golden on horseback to save her and bring her home to your ranch. Admirable. And you left the safety of the bunker to save her once more. And here she was, thinking she'd be a spy on us to see if she could save her people. It's the stuff that myth and legends are born of. Your community is definitely worth keeping around."

"What?" How could they know about his underground shelter already? They had just gotten here. And did he say Mckenna was going to become a spy to help them? He could only shake his head, trying to make sense of it all. One thing stood out. He said his community was definitely worth keeping around. "What's the deal then?" Connor cut straight to the case.

"My Celia and baby Arthur need a good home, a place for Arthur to grow up strong and free. I want them to become an important part of Braveheart. Accepted and protected by the community. Of course, I will be here to see to their needs. I'm Eastwood, by the way."

"Eastwood?" The name rang a bell, but he had no time to ponder it. He reminded him of a younger version of Mayor Hazzard. He had a son, but his name wasn't Eastwood. Or at least he didn't think so. The name now had a slightly sinister tone after Connor had been told about the sentient computer housed in Washington naming himself Eastwood.

"Are you related to Mayor Hazzard? He lives in Anchor."

"Yes, my DNA is."

What did he mean by that? Maybe he disliked his dad?

"So, do we have a deal?"

"How can I be certain these military bots aren't a danger to my people? I've been told by good sources this event was caused by AI run amuck." Did this guy know something about what was going on in Washington? He couldn't be the actual sentient computer. No way was a sentient computer inside a human being. The technology wasn't invented yet, right? It made no sense. Maybe it was the world's oddest coincidence they shared the name, or the guy liked to play practical jokes. He certainly looked smug enough for them.

"I can assure you they are no danger to anyone if my family is not attacked. They are here to be of service. Help with the rebuild."

"I want to be clear. My people are not to be harmed. They're good people, trying their best to make it in a world gone to shit all around them except right here at Braveheart. I don't know how long until the real world tries to break in. The gate has been destroyed, meaning we are now vulnerable."

"Jessie James and Wild Bill can fix that." The man calling himself Eastwood turned and pointed at two of the bots standing behind him. "Go and see to the creation of a new gate to replace the one that was destroyed earlier."

"Yes, sir!" The two military bots marched off in unison.

"What's to stop you from harming my people if you don't like something they say or do?" The guy had too much firepower on his side of the equation. And he didn't trust him one iota. Too many unanswered questions.

"You don't. But I want a community for Celia and her son. It's of great importance to her, and I want to keep her happy, like men do with their significant other."

"Connor, maybe we could talk about this away from here?" Mckenna spoke up, looking restless.

"I want to say something." The woman he'd been told was Celia handed the baby to the man sitting at her side. "I've been traveling with Eastwood for a number of days now. He rescued me from a bad situation. Arthur and I would have starved if not for him. He's a man of his word. If he says he won't hurt anyone, he won't. And he has lots of great ideas about how to move forward and rebuild the world. You should be thanking your lucky stars he's decided to come here instead of heading somewhere else."

"Duly noted," Connor said.

There was a lot more going on here than was being said. They'd barely scratched the surface of whatever it was. But it did let in a small ray of hope that maybe things could go on at the ranch as they were before. That his people could live in the sunlight and carry on. If the guy had wanted to kill them, with those military bots at his disposal, they'd already be dead. "I think Mckenna and I should discuss this on our own for a few minutes."

"Of course, take all the time you need."

Mckenna got up and hurried to his side. They quickly walked from the room and into the kitchen. Connor pulled her into his arms. They hugged for a good long moment, each needing to absorb the strength their relationship offered.

"Thank God you're okay. What were you thinking running off like that again?"

Mckenna stiffened and pulled out of his arms. Then she relaxed and laid it out. "This is not the time to rehash what is done. I'm sorry, but I'm built the way I am, no changing it. But all that matters now is what are we going to do? Do you trust them to keep their word?"

"Hell, who can know for certain." Connor raked his hands through his hair. "But I think it's the best offer we're going to get."

"Yeah, me too." Mckenna shook her head. "You know, my cup must still be half full because I sense this might all work out. I like Celia. She's a mom just like me. Wants what's best for her baby. Eastwood is pretty much wrapped around her finger, I think, is my take on it."

Connor leaned down and kissed her. "Thank you."

She gave him a surprised look. "For what?"

"For being you. I would have traveled to the ends of this earth to find you. You know that, right?"

"Good thing it was only down to Golden." She smiled, letting him know it was no small thing.

"Good thing. Shall we tell the others?" Connor asked.

"Yeah, I think it's the best option. But we got to let them decide for themselves." Mckenna pulled him down for another kiss. "I love you, Connor Hale. Now let's go and finish the negotiations. I want to sleep in my own bed tonight."

Connor stopped for a moment to look out the view from the kitchen window. The crabapple trees were budding in the orchard, the first sign of spring and an inspiring sight after the carnage of the last nine days. The spot was close to where his mom and dad were buried. He would visit them later and share the news. Maybe the fighting wasn't totally over yet, but it was a new beginning. One he could live with for now. But he'd definitely be keeping his eye on this Eastwood character. He'd get to the bottom of what was going on, one way or another.

# A LOOK AT:
## DEATH SECRETS

In the shadow of Alaska's towering peaks, Anna Hale is haunted by a past painted in flames and betrayal. Marked by the tragic death of her mother and the scars of a childhood marred by violence, Anna has fought tirelessly to build a semblance of normalcy, only to have it shattered again and again. The latest blow comes when her sister, Tia Pace, vanishes without a trace, reigniting old wounds and casting Anna into a nightmare where she's the prime suspect.

As she grapples with her stepfather's execution and the weight of suspicion, another crisis looms: Zoe Pace, her other sister, has disappeared in an eerily similar manner. The only clue a sinister black rose and a chilling letter. When her brother Josh, now a dedicated cop in the Anchor Police Department, begs for her assistance, Anna is pulled back into the fray. Despite the agony of reopening old wounds, she embarks on a desperate quest to unravel the mystery of her sisters' disappearances.

Faced with the unforgiving Alaskan frontier, Anna must confront a tangled web of corruption and deceit, with a copycat killer moving in the shadows. With every tick of the clock, Anna's hope for a normal life slips further away, but her resolve to find her sisters and bring them home burns fiercer than ever. Will Anna's journey through the cold, dark paths of Alaska lead her to her sisters, or will she find herself lost in the depths of a conspiracy that threatens to consume everything she holds dear?

*AVAILABLE NOW*

# ABOUT THE AUTHOR

January Bain is an award-winning author who firmly believes that stories unite us, that good stories help us to discover the commonality of the human experience by supporting values, empathy and understanding. She has had the pleasure of select novels being turned into games, and her work is also available in different languages.

She and her husband live in rural Canada on peaceful acreage where a variety of wildlife comes to visit regularly and expect to be fed and paid attention to.